PRAISE FOR

THE SOCIAL GRACES

"Rosen's novel opens with a sly wink to that grande dame of the Gilded Age, Edith Wharton, before she deftly spins a captivating tale of her own based upon the legendary rivalry between Caroline Astor and Alva Vanderbilt. And what a rich story it is, full of opulent balls and monstrous mansions, yet firmly rooted in the parallel struggles of two very different heroines as they fight for their dignity and rights as wives, as mothers and as women."

—Fiona Davis, *New York Times* bestselling author of
The Lions of Fifth Avenue (GMA Book Club Pick)

"As ever, Rosen shines with impeccable research and eloquent prose. Readers will relish this peek behind the curtain of New York's most rich and famous families and follow with interest, amusement and even shock the escapades of these strong and savvy women. Enjoy!"

—Pam Jenoff, *New York Times* bestselling author of *The Lost Girls of Paris*

"*The Social Graces* transports readers to the glittering and cutthroat world of Gilded Age New York, where two compelling heroines—Caroline Astor and Alva Vanderbilt—vie for social supremacy as they navigate a sea of tragedies and triumphs. Both an intimate portrait of two intriguing women and a sweeping depiction of Gilded Age society. Rosen's characters leap off the page with vivid description and poignant emotion. Richly detailed and meticulously researched—historical fiction readers will love *The Social Graces*!"

—Chanel Cleeton, *New York Times* bestselling author of
The Last Train to Key West

"I was all in with Alva and Caroline from page one. Renée Rosen brings the Gilded Age to vibrant life through the eyes of the two ferociously independent women who vied for the reins of society. By turns tender and devastating, this beautifully written novel kept me in thrall to the end." —Kerri Maher, author of *The Girl in White Gloves*

"Meticulously researched and absolutely absorbing, *The Social Graces* chronicles the eye-popping extravagances and catty magnificence of the brassy nouveaux riches who fought to seize control of high society during the Gilded Age. I can't remember the last book that made me gasp 'Oh, no!' as many times at unexpected reversals. The pages all but turned themselves!"

—Julia Claiborne Johnson, bestselling author of *Better Luck Next Time*

"*The Social Graces* is Renée Rosen at her finest! Pulling back the curtain on the blood-sport world of Gilded Age high society, Rosen's captivating story of rivals Alva Vanderbilt and Caroline Astor shows what happens when an unstoppable force meets an immovable object."

—Bryn Turnbull, author of *The Woman Before Wallis*

PRAISE FOR
PARK AVENUE SUMMER

"A delightful and empowering read."

—PopSugar

"Renée Rosen is my go-to for whip-smart heroines who love their work. . . . *Park Avenue Summer* is a delightful summer cocktail of a read!"   —Kate Quinn, *New York Times* bestselling author of *The Rose Code*

"Filled with wit, heart and verve, Rosen's novel dazzles and empowers. Simply wonderful!"

—Chanel Cleeton, *New York Times* bestselling author of
The Last Train to Key West

"Part historical fiction, part coming-of-age story, this is a novel for our keeper shelves, to read and reread when we begin to doubt that there is still time to become the best version of ourselves. Lovely prose, a unique story line and a heroine who will stay with you for a long time make this a book I highly recommend."

—Karen White, *New York Times* bestselling author of
The Last Night in London

"A breezy, delightful novel that celebrates female friendship and ambition."

—Jamie Brenner, *USA Today* bestselling author of
The Forever Summer and *Summer Longing*

"Rosen's command of historical detail is masterful; so, too, is her ability to create fictional characters, among them her heroine Alice, who are as fully realized and compelling as the beguiling Brown herself."

—Jennifer Robson, *USA Today* bestselling author of *Our Darkest Night*

"Rosen delivers a cast of complex and ambitious female protagonists to truly root for. *The Devil Wears Prada* meets *Mad Men*, *Park Avenue Summer* is pure joy from cover to cover. I loved it."

—Hazel Gaynor, *New York Times* bestselling author of
When We Were Young & Brave

"Renée Rosen combines meticulous research with a true affection for her characters to bring this heady time movingly to life."

—Elizabeth Letts, #1 *New York Times* bestselling author of
Finding Dorothy

"*Park Avenue Summer* is a frothy and fun cocktail of fact and fiction, perfect for anyone who has ever been a 'Cosmo Girl.'"

—*The Augusta Chronicle*

"*Park Avenue Summer* is a fascinating behind-the-scenes glimpse into the world of the iconic *Cosmopolitan* magazine and its equally iconic editor, Helen Gurley Brown. . . . The story line is fast-paced and utterly absorbing: a delight from start to finish."

—*Historical Novels Review*

"Instantly absorbing, thoroughly researched and a fun, breezy read. It's like revisiting *Mad Men*, but from Peggy's and Joan's points of view."

—Bookreporter

THE
SOCIAL
GRACES

Renée Rosen

BERKLEY
New York

BERKLEY
An imprint of Penguin Random House LLC
penguinrandomhouse.com

Copyright © 2021 by Renée Rosen
Readers Guide copyright © 2021 by Renée Rosen
Penguin Random House supports copyright. Copyright fuels creativity, encourages diverse
voices, promotes free speech, and creates a vibrant culture. Thank you for buying an
authorized edition of this book and for complying with copyright laws by not reproducing,
scanning, or distributing any part of it in any form without permission. You are supporting
writers and allowing Penguin Random House to continue to publish books for every reader.

BERKLEY and the BERKLEY & B colophon are registered trademarks of
Penguin Random House LLC.

Library of Congress Cataloging-in-Publication Data

Names: Rosen, Renée, author.
Title: The social graces / Renée Rosen.
Description: First edition. | New York: Berkley, 2021.
Identifiers: LCCN 2020040654 (print) | LCCN 2020040655 (ebook) |
ISBN 9781984802811 (trade paperback) | ISBN 9781984802828 (ebook)
Subjects: LCSH: Belmont, Alva, 1853–1933—Fiction. |
Astor, Caroline Schermerhorn, 1830–1908—Fiction. | GSAFD: Biographical fiction.
Classification: LCC PS3618.O83156 S63 2020 (print) | LCC PS3618.O83156 (ebook) |
DDC 813/.6—dc23
LC record available at https://lccn.loc.gov/2020040654
LC ebook record available at https://lccn.loc.gov/2020040655

First Edition: April 2021

Printed in the United States of America
1   3   5   7   9   10   8   6   4   2

Book design and family trees by Nancy Resnick

This book is a work of fiction. References to real people, events, establishments,
organizations, or locales are intended only to provide a sense of authenticity, and are
used fictitiously. All other characters and all incidents and dialogue are drawn from
the author's imagination and are not to be construed as real.

To my family with love

Pray to God. She will help you.

—ALVA VANDERBILT

THE ASTOR FAMILY TREE

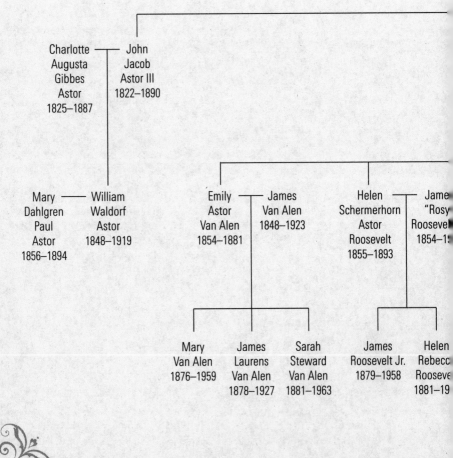

Charlotte Augusta Gibbes Astor 1825–1887 ─┬─ John Jacob Astor III 1822–1890

Mary Dahlgren Paul Astor 1856–1894 ─── William Waldorf Astor 1848–1919

Emily Astor Van Alen 1854–1881 ─┬─ James Van Alen 1848–1923

Helen Schermerhorn Astor Roosevelt 1855–1893 ─┬─ Jame "Rosy" Roosevel 1854–1

Mary Van Alen 1876–1959

James Laurens Van Alen 1878–1927

Sarah Steward Van Alen 1881–1963

James Roosevelt Jr. 1879–1958

Helen Rebecc Rooseve 1881–19

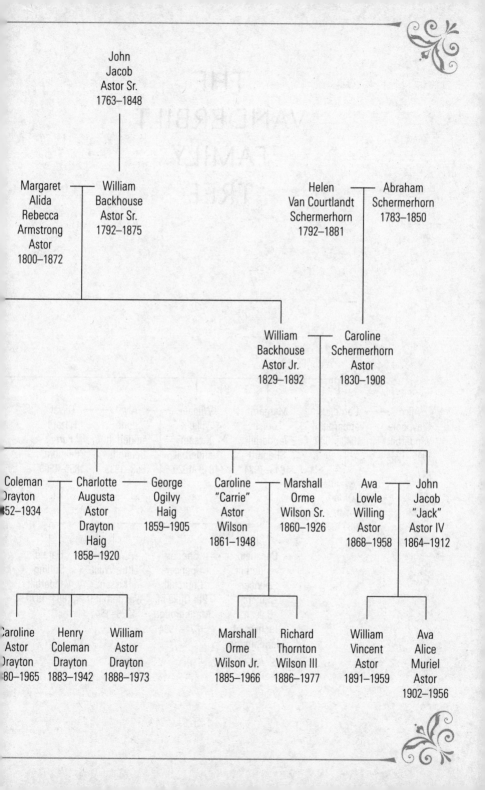

John
Jacob
Astor Sr.
1763–1848

Margaret
Alida
Rebecca
Armstrong
Astor
1800–1872

William
Backhouse
Astor Sr.
1792–1875

Helen
Van Courtlandt
Schermerhorn
1792–1881

Abraham
Schermerhorn
1783–1850

William
Backhouse
Astor Jr.
1829–1892

Caroline
Schermerhorn
Astor
1830–1908

Coleman
Drayton
52–1934

Charlotte
Augusta
Astor
Drayton
Haig
1858–1920

George
Ogilvy
Haig
1859–1905

Caroline
"Carrie"
Astor
Wilson
1861–1948

Marshall
Orme
Wilson Sr.
1860–1926

Ava
Lowle
Willing
Astor
1868–1958

John
Jacob
"Jack"
Astor IV
1864–1912

aroline
Astor
Drayton
80–1965

Henry
Coleman
Drayton
1883–1942

William
Astor
Drayton
1888–1973

Marshall
Orme
Wilson Jr.
1885–1966

Richard
Thornton
Wilson III
1886–1977

William
Vincent
Astor
1891–1959

Ava
Alice
Muriel
Astor
1902–1956

THE VANDERBILT FAMILY TREE

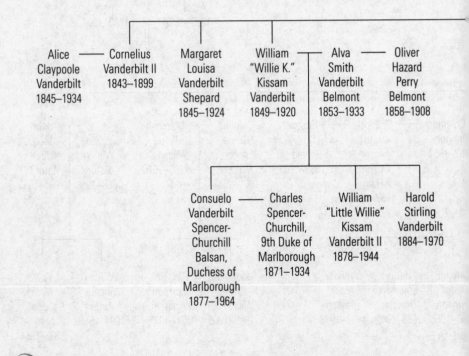

Alice Claypoole Vanderbilt 1845–1934 —— Cornelius Vanderbilt II 1843–1899

Margaret Louisa Vanderbilt Shepard 1845–1924

William "Willie K." Kissam Vanderbilt 1849–1920 —— Alva Smith Vanderbilt Belmont 1853–1933 —— Oliver Hazard Perry Belmont 1858–1908

Consuelo Vanderbilt Spencer-Churchill Balsan, Duchess of Marlborough 1877–1964 —— Charles Spencer-Churchill, 9th Duke of Marlborough 1871–1934

William "Little Willie" Kissam Vanderbilt II 1878–1944

Harold Stirling Vanderbilt 1884–1970

Sophia Johnson Vanderbilt 1795–1868 — Cornelius "Commodore" Vanderbilt 1794–1877 — Frank Armstrong Vanderbilt 1839–1885

Maria Louisa Kissam Vanderbilt 1821–1896 — William Henry "Billy" Vanderbilt 1821–1885

Cornelius Jeremiah Vanderbilt 1830–1882

Emily Thorn Vanderbilt Sloane White 1852–1946

Florence Adele Vanderbilt Twombly 1854–1952

Frederick William Vanderbilt 1856–1938

Eliza Osgood Vanderbilt Webb 1860–1936

George Washington Vanderbilt II 1862–1914

THE
SOCIAL
GRACES

PROLOGUE

Society

NEW YORK, 1876

THEY CALL US THE fairer sex. Something we find flattering and maddening in equal measure. Dainty. Delicate. Weak. Come now, if a man donned a corset, laced so tight as to shave four inches off his waist, he'd pass out on the first deep breath. And need we broach the subject of childbirth? *The fairer sex, our bustles.*

We are the wives and daughters of wealthy men, though our family fortunes are recent. A generation or two ago you would have found our mothers and grandmothers standing over wood-burning stoves and mending socks, knitting woolen blankets. For the most part, our fathers and grandfathers worked hard, in legitimate businesses—although some *may* have taken advantage of circumstances after the War Between the States. They call it war profiteering but we like to think of it as seizing the moment.

We are the nouveau riche. The new money. Enemy of New York's old money, those insufferable yet enviable snobs called Knickerbockers.

In our best efforts to emulate the old money, our calendars, like theirs, revolve around two seasons: winter and Newport. Winter takes place in Manhattan and lasts but twelve weeks. The festivities begin in November, and the recent debutantes among us are put on display in hopes of landing husbands. Gentlemen in search of wives do not care if we are fluent in five languages, or none. In fact, some might prefer the latter. They are not impressed that we've been educated in France, can play the harp and piano and have studied ballet. These suitors are only concerned with the size of our dowries, the length of our slender necks, and our doe-like eyes, which we enhance with belladonna-berry juice. Thankfully, by the start of the first waltz, the tearing and stinging subsides, and our vision *usually* returns to normal.

The married among us feel relieved and perhaps a bit smug. We may not be sitting behind mahogany desks or holding positions on the boards of big corporations, but we do exercise a different kind of currency. Social currency. It's our form of gold. Our means of trading— for better invitations, more status and greater influence.

When you first come into money, no one tells you that being rich takes some getting used to. There is a rhythm to a wealthy woman's day, set routines that leave no room for spontaneity, no room for error. We've come to learn that there's a proper way of doing everything— and we do mean *everything*. From how we dress to how we sit, how and what we eat, down to how we greet a gentleman on the street. This is the price we pay to keep our influence.

Now lest that sounds too dreary, rest assured we *do* have every comfort we could ask for. Liveried servants, dressing rooms with armoires of French couture meticulously organized by our lady's maids, whose chores include keeping the ostrich and osprey feathers faced out on our Reboux hats. We have cedar closets filled with garment bags guarding the delicate beading and fabrics of our ball gowns, still stuffed with the tissue paper and perfumed sachets they were packed in prior to making their journeys from Paris, arriving to us without a wrinkle.

Of course, not one stitch of clothing, not even a pair of kid gloves, belongs to us outright. They are the property of our husbands. As are we. We indulge at the pleasure of these men. And do we ever indulge! We throw ourselves into the fray. We feast on nine-course meals and dance until dawn, still twirling when we return home, or perhaps it's just the room that's spinning from too much champagne. Our social calendars are full. We attend luncheons, teas and recitals by day, receptions, dinner parties and balls by night. And of course, the most special night of the week is always Monday.

On Monday nights we attend the opera, dressed in our finest gowns and jewels, accompanied by our husbands, fathers or perhaps our wooers, along with a grim-faced chaperone, there to ensure no hand-holding or other debauchery takes place.

In the snow, peppered with coal dust and soot, we make our way to our horse-drawn carriages bound for the Academy of Music. The doors open at half past eight, and we arrive precisely ten minutes after that. The orchestra is already playing the overture, but that is of no concern. We are not there for the music. Heavens no. Most of us don't particularly like opera, and yet, we faithfully attend because this is what society does, and being there, being seen there is all part of the game. And we aim to play. We aim to be victorious. Eventually.

Our seats are on the main floor, where anyone who can afford a ticket sits. At first blush the red and gilded auditorium appears the very essence of splendor. It's only upon closer examination that we notice the threadbare carpets, the cracking plaster and peeling paint. The theater holds 4,000, and by the end of the second act, rest assured, every seat will be taken just in time for the arrival of the Academy's most honored guest. As if perfectly planned with an orchestral crescendo, she steps into her velvet box in the balcony, high above us all. In kind, we turn to her like flowers to the sun.

There she is—Caroline Webster Schermerhorn Astor. Mrs. Astor. While our ancestors were biding their time in Europe, hers were already walking these very streets—the first Dutch settlers to arrive in New York. That makes Mrs. Astor a Knickerbocker, American royalty.

We always yearn for intermission, our bottoms aching from the aging springs in our seats. While the smart set lines up outside Mrs. Astor's box, waiting to pay homage to their reigning queen, we congregate in the lobby to stretch our legs and mingle. Creatures of habit, we will have the same conversations we had the Monday before and the Monday before that. Penelope Easton will comment that if this were Wagner, we'd still be stuck in the second act, and Mamie Fish will tell us her favorite musical instrument is the comb. There are never any surprises.

But tonight, just after Faust has seduced Marguerite in the third act, our lorgnettes rise in unison. Across the way, rustling in gold lamé, trimmed in silver tulle, is Alva Smith. No, pardon us, Alva *Vanderbilt*. The new Mrs. Vanderbilt is accompanied by her handsome husband. Her vibrant red hair is crowned with a tiara, and she wears a thick rope of pearls rumored to have once belonged to Catherine the Great. She's also adorned with a diamond stomacher, sparkling earrings and half a dozen bracelets riding atop her supple gloves. If there were such a thing as being overdressed for the opera, this would be it.

Finding the performers more engaging, most eyes return to the stage, but for those of us still paying attention to Alva Vanderbilt, we see—but for a moment—that she does the most outrageous thing. She turns toward the balcony where Mrs. Astor is sitting, looks directly at the Grande Dame. And smiles. Suddenly the cymbals clash, the kettledrums thunder and for an instant we fear this is Mrs. Astor's wrath. But then the flutes, the violins and other instruments join in, and our attention is lulled back to the stage as we settle in for the final act.

It's only much later, while the moon slips out from behind the clouds, sending predawn shadows through our bedroom windows overlooking Fifth Avenue, that we sense some infinitesimal shift has occurred. This is the start of something. We just don't know what that *something* is yet.

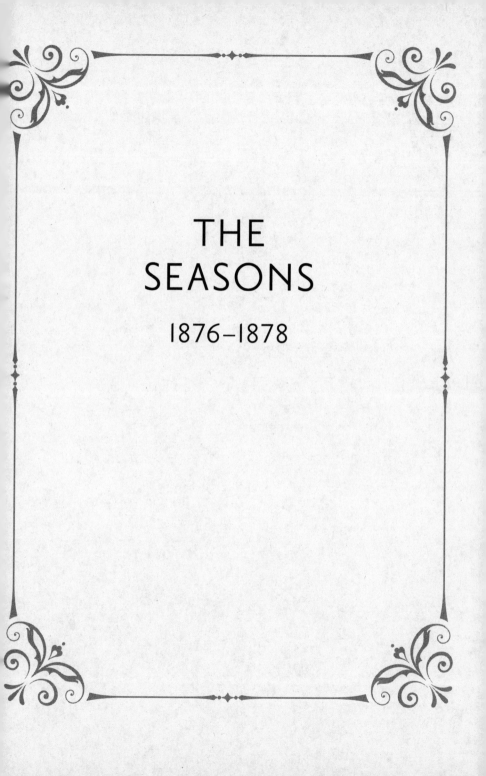

THE
SEASONS

1876–1878

CHAPTER ONE

Caroline

NEWPORT

CAROLINE LET THE NEWS sink in, though it didn't have far to travel. A headache was already forming behind her left eye, gathering strength as the pain spread to her chest. Or, more accurately, her heart. She looked at Augusta's handwriting again: *Your husband was seen with . . .* Her sister-in-law probably thought she was doing the Christian thing. It shouldn't have come as a surprise. And truly it didn't. Caroline's husband did as he pleased, with whom he pleased, while she went mute, tolerating, enduring. What other choice was there? Caroline tore the letter in half and then quarters and eighths and so on until she had reduced William's infidelity to confetti.

Abandoning the scraps, she went out on her bedroom terrace overlooking the cliffs and the Atlantic. Fingers resting atop the marble balustrade, she was bathed in sunlight. Giant swells from the ocean rushed the beach, breaking against the cliffs as blankets of sea foam, left in their wake, were dragged back to the surf. High tide was approaching, and just as the waves gained momentum, rising to full strength, Caroline, too, felt a surge within herself. Not that long ago, William's dalliances had crushed her, sending her into a spiral of self-pity, unable to leave her bed for days on end. But here she was, still standing. Yes, her head throbbed, and her heart ached, but she wasn't crumbling. She'd been here before with him. She'd be here again.

Wisdom was the only benefit of growing older, the trade-off for the faint lines around her eyes and mouth. Like a wave that rises, peaks and breaks, at forty-five Caroline Astor was at the midpoint of her life, having spent all those years harnessing her energy until now, at last, her boldness was cresting. How long could she sustain this before it all collapsed? She couldn't say. She didn't want to think about that, about what came next, when she was no longer vital, no longer so important. It was inevitable. It happened to everyone, sooner or later. The elders, who should have been revered, sought out for their knowledge and experience, instead were pushed into corners, forgotten and invisible to those whose time had come. But for now, surely Caroline was at her peak. No longer riddled with self-doubt, apologizing for who and what she was. She wished she could stop time, stay in this spot forever.

Yes, William had a reputation, and if Augusta knew about his latest lapse, others were already talking. If there was one thing Caroline detested, it was gossip. She imagined the matrons strolling down Bellevue Avenue saying, *If it weren't for her pedigree, he never would have married her.*

William Backhouse Astor Jr. was still a handsome man. Though slightly balding now, he had large brown eyes and that lovely horseshoe mustache that called attention to his cleft chin. Caroline knew she was no beauty, having inherited her grandfather's square jaw and prominent nose, but what those society ladies didn't know was that no matter how many women caught William's eye, no matter how many he'd take up with, she would be the one he'd come back to. Every time. Always.

She heard footsteps and turned to see Emily standing in her bedroom. She seemed tentative, even skittish. A random noise in the hallway had just made her jump, and that made Caroline forget about her headache and all that had caused it.

"What is it? What's wrong?"

"Nothing," said Emily, her fingers reaching for her necklace, touching each peridot, every emerald. Knowing Emily, she was adding up the number of gemstones in her head. Some people related to the world in terms of words or colors, maybe sounds or music. For Emily it was math. She'd look at a wheel and focus on the number of spokes. A bouquet translated into the number of flowers, sometimes down to the number of petals. Before her second birthday she had learned to count to five—holding up one finger at a time. Numbers never lied, never changed. Their absoluteness had always reassured her.

"I'd like to talk to you about the clambake," Emily said, her shoulders rising with a deep inhale as if conjuring some inner courage. "I would very much like to extend an invitation to Mr. James Van Alen."

"I see." The headache was back. Caroline paused before a curio cabinet and rearranged her bronze garnitures while considering her response. Emily, now twenty-two, was her eldest, and Caroline was eager for her to marry, just so long as she didn't marry James Van Alen.

"I'd like to invite him," Emily repeated.

"Well." Caroline set the figurine down. If she said no, she feared she'd only drive Emily further into Van Alen's arms. "I suppose we *could* have one more guest."

"And—"

"And?"

"I—I would like Mr. James Van Alen to be seated at our table." She nodded—*There, I said it*—and reached down, touching her necklace once again.

Caroline laughed though she didn't find it funny. "Oh, I'm afraid *that* would be most inappropriate. Seating Mr. Van Alen at our table would send the wrong message. Everyone will assume you're already spoken for."

"But I *am* spoken for, Mother. I am."

"Oh, please don't let your grandmother hear you say that. You'll give her heart failure." Caroline's own heart clenched at the thought. James Van Alen was altogether wrong for Emily just as Horace Wellsby had been wrong for Caroline when she was a young girl. Back then, Caroline's mother had forbidden her to see him, and that was that. No protest, no questions asked. Going against her mother's wishes would have been akin to breaking the law. But Emily wasn't quite as dutiful, and Caroline could picture her sneaking off to meet Van Alen, secretly writing him love letters. Caroline didn't want to put Emily in a position to have to lie. She didn't want Emily tempted by Van Alen in the first place.

"Oh, Emily," Caroline sighed. James Van Alen was a widower. He should have been mourning his wife, who had passed less than a year ago, rather than courting another woman. She wanted to say that James Van Alen did not come from good stock. That despite his father being a brigadier general, James Van Alen Sr. had invested heavily in the Illinois Central Railroad and had taken advantage of his workers. She wanted to say that James Van Alen Jr. was a laughingstock, that after attending Oxford for a year, he had returned to the States with a phony British accent and a fake monocle.

She wanted to say all that and more, but instead she took Emily's hand and coaxed her to the side of the bed and sat beside her. "My darling girl, don't be in such a rush. James Van Alen is only one man. There are others, I assure you."

"Oh, but he's wonderful. He's handsome and intelligent and kind."

"Don't underestimate yourself, Emily. You have beauty and breeding. You can have your pick of eligible gentlemen."

"But he's the one I want."

"I know you think that now, but there are several fine bachelors coming to the clambake. I invited them specifically for you."

"Can't you introduce them to Helen and Charlotte instead?"

"I've invited other gentlemen for your sisters."

"What about Carrie? She's fifteen. She's old enough for a beau."

Caroline stood up and reached for Emily's chin, tilting her face until their eyes met. "Right now, I'm more concerned about you. Now I'll agree to invite your Mr. Van Alen to the clambake, provided you don't allow him to monopolize all your time."

Emily was about to say something else when Caroline's butler, Hade, interrupted, announcing that Mr. Ward McAllister was there to see her.

"Mother, can we finish talking about this after you meet with Mr. McAllister?"

"I'm sorry, Emily, but having James Van Alen at our table is out of the question."

Emily's brow crinkled; her lips trembled ever so slightly. She was on the verge of tears, which she knew better than to shed in front of Caroline. Just as her own mother had done, Caroline raised her daughters to be strong, disapproving of any show of weakness. Emily brushed past Caroline, muttering, "You don't understand . . ."

Caroline smoothed the front of her gown. She would deal with her own heartache and her daughter's disappointment later. She could do that—push unpleasantness aside whenever needed. Some mistook that trait of hers for being cold and callous when really it was all about efficiency and the ordering of one's thoughts. And so, for now, she was Mrs. Astor and society awaited. She followed Hade down the grand staircase, moving in her usual slow manner, as if she carried the weight of her Dutch ancestors on her back.

Ward McAllister was in the sitting room, a short and stout man with a noticeable paunch and a slightly unkempt goatee. Despite his elfin appearance, he had somehow become *the* leading authority on style and etiquette, the expert on wine, food and entertaining. Together, Ward and Caroline had organized society and ran it in much the same way the Astor men ran their real estate empire.

Caroline had met Ward years ago when he was a lawyer. And not
a particularly successful one. He had recently returned from England
and France, eager to put what he'd learned about etiquette and all
things fashionable to work in America. Caroline had been at a lawn
party in Newport when she'd spotted a young Ward pouring his drink
into the hostess's flower bed.

"Do you disapprove of the champagne, or are you merely assisting
the gardener?" she'd asked.

"Actually, the former. One should never scrimp when it comes to
champagne," he said with mock horror that had made her laugh.

"Might I remind you," she said, knowing that he himself could
not have afforded much better, "not everyone has the means not to
scrimp."

"Then one should acquire the means." His eyes widened as he
playfully twisted the tip of his mustache.

Years later, he had done just that—acquired the means—by marrying a wealthy woman. Unfortunately, soon after, an illness left her
bedridden, which meant Ward was on his own to navigate society's
amusements. William had never cared for Ward and used to joke,
calling him an invert. *The man sits around with you hens all day discussing centerpieces and dance steps.*

"Apologies for the intrusion," Ward said, rising with his walking
stick in hand, "but we are in the midst of a crisis."

"Oh?" Caroline detected a slight thrill beneath his alarm, knowing that her friend liked nothing more than to be in the center of a
societal storm.

"Mamie Fish is hosting a fish fry."

"Well, that's certainly one fish too many for me." Caroline waved
her hand, brushing it aside. Mamie Fish was new money, and Caroline had no use for her or the other members of the nouveau riche.

"But don't you know," said Ward, the buttons on his vest straining as he breathed heavily, "she's *deliberately* having it on the same night as your clambake."

"Is that so?" Caroline actually welcomed this minor hitch. It gave her something to *work on*, and correcting *anything* always restored her sense of control. She might not have been able to do a thing about her husband's most recent affair, or Emily's poor taste in men, but society still looked to her, and Mrs. Stuyvesant Fish was not about to challenge that.

"Mamie's fish fry is all people are talking about, don't you know," Ward said, repeating his favorite catchphrase.

"Really?" Caroline crossed the room to straighten a calla lily leaning too far left in its delft blue vase. It had been bothering her since she'd entered the room.

"They say she's having a chamber orchestra!"

"Hmmm." Caroline paused, her hand on the stem. "Only a chamber?" She positioned the lily back in the vase. "We're having a symphony."

"A symphony orchestra?" His left eyebrow arched.

Reaching for the pull cord, Caroline rang for Maria de Baril, her social secretary, who immediately appeared, as if she'd been perched outside the door, waiting. She was a petite woman with very dark hair and an olive complexion. She always wore a fanciful array of beads about her neck.

"Maria, we're going to be making some changes to our clambake."

"Very well, madam." She produced a pen and small leather-bound tablet, her hands poised for dictation.

"Send word to the Academy of Music. Tell them I'm requesting that their orchestra perform for my guests along with Christine Nilsson."

Ward gave her an admiring nod, which she returned with a look—*What did you expect?* She was on the opera's board—as was

Ward—and was well acquainted with Miss Nilsson, the star Swedish soprano.

"Also," she said to Maria, "inform the chef that we'll be adding a few more courses to our menu." She began ticking items off on her fingers. "Lobster croquettes, *truite à la meunière* and *crevettes au beurre blanc*. Instead of the Riesling, we'll be serving Chassagne-Montrachet, and see to it that an additional case of the 1860 Moët et Chandon is chilled."

This time, Ward gave her a conspiratorial yet all-impressed look, as if he hadn't anticipated her going to such lengths, sparing no expense. *This* was what she did. It was what made her Mrs. Astor. Not just any hostess, and certainly not Mamie Fish, could entertain the way Caroline did. She had it down to a science. Off the top of her head she was able to put together an exquisite French menu, paired with the perfect wines. She could envision the table settings down to the centerpieces.

"Will there be anything else?" asked Maria, still taking notes.

"Yes. See to it that Mrs. Stuyvesant Fish receives an invitation."

"You're inviting Mamie?" Ward was aghast, leaning forward on his walking stick. "But Stuyvesant Fish is railroad money. If you extend that invitation to Mamie, there's no going back. You'll be officially welcoming her into society."

"It's better to have her *in* society than on the outside. I don't wish to hire the Academy's symphony and their leading soprano every time Mamie Fish decides to throw a party."

CHAPTER TWO

Alva

THE FIRST ANNUAL STUYVESANT FISH *fish fry has been canceled until further notice.* Alva sat at the table in the morning room and studied the ornate calligraphy, the raised black ink on the thick vellum, turning it over as if expecting an explanation on the back. Her only worthwhile invitation of the Newport season had just been revoked.

She plunked Mamie's note down, pushed away from the table and wandered down a long corridor lined with portraits, three generations of stern-looking, mustached and muttonchopped Vanderbilt men. Alva thought Willie K., whose portrait hung at the end, was the handsomest of them all, perhaps the most handsome man she'd ever seen.

She'd had no idea who he was the first time she set eyes on him, from a distance, on the field at the Westchester Polo Club. The game was new in the States and she'd never been to a match before, didn't fully understand how it was played, but that didn't matter. She was captivated by the athletic man with the wavy dark hair, charging down the field, his mallet whacking the wooden ball, driving it through the goalposts. There were cheers from the stands, and Alva was on her feet, not to applaud but to get a better look at him. After begging her friend Consuelo Yznaga—Alva's only remaining friend from childhood—to introduce them, she found him even more handsome up close. She

soon learned that the expression *opposites attract* was true. Where she
was intense, he was lighthearted. Where she was poor, he was rich.
Consuelo had casually mentioned that Willie's grandfather, the Commodore, was a millionaire many times over.

Alva continued roaming through the Vanderbilt cottage—one
of three his family owned—where she and Willie were staying that
season. The fact that they called it a cottage was absurd to her. A cottage with nineteen rooms. Each one had been decorated in variations
of the same forest green, pale yellows and soft browns found in their
city homes. For a moment she lost herself in admiring the amaranth
wainscoting in the parlor, the Florentine glass pendulum chandelier
in the main dining room, the mother-of-pearl inlays in the staircase
banister. Sea air and sunlight poured in through the French doors,
casting a golden haze over the sitting room at the end of the hall. She
paused, leaning up against a fluted column, thinking again about all
the Newport parties she hadn't been invited to, including Mrs. Astor's clambake.

Being left out was nothing new to her, and yet, each time, it caught
her off guard like a shock from touching a charged surface. She thought
being married to William Kissam Vanderbilt would have remedied the
problem, his family money catapulting her to the top of every guest
list. She'd been mistaken.

Willie K., as she affectionately called him, was at the archery
range with James Van Alen. No one was around, not even a servant.
Alva was still relatively new to the Vanderbilt ways, their exorbitant
tastes, spending more on a single chair than most families had to live
on for a year. Or longer. A stab of guilt hit her before she let it go.
Gradually, she found herself easing into these comforts, luxuriating
in their opulence like she would a deep bath. Still, it was so much
house for just the two of them and their servants. The walls held the
quiet when no one was around, and Alva didn't do well when left on
her own. From the time she was a child, she had unapologetically

required an audience—even if of one—needing someone to hear her, to pay attention to her. It was terribly lonely in that cottage without Willie. It made her wish her sisters had changed their minds about visiting, but they were back in the city, claiming Newport was too rich for their blood.

Alva thought she heard someone downstairs, but it was only the ocean breeze blowing a porch door shut. She returned to the morning room, picked up the newspaper already rustled through by the men. Slipping out of her new beaver-cloth shoes, she rested her bare feet on the seat of Willie's chair and began reading the *Newport Daily News* while absentmindedly twisting a lock of her red hair. She knew it wasn't any more ladylike to have her nose in a newspaper than it was to twirl one's hair, but she needed the distractions.

Alva reached for a slice of toast spread thick with butter and raspberry jam. The first bite sent a shooting pain from her jaw to her temple. She'd been grinding her teeth at night again. A new habit she'd formed. Some mornings she could hear her jawbone click each time she opened her mouth. But the flavors overrode the pain. The jam was so sweet, the butter so creamy and the toast so airy and crusty— nothing like the dense, tasteless black bread she and her family had eaten with every meal just to fill their bellies. Even now, there were certain foods she tried to avoid: cornmeal, beans, cabbage and potatoes. Those had been the staples of her diet for six years and now carried the aftertaste of scarcity.

Before she was Alva Vanderbilt, she'd been Alva Smith from Mobile, Alabama. After the War Between the States, when she was sixteen, her mother died, and within a year, her father had squandered the family's fortune, which had been considerable by non-Vanderbilt standards. Suddenly poverty-stricken, the Smiths found that the world had turned on them. People who used to be their friends openly shunned them, crossed their names off their guest lists for barbecues and other entertainments, too. Alva's sisters, Armide, Jennie and Julia, quietly accepted the rejection. But not Alva. Alva fought back, pushing a girl in the park who'd made a snide remark about her out-of-date dress. When someone ignored her on the street, she'd call out their name—*Oh, Mary Lou, I see you—hell-low! Well, hell-low there, Mary Lou.* Adversity had always fueled Alva, and she vowed that the Smiths would be walking in high cotton once again. She owed her mother that much.

Alva heard someone coming. It wasn't the porch door this time, and she dropped her feet to the ground, shoved aside the newspaper and sat up straight. Willie and James Van Alen were back, their bows and quivers in hand. Willie's dark hair was windblown and tousled, a hint of his cowlick poking up, his cheeks tinged pink from the sun. He was squinting, his pale blue eyes adjusting to the light inside the room. Though his lips remained downturned, she could tell he was smiling at something Van Alen had just said.

". . . I beat you fair and square, mate," he said to Willie.

"If you say so." Willie laughed.

"Oh, don't be such a Podsnap," he said, adjusting his monocle. "You're always so bloody chipper."

Alva smiled, recalling how she'd initially been charmed by James Van Alen's accent before discovering it wasn't real. Neither was the eyepiece. Nothing but a circle of glass. He'd spent a year in England and had returned home a myopic Brit. But she didn't hold it against him. Not like the others, who themselves all spoke with a heavy stilted inflection that didn't sound quite American or British—but rather something unnatural in between. Even Alva had been known to play the role of a Southern belle when it suited her or, conversely, a worldly sophisticate, peppering her sentences with French.

"I suppose you heard about the fish fry being scratched," said Van Alen.

Alva reached for Mamie's card and held it up.

"Pity you won't be joining us for Mrs. Astor's clambake."

"*You* were invited?" She plunked the card down, hoping she hadn't sounded rude, though judging by the way Willie's eyebrows arched, she guessed she didn't pull it off. At least Van Alen hadn't seemed to notice.

"Indeed," he said. "Emily's parents are warming to the idea of me. With any luck, I'll be seated at the family table. It's going to be marvelous."

"Oh, cheer up, darling." Willie leaned over and kissed her cheek. "You don't even like clams."

Alva stood up, perhaps too abruptly. "If you boys will excuse me," she said, forcing a smile, "I think I'll go for a swim."

As she rushed up the stairs to change, she overheard Willie saying, "I don't know what's gotten into her. She always says clams are too chewy."

Up in Alva's room, her maid set out three flannel swimming outfits to choose from, each with woolen stockings along with outdoor slippers. She had a dozen or more hanging in her closet. There was a time she didn't even have a dozen dresses, let alone swimming costumes. She settled on a black-and-gray-striped suit, knowing that any of them would weigh her down once they got wet, making swimming too far out nearly impossible. This frustrated her to no end. Men didn't need to cover every inch of flesh. They could swim freely whereas she could only go wading at best.

After saying goodbye to Willie and Van Alen, she set out for the beach. Wandering down the tree-lined street, she passed a cluster of women, chatting away as they strolled leisurely in their best day dresses, their parasols hoisted above their shoulders. Alva felt a stab of envy. A simple afternoon walk with friends. *They make it look so easy.* Sometimes she tagged along with the other Vanderbilt women on their walks, listening to them wax on about their children and relations she'd never met, and family lore about the Commodore. There wasn't an opening or even a crack for her to enter the conversation, and she found herself lonelier in their company than when she was by herself.

When Alva reached Ruggles and Bellevue Avenues, she decided to take a detour and turned down the dirt pathway that led to the cliffs. Cliff Walk was a much prettier route, and as she hiked along, the trail grew more winding, even a bit treacherous in places, requiring a steady foot to navigate. The tomboy in Alva that fished, golfed and performed calisthenics every morning with Indian pins loved the challenge. She placed her slippered feet with nimble grace from one rock to the next while holding on to her bonnet. The pulse of the ocean, steady as a heartbeat, whooshed in her ears. Up ahead, around the bend she could see the rocks in the distance, those massive slabs of black shale and sandstone. She watched as a gull walked about with a clam in its mouth, dropping the shell against the rocks until it cracked open, before reaching inside to pull the fleshy meat out with its beak. Willie K. was right; she didn't like clams. She had to look away, and when she did, she saw a young woman sitting on the ledge of a cliff, elbows to knees, head in hands. The wide lavender ribbons on her hat were fluttering in the breeze. She appeared to be crying.

"Are you all right up there?"

The woman lifted her face, and Alva saw that it was Emily Astor. Even from a distance and even while Emily was sobbing, Alva thought what she always thought when she saw her: *Good lord, what a beautiful girl.* How was it possible that anyone could have such enormous dark eyes, such a straight, perfect nose and a flower bud of a mouth?

"Please, just let me be." Emily buried her head in the folds of her arms, shoulders shaking.

Alva squinted, trying to block the sun. "Be careful getting down from there."

"Just please—please, just go."

"Okay, fine. Fine." Alva slapped her hands to her thighs and walked on, wondering why she'd even bothered. James Van Alen had introduced Alva and Emily on three separate occasions, and each time, Emily had said, *How do you do?* discounting their previous meetings. And Alva knew where she got that from, too. Her mother, the great Mrs. Astor, always looked through Alva, as though she weren't there or wasn't worth the time it would take to acknowledge her presence.

It seemed that everywhere Alva turned she was met with some form of slight. The world had been trying to rein her in from as far back as she could remember. When Alva was four, her brother died of consumption. He was just thirteen. Alva remembered her father sitting in the church pew, shoulders shaking as he wept into the crook of his arm, asking God out loud why he'd taken his son and not one of his daughters. Alva had been crushed and ran out of the church. She hid in the cotton field until Armide found her and practically dragged her back inside the house. Alva couldn't look at her father, knowing that he'd loved his son more than her or her sisters. But Alva couldn't accept that. She was just as good as a son, and she vowed to prove that to her father, to everyone. She wouldn't be kept down, wouldn't be rendered second-rate. But the world wasn't quite ready for Alva. Her own mother punished her for playing town ball and climbing trees. As a young woman, she couldn't attend debutante balls because she was poor. Later, she wasn't allowed to go to college or study subjects like politics and architecture just because she was a girl. Now she couldn't go to Mrs. Astor's clambake, and not because she was a woman, and not because she wasn't rich enough, but because she wasn't good enough. Not being good enough—it all boiled down to that simple truth.

At times like this Alva questioned why she wanted to be part of society in the first place. But she knew why. Society was the only arena where women didn't have to answer to men. They had created their own little world, governed by their own rules, set in place by their own rulers. It was the only realm where she could hope to have any say about *anything* at all. If she wanted respect, if she wanted power, she had to make her way in society.

A seagull squawked overhead, strident to her ears. Alva kicked a loose pebble out of her way and had just reached a bend in the path when she saw a hat being carried away over the cliff. She saw the lavender ribbon flapping in the breeze and realized it was Emily's. A second later she heard an ear-piercing shriek that sounded more animal-like than human. There came another shriek and Alva rushed back to see that Emily had slid down a five-foot drop, her fall broken only by another ledge jutting out. There was no way to hoist herself back up.

"It's okay—you're all right," Alva called out. "Just stay right there. Don't move. I'm coming." Alva's heart was racing as she advanced from one rock to the next, keeping her eye on Emily as she struggled, gripping the jagged ledge for support.

When Alva got close enough, she reached for Emily's hand. "Just grab hold of me."

But as she groped for Alva, Emily stumbled again and skidded off the rock, clinging onto another serrated section of stone overlooking a twelve-foot drop. Alva cried out even before Emily did. She tried reaching for Emily, their fingertips straining but not connecting. Alva leaped forward to the next rock, her heart hammering when she grabbed hold of Emily's forearm. Emily's cheeks were puffing in and out, every part of her laboring to hang on. Alva still had hold of Emily, even as her own feet were slipping.

"Help," Alva shouted out, panic rising in the back of her throat. "Somebody, please, come help us!"

But there was no one around. Alva was on her own. She slid closer still toward the drop-off, managing to wedge her foot between two overlapping rocks. Using that as her anchor, Alva got hold of Emily's other arm. With all her might, Alva drew a deep breath, her limbs aching as inch by inch she dragged Emily back onto a flat rock. The two women collapsed side by side, panting, sweating. Emily was shaking, her face streaked with blood and dirt, her kid gloves shredded. Her dress was torn along the bottom and sides. Blood oozed from the cuts and gashes along her forehead, arms and legs. Alva herself became aware of a salty, metallic taste in her mouth. She must have cut her lip. When she wiped the sweat from her brow, her fingers came away tinged with blood, and the palms of her hands were deeply pitted with gravel and grit.

She had no idea how long they stayed there, breathing hard, unable to move. Though she'd gotten them both this far to safety, she was still expecting someone to help them. It took a moment before she realized the rest was up to her.

After she'd gotten Emily on her feet and made sure nothing was broken, she asked what she'd been doing up there to begin with. "Don't you know that people have fallen to their deaths on Cliff Walk?"

Emily didn't answer. Alva didn't ask again.

Together they slowly inched along from one jagged rock to another with Emily leaning on Alva. Every few steps she had to stop and shift Emily's weight, pressing into her hip and shoulder. It seemed to take forever before they came to the paved pathway. By then Emily had begun talking—chattering really—going on and on about her mother's clambake, about James Van Alen and then back to the clambake. Alva paused and looked at her in such a way that made Emily stop, her eyes wide, her mouth open.

"What is it?" asked Emily. "What's wrong?"

"It's nothing." Alva shook her head, smiling.

"No, tell me. What is it?"

"You." She pointed, her amusement building.

"*Me*? What did I do? Tell me. Oh, please tell me. Did I say something funny? Did I do something wrong? Oh, what is it?"

"It's *that*—what you're doing right now!" Alva covered her mouth, laughing out loud. "You're—you're babbling."

Emily looked affronted. "I do not babble."

"Oh, yes you do," said Alva, howling. "I'm sorry—I'm sorry," she said, trying to catch her breath, "it's just that I never thought you Astors *babbled*. It makes you seem *almost* human."

Emily pressed her fingertips to her mouth, and Alva was sure she'd offended the prim and proper Miss Astor, when suddenly Emily's shoulders began to shake as she let out a high-pitched giggle.

"I suppose you hiccup and snore and do all kinds of other graceless things, too."

With that, Emily burst into a fit of chortling. Both of them were now laughing so hard that Alva was doubled over, unable to speak, holding her midsection while still propping Emily up.

"Oh God, stop," said Emily, trying to recover, sopping the tears from her eyes. "Oh, it hurts—don't make me start laughing again."

When they were both finally able to compose themselves, the pendulum swung the other way and Emily grew serious, somber. "I could have died today, couldn't I have?"

"But you didn't." Alva pushed the words past the lump in her throat.

"You saved my life. And you could have died, too," she said, as if this just dawned on her. Reaching for Alva's hands, she said, "I won't ever forget this. I mean it. Thank you."

Alva never knew what to do when someone turned soft and emotional. Usually she cracked jokes or changed the subject. Her sisters and Consuelo always accused her of that. So did Willie. This time she said nothing.

In silence, she helped Emily along the pathway, concentrating on not buckling or letting Emily fall. Meanwhile Emily went back to chattering about James and how much she wanted to marry him, how funny Alva was and how she couldn't remember the last time she'd laughed like that.

Alva was only half listening because now something quite splendid was taking root in her mind. About fifty yards back, it had dawned on her that a golden opportunity had just presented itself. This was Alva's chance to meet Mrs. Astor—and under the most advantageous circumstances. Alva would walk Emily home and return her safely to her mother. Mrs. Astor would be so grateful—so indebted to Alva for rescuing Emily—that her frosty veneer would melt away and she would insist that her daughter's savior attend the clambake, and welcome her into society.

They'd made it to where Victoria Avenue intersected with Bellevue, when Emily turned to Alva and said, "Thank you. For everything." She let go of Alva, wincing as she attempted to hobble away.

"Wait—" Alva grabbed Emily just before she stumbled. "You can't walk on that ankle. I'll help you the rest of the way."

"No." Emily shook her head. "I'm all right. It's best that I go alone. I can make it."

"Don't be silly. You can hardly put any weight on that foot. I'll help you back home and we'll explain what happened to your mother and—"

"No!" Emily blurted out. "Mother can't know I was on Cliff Walk. She's always forbidden me to go there."

"But . . ." Alva's voice trailed off, her mind scrambling, trying to salvage her plan, find another way in. She needed Emily's help in this. Alva couldn't just knock on Mrs. Astor's door later on and say, *By the way, I saved your daughter's life, now invite me to your clambake and let me into society.* Alva supposed somewhere down the line she could ask Emily for an introduction, but that wouldn't be enough. That could be easily dismissed. No, she needed more leverage than a simple *how do you do.* Alva was still thinking when Emily attempted another step forward and nearly collapsed.

"Come on now." Alva had hold of her again. "You can't walk the rest of the way by yourself."

Emily lowered her eyes and nodded, surrendering to Alva for

help. "You just can't say anything about this to Mother. Please? Promise?" Emily gripped Alva's free hand. "I'm asking. As a friend."

A friend? Alva hesitated, her chest growing warm. She was desperately lonely and so in need of a friend. She never would have assumed that Emily considered her a peer. Much to her surprise, Alva *did* like Emily, and not because she was Mrs. Astor's daughter. She was different one-on-one, nothing like the times they'd met before. There was a sweetness and an innocence to her that Alva found endearing. And her laughter was infectious.

"Please?" Emily's eyes were big and pleading.

Alva had a decision to make. She could use this as a means to enter society, or she could have a new friend. She looked at Emily and nodded. "This will be our secret. I won't say a word."

CHAPTER THREE

Society

FAINT TRACES OF SEA spray waft in the air all around us. Those invisible salt crystals cover every surface of this town just like the gilding so favored by Newport's elite, most of whom—including us—are oblivious to the slow rot underneath.

Still, there is no place like Newport in the summertime. Six weeks filled with six-course dinners, lawn parties, teas and luncheons each day and balls that last till dawn every night. Most of us have ninety or so gowns on hand just to get us through the season.

In the afternoons, while the men are off sailing their yachts or playing lawn tennis, we ladies seek our exercise and a chance to show off our best day dresses and gems by taking daily strolls down Bellevue Avenue. We keep our parasols open to block the sun, as freckles and suntans are regarded as common and must be avoided at all costs.

The Knickerbocker matrons make their own daily parade in a string of horse-drawn carriages led, of course, by Mrs. Astor. Just now as she passes by, we practically stand at attention, not that she even notices us here, in the heat of the day, our corsets and petticoats a heavy second skin, our coiffures wilting beneath our wide-brimmed hats.

Tomorrow and the next day, and the day after that, we'll be right back here, in this very spot. All will be the same, save for our finery.

CHAPTER FOUR

Caroline

CAROLINE WAS NEARING THE end of her daily carriage ride down Belle-vue Avenue. She was accompanied by Charlotte, which was highly unusual. Could it be that her daughter was suddenly taking an interest in society? At eighteen, Charlotte preferred sailing and hunting with her father over anything having to do with society.

Caroline glanced at her daughter's gloved fingers curled atop the handle of her parasol, fingertips drumming impatiently as if she couldn't wait for this to be over with. So why had she asked to come along? Why was she wearing one of her best day dresses with the open neckline trimmed in satin ruffles? And why had she pinned up her buttery blond curls, securing them beneath her favorite bonnet? Caroline focused on one strand of Charlotte's hair that had broken ranks and was now dangling down her long neck.

Charlotte must have sensed her staring because she turned, pressed her lips together tightly and looked away again. Charlotte was so hard to catch hold of, to pin down even when she was right there beside her. Caroline wanted to say something, but the moment had passed. Now she eased into the slow, steady rhythm of the carriage while listening to the hooves striking the cobblestones, the jangle of the bridles. She turned to gaze out the open carriage, the breeze carrying the smell of the sea punctuated here and there with horse manure.

Just as their barouche was turning at the bend, Caroline felt a sharp jolt as a four-wheel trotter came charging out of nowhere. With a woman at the helm, it whooshed past them, making their horses roar violently and rear up. Caroline and Charlotte were thrown about in the back seat; their hats and parasols went flying until their coachman was able to regain control of the horses. He brought the carriage as well as the rest of the procession to a halt before jumping down from his box and coming around to the side to check on them.

With his cap in hand, his dark lank hair hanging in his eyes, he said, "My apologies. I hope neither of you was hurt."

"We're fine, Duncan." Charlotte retrieved her bonnet and patted her hair in place. "Thank you."

"Women drivers," he muttered.

Women drivers indeed, thought Caroline, remembering the days she used to take her own coach out. Years ago, she had so enjoyed sitting up on the box, the breeze sharp against her cheeks, the leather ribbons steady in her riding gloves as she drove her four horses as fast as they could go. People would stand on the sidelines, clapping as she sped past them. Now, of course, taking the reins herself was out of the question as were so many other things, like playing croquet or lawn tennis.

"You're sure now?" asked Duncan. "No one's hurt?"

"Not a scratch on us," said Charlotte. "You handled the horses so expertly." She flashed a smile, which he returned as he bowed before replacing his cap and climbing back up to his seat.

The puzzle pieces quickly fit together—Charlotte wasn't remotely interested in society. *This was all about the coachman!* Caroline's chest tightened.

"What was *that*?" she asked as the carriages began moving again.

"What was *what*?"

"That little exchange with you and the coachman."

"Who? You mean Duncan?" she asked, as if it could have been

anyone else. "He is awfully handsome, isn't he? Even Helen thinks so and she's madly in love with Rosy."

"That's enough, Charlotte. Your behavior is most inappropriate." She was going to say more but found herself distracted by two women walking up the sidewalk, right by the blue boxwood shrubs that lined the Astors' cottage. They were leaning into each other, the one with red hair slightly taller than the brunette, something broken in their gait. Neither one had gloves, or hats, not even a parasol to protect them from the sun. The redhead was in a bathing costume. They looked mangy and scraggly like a couple of strays. Caroline assumed they were trespassers, locals from town who had wandered up to Bellevue, but on closer examination, something about the woman in the dress caught in her mind. She knew that dress. Her eyes moved up. She knew that woman! Her nerves started crackling, her mouth dropped open.

The look on her face made Charlotte turn. "What is—what—oh my!" Charlotte gasped. "Is *that* Emily? What's wrong with her? Who's that with her?"

Confusion gave way to alarm as Caroline realized Emily was hurt. The carriage was turning in to the long drive just as Emily and the other woman staggered up under the portico.

"Emily—" Caroline called out. She didn't even wait for Duncan to help her down from the carriage. Her hem caught on the fold-down steps, and she heard the fabric tear as she pulled herself free, rushing to Emily's side. "Heavens, child, are you all right? What happened?"

"She tripped," said the redhead with a slight Southern accent. "And over her own two feet if you can believe that." She tacked on a slight laugh, as if it were nothing.

Emily hobbled, still holding on to the redhead.

"You're limping!" Caroline's voice ticked up as she stepped in to take the redhead's place. *She needs her mother now, not you.* "Have you broken anything?"

"She's just good and sore," said the redhead, acting overly protective, almost possessive of Emily, who hadn't yet said a word.

Caroline saw a raised bump on Emily's forehead, already starting to purple, a thread of dried blood running to her brow. Caroline reached over and brushed the hair from Emily's eyes with her fingertips. She looked frightened, shaken. "Charlotte," Caroline called over her shoulder. Her other daughter was still in the carriage. "Go get Hade! Have him send for the doctor."

"I think some bed rest is probably all she'll need."

Who asked you? Caroline wanted to say to the redhead, and then noticed that she also had scratches and bruises on her face, though not as severe as the ones on Emily's. Otherwise, she seemed unharmed and was now saying something about soaking in Epsom salt. Caroline wished she'd stop inserting herself in the middle of this. She just wanted to take care of Emily. All this chattering—Caroline couldn't hear herself think. "Charlotte," she called out again. *What was the matter with her—just sitting there talking to the coachman.* "Charlotte, go get Hade. Have him send for the doctor. Now, Charlotte!"

"I'm Alva, by the way," said the redhead, thrusting out her hand. "Alva Vanderbilt. It's a pleasure to finally meet you, Mrs. Astor."

Caroline didn't catch the first name, but *Vanderbilt* registered. Everything she knew about the Vanderbilt family, she didn't like. The patriarch, Cornelius Vanderbilt, whom everyone called the Commodore, was notorious for his unethical business practices and deplorable manners: cheating his competitors, chewing with his mouth open, picking his teeth at the table. He'd made his fortune in railroads, and Caroline didn't care for railroad money. She believed one's wealth should be inherited, not earned, as she herself had inherited a good sum in addition to marrying yet more money. Caroline never acknowledged William's grandfather, the late John Jacob Astor, who had indeed *earned* his fortune—as a fur trapper, no less—and whose ruthless business practices and despicable table manners rivaled the

Commodore's. She knew the only difference between Astor and Vanderbilt was that John Jacob Astor had gotten a head start, some twenty years before Cornelius Vanderbilt began his business. Caroline didn't address this parallel and made it a point to never speak of the Astors' humble beginnings.

The Vanderbilt woman was still talking. ". . . You'll have to forgive my appearance"—she tugged on her flannel top—"I was on my way to the beach and—"

"If you'll excuse me, I want to get Emily inside."

"Of course. Of course," she said, stepping in, taking hold of Emily's other side. "I'll just help you get—"

"That won't be necessary, I assure you."

The Vanderbilt woman backed off but only after Hade appeared with Charlotte trailing behind him.

"Lovely to meet you," Alva called out as Hade carried Emily inside.

Caroline reached the doorway and looked back over her shoulder. "Charlotte, are you coming?" But Charlotte had drifted back over to the carriage, to the coachman.

On the day of the clambake, Caroline took extra care with her toilette, knowing that all eyes would be on her. And her family. Though Emily had covered those mysterious scratches along her brow with face powder, the sunlight was unforgiving, making her attempt at camouflage obvious. *And oh, what fodder that will be for the gossips.* Thank goodness they didn't know about Charlotte pining away for that coachman. *My lord, they'd have a field day with that!* Sure, the other matrons would smile and fawn over Caroline, but as soon as she turned her back, they'd start chattering about her daughters, speculating about her marriage.

How odd, she thought, that no one ever questioned her relationship with Ward McAllister, who had escorted her to countless social engagements. No one said a word about that. But if William was seen speaking to a woman at the polo field, or down by the yacht club, it was scandalous.

Oh, let them talk. Caroline knew she couldn't stop them, and though her pride was wounded, her core was stronger than ever. She could take it, and later, after she received her two-faced guests, she would walk the grounds with William at her side and put that rumor to rest. Now she just needed an explanation should anyone ask what happened to Emily's face.

Caroline heard the *thump*-shuffle-shuffle, *thump*-shuffle-shuffle, *thump* of her mother approaching moments before she appeared, her cane pushing open the dressing room door. "*That's* what you're wearing tonight?" she asked.

Caroline studied her choice in the mirror, the neckline enhanced with a silk ribbon, the satin bows along the bodice, the deep purple polonaise bustle.

"Need I remind you, Lina, that a lady of true gentility never dresses in the height of fashion."

"It's not as if I'm wearing Worth, Mother."

"Thank heavens for that. His designs are positively gauche." She switched her cane from her left hand to the right. Caroline's mother— Helen Van Courtlandt White Schermerhorn—was still a regal-looking woman, even at eighty-three. Her once glossy black hair was now white, and the face may have been well creased, but the eyes—the eyes remained icy blue and didn't miss a thing.

"You mustn't feel you need to compete with the new money, Lina. It's beneath you," her mother said, reaching for a bar of soap, wrapped in lavender paper. "I do so hate the way our people are being influenced by the nouveau riche." She smelled the soap, made a face and set it back down. "I thought you and Mr. McAllister were supposed to guard against that sort of thing."

"We're doing our best, Mother, but times are changing and—"

Caroline was silenced by her mother's exasperated sigh, which led to a maddening standoff, one that Caroline knew she'd never win. She never had before. She turned away and busied herself with her earrings.

As tough as Caroline was, she was no match for her mother, whose strength had been forged in tragedy. Here was a woman who had buried six of her nine children. Two of the three remaining daughters were sickly and for the most part bedridden. That left Caroline—Lina, as they called her. It wasn't enough to survive; Lina had always been expected to thrive. She was the one her mother had pinned her hopes on, and when the opportunity came for Caroline to take over society, it was her mother who had urged her to do so. "You must protect our people from this assault by the nouveau riche," she'd said to Caroline one day, while tapping her cane to the floor. "You have the breeding and lineage—and the means." *Tap, tap, tap.* "You must take the reins and put an end to these interlopers." *Tap, tap, tap.* "Our way of life is meant to inspire refinement and decency, and there is absolutely nothing inspirational about that lot . . ."

That had been her mother's sermon back in 1872, just before Ward McAllister had come to her to discuss a plan of his own for preserving society. "The women with their tiaras and coronets, the men with their fat cigars and bejeweled walking sticks," he'd said in disgust. "They all reek of newly minted steel and railroad money. They're trying to buy their way into society and it's our duty to keep them out."

"And how do you propose we do that?" Caroline had asked, slightly bemused by his passionate stance.

Well, it just so happened he'd had a plan. Like British nobility, he explained how he wanted to hand-select members of their peerage. "And I'm going to need a hostess of the finest and highest caliber, like you, to assist me in organizing this new chapter in society."

Caroline knew better than to have been flattered. "And why me?" she'd asked pointedly.

"The question is, why *not* you? I can think of no other society hostess who possesses your sense of taste and refinement."

"I think what you *really* mean is that you can think of no other hostess who possesses her own money."

He'd laughed, a bit contrite. "Well, perhaps that does give you an advantage."

Unlike other hostesses, Caroline had inherited a fortune of her own after her father passed away. She didn't have to ask her husband's permission or present a weekly ledger of household and personal expenses for his approval. That level of independence for a woman was unheard of, and it distinguished Caroline from every other society hostess. It had helped make her society's queen—that and Caroline's desperate need to please her mother.

Since then Caroline and Ward had spent hours holed up in her parlor, scrutinizing guest lists and seating arrangements, discussing which china setting and sterling silver to use. A debate over what wine to serve could last an hour or more. Ward took society very seriously, and over time, Caroline came to believe that all this mattered. William, on the other hand, thought society was frivolous. It occurred to her, only much later, that perhaps her husband had hoped she might have taken an interest in one of his pastimes or hobbies—yachting, horse breeding . . . He always seemed to ask if she'd join him when she had something else scheduled; a luncheon or meeting, a ball or opera to attend. His timing was impeccably off, and she sometimes wondered if he'd asked knowing she wouldn't be available.

It had never occurred to her that it stung her husband, her preferring the company of others, especially Ward McAllister. It also never occurred to her that her husband's pride might have been hurt, knowing his wife's appointment book was more full than his own. She hadn't thought about those things because to Caroline, society was vital. For the first time in her life, she'd done something her mother could boast about. For the first time ever, Caroline was respected; she was important and valued for things separate from her role as wife and mother. By now this business of society was so deeply ingrained in her that she was certain that if it no longer existed, if it no longer mattered, she, too, would no longer matter.

"Well," her mother said, "I can see this conversation is getting us nowhere. I'll be downstairs in the parlor."

Even after she left, the sound of her mother's voice was still the loudest in Caroline's head, and her poise slipped. She tugged off her earrings and tossed them on the dressing table, surprised her mother hadn't said anything about them being too ostentatious for a woman in her position.

Another moment passed and she went to her closet, where a simple blue gown without a single ribbon or flounce was hanging.

She rang for her lady's maid to help her change.

CHAPTER FIVE

Alva

WHILE JAMES VAN ALEN and everyone who was anyone were getting ready for Mrs. Astor's clambake, Alva was steeling herself for dinner with Willie's family at his parents' cottage. As the newest member of the Vanderbilt family, she still felt like an outsider. She didn't understand their ways. There was something *uniquely Vanderbilt* ingrained in them, a sensibility that she couldn't define or grasp. She didn't always get the jokes, nor was she able to follow the non sequiturs that had them shifting from topic to topic like trains switching tracks. At times it was as if they spoke a different language.

Standing in her dressing room, Alva was faced with a new dilemma—deciding what to wear. How was she to choose between the gowns with opals, gowns with pearls and diamonds, satin and silk ribbons, delicate lace fringe, gold and silver threading? She couldn't imagine how she'd once managed with only a handful of dresses that she'd mended over and over again. Just remembering those days had planted a horrifying thought in the back of her mind: *What if this all goes away?*

Though Alva knew the Vanderbilts were one of the wealthiest families in the country, old fears persisted. Having seen a man's fortune vanish once before, she didn't trust that it wouldn't happen again. For that reason, Alva always took a few greenbacks from her weekly allowance and placed them in a hatbox hidden in the back of her dressing room closet. Just in case.

This fear of it all going away might have explained why Alva never saved the best for last. She was afraid that any delay might cost her the very thing she'd been holding out for. She didn't want to put off her happiness for even a second. She wanted the best and had no intention of suffering through something inferior or unsatisfying just to get to it. She'd always wanted her reward up front and couldn't understand why her sisters would suffer through the tasteless vegetables, dried-out meat and pasty rice just to get to dessert. She'd sneak the cake, the pudding, the tarts despite the consequences for eating them before her supper.

"Alva?" She heard Willie K. calling to her from downstairs. "Hurry up now, darling. We mustn't be late for dinner."

"Just finishing up," she said, still sorting through her closet, pausing over the dress she'd planned to wear to Mamie's fish fry, the dress she would have worn to Mrs. Astor's clambake had she been invited.

Alva pulled out the gown and held it up beneath her chin, wondering if the neckline was high enough and the sleeves long enough to cover the remnants of her scars and bruises. Thankfully the one on her face had faded from purple to jaundice, barely noticeable anymore especially if she wore a bit of powder. But her muscles and joints still protested each time she moved, and it had been a week.

But truly, what hurt even more—what refused to heal—was the way Mrs. Astor had treated her that day. Though, in her defense, Mrs. Astor hadn't realized that Emily had been on Cliff Walk, a mere slip away from death had Alva not come along. Mrs. Astor didn't know any of that but still, she had treated Alva as if she'd been a delivery boy dropping off a parcel. And of course Emily had been too afraid of her mother to speak up. Two days later James Van Alen had stopped by to convey a message from Emily. She'd wanted to thank Alva again and hoped to see her soon. Not a word about her mother, nothing about the clambake.

Alva moved over to the mirror, holding up her elbow to examine the scab that had formed. She'd been fighting with herself to keep from picking at it, which was proving harder to do than keeping her promise to Emily.

For all of her flaws—and Alva knew she was no angel—she did take promises seriously. Mrs. Astor would never know that Alva had saved her daughter's life. There was no going back on that, which just meant Alva would have to find another way to get the Grande Dame's attention.

CHAPTER SIX

Caroline

THE ORCHESTRA WAS WARMING up, musicians tuning their violins, violas and other instruments. Christine Nilsson, in an ivory silk faille gown, stood off to the side, practicing her vocal scales—*Ah-ha-ha-ha-ha, ah-ha-ha-ha-ha.* Caroline's first footman, dressed in elegant green livery—ordered specifically for this event—was stationed at the front door, ready to inspect invitations before admitting each guest. A second footman, also dressed in livery, was off to the side, waiting to adhere white boutonnieres to the gentlemen's lapels. Sixty round tables with gilded chairs were stationed on the lawn, overlooking the cliffs. Each table was graced with a white damask tablecloth, the edges fluttering in the breeze, the napkins weighted down with fourteen-karat-gold cherub rings. A spread of silverware flanked the china at the place settings, and a dozen American Beauties sat at the center of each table. It was a flower that Caroline had introduced to this country, and at $2 a stem, American Beauties were a rare extravagance. Few hostesses could ever convince their husbands that the expense was necessary.

Normally Caroline's parties didn't begin until eleven in the evening, but her clambake was called for five o'clock, with supper being served at eight, followed by dancing till dawn and two buffets, one at midnight and a second one at six a.m.

Even at this hour, the day's heat was nearly unbearable. Caroline stood at the foot of her yard with Ward McAllister, waiting to receive their guests. Among the first in line was Caroline's brother-in-law.

John Jacob Astor III stepped forward. He had bristly muttonchops and a mustache that had already turned gray despite his dark brown hair. He took both her hands in his. "Caroline" was all he said.

She didn't expect more. Her reply was simply "John."

Her sister-in-law, Augusta, was next. She had a squarish, boxlike face but beautiful blue eyes that drew you in. "The letter . . . ," Augusta said, her mouth twisted up, giving Caroline a pitying glance, the rest implied. "I prayed for you. And for William, too."

There was something ever so smug in her delivery, as if she had taken some pleasure in writing that letter. Caroline pressed her lips together and raised her chin, remembering the Augusta who once loved hunting and gun collecting before trading all that in for the Bible. How many times had Augusta forced Waldorf to his knees, making her son repent for singing or playing hide-and-seek in the dumbwaiter with his cousins on a Sunday?

Waldorf was next in line. He had grown into a handsome, politically ambitious man, now in his twenties with his eye on the United States Senate. "Aunt Lina," he said, planting a perfunctory kiss on her cheek before walking off, just as dismissive as his parents had been.

Caroline turned to her other guests, pleased to see everyone enjoying themselves; admiring the view along the cliffs, women gingerly removing their gloves just long enough to nibble a clam or prawn before replacing them, men holding their boaters in place while playing bilboquet or croquet. Young ladies fluttered about with dance cards fastened to their wrists, penciling in the names of gentlemen to whom they'd promised dances when the ballroom opened.

After receiving so many guests, Caroline was hoping William would join her on the lawn but he was nowhere in sight. Instead, she somehow found herself walking alongside Ward McAllister and Mamie Fish—of all people. Although she'd wanted to keep an eye on Mamie, knowing she had hopes of rising up in society and taking Caroline's place. She wasn't threatened, though. It would take a much shrewder and more powerful woman than Mamie Fish to replace her.

Caroline now observed Mamie with great curiosity. She was wearing a gown so heavily embellished with diamonds and pearls that she appeared to have a difficult time walking. The brim on her hat was wide enough to provide shade for Caroline and Ward, too. Caroline would have expected this from new money, but that day, she noted that the smart set wore gowns that were equally ornate. Everywhere she looked Caroline saw more sparkled beading, rays of sunlight glinting off the jewels. Everyone was fascinated with those Worth gowns. Nowadays gemstones and trinkets were becoming as essential to a society lady as her calling card.

Caroline looked down at her own dress, regretting that she'd changed. For once, her mother had been wrong. Times *were* changing and Caroline was torn, caught between two worlds: her mother's and her own. Admittedly, she didn't know what to do with her own world. As the head of society, she'd been so busy preserving the etiquette and traditions from the past that establishing any sense of modernity hadn't occurred to her. She had many strengths and talents when it came to her role, but being an innovator was not one of them. She sometimes felt like someone with no imagination and absolutely no artistic abilities standing before a blank canvas. She had no clear vision for the future. She certainly couldn't have predicted that women would ever dress as eccentrically as they did now. And what if she, too, *had* appeared that day in a Worth gown? *So what?* It might have been refreshing, might have shown her guests a lighter side of her. Her mother wouldn't have approved no matter what she wore, and with all the gossip about her marriage, if ever there was a time for Caroline to sparkle, it had been then.

A group of gentlemen in linen summer suits and straw boaters were off to the side playing battledore and shuttlecock. Mamie's husband, Stuyvesant Fish, was among them and had nearly collided with August Belmont. The two of them were now batting away and still missing the shuttlecock. Well, that got Mamie laughing. *And oh, that laugh!* People turned to see where all the *noise* was coming from.

Caroline could take no more and excused herself, heading for the stone stairs overlooking her yard. Doing a lighthouse sweep of the lawn for William, Caroline observed her youngest, Jack, plucking canapés off a footman's tray. The boy's appetite was insatiable. He was only twelve but ate more than most grown men. And to think, of all her children, he'd been the smallest at birth, weighing a little over five pounds. She sometimes blamed herself for trying to fatten him up, but the doctor assured her he was just a growing boy. Still, Caroline worried and summoned his governess. "Keep Jack away from the hors d'oeuvres. He's going to make himself sick, eating like that." The governess scampered across the lawn to reprimand Jack, who'd gotten hold of one last prawn before being tugged away.

Caroline still couldn't locate William. She hadn't seen him since the guests began arriving, which wasn't a good sign. She feared he was in a drunken stupor and that people were talking about his affair. The only way to quash the gossip was for the two of them to appear together, unified, with smiles in place.

She went inside to look for him, passing her butler, standing regally in the grand foyer. "Mr. Astor is in the library with Miss Charlotte," Hade said without her even having to ask.

Sure enough, there was William, in the library, sitting in his leather armchair with a glass of whiskey at his side. Charlotte was with him, the two of them playing cards.

Of all her children, Charlotte was William's favorite. He made no attempt to hide it. He called her Charlie, and unlike the others,

William had taught her to fish, golf, how to shoot and clean a gun. In many ways, Charlotte was more like a son to him than Jack.

"Who's winning?" Caroline asked, sliding the pocket door shut behind her.

"We're tied," said William.

"Not for long." Charlotte played the king of spades and that was that. Game over.

"Good thing this wasn't poker," said William. "She'd have cleaned me out."

"Oh, poker!" Charlotte lit up. "Let's play."

"Oh, no. No you don't," said Caroline. "In case you haven't noticed, we're entertaining guests, and you, young lady, should be outside. You too," she said, eyeing William.

"Oh, Mother, must I? Those people are so boring."

"Charlotte."

"I agree with Charlie. *Must we?*" William laughed as he gathered up the cards.

Part of Caroline would have loved to stay and play a hand or two with them, avoid the small talk outside, the exchange of pleasantries, the adoration as well as the scrutiny. "Yes," she said, "you *must* join the party. Both of you."

"Well," said Charlotte, "maybe I'll go down to the stables first and see what Duncan is—"

"Charlotte!"

"Oh, Mother." She burst out laughing. "Don't worry. I'm teasing. I would *never* do that." She dramatically stood up, palms faced out. "Look—I'm going back to the party—see? I'm going."

After she left, Caroline turned to William, who was roaring with laugher, pointing. "You should have seen the look on your face."

"You shouldn't encourage her. She's becoming a little too familiar with that coachman. I don't like it," she said, noticing with some minor irritation that someone hadn't put a book back where it belonged on the shelf. *Is it so hard to line them up according to height?* she thought as she crossed the room to fix it, the orchestra music filtering in from outside. "What are you waiting for?" she asked. "You should be mingling with our guests."

"They're your friends." He set the cards aside. "Besides, I doubt any of them would notice if I was out there or not."

"You promised, remember?" Caroline was about to say something else when the pocket door slid open and in walked James Van Alen. Hade appeared behind him, breathless—as if he'd rushed down the corridor after him—apologizing for the interruption.

William waved off the butler's concern, and Caroline braced herself. There was only one reason why Van Alen would dare approach William, and she couldn't bear to witness it. "I'll leave you two gentlemen to your business."

"You'll do no such thing." William glowered at her.

Of course, this was the moment he wanted her by his side. Obviously, William knew what was coming, too. Their dislike of James Van Alen was one of the few things they agreed on these days. Though she was certain that William was blaming her for inviting Van Alen to the clambake. At that moment, she was blaming herself, too. In a rare show of wifely obedience, Caroline dropped into the chair near the window.

"Forgive me," Van Alen said, adjusting his monocle. "I was hoping I might have a word, good sir."

"I'm occupied," William said, polishing off his drink.

"But it is a matter of great importance."

William sighed. He was a prankster with a vicious streak, and just then he had *that look* in his eye. Caroline knew Van Alen would soon regret ever stepping foot inside that library. "Well, in that case"— William motioned to the butler and held out his empty glass—"a refill for me, Hade, and one here for Mr. Van Alen."

Van Alen politely raised his hand. "Ah, actually, I don't drink—"

"Don't tell me you're not a whiskey man," said William, incredulous.

For all of Van Alen's faults, Caroline and William both knew that drinking wasn't one of them.

"Ah, yes," said Van Alen, poorly hiding his trepidation. "Whiskey. Capital idea."

"Oh, and, Hade, leave the bottle," William said as he handed Van Alen his drink.

After Hade disappeared, William raised his glass. "To your health, young man."

Van Alen took an obligatory sip.

"It's not a cup of tea, you know," said William. "If you're going to drink, *drink*." He clanked his glass against Van Alen's. The young man winced after taking a healthy swallow. "Now that's more like it," said William, who continued talking at length—something about *the best whiskey he'd ever had*—and kept gesturing for Van Alen to keep drinking.

"Well then, Mr. Astor, Mrs. Astor," he eventually managed to slip in, offering a slight nod to them both, "I wanted to talk with you about my intentions for your—"

"Excellent intentions, I am sure. Let me top that off for you," said William, reaching for the bottle.

"No, no, I'm quite fine, thank you." Van Alen covered the glass with his gloved palm.

"Oh, nonsense." William pushed Van Alen's hand aside and refilled his glass.

"Thank you, sir." Van Alen took another sip. "The reason I wanted to speak with you is—"

"Now there's a man who appreciated a good glass of whiskey." William cut him off, pointing to a photograph of his grandfather resting on the fireplace mantel. "John Jacob Astor," he said with a puff of pride. "Yes sir, he appreciated his whiskey."

"I believe Emily mentioned that." James smiled weakly. "And speaking of Emily, I wanted to ask you about—egads," he said while William refilled his glass yet again and motioned for Van Alen to drink up, which he reluctantly did.

"Now as I was saying." Van Alen adjusted his monocle. "I've been seeing a good deal of your daughter and well . . ." He paused and took another sip for courage. "Well . . . well, you see . . ." He began to ramble, repeating himself. "Mr. Astor, I've grown awfully fond of the girl. Awfully, *awfully* fond of her. Actually, it's more than a fondness and—"

"Tell me," William interrupted, "how's the general doing?"

"The general?" Van Alen's eyes flashed so wide his monocle nearly slipped.

"Yes, yes," said William. "Your father, the general. How is he?"

William despised General Van Alen.

"My father's doing very well." Van Alen tucked a couple of fingers inside his collar to loosen it as he took another long pull. Caroline observed that his whiskey appeared to be going down more smoothly now. "And I should make you aware that I'll be inheriting a good sum of money. Upwards of one million, plus—" Van Alen stopped, as if he'd lost his train of thought. He pressed his glass, sweating with condensation, against his forehead. "It's suddenly rather balmy in here, isn't it?"

"*Balmy?*" William turned down his lower lip. "No, I don't find it *balmy* at all. I'm actually quite comfortable. Dear?"—he turned to Caroline—"are you finding it *balmy?*"

Van Alen removed his gloves, using them to pat the perspiration from his brow. "I'm s-s-suddenly verry warm."

"Perhaps we should table this conversation," suggested William. "You seem to be in the cups at the moment."

"Nooo, no, ssssir, not at all," he slurred just before coming out with it: "By golly, it's love. Forsooth there's no one I love more than your daughter, sssssir, and I've come to ask for your hand in marriage."

"I beg your pardon." William leaned forward, hand to ear. "I don't believe I heard you correctly."

"I s-said, sir, that I've come to ask for your hand in marriage."

William sat back, cracking a sly smile. "I'm afraid I'm already spoken for."

"Nooo, noo, noooo." Van Alen shook his head. "What I meant was—"

"I know what you meant, and not only can you not have *my* hand in marriage, but you cannot have my daughter's, either."

"But, good sir, I—"

"You, good sir, are an ass, or as you might put it, an arse. I don't care about you inheriting your father's millions. The Astors and the Van Alens shall not mix. I will never let my daughter marry into your moneygrubbing family." William called for the butler. "Hade? Hade, get him out of here."

Van Alen mumbled something as Hade got him to his feet and escorted him out. "Well now"—William dusted off his hands triumphantly—"that was jolly grand fun."

"Good show, ole chap," Caroline quipped. "But your work here isn't done yet. Supper is about to be served. And you *will* be joining us."

The orchestra continued to play as the guests took their seats. The candles on each table were lit as the sun began to set, flickering in the breeze, illuminating the yard.

Caroline's family, along with Ward McAllister, were seated at the head table. She was aware of her mother watching her, just as she was watching her own children. Her daughters were lovely, with William's beautiful eyes. The two oldest girls, Emily and Helen, were just a year apart and looked so much alike—the same dark hair, dramatic dark eyes, cherub-like faces—they were often mistaken for twins. Carrie, her youngest daughter, had worn her light brown hair pinned up that night, like her older sisters did, accentuating her long neck. It was the first time she'd styled her hair that way, and Caroline felt a tinge of sadness to see her growing up so fast.

There were several side conversations taking place all at once, and Caroline found herself dipping in and out of them, catching only fragments here and there: her husband laughing conspiratorially with Charlotte; Jack asking for the first course; her mother's horror over Victoria Aarden, an unmarried woman, wearing a tiara. On the other side of the table she heard Helen saying something about Rosy.

"Oh, so it's *Rosy* now, is it?" Caroline teased. "Mr. Roosevelt has certainly expressed a great deal of interest in you lately."

"No more than usual." Helen smiled, the color of her cheeks growing pink as she lowered her eyes.

It was just like Helen to downplay the romance, not wanting to upset Emily. Everyone approved of Rosy, whereas no one approved of James Van Alen. Of all of Caroline's daughters, Helen was the most congenial, the family arbiter, the one most likely to have forfeited a wooden penny doll when they were younger or a piece of Turkish delight if it meant keeping the peace between Charlotte and Carrie. Or Charlotte and Emily. Even Charlotte and Jack. Charlotte was always in the middle of everything.

Caroline turned her focus toward Emily, who hadn't said much about Rosy. Or anything else for that matter. She was jittery, looking around. Maybe she was adding up the number of pink plumes in the ladies' hats or counting the straw boaters while no doubt searching for James Van Alen. Caroline wondered if Emily had any idea that he'd asked for her hand.

A footman, dressed in Astor livery, handed each of them a menu engraved with the eight courses. Caroline's mother raised an eyebrow as if to say, *Is this necessary?* And her brow rose higher still when the footmen presented the first course of caviar and oysters on the half shell.

"Service *à la russe* is much more elegant than service *à la fran-çaise,*" her mother said.

Caroline knew her too well to assume this was a compliment. She took a sip of champagne and braced herself.

"Serving each course one at a time rather than bringing the food out all at once is very European," her mother added. "Of course, it's also a much more dramatic presentation. Tell me, Lina, how many additional liveried footmen did you hire just for this?"

"I told you, Mother"—Caroline looked across the way at Mamie, her fish fork scooting an oyster about—"I did what I had to do." Caroline set her glass down. "I don't suppose you approve of the favors, either."

"There was nothing wrong with the nosegays and handkerchiefs," she said with a hand flourish, "but if you feel the need to impress your guests with expensive trinkets, far be it from me to say anything."

Caroline pressed her lips tight, willing herself not to scowl. There were too many eyes on their table and on her.

The supper pressed on with one course followed by another. When the footmen served the Roman punch, William pushed his cup aside and Jack reached for it, plunging his spoon into the sweet meringue before Caroline could stop him. William dabbed his mouth and tossed his napkin onto the table before turning to Caroline and saying wryly, "May I be excused now?"

She wanted to say no, but he wasn't asking her permission. In fact, he had already stood up and taken his first step away from the table, and there was no graceful way to counter. She had to let him go and without revealing even a hint of disappointment. He had barely made it inside when Caroline realized she had a far bigger problem to contend with.

James Van Alen had somehow managed to find his way back into the party. She watched in horror as he stumbled and tripped across the grounds. Caroline didn't know what to do, but she was on her feet now, heading toward him.

Her nephew sprang up from his table and grabbed Van Alen by the lapels, shouting, "Get hold of yourself, man."

"Please, Waldorf," said Caroline, catching up to them. "That's enough, thank you. People are staring. Let us not draw any more attention to the matter." But of course, it was too late for that. Her guests were watching them while finishing their cherry compote, as if this were part of the evening's entertainment.

Emily was at Caroline's side now, too. "James? Oh James, what's—" She stopped and brought a hand to her chest. "Have you been drinking?"

"Yesh, yesh I—I have," James stammered, belched and hung his head, teetering, his balance unsteady. "I'm verry tired," he said, his backside already butting up against one of the tables, making a few of Caroline's guests abandon their chairs.

A footman took hold of him, and Waldorf held Emily back as Van Alen was escorted away from the clambake once again. Emily broke free from her cousin's hold and stormed off toward the cottage. Caroline, all stilted smiles, followed, finding Emily already in the library confronting her father.

"You know James doesn't drink," Emily was saying. "You've gone and made a fool of him."

"My dear, James Van Alen needs no assistance from me in that department."

"Don't you see, he wants to marry me, and I want to marry him. I'm going to be his wife."

"Over my dead body."

And with that, Emily's eyes grew glassy, her indignation faltering as she covered her face, sobbing into her hands. Though she hated to see her daughter in such pain, Caroline was relieved, certain they'd seen the last of James Van Alen.

CHAPTER SEVEN

Alva

WHEN ALVA AND WILLIE K. arrived at the Vanderbilts' cottage for dinner that night, her father-in-law, Billy, nearly stampeded them in the drawing room. "Well, look who's finally here."

It was obvious that Willie's good looks came from his mother, Louisa Kissam, for his father was a stocky man with scraggly whiskers that irritated Alva's cheek when he leaned in to kiss her hello.

All the Vanderbilts were there, including the Commodore, a stoop-shouldered man with tufts of cottony white hair. He was accompanied by his second wife, Frank, named after her father's best friend. She was forty years younger than the Commodore and a good twenty years younger than some of her stepdaughters. She also happened to be the Commodore's second cousin, which no one thought odd seeing as his previous wife had been his first cousin.

When one of the footmen held out a tray of aperitifs, the Commodore reached for a glass, dismissing the cocktail napkin with a swat of his hand. "Hmmmph," he said, looking disapprovingly at the fluted sherry glass. "What a bunch of poppycock."

The Commodore had no use for society or manners. Willie's grandfather had grown up penniless on Staten Island and had worked sixteen- and eighteen-hour days trying to get his own ferry business started. Back then, there was no need for etiquette. He downed his sherry in two gulps.

Billy reached for an aperitif, raising his glass to his eldest son, Cornelius II. The two of them were talking about a new railroad line that would yield the family another million by its completion. Alva's ears perked up at that. *Another million.* She still couldn't get used to their tossing such staggering amounts of money around like a handful of coins. It would have been nice if some of that money found its way to a worthy cause, but the Commodore was not a big believer in philanthropy. He'd often said, *Let others do what I have done, and they need not be around here begging.*

Alva pretended she wasn't eavesdropping on the men while she stood with Willie's sisters, Margaret and Florence, all encircling Cornelius's wife, Alice. Alice Vanderbilt was ten years Alva's senior, and despite Willie's mother being alive and well, Alice considered herself the Vanderbilts' matriarch. Alice had an interesting face, long and slender with a dark sprig of tightly wound curls resting on her forehead. Her small, narrow eyes made her appear as if she were always squinting. The other women were listening intently to her talking about how her young sons, Bill and Neily, were constructing a toy railroad of their own.

"It must be in their blood," said Alva.

"Why, of course it is." Alice looked at Alva as if she'd said something not only absurd but also obscene.

Alva was thinking of her response when an unsavory-looking man barged into the room. At first, she thought he was an intruder, come to pick their pockets and help himself to all the women's jewelry. But no one else was alarmed. Maybe he was a deliveryman or perhaps a servant out of livery. Wrong again. The tall, lanky, almost gaunt man in the threadbare suit was Cornelius Jeremiah Vanderbilt, whom they all called Jeremiah.

"I don't believe we've met," he said to Alva moments later, after having made his rounds to the others. He reminded her of those vagrants who slept in doorways and stole apples and grapes off the carts down on Fourteenth Street and Third Avenue. "And tell me, how are you related to all this?" He gestured to the others, to the room and all its excess.

"I'm Willie's wife. And you?"

"I, my good lady," he said with a grandiose bow, "am the Commodore's ne'er-do-well son."

"I didn't realize the Commodore had another son."

"And *I* didn't realize Willie had a *wife*."

"Oh my," said Alva with feigned alarm, "do you think we're at the right dinner party?"

At that Jeremiah threw his head back, raised his hand to his chest and laughed. He had long slender fingers except for two on his left hand. They were misshapen, slightly bent, the knuckles gnarled. Each time he blinked, his long lashes stirred the tips of the hair hanging down in his steely-blue eyes. Looking past the beard, she could now see a family resemblance, Jeremiah looking more like the Commodore than his brother Billy.

"So, where have they been hiding you?" asked Alva. "And why weren't you at our wedding?"

"I wasn't invited. I told you, I'm the ne'er-do-well son." He sounded proud of the title, as if that distinguished him from the others. The footman came by with a tray of aperitifs. Jeremiah took two glasses, passing one to Alva. "It's a rough crowd here tonight. Billy can't stand me. Neither can Alice. Watch out for her. She doesn't like you one bit, I can tell already."

"Thanks for the warning."

"Well," he said, conspiratorially, "we interlopers have to stick together."

Alva raised her glass and an eyebrow in unison. Regardless of what the Vanderbilts thought, she liked Jeremiah. Felt an instant connection with him. Later she would learn that being the family wastrel wasn't entirely his fault. Jeremiah had been born with epilepsy, and after his first seizure, complete with frothing from the mouth, the Commodore had put him in an asylum. After his release, Jeremiah picked up a gambling habit and some other vices. But that was years ago and according to Willie, Jeremiah had been behaving himself, and for now anyway, was back in the Commodore's good graces.

Twenty minutes later, dinner was served, and they'd all moved into the dining room, sitting around a table made of rosewood and mahogany trimmed in bronze. Two footmen brought out enormous serving dishes and tureens, steaming platters of capon, bass and lamb, the various aromas melding together, clashing and at times pungent. Alva had lost her appetite because they'd begun talking—of all things—about Mrs. Astor's clambake. She would have given anything to be there instead that night.

"I hear they're bringing the Academy's symphony in from New York," said Willie's mother.

"I wonder how much that will cost them," said Cornelius, tucking his napkin in his shirt collar.

"Speaking of the Academy of Music," said Alice, "with any luck we'll be purchasing a box this coming season. I'm hoping to set up a meeting with the impresario when we return to New York."

The others thought that was splendid. The Academy of Music was the city's opera house, the fountainhead of the Knickerbockers' existence. Alva didn't respond. She knew Alice had been denied such a meeting for the past three seasons. What made her think this year would be any different? The expression on Jeremiah's face said pretty much the same thing.

Alva took a good hard look at her new extended family. The people gathered around that table represented more wealth than was fathomable. Even more wealth than the Astors possessed. The Commodore was worth millions, which, upon his death, would be cut up like a pie and served sliver by sliver to his thirteen children and their descendants. The largest piece, of course, would go to his eldest son, Billy.

The Commodore, seated to Alva's right, was eighty-two, and his mind and vision were beginning to wane. He'd already mistaken Alva's gown for his napkin, and when he bent over to dab his mouth on her dress, she yelped. The others looked on horrified, but not quite as horrified as they'd been when he splashed about in his finger bowl and then slurped it down the hatch.

Looking around the table again, Alva saw exactly what she was up against. Yes, the Vanderbilts had enormous wealth, but no amount of money could buy the one thing they lacked: breeding. She was all too aware that Billy was using his oyster fork for his salad, Jeremiah had bread crumbs in his beard, Cornelius had his elbows on the table, and the Commodore was chewing with his mouth open.

Though each new generation possessed slightly better manners and greater sophistication, the Vanderbilts hadn't evolved enough for society. Frankly, they hadn't evolved enough for Alva, either. It was obvious now that it was going to be up to her to get the Vanderbilts recognized by society.

CHAPTER EIGHT

Caroline

OVER MY DEAD BODY. The day after the clambake, those words came back to haunt William Backhouse Astor Jr. Caroline was passing by the conservatory just as her husband was about to receive a most unusual visitor, an eager-looking gentleman with broad, square shoulders and an obedient stance. Hade announced him as George Pendergrass, General Van Alen's second.

"Van Alen's *second*?" William laughed and looked at Caroline, who was now curious enough to join her husband in the chair beside him as the breeze coming through the open windows stirred the drapes.

Pendergrass ceremoniously handed William a sealed envelope. "General Van Alen asked that I deliver this letter to you personally."

No one said anything. The sound of water trickling from the marble Apollo fountain in the center of the room was suddenly amplified.

"Very well," said William eventually. "You've delivered his letter, and now, if you'll excuse me, I don't have time for this nonsense." He gestured toward the door.

"I've been instructed to wait while you read the general's letter." Pendergrass stood solid and stoic, hands clasped behind his back.

"Utterly ridiculous," said William with a wave of his hand. "I won't be told what to do. Especially not in my own house and certainly not by Van Alen."

"Very well then, sir." Pendergrass retrieved the envelope from William. "I've been instructed to read it to you, if by chance you refused to do so yourself." He unsealed the letter, cleared his throat and began:

Sir—

Having learned of the unfortunate events that occurred on your property yesterday, Thursday, the tenth of August, I am gravely offended. You have not only humiliated and insulted my son, but you have besmirched my family's good name. I demand you retract your statements and offer an apology at once to my son, and to each guest in attendance. Furthermore, I demand that you grant permission thereby allowing Miss Emily Astor to wed my son, James Van Alen Jr. If all of the above, as well as a formal written apology to me, are not forthcoming within the next twenty-four hours, I will have no choice but to challenge you to a duel using Colt pistols as our weapons. The time and place to be—

"Enough!" William shouted, making Pendergrass take a half step back.

A duel? Caroline shook her head. It was preposterous.

"I refuse to waste my time listening to one more word." William looked at Pendergrass and added, "You tell General Van Alen he's every bit as pompous as his son." He snatched the letter from Pendergrass, crumpled it into a tight ball and deposited it back into Pendergrass's hand. "There's his apology. What he chooses to do with it is of no concern of mine. However, if he's looking for suggestions, I can offer a prime location as to where he may shove it."

Caroline listened to her husband hurling insults about General Van Alen, and when his language became too colorful, she excused herself, doubting that anyone noticed she'd left the room. With the sound of William's bluster echoing off the walls, Caroline went upstairs to check on Emily, who had not stepped out of her room since the clambake.

When she knocked on the door, there was no answer. She tried the knob, surprised when it turned. Letting herself in, she saw Emily on her side, facing the wall. She didn't stir at all, and at first, Caroline thought she was asleep. But then Emily craned her neck, rolling onto her back.

"I haven't heard from James since the clambake. It's over. I've lost him. Lost him for good."

"Shhhhh." Caroline sat on the side of the bed, smoothing her hands over the coverlet while General Van Alen's ultimatum rang out, again and again inside her head. She couldn't shake it loose.

"I feel like part of me has died," said Emily. "It hurts so badly. Sometimes I can hardly breathe."

"Your first heartbreak always hurts the most," said Caroline. "But you'll see"—Emily rolled back onto her side—"your heart will mend, stronger than it was before. I promise you that. The heart is resilient. The more it breaks, the stronger it becomes."

"I can't talk about this right now. Please, just let me be."

But Caroline didn't know how to let *anything* just be. It wasn't in her nature. She was a doer, an organizer—the one who smoothed ruffled feathers, who made problems disappear, who—in the eyes of her children—possessed mythic powers. But for once, Caroline was at a loss. There was no good outcome for this.

No one teaches you how to be a mother, she thought, easing off the bed. They teach you everything else—how to set a proper table and dance the cotillion, speak French, but there were no lessons for raising children. Unlike her own mother, and despite having a staff of nurses and governesses, Caroline had always been involved with her children. She'd bathed them herself, changed them, read them bedtime stories. It was all trial and error, and Emily, being her first, was the recipient of more than her share of mistakes. Caroline feared she was about to make another one where Van Alen was concerned.

She wandered into her bedroom and leaned up against the back of the door, staring about the room. It was large, large enough to double as her office, and in the corner was her desk, designed for her in Paris by Alfred Emmanuel Louis Beurdeley. She'd fallen behind in her correspondence and thought some letter writing would take her mind off things. Removing a piece of vellum stationery, off-white with her name engraved at the top, she began a letter to Matilda Browning, a cousin twice removed who'd been seeking advice on her daughter's debut. An acrid scent escaped from the crystal ink bottles on the silver footed tray as she studied what she'd written. She was unhappy with her penmanship. The D in *Dear* was not in alignment with the C in *Cousin* or the M in *Matilda*. She tore it up and started over again but only got halfway through before she tore that one up as well.

Caroline gave up and went over to the leather club chair where she had a splendid view of the cliffs and the water. The sound of the waves breaking usually brought her solace, but not on that day. Resting her head in her hands, she asked, *What am I to do? What have I done wrong?*

When she considered all her daughters, Helen was the only one who seemed content to follow in Caroline's footsteps and build her life in society, whereas Charlotte, well, Charlotte was a rebel. Contrary in nature, she'd deliberately take an interest in just about anything and anyone that Caroline would oppose. And then there was Carrie. Her youngest daughter loved to draw, to paint, rendering portraits of her sisters, her brother—anyone willing to sit still long enough for her to capture. And she wasn't without talent . . .

Caroline recognized that her daughters were coming into their own, developing their own interests and passions, but she didn't know how to let go and trust that they'd find their way. She'd tried so hard to wrap her arms around them all, contain them, keep them from straying into unknown territory, but she was losing that battle. The one thing she knew was that she didn't want to be like her mother. Caroline cringed each time she'd catch herself saying things like *Did you do something to your hair?* Meaning, whatever it was, she didn't like it. Or *Why? Because I say so.* Or *Shoulders back, young lady* and *What did I tell you about ___?*

But she couldn't dwell on that just now. Her mind was blistering with worry over Emily and fears about the duel. By ignoring General Van Alen's request for an apology, William had as good as accepted the challenge, and the very thought of her husband dueling with Van Alen left Caroline with a pit in her stomach. Van Alen was an expert marksman. A duel with him was a death wish.

There was a knock on the door, and Hade appeared with a decanter and a crystal tulip-cut copita glass on a silver tray. "I thought perhaps a bit of sherry might be in order, madam."

Hade had been with Caroline for only a few years, having replaced her previous butler who'd perished in his sleep one night. Hade had come to the Astors highly recommended and quickly proved himself to be a gentleman, devoted to a life of service. Nearly middle-aged, he had a tinge of gray in his otherwise dark hair. He was tall and lean and spoke with a deep, rich baritone. One of Hade's greatest assets, aside from her children adoring him, was his uncanny ability to anticipate Caroline's every need, whether that be adding a log to the fire or bringing her a cup of tea—or, in this case, something stronger.

Caroline never drank in the afternoon, but she made an exception that day and was grateful that Hade had left the decanter for her. She took a sip, feeling the warmth spread across her chest. After finishing the one sherry, Caroline contemplated another. Emily was still in her room, Helen and Charlotte were at the beach, Carrie was sketching her grandmother on the veranda, and Jack was out walking with his governess, who had promised him biscuits in exchange for a little exercise. Caroline poured a second glass and sipped it while rehearsing her lines. When she felt prepared, she finished the last of her sherry, set the decanter aside and went off in search of William.

She found him in the game room, sitting on the edge of the settee, surrounded by his various sailing trophies. He was lacing up his white balmoral footwear with the rubber soles that he always wore on his yacht.

Her heart sank. "You're going sailing?"

"Yes, and why not?"

"Today of all days?" She was still standing in the entranceway, squeezing the doorjamb, staring at the billiard balls scattered across the table.

"And what would you prefer I do? Sit here, fretting, waiting for Emily to appear? She'll come out of her room when she's good and ready."

Emily? She wasn't nearly as worried about Emily as she was about him. Her gut tightened. "William, you absolutely must stay here and write your apology to—"

"I'll do nothing of the kind."

This was exactly what she'd feared; he was too proud to back down. She made her way over to a chair, perched herself on the edge, trying to think of a way to reach him. She wanted to say she feared for him, that his children needed him, that *she* needed him. She wanted to say she loved him, but what she said instead was: "You're a fool. Van Alen is a brigadier general. Your hands shake unless you're holding a drink. He'll kill you on the count of ten."

William stood up and crossed the room, turning his back to her, feigning interest in something outside the window. But she could see his reflection in the glass, the way his face was locked in a grimace. He was rattled. They both knew she was right.

"Did you hear what I said, William? You cannot go through with this duel."

"I have to." Still turned away from her, he added, "Would you prefer I apologize, give my blessings to this preposterous marriage and let my daughter marry a man who would be an utter embarrassment to this family? Is that what you want me to do?"

Caroline got up from her chair, went to her husband's side, placed her hand on his and simply said, "Yes."

And that was how her daughter Miss Emily Astor became engaged to Mr. James Van Alen Jr.

CHAPTER NINE

Society

NEW YORK

FROM DRAWING ROOM TO drawing room, there is only one thing we talk about these days: the Astor wedding. Or more specifically: Why on earth is Emily Astor marrying James Van Alen? These days fashionable ladies—debutantes without half the pedigree of Emily Astor—marry dukes, earls, viscounts, barons—men with *real* British accents!

Alice Heine is now Duchess de Richelieu; Jennie Jerome is Lady Randolph Churchill. Consuelo Yznaga has recently become engaged to Viscount Mandeville, and just last week we learned that Minnie Stevens has become affianced to Captain Arthur Paget, whose grandfather is the first Marquess of Anglesey. Soon enough we'll be calling her Lady Paget. How is it possible, then, with all the world marrying into nobility, that Mrs. Astor's eldest daughter would marry someone who not only *isn't* a Knickerbocker but *is* a Van Alen? Simply unheard of.

Already so many details of the wedding have begun to surface. Ophelia heard the guest list includes President Grant and the British prime minister. The menu is rumored to have grown from six to nine courses. The flower arrangements are expected to be so elaborate that one florist can't possibly handle the order, so Mrs. Astor has employed both Howard Fleishman and Klunder, Hodgson, Wadley & Smythe. It's obvious that Mrs. Astor is determined to surpass even her own superlative standards for entertaining, and for the next two weeks, each of us frantically checks our mail, hoping to receive a coveted invitation to what is being hailed *the wedding of the decade*.

CHAPTER TEN

Caroline

IF WILLIAM LOOKED AT his timepiece once more, if he clacked it open and snapped it shut again, Caroline was going to scream. And she never screamed. Instead, she waited, counted to ten. In less than twenty-four hours, their daughter was getting married, and William had just announced that he was not going to walk Emily down the aisle. Caroline knew he didn't mean it, that he simply liked the sound of it, that it gave him some false sense of control over the situation.

"Why not just have Waldorf give her away?" he said. *Clack. Snap.* "He's running for the senate. Surely that should impress everyone."

"Waldorf is not her father."

"Oh, come now, Lina. You're not fooling anyone." He set the time-piece down. "You can invite as many presidents, as many dukes and duchesses—invite the goddamn queen of England—it won't change a thing."

Maybe it wouldn't change the situation, but it was certainly providing enough dazzling distractions to give the gossips something else to focus on. She had painstakingly curated the guest list, one that was so ultra-exclusive she'd even crossed off several of the bride and groom's requests. As she explained to Emily, there simply wouldn't be room for several of James's friends such as that young Vanderbilt and his brash wife.

"I tell you, Lina," William said, reaching for his timepiece again, "everyone knows this wedding is a farce."

"This marriage may be a farce, but it saved your life, and now I'm going to save Emily's reputation. And I don't care how many dignitaries it takes to do it."

"But you—"

"You *are* going to walk your daughter down the aisle tomorrow, and you *will* play the part of the proud father. Because if you don't, you'll only fuel more talk."

"But you can't *stop* them from talking," William said, flailing his arms until a streak of pain crossed his face, his thrashing about becoming less vigorous. She knew his shoulder was bothering him. A remnant from a riding accident when he was eighteen. Thrown from a horse, he'd dislocated it. It had started bothering him in recent years, on damp days, cold days, nights when he'd slept wrong.

She went over to massage the spot she knew so well, the spot she'd rubbed many a time with liniment oil. He allowed himself to sink into her touch for a moment before shaking it off.

Changing his tone, he took on a British accent. "Van Alen's probably spit shining his monocle right now—egads!" He laughed.

She didn't.

"Oh, come on now, Lina. You used to find it funny whenever I imitated that buffoon."

"That *buffoon* is about to become a member of our family."

"This wedding is a sham," he said, returning to his earlier argument, picking up the timepiece again. He muttered something else under his breath and sighed. "Well, I'm not staying for the reception, I can tell you that right now . . ." *Clack. Snap.* "I'm getting on my yacht and . . ."

She had allowed him to sound off, much in the same way that she tolerated little Jack's tantrums when denied a second fruit tart or chocolate biscuit. She half expected William to stomp his foot. "Well," she said, picking a piece of lint off his lapel, "unless you have anything more to say, I suggest you get a good night's sleep. We have a big day tomorrow."

She turned toward the door. Their argument was over. She had conceded on his behalf. He was going to give his daughter away the next day and he would attend the reception, too. There wasn't a thing he could do about it, either. She was the queen of New York society, but that didn't make him the king. And he knew it. As a mere wife, she might not have any legal rights, but she had other means available to her. If she'd wanted, Caroline could have had William banished from every men's club including his precious yachting club. She could have seen to it that he would never again be welcome at another poker table or invited on another fox hunt or coaching party. Of course, she never would have done any of those things because, heaven help her, she still loved him.

Caroline hadn't been a young bride when she married William. Until she met him, her heart had belonged to Horace Wellsby, the son of her father's lawyer. One day while Mr. Wellsby was behind closed doors with her father, Horace had smiled at her, and she lived on that for a week. After a month of secretive courting, he worked up the nerve to kiss her. She was twenty years old. It was her first kiss.

Caroline couldn't contain her excitement, and when she returned home that day, she blurted out, "Oh, Mother—I think I'm in love."

Her mother had seemed pleased, as if to say, *It's about time.* Resting her embroidery hoop in her lap, she wanted to know more. "Who is he? Do we know the family? Who are his people?"

"Actually, I've known him quite some time. It's Horace. Horace Wellsby, Mr. Wellsby's son."

Her mother's expression sagged, changing entirely. "Oh, Lina."

She shook her head. "The lawyer's son? No, no, no." She placed the embroidery hoop on the side table. "You must put an end to this. Now. You are not to see that boy again. Do you understand?"

Caroline did understand. She understood because Caroline had never once defied her mother, had never challenged her on anything. So she never saw Horace again because going against her mother's wishes would have been blasphemous.

Two years had passed since her first and only kiss. Caroline was beginning to fear it might be her last and that she'd end up a spinster, when suddenly William Backhouse Astor Jr. came into her life.

Her mother had arranged it, inviting William and his parents for dinner. Though William was only two years older than her, he seemed so much more mature. One look at his whiskers, his broad shoulders, and Caroline was terrified. He was a man whereas Horace had still been a boy. *What is Mother thinking?* He would never be interested in someone like her. William had recently returned after living abroad for two years and regaled them with stories of his travels. Caroline hardly said two words throughout the meal.

After dinner, the two of them sat in the parlor. Caroline was afraid of being alone with him and couldn't bring herself to look him in the eye.

"Our mothers cooked this whole thing up, you know," he said conspiratorially.

Caroline kept her eyes trained on her hands. "I know. I'm sorry about that."

"Sorry?" He rocked back and laughed. "I'm not."

Speaking into her hands she said, "Please, don't make fun of me."

"You know what your problem is? You don't see yourself the way others see you."

That was just the thing. She was afraid she did. She was certain that her most appealing attribute was her Dutch ancestry.

"You're an interesting girl, Caroline Webster Schermerhorn. You're very different from the other girls—I'll give you that. But you've got something"—he reached over for her hand—"something special."

She looked at him, still not sure of what to say. She knew by the heat rising on her face that her cheeks were turning red.

He suggested they spend more time together, get to know each other better. If they'd had a chaperone with them, Caroline couldn't recall it. All she remembered was him—William Backhouse Astor Jr. The first time he kissed her, well, she realized her kiss with Horace hadn't counted. William had melted her on the spot.

They were married, and nine months later, Caroline gave birth to Emily. William's disappointment at having produced a daughter was not lost on anyone. Especially Caroline, who felt she'd failed him. One year later, Helen was born, and over the next six years, two more daughters arrived, Charlotte followed by Carrie. The girls were each so different, as if they'd come into this world with their personalities already intact, just waiting to open and blossom.

William had all but given up on a male heir. Perhaps that was why he'd gravitated to Charlotte. His *Charlie* wasn't like the others. She didn't cry, wanting to be picked up and coddled. No, she'd fall and get right back up, ever more determined.

As the girls grew older and no longer needed Caroline as much, she found herself becoming more involved in society, hosting dinner parties and balls. She was busy, almost too busy to realize what was happening to her marriage.

That was when William began spending more time on his yacht or out with his horses. She suspected there was another woman—or women—but pushed the thought from her mind until her suspicions were proven true. The perfume and rouge she'd discovered on his handkerchief could only mean one thing. Caroline was crushed, certain it was the baby weight she'd failed to shed that had driven him away. Over the next three months, she'd starved herself back to a twenty-two-inch waist. Still William kept his distance. She was furious but also heartbroken. Each time he was out late, or didn't come home till dawn, Caroline sat up, waiting, going to the window, looking, watching, hoping he'd appear. And when he did finally show up, drunk and unapologetic, Caroline did what she'd seen her mother do when *her* husband strayed: she looked the other way.

Just when she was sure she'd lost William's affections forever, one night, he decided not to go out after dinner and instead, later that evening, he came to her room. That was the night that John "Jack" Jacob Astor IV was conceived. At last, a son.

It was also the last time William had stepped foot inside her bedroom.

CHAPTER ELEVEN

Alva

IT WAS NOVEMBER AND a new season was already underway. Any hope Alva had about her Cliff Walk rescue ingratiating her with Mrs. Astor had been dashed when she and Willie K. were not invited to Emily's wedding. Alva had even had a special dress made, had bought their wedding gift—a pair of Venetian enamel vases once owned by an eighteenth-century viscount. She'd boasted to Alice and the rest of the Vanderbilts that she would be attending the wedding, hobnobbing with Mrs. Astor's smart set. Alva had been mortified by the rejection.

And then, as luck would have it, luck that turned to misfortune, Alva had spotted Mrs. Astor one day at Tiffany & Company on Union Square. The Grande Dame was at the counter, looking at an array of diamond brooches the clerk had set before her on a black velvet tray. Alva inched closer while they pared down the selection.

"I'm torn between these two," Alva overheard Mrs. Astor saying.

Alva peered in closer. One was a lovely oval amethyst stone set in an elaborate laurel wreath of rose-cut yellow diamonds. The challenger was a cluster of deep blue sapphires set in a flower head pattern of diamonds.

"They're both lovely," said the clerk. "I'm certain that Mrs. Van Alen will be delighted with either one."

Mrs. Van Alen? Emily? This is for Emily?

"I just can't decide which one would suit her best," Mrs. Astor lamented.

That's when Alva spoke up. "Pardon me—I couldn't help but over-hear." She felt Mrs. Astor tense up beside her. *Keep your mouth shut, Alva. Don't say another word. Don't, don't, do not*— "With Mrs. Van Alen's coloring," she said, "I think the amethyst would be better."

"Very well then," said Mrs. Astor to the clerk. "I'll take the sap-phires."

Alva sulked and then, a few weeks later, she decided the time had come to pay a social call to Mrs. Astor. Yes, there were rules about this sort of thing, but as far as Alva was concerned, rules were meant to be broken. While it was customary to drop off one's card ahead of time and wait—sometimes up to a week—for Mrs. Astor's reply, Alva wasn't willing to do that. She'd already followed the proper etiquette and had dropped off her card not once, not twice, but three times. She was tired of waiting. Hers wouldn't be one of a hundred or so cards awaiting Mrs. Astor's approval. Alva had never been passive about anything she'd wanted before, so why this?

She checked herself in the mirror one last time. She had decided to wear her pale green dress with the emerald beading along the bodice and the creamy strand of pearls that Willie said had once be-longed to Catherine the Great. Those pearls along with her mink coat would make a statement.

It was snowing that day, the first measurable snowfall of the year. When the family's coachman brought the brougham around for her, a dusting of flakes had already accumulated on the two black horses, steam coming from their muzzles. The driver lowered the carriage steps and helped her inside. Alva, who had walked the city till the soles of her shoes wore away—who had ridden crowded omnibuses alongside men with mud-caked boots and rank breath, women in threadbare clothing with children on their laps—would never take a private coach and driver for granted. She stuffed her gloved hands deep inside her silk-lined muff while the brougham eased forward.

By two o'clock that afternoon, a good four inches of snow had already fallen, with a gray sky promising more. Alva's coachman negotiated the ice and snowdrifts, staying within the deep tracks laid down by previous carriages that had trekked up Fifth Avenue. Clearing a porthole in the window fog, Alva was mesmerized by a city that seemed to be growing skyward as much as it stretched outward. Those buildings, their stature and sense of permanence, left her in awe. She could only imagine what it must have been like to create something that solid, that enduring, something one could put their name on.

When she arrived at Thirty-Fourth Street, Alva gazed out at a rather unremarkable four-story townhouse. *So, this is where the great queen lives?* Alva had been expecting something much grander and noted that it was a tad bit smaller than the home of her brother-in-law, John Astor III, right next door. And, of course, the Alexander T. Stewart mansion across the street dwarfed them both.

Before the coachman helped her out of the carriage, he offered to deliver her calling card on her behalf. Alva thanked him anyway, and though it was out of the ordinary—highly so—she needed to meet with the Grande Dame in person, look her in the eye and win her over. She wouldn't mention Emily's rescue, wouldn't say a word about the incident at Tiffany & Company. No, Alva would appeal to Mrs. Astor just as any other young society lady might do. She would make Mrs. Astor see that she could contribute to society, that not *all* railroad money was bad.

Alva proceeded, allowing her driver to guide her up the front stairs and tug the bell pull, before sending him back to the carriage. Alva clutched her calling card, practicing her lines: *Why, Mrs. Astor, what a lovely home you have . . . It's a shame the two of us haven't met properly yet . . .* Soon the front door opened, and Alva was face-to-face with Mrs. Astor's butler, a tall, slim gentleman with a long, solemn expression and heavily lidded eyes that made him appear sleepy. He bowed respectfully and, without a word, held out a silver tray.

As Alva placed her card on top, she smiled and asked, "Is she in?"

His eyes flashed, breaking from his stuffy composure. "I—I beg your pardon?"

"Is Mrs. Astor in? I'd like to have a word with her." Alva wasn't sure if it was her request or her Southern accent—which she'd played up—that had confounded him. She smiled in that way that had opened many a door for her in the past and was about to step inside, when the butler deftly blocked the entranceway.

"I'm afraid Mrs. Astor does not receive guests in this manner." He bowed again and, in his deep voice, wished her a good day and closed the door.

Alva stared at the bell pull, stunned, as if expecting him to open the door again. Through the stained-glass windows she saw him disappear down a long dark hallway. She'd been dismissed. By the butler. Forcing herself down the front stoop, her heart in her throat, she kept her shoulders high and dignified as she walked back to her carriage.

"Take me to Miss Yznaga's home," she said as her coachman helped her into the brougham.

She stuffed her hands inside her muff, fingers balled into fists. She needed Consuelo's advice. Thankfully her friend was back in New York, preparing for her marriage to George Victor Drogo Montagu, Viscount Mandeville, the future eighth Duke of Manchester. At least that was one wedding she'd be invited to. Thankfully none of those ridiculous social formalities mattered when it came to Consuelo.

The two had met as young girls in Newport. Consuelo's father had been a wealthy Cuban sugar plantation owner, and Alva's father had run a successful cotton plantation. Both girls had grown up in the South, Consuelo in Louisiana, Alva in Alabama, their summers spent in Newport. Consuelo was the only one who had stuck by Alva after her family lost everything.

When she arrived at the Yznagas' home, she found Consuelo in the music room, practicing her banjo, which accompanied her just about everywhere. Alva had seen her friend strumming away at lawn parties and dinner parties, and only Consuelo was charming enough to get everyone applauding and encouraging her to play more. She soaked her fingertips in a dish of butter each night to keep them from becoming calloused.

Alva whipped her muff and hat across the room and pulled her traveling gloves off with her teeth before relaying what had happened with Mrs. Astor's butler.

Consuelo strummed a few chords and said, "Well, what did you expect? You know better than that, Alva. That little gesture of yours probably did more harm than good. You can't go around bullying everyone—especially not Mrs. Astor."

"And apparently not you, either."

Consuelo laughed. "You've always been such a terror. When we were little, you'd do just about anything to get your own way."

"And it worked, didn't it?"

"That was then. This is now." Consuelo accented her point with a C chord. "Society won't give an inch. I'm warning you. And you have to stop following Mrs. Astor around in stores."

"I wasn't following her. She just happened to be there."

"And you should have had the good sense to keep your mouth shut."

"Well, I've about had it with *society*. I can't seem to do anything right by these people."

Consuelo laughed, set her banjo aside and patted her tight dark curls in place.

"It's not funny. Oh, heaven help me!" Alva dramatically pressed the back of her hand to her forehead as if about to faint. "How dare I call on the great Mrs. Astor? At least I waited until two o'clock." Alva had observed the rule that it was impolite to make a social call before two in the afternoon and even worse to stay past four.

"I think asking her butler if you could speak to her was probably the greater offense."

"Lord have mercy," said Alva. "I didn't realize it's such poor form to ask to be received by the high-and-mighty Caroline Astor."

"Now you're just being a brat," she teased. "And really, you mustn't speak that way about Mrs. Astor. She's a very powerful woman, and like it or not, Mrs. Astor is the only one who can grant you entrée into New York society."

"But she's too old-fashioned. Too set in her ways. And she's cold. I tell you butter wouldn't melt in that woman's mouth."

"Now, Alva."

"Okay, all right." She raised her hands.

Consuelo went over to Alva and cupped her face in her hands. "Calm down. You're a very bright girl—you *will* figure this out. If Mrs. Astor is standing in your way, maybe it's time to try another avenue."

"Like what?"

"I don't know"—she dropped her hands and shrugged—"maybe the Academy of Music."

"I've already tried buying a box. They won't even meet with me to discuss the matter."

"Well, try again. I've known you a very long time and you're not a quitter. You've always gotten everything you've set your heart on, including Willie Vanderbilt. If you put your mind to it, Mrs. Astor and the Academy of Music won't stand a chance."

CHAPTER TWELVE

Caroline

CAROLINE WAS ABOUT TO start a new book and had settled into her favorite Herter Brothers armchair, across from the crackling fireplace, near the upstairs bay windows. It was a crisp, sunny fall day, and most of the leaves from the Norway maples out front had withered weeks ago, giving her a clear view of Fifth Avenue through the tree branches.

She'd yet to open the book resting in her lap and was instead gazing out the window, watching the family brougham pulling up out front. The coachman jumped down from his box and when he opened the carriage door, Charlotte stepped out. She smiled and leaned toward him while he held her by the waist, raising her up like a ballerina, her feet fluttering the hem of her coat. They were laughing, the winter sun glinting off the brass buttons on his uniform.

Caroline got up, moved closer to the window, pulling back the drapes, watching the two of them, the rush of her pulse beating up inside her head. She stood there, transfixed, until Charlotte left the coachman and came inside.

When she heard her coming up the stairs, Caroline met her at the top of the landing. "Might I have a word with you, young lady?"

Caroline knew she had to say something, but she was so unprepared to deal with this. She was still thinking of what to say when Charlotte spoke up.

"I saw you watching us just now," she said smugly, as if she'd done it intentionally, performing for Caroline's benefit. Was Charlotte taunting Duncan Briar or Caroline? She couldn't tell.

"He's a very interesting man. You would realize that if you'd ever bothered getting to know him."

"I don't need to get to know him. And neither do you. For heaven's sake, Charlotte, he's a coachman! You are not to go out riding with him again without a chaperone. Do you understand?" My goodness, she sounded just like her mother. Hadn't she uttered that very same sentiment to Caroline when she'd learned about Horace Wellsby?

Charlotte smirked. "Don't worry, Mother, I'm not going to marry him."

"Of that you can be certain."

Charlotte folded her arms across her chest. "Will there be anything else?" She stood, drumming her fingers along the sleeve of her dress. "I promised Father I'd beat him in another chess game."

Caroline was at a loss. She shook her head and waved Charlotte away.

Later that day, Duncan Briar stood before Caroline in her sitting room, head bowed, hat in his hands, fingers crumpling the brim. He'd brought the smell of the horses in with him from the livery stables out back.

Caroline set her teacup aside and folded her hands in her lap. "I'm afraid your services will no longer be needed here."

His head shot up, surprised. He had shaggy brown hair and a strong chin. His blue eyes opened wide. "If this is about repairing the carriage wheel—"

"I assure you it has nothing to do with that."

"Then may I inquire as to why I'm being dismissed?"

There was an earnestness in his eyes, as if he had no idea what was coming. Caroline thought for a moment, weighing her response. The less said the better. "I would be happy to provide a reference for your future employer."

As Duncan bowed, thanked her and walked away, Caroline felt a twinge of guilt. After all, he'd been a fine driver, a loyal employee, but Caroline had to get rid of him.

Later that afternoon Caroline found Charlotte in her bedroom, holed up in the little nook built into the bay window. A magazine lay facedown on the seat cushions alongside her stocking feet.

"You didn't have to let him go," she said, staring out the window, wiping her eyes with the back of her hand.

So she'd already heard. Maybe Carrie or Jack had told her. "I did it for your own good."

Charlotte reached for the magazine and began leafing through its pages. Her eyes were shimmering, and Caroline could tell she was beating back more tears. "He didn't do anything wrong. If you want to punish someone, it should be me, not him."

Caroline didn't want to punish Charlotte. She had simply wanted to remove the temptation. "I'm only trying to protect you."

"Protect me, huh?" she said bitterly, chucking the magazine aside. "I don't need protecting."

Caroline knew better than to press the matter. If she backed off now and said no more, it would simmer without boiling over into an argument. As she turned to leave Charlotte's room, she saw her daughter's shoes pushed into the corner, caked in mud with a few straws of hay stuck to the soles. Obviously she'd been down to the stables to see Duncan Briar one last time.

CHAPTER THIRTEEN

Alva

NEW YORK, 1877

MONTHS PASSED AND NOTHING changed. Consuelo was in Europe with her future husband, and other than attending a few dinner parties with Emily and James Van Alen, Alva felt abandoned. With no one else to turn to, she found herself gravitating toward the only person who seemed to understand her: Jeremiah Vanderbilt. As of late, they'd become quite good friends. He would come to her house or she would go to his, a modest brownstone equally modest in its furnishings.

"For a Vanderbilt, you really don't know how to spend your money," she'd said the first time she was invited to his place.

He laughed, reaching for a cigarette.

"Have you noticed," she'd said, "that *all* Vanderbilt houses look the same inside? Everything is always done in that god-awful mossy green."

"Well, you know what they say, just because you have money doesn't mean you have taste." He'd laughed again.

"You're certainly right about that."

He struck a match, and there, with his handsome face inches from the flame, she saw a hint of madness, but also a flash of genius. His wit and timing were uncanny. And yet, when he wasn't uttering quips and being sarcastic, he could be intensely deep and sensitive. He knew when and how to make her laugh and when to keep quiet and commiserate. He'd done just that when Alva learned she wasn't invited to Emily's wedding, when Mrs. Astor snubbed her at Tiffany & Company and again after Alva had dropped off her third calling card for Mrs. Astor.

The more time they spent together, the more she marveled at his uniqueness. He was a true original who did his own thinking and didn't care what others thought of him.

Alva remembered the first time she'd met Jeremiah's companion, George Terry. He was a short, stocky man with a handsome face and round oversize spectacles, which he'd removed upon their introduction, as if to get a better look at her.

"So this is Alva," he said, shaking her hand. "I understand that you've been a very good friend to Jeremiah. He needs a good friend like you."

She was moved by what he'd said and hadn't realized until then just how difficult life must have been for someone like Jeremiah.

"I'm not ashamed," he'd said to her one day, unprompted, out of the blue. They were walking down Seventh Avenue. Jeremiah liked walking. Said it cleared his head and swore the exercise kept his *spells*, as he called them, at bay. "George is my best friend. My favorite person on the planet."

"I thought *I* was your favorite person on the planet," she teased.

"Next to you of course." He looped his arm through hers. "If we had half a brain, George and I would move to Paris."

"Why don't you? I'll come visit."

"Takes money," he said. "Now you'd think my father would like it if I'd—*poof*—disappear. But no. He's cut my allowance. Again. So now I can't leave. I'm stuck here. At least for the moment until I can turn things around." Jeremiah was on a losing streak. "The Commodore—" He shook his head and laughed. "Come on now, who calls themselves 'the Commodore'? It's ridiculous. The man's an absolute loon. And don't be fooled by his old man act. Watch him, I mean it. He's calculating. And mean. Do you know that he once put my hand in a keystone press?" He held out the evidence.

Alva studied the mangled fingers, having always wondered what had happened to his hand.

"And that's nothing compared to what Billy used to do to me. He used to chase me around with a hook wrench. He'd catch me right in the collar and drag me around. So much for brotherly love, huh?" He laughed.

Alva thought about her own sisters. There were times she'd chased Julia and Jennie around the house with her hairbrush or anything else she could get her hands on. Armide was bigger than her, so she never dared. Their fights were always verbal.

"Sometimes I can't believe Billy and I have the same blood running through our veins," Jeremiah was saying now. "I don't think like a Vanderbilt."

"Well, thank goodness for that."

"You want my advice? Be careful. Keep your guard up. The Vanderbilts are ruthless people. They get in your system. They'll warp your mind if you let them. Given half a chance, they make you think you've gone mad."

Alva decided to follow Consuelo's advice, and after several more attempts, she was finally granted a meeting with August Belmont, the Academy of Music's impresario.

It was raining the day of her meeting, a steady downpour, peppered with sleet, the temperatures on the brink of changing to snow. The Academy was located on East Fourteenth Street and Irving Place, in a pocket of Manhattan that had once been the pinnacle of New York society. Now that had changed. Alva passed by a sign for Tony Pastor's, a raunchy vaudeville house in the basement of Tammany

Hall, located next door to the opera house. The sidewalk was crowded and she had to weave through clusters of protestors, men and women, hoisting signs that read **EMPLOYMENT FOR JOBLESS MEN**, **WE SHALL FIGHT UNTIL WE WIN**, **WORK OR RIOT**. Some of the lettering blurred, the paint running in the rain. As she passed them, she recognized the same anger and determination etched in their faces, regardless of their causes. She wondered what pushed a person to the point that they'd stand on a street corner on a miserable wet day like that.

After shaking the rain from her umbrella just outside the front door, Alva found a young woman with a very pointy chin waiting for her inside. She was polite, and overly formal as she showed Alva into a dark, cavernous office just off the lobby. "Mr. Belmont will be with you momentarily, Mrs. Vanderbilt." She practically bowed as she closed the door.

Alva took one of the chairs opposite the desk, hooking her umbrella over the arm. A puddle of rainwater immediately began collecting on the floor, and she regretted not having left the umbrella in the lobby. She scooted her chair over just a bit to hide the one puddle while another, slightly smaller one began forming.

On her carriage ride over, Alva had recalled Tessie Oelrichs saying that Mr. Belmont was a Jew—the only Jew to have gained acceptance into society, as far as she knew. She had been nervous about the meeting, but once Mr. August Belmont walked in, all her foreboding seemed to have been for naught. August Belmont, a slight man, clean-shaven with distinguished graying temples, could not have been more welcoming, apologizing for keeping her waiting, even offering her tea and biscuits.

"Now tell me, what can I do for you, Mrs. Vanderbilt?" He smiled and sipped his tea as his spectacles rode down his nose.

"First, I'd like to thank you for making time in your busy schedule to meet with me," she said, sounding as if she'd just arrived from the Deep South.

"The pleasure is all mine." He resettled in his chair. "Although I do have another appointment coming up," he said, checking his pocket watch, "so perhaps we should begin."

"Very well then," said Alva, "I requested this meeting because I would like to purchase a box at the Academy."

"I see." He hesitated, setting his cup down and squaring his elbows on his desk. "We of course do appreciate your interest; however, the matter of boxes remains a rather complicated one."

"How so, Mr. Belmont?" She felt the tug of resistance. The trepidation she'd experienced earlier was starting to return.

"Well, for one thing, our members are all quite passionate about the opera and—"

"I can assure you, the Vanderbilts are extremely passionate about music. About all the arts." Alva sipped her tea, her voice calm, polite, proper.

"I'm afraid there's more to it than that." He pushed his glasses up his nose with the tip of his finger. "Boxes at the Academy are extremely rare. When one does become available, it's generally passed down to the family's next generation. But even more than that, there are commitments to owning a box."

"And what might those commitments be?" She tilted her head, fluttered her lashes.

"Because they're of a financial nature, this might be a conversation more suited for Mr. Vanderbilt."

"Oh, I assure you, I'm perfectly capable of talking finances, especially where my family is concerned." She could see this had thrown him. *Good.* "Please, Mr. Belmont, as you were saying? The commitments?"

He cleared his throat, reached up for his spectacles again. "Actually, there is a *significant* financial commitment that comes with owning a box. For example, even a mezzanine box, seating just four guests, starts at $400 per season. And the price only rises from there." He gestured with his hands, as if to say, *There, that explains it all.*

She recognized a polite rebuff when she encountered one. Refusing to be put off, she said, "Naturally, I'm prepared to pay whatever the asking price is. And it goes without saying that a balcony box would be most desirable."

"Well now," Belmont laughed, suggesting she was out of her depth, "those are quite pricey. They start at $800 per season."

"I'll pay twice that much," Alva shot back with a smile.

"Excuse me?"

"Mr. Belmont, you should know that I'm prepared to pay well above your asking price."

He cleared his throat again. "I'm afraid it's not as simple as all that."

Alva set her cup down and leaned forward in her chair, her eyes zeroing in on his. "I would think the Academy would welcome the Vanderbilts' contribution. I know for a fact that the Academy is in debt." She watched him shift in his chair. She kept going. "According to the article in the *New York World*, you're $50,000 short for the season. Your building is in constant need of repair. The roof leaks, the walls and ceiling are crumbling, the boiler is failing. They said Adelina Patti demanded $4,000 for her last performance. Christine Nilsson wants $4,500 for her upcoming engagement."

Belmont removed his glasses. "I see you've done your homework, Mrs. Vanderbilt. I'm impressed but—"

There was a knock on the door as the young lady from the lobby tucked her head inside. "Mr. Belmont, please forgive the interruption, but Mrs. Astor is arriving."

"Oh dear, she's early." Belmont sprang up from his chair, collected Alva's teacup and the platter of biscuits, handing both off to the woman. "I'm afraid we'll have to conclude our meeting."

"Well, I was—"

"Please, Mrs. Vanderbilt." There was a hint of panic in his voice as he opened another door, which Alva hadn't even noticed was there before. "Mrs. Astor is here!"

"But I—"

He stepped in and coaxed her out of her chair.

Alva was stunned. She was being ushered out as if he feared being seen with her there. She reached for her umbrella but then thought better of it and left it there hooked on the arm of her chair.

"Please, hurry."

With as much dignity as she could muster, she went to the doorway. "I do hope we can continue our discussion later—"

"Just follow the stairs at the end of the hallway," he said. "It leads to the rear of the theater."

She heard the door close behind her and found herself in a musty back hallway lined with murals of rolling hills in clover, balconies, backdrops of gardens, cluttered racks of costumes, throne-like chairs and other props. Forcing herself down the rickety staircase, her anger intensified with each step. Mrs. Astor was early—she should have been asked to wait while Alva finished her meeting.

Standing outside under a dripping awning, she counted to one hundred, drew a deep breath and walked back around to the front, past the protestors outside Tammany Hall. Another deep breath and she breezed through the lobby, past the pointy-chinned young woman who attempted to stop her. "Wait, Mrs. Vanderbilt, please, you can't go in there! Mr. Belmont is—"

Alva was already back inside Belmont's office.

His face blanched as his mouth dropped open. Mrs. Astor was seated beside him on a velvet settee, a fresh pot of tea and plate of biscuits on the table before them.

"Why, Mrs. Astor," said Alva, "so lovely to see you again." She paused, waiting for some sign of recognition. Not even a hint. "I'm Alva. Alva Vanderbilt—Emily's friend?" If Mrs. Astor had remem-

bered meeting her—not once but twice now—she wasn't going to
acknowledge it. Alva remained undeterred. She was going to finish
her meeting with Mr. Belmont—and in the presence of Mrs. Astor.
She'd plead her case to the Grande Dame, she'd reiterate the Academy's financial troubles and offer a solution: one box for which Alva
would gladly pay handsomely.

"Mrs. Vanderbilt, please—" Mr. Belmont stood up, befuddled.

"Oh, do forgive me. I forgot my manners right along with my
umbrella."

"I do apologize," Belmont said to Mrs. Astor, who had yet to utter
a word.

With her umbrella in hand, Alva was about to launch into her
speech, but before she could get the first word out, Belmont steered
her out of his office.

It all happened so fast and the next thing Alva knew, she was just
outside his door, listening to Mrs. Astor say, "What on earth was *she*
doing here? Everywhere I turn, there she is. And her manners are no
better than the Commodore's. I tell you, the Vanderbilts do not belong at the Academy of Music."

Alva's grip tightened on her umbrella as her heart pounded. She
knew she'd just ruined her chances of ever getting a box at the opera.

CHAPTER FOURTEEN

Society

SO ALVA VANDERBILT CAME to us. By default. Actually, it was Lady Paget—formerly Minnie Stevens, who has taken to wearing twenty pounds of jewelry along with her title—who first brought Alva into our circle. Most popular among us is Kate Strong, nicknamed Puss on account of her affinity for felines. She has blond Little Bo-Peep curls, and always wears a diamond brooch shaped like a cat. Also in our set is Mrs. George Cavendish—Peggy to us—a gracious hostess with a pronounced stutter that makes her try all the harder. Peggy's oldest and dearest friend is Lydia, the romantic among us, who adores the books of Jane Austen and the Brontë sisters. There's also Tessie Oelrichs and of course Mamie, as well as Penelope, Ophelia, Fanny and Cettie. Together, we're the lower-ranking class of society ladies. The whole lot of us have been lumped together and labeled the robber barons' wives, married to men like John Pierpont Morgan, Jay Gould and John Rockefeller.

Alva should be grateful that we've welcomed her in, but we can tell our friendship feels like a consolation prize. While we invite her to our dinner parties and luncheons, she rarely reciprocates. Lady Paget insists it's because Alva thinks her home is too modest. We aren't convinced that's the reason, and yet we understand Alva's ambivalence about being one of us. Some of us don't even want to be *one of us*, either.

This afternoon, we're gathered in Cettie Rockefeller's drawing room, sitting in a semicircle, our spines uniformly eight inches from the backs of the caned Louis XV chairs, while we balance Coalport china plates of finger sandwiches on our laps. The only exception is Puss, who has traded in her plate for Mr. Fritzy, a rather well-behaved Persian lounging peacefully while she strokes his ears.

The conversation today, like most days, begins with a recap of last night's dinner parties, balls, the ballet. It's agreed that so-and-so's dress was too tight, too embellished, too bland, too something. We share snippets of gossip about so-and-so's daughter, husband, mistress, and it doesn't take long before we find ourselves talking about Ward McAllister and Mrs. Astor.

The mere mention of Mrs. Astor's name piques Alva's ire. While we're talking about ways to impress her, Alva is talking about ways to bring the Grande Dame down.

She suggests throwing a lavish ball and inviting everyone *but* Mrs. Astor. Penelope insists this will never work. If people knew she was trying to exclude Mrs. Astor, no one would come for fear they'd be cut from her guest list forever. We all saw what happened when Mamie tried hosting a fish fry on the same night as her clambake. Though Tessie is quick to point out that Mamie's attempt *did* get her into society.

"Well, I don't want in through the back door," says Alva. "When I enter society, it will be through the front door."

Alva is certainly a bit more haughty than usual. We suspect this has something to do with the inheritance. At the start of the new year, on the fourth of January, the Commodore passed away. Eighty-two years old and worth $100 million. The day after his funeral, they did the reading of the will, as if they couldn't wait another second to see what he'd left them. They say the bulk of his estate, some $75 million, went to Alva's father-in-law, Billy, and the rest was divided among the male heirs.

It hasn't been that long—just a few weeks—but already we can see the change in Alva. She's always dressed with a flair, but even more so now, despite her being pregnant. Even with her belly showing, she isn't afraid to wear bright reds or oranges regardless of their clashing with her hair color. And yet, she knows—or at least she *should* know—that even her husband's newly acquired millions won't make a difference as far as Mrs. Astor is concerned.

So like it or not, she's stuck with us, and us with her.

CHAPTER FIFTEEN

Alva

$2 MILLION CHANGED EVERYTHING. Alva had always known her husband was wealthy, but now he was wealthy beyond anything she could have imagined. This wasn't just money, this was a fortune. She couldn't get that glorious dollar amount out of her mind. Knowing she could afford anything her heart desired was a heady thing. No price tag was beyond her reach.

Though she'd done absolutely nothing to contribute to her husband's vast wealth, she felt it belonged to her as if she'd earned it herself. And in truth, Willie hadn't earned it, either. She told herself she'd be generous, that she'd be charitable, but still she was reluctant to part with too much just yet—even to the worthiest of causes. There was the fear there wouldn't be enough left for Alva and Willie. And there were so many things they needed, wanted, or simply had to have.

As much as she tried to conceal it, Alva felt a bit smug. She now had an edge over Mamie, Tessie, Penelope, Puss and the rest of her peers. She felt almost sorry for them. *Almost.* The one she truly did feel sorry for, though, was Jeremiah, who'd received only $200,000. *Only $200,000—do you hear yourself, Alva?* She knew plenty of people who could have lived comfortably off that amount for the rest of their years. But not a Vanderbilt, definitely not a Vanderbilt—not even Jeremiah Vanderbilt.

She tried not to dwell on that and instead focused on the fact that she and Willie K. were moving up. Alva had been seven months pregnant at the reading of the will, and she and Willie had immediately begun talking about building a new house, a bigger house, a house that she could decorate as she saw fit. It was time.

Nearly two months to the day of the Commodore's passing, on the second of March, 1877, Alva gave birth to their first child. When the midwife placed the baby in Alva's arms, she was speechless. The little girl was a sheer delight, beautiful with Willie K.'s dark hair and Alva's blue eyes. With tears running down her face, Alva was stunned by the wonderment of it all, that this child had come from her. She had created this little girl and now she belonged to Alva. Forever.

Just then that tiny face scrunched up red and began sputtering, tears flowing, chest heaving. Alva froze. "What's wrong with her?"

"Oh, nothing's wrong. She's just hungry is all," said the midwife, who had been in favor of bringing in a wet nurse. But Alva had objected, insisting on feeding her baby herself, just as her own mother had done.

The midwife positioned the baby on Alva's chest, but when the infant's mouth clamped down on Alva's breast, her suckling wasn't strong enough. Nothing happened. Her milk wouldn't flow. She had nothing to give her. It was then that she realized this new life was so fully dependent on her and already she was failing her. Unable to feed her—the most basic thing a mother could do—Alva was flooded with fear. She wasn't ready. She couldn't do this on her own. She panicked and began to sob until the midwife stepped in and took the baby from her.

"It's okay," the midwife assured her. "We'll just bring in a wet nurse if you can't manage it."

But the baby was still crying and so was Alva. She couldn't help it. She desperately wanted her mother, wanted her alive and by her side to show her how to do this. She didn't want Alice and Louisa there, telling her everything she was doing wrong, making her doubt herself and second-guess her every move. Her sisters were still making their way from Mobile, where they'd gone to visit an elderly aunt. Besides, none of them were married and they wouldn't have known what to do, either. Consuelo was in Europe, Emily had her hands full with a baby of her own, so the only friend left was Jeremiah, and he was of no use in this situation. Alva had never felt so alone. She cried harder, unable to stop. Her head was congested, temples pounding; her body felt wrenched.

At some point she wore herself out and drifted off into a chain of restless dreams. When she awoke early the next morning, Willie K. was fast asleep in the chair next to her bed, his hair as rumpled as his clothes, a shadow of whiskers coming up on his cheeks and chin. She worried that he was going to wake with a kink in his neck. The maid said he'd been there all night, wanting to make sure "both his girls" were okay.

Alva watched him sleeping and realized that, in fact, she wasn't alone. She had Willie K. and she had her baby. A family of her own. Why this very obvious fact hadn't entered her mind before, she couldn't say, but this time when her little girl cried, Alva didn't panic. She knew what her baby needed. As the nurse placed the infant in her arms it felt as natural and as right as anything ever could have. When that tiny mouth latched onto her breast, Alva felt her power coming back.

In that moment Alva realized that everything—*everything*—was different now. She was seeing the world through the eyes of mother-hood, a kind of double vision; one eye on her daughter's future, the other on her own. Her priorities shuffled, falling into different places. All at once society seemed a shallow pursuit for herself and yet abso-lutely essential for her daughter. Alva vowed to do whatever was necessary to ensure that her daughter would be received by the finest families, welcomed in the very best circles. She looked at the child in her arms, those eyes staring up at her, all innocence, and she vowed that her girl would never know the kind of rejection that Alva had faced since she was sixteen.

Willie awoke shortly after she'd finished feeding the baby. "You're peacocking," she said, pointing to his charming little cowlick, right on the top of his head. It was sticking straight up like it usually did in the mornings. The first time she'd seen it, she'd laughed, said he looked like a peacock.

He smiled back at her, flattened his hair down with his palm. He asked how she was feeling and asked if he could hold their little bundle.

"'Little bundle.'" Alva smiled as she placed the baby in Willie's arms. "We can't call her that. What do you think of the name Consuelo?"

"Really? After your friend? I was thinking maybe Louisa, after my mother."

"But Consuelo introduced us. And we already agreed she would be our baby's godmother."

And so, it was settled. The newest Vanderbilt heiress would carry on with the curious moniker, and Alva, a new mother and the wife of a man $2 million richer, would carry on in her quest to be accepted into high society with even more vigor and greater urgency. She wasn't doing it just for herself and the Vanderbilts now, she was doing it for her daughter, too.

Later that morning, after Willie had cleaned up, shaved and changed his clothes, he returned to Alva's bedroom, kissed the crown of her head and announced that he'd been called away for a meeting at his father's home.

"Now? But—"

"I'm sorry. My regrets to your sisters. It really can't be helped. Family emergency. They've asked us all to be there—Cornelius, George, Fred, Mother—everyone. I'll be back as soon as I can."

After he left, Alva sat up in bed, her pillows fluffed, propping her up from behind. The baby was sleeping in her bassinet in the corner of the room. Alva wished she could have rested as well, but she was too curious and mildly irked, wondering what constituted a family emergency. What could have been more important than their coming over to meet the newest member of the Vanderbilt family?

She'd never understand her in-laws. They were cold people. Such a contrast to her sisters, who had ridden a train all night just to be there. And as soon as they'd arrived, they had gathered around baby Consuelo, taking turns holding her, cooing, marveling at her tiny fingers and toes. Jennie thought she looked like Willie. Julia thought she was "all Alva."

Armide, with her dark brown hair piled high and pinned slightly off-center, disagreed with them both. "She's the spitting image of Mama."

Mama. They all sighed. A swell of pride, of longing. Each year the sisters made a pilgrimage to her gravesite on the anniversary of her death. Their father's grave, as far as Alva was concerned, just happened to be there. She couldn't speak for her sisters, but she herself would never have gone out of her way to pay her respects to him.

"How did Mama manage with all of us?" Alva said, dreamily looking at Consuelo nestled in Jennie's arms. "Four daughters."

"She had help," said Julia, resting her foot on the stand of the baby cradle.

"Oh, be careful, Julia," Alva said, pointing.

Julia removed her foot and raised her hands, giving her other sisters a look. "Is it okay if I touch this chair?"

"Oh, stop it, Julia—I'm sorry, but that's a very expensive cradle. That wood is imported from Africa. It's very rare."

"Oh, 'it's very *rare*,'" mocked Julia.

"Now *you* were a handful," Armide said to Alva, changing the subject, restoring peace.

"That's not so," Alva attempted to protest before her argument collapsed and they all broke into a fit of laughter. From a young age Alva had it in her head that the rules and conventions that everyone else abided by did not apply to her. She played by her own rules, repercussions be damned.

"You knew how to manipulate and bully everyone," said Jennie.

"It's because of her thumbs," Julia said to the others, as if Alva weren't there.

"That's right—she has those crooked thumbs," said Armide.

"Oh, no," said Alva. "That's an old wives' tale."

"Put 'em up," said Jennie, volunteering, raising her thumbs and joined by Julia and Armide—all of them perfectly straight. "Alva?" Jennie taunted. "Come now—your turn."

Alva was already laughing as she raised her thumbs—definitely crooked and curving outward. "That doesn't prove anything," she said, still cackling so loud, she snorted.

"Remember what you did to Miss Naisy at the beach?" asked Armide.

"You mean our governess?" Alva shook her head, remembering the day Miss Naisy refused to let Alva go swimming. Well, Alva wasn't having it. In great defiance and with great delight, she ran away from the governess and plunged into the water. She refused to come out, eventually making Miss Naisy go in after her, clothes and all. Alva's mother got the strap out after that, but Alva never regretted her actions for a second.

"And didn't you torture your reading tutor?" asked Jennie.

"I didn't *torture* her—please, I wasn't *that* bad. I may have nudged her off her stool once."

"That's right—you shoved her right onto the floor."

"Well, I didn't like her, and I didn't want to read the book she selected," said Alva with a shoulder shrug. "She quit on the spot."

"And you got another lashing for it," said Julia.

"Yes, but I didn't have to read that book," said Alva with a tinge of pride. She would willingly accept any punishment in exchange for getting her own way first. The one thing she could not and would not tolerate was being controlled. By anyone. Fearless and emboldened by that very fearlessness, she did as she pleased, bending and often breaking the rules.

"Mama couldn't take her eyes off you for a second," said Jennie, passing baby Consuelo on to Armide, who was sitting in the rocking chair in the corner.

"Alva wouldn't let her," Julia laughed, crouching down to look at the baby in her sister's arms. "You *always* had to have Mama's attention. *All* of her attention. You'd do things just to rile her up. You'd rather she get out the riding crop than ignore you."

Alva couldn't deny that. They were playfully ganging up on her, three against one, but she didn't mind. She was enjoying it, welcoming more teasing, when suddenly Consuelo let out a robust wail. It was hard to believe that such a tiny figure could have produced something so loud, so shrill. In an instant everyone's focus was back on the baby. As her sisters circled even closer around Consuelo, Alva realized it was the first time she'd been willing to be overshadowed. Call it a mother's pride, but her daughter was an extension of herself. Alva understood that, for the rest of her life, she would be sharing center stage with her daughter.

When Willie K. returned, he came upstairs and, without a word, dropped down in the chair beside her bed. He was exhausted.

"Has the family *emergency* been resolved?" she asked, adjusting the baby blanket, tucking it under Consuelo's chin.

"Hardly," Willie said, scrubbing his hands over his face. "Uncle Jeremiah is contesting Grandfather's will."

"Can you blame him?" *Good for you, Jeremiah*, she thought. *Good for you.*

"He's being very stubborn. If anyone ever questioned whether or not the man is raving mad, well"—he shook his head, bewildered—"here's your proof. Father even offered him an additional $250,000 and he turned it down."

"That's an insult coming from your father, and you know it." She heard herself and thought, *Since when is $250,000 an insult?* Jeremiah's words echoed in her head: *The Vanderbilts are ruthless people. They get in your system. They'll warp your mind if you let them* . . .

"That's not the point. My uncle is not a responsible man. Never has been. It's for his own good. I know you're awfully fond of him but please, Alva, do us all a favor and cut ties with him."

"Pfft." That was not about to happen, and the mere suggestion made her all the more determined to see Jeremiah as soon as she'd recovered from the birth.

"I mean it, Alva. He's trouble." Willie blew out a deep breath and stared at the floor. "Uncle Jeremiah is holding us all hostage. The money's locked up until this whole mess gets resolved. There's nothing we can do now but wait. And who knows what will be left by then and what we'll end up with."

What we'll end up with? Alva looked at him, feeling her eyes growing wider.

"We'll have to put the new house on hold for now."

"What?" She was crestfallen. She thought that whatever Jeremiah was owed would have come directly out of Billy's money. It didn't occur to her that Jeremiah could interfere with Willie's inheritance, too. She'd been counting on that money for their new house, to help them establish all the Vanderbilts in society, to pave the way for their child and more children to come.

The *family emergency* had just taken on a whole new meaning for her, too, because now this was affecting her plans. It was endangering her daughter's future. She found her heart conflicted, her support of Jeremiah collapsing, sudden as an avalanche. Perhaps she was becoming a Vanderbilt after all.

CHAPTER SIXTEEN

Caroline

CAROLINE HEARD THE PIANO music trilling from the ballroom as the Pendletons' butler escorted her down a long hallway, graced with family portraits and enormous tapestries. Caroline was hoping to slip quietly inside but she was hardly inconspicuous. She attracted attention and altered the atmosphere of every room she entered. So when she stepped inside the Pendletons' ballroom, she was not surprised that all eyes turned her way. The cotillion leader, Peter Marié, stopped calling out figures, and the dancers came to a standstill. The fifteen or so chaperones—including Ward McAllister—seated along the perimeter of the ballroom rose to pay homage to her.

Everyone seemed pleased to have her there except her daughters. She saw Charlotte and Carrie flatten down, their wings clipped. Charlotte had rolled her eyes when Caroline first entered the room and Carrie's brow had creased, her cheeks flushed pink. Caroline felt a stab to her heart.

When had she become the enemy? There was a time when they always wanted to be around her, the closer the better, all of them fighting over who got to perch on her lap, hold her hand, sit next to her. Now they behaved as if wanting nothing to do with her. Didn't they understand that Caroline had already lost Emily to James Van Alen? Caroline wished now that she'd used a firmer hand with Emily and had put her foot down when the couple first started courting. And even though Helen was now engaged to Rosy Roosevelt and Caroline had gotten rid of Duncan Briar, she still couldn't risk Charlotte or Carrie marrying the wrong man.

"Please," Caroline said to everyone with a dismissive wave of her hand, "continue."

Mrs. Pendleton offered Caroline her chair, a throne-like Henry Williams with gilt trim, velvet upholstery and lovely roundels. Ward McAllister was seated next to her on a walnut hardback. It was only Wednesday and she'd already seen Ward three times that week. They'd met on Monday to schedule next year's operas for the Academy, on Tuesday afternoon he'd assisted with the seating arrangements for an upcoming dinner honoring the visiting Alexander II, and Tuesday night the two had dined lavishly at the home of a mutual friend, Mr. Frank Gray Griswold. You'd think they'd have nothing left to say to each other, but Ward had already informed her that Mrs. Alva Vanderbilt had been overheard saying some rather unflattering things about Caroline.

"The nerve of her," he said. "Calling you snobbish and rude. Why, I've never known you to be rude unless provoked."

"Well, Mrs. Vanderbilt has certainly provoked me," Caroline said while keeping an eye on her daughters, watching them move through the various figures and the complicated windmill steps. Of course, she knew her girls weren't merely interested in learning those cotillion routines. The real reason they were there, the reason they had both taken such extra care with their morning toilette, was because of the young men at the rehearsal that day.

"Well, well, well," Ward said, in a conspiratorial whisper, "would you look at that." He motioned with a tilt of his head toward Charlotte, who had just dropped her glove while looking into Peter Marié's eyes.

Caroline was stunned. Charlotte was never clumsy, and dropping her glove was no accident but rather a coded declaration of love. Her girls probably couldn't have imagined that she, too, had once been a debutante, sending secret messages to William Backhouse Astor Jr. across the room by dropping her glove, or holding her fan in a particular way, or twisting her kerchief, certain that she'd fooled her chaperones, too. But Caroline knew all those tricks, all those hidden signals. Times may have changed, but that secret language of love hadn't.

"Very good," said Peter Marié with a single clap of his hands. "That was excellent. Excellent. Let's do it again. Places, everyone! Places." He walked over, letting his hand rest on the small of Charlotte's back, whispering something in her ear that made her smile.

Was Peter Marié flirting back with her? Caroline observed that the entire time Charlotte was dancing with other men, she had not been able to take her eyes off Peter Marié. Mr. Marié was tall and fit, with dark hair, beautiful dark eyes and a face to be admired. But he was too old, had already declared himself a chronic tease and a confirmed bachelor.

Meanwhile, Caroline's youngest, Carrie, who was just sixteen and had only recently been introduced to society, flitted and twirled from one dance partner to the next. So bold, so self-possessed her youngest was. She was nothing like her eldest. When Emily was a debutante, she'd been all hesitation and self-consciousness. While the other girls danced about, her precious Emily had kept herself small, those delicate shoulders rounded, her big brown eyes trained on her feet, her lips moving, counting her steps. Caroline had felt a special tenderness toward Emily then, recalling how she herself had been timid and awkward at her first dances. All this was floating through her mind when she saw Carrie stealing lovesick glances at the Reinhardt boy across the room and while exposing her ankles!

Caroline was appalled. When had her daughters developed such passions? The other young ladies managed to control themselves. But not her girls. They let their hearts lead them about, rather than their good sense.

When they arrived home, Caroline marched her daughters into the drawing room. They were seated side by side on the satin settee, backs straight, hands in their laps. Hade appeared just in time to bring Caroline a much-needed cup of tea and to stoke the fire. The room was quiet, the girls were waiting for her to speak, but Caroline wasn't ready, though she understood her silence was torturing them. Of course, she knew her daughters were burdened by her position, that they were scrutinized more closely, held to a higher standard than other girls. But that was all the more reason why they had to be careful about their behavior. Especially Charlotte. Caroline always knew she was precocious, just like her father. No wonder the two were thick as thieves. Caroline was tired of watching her make a spectacle of herself, first with that coachman, now today with the cotillion leader, flitting from one inappropriate man to another like a bee going from flower to flower.

While watching Hade tend to the fire, Caroline took a sip of tea and finally said, "You must remember that you are not just ordinary girls. You are the Astor girls, and you must conduct yourselves accordingly."

Charlotte exploded. "Why were you even there today? We're not babies, you know. And plenty of other chaperones were there."

"Excuse me, young lady," said Caroline. "Those other chaperones are not your mother, and none of them would tell you what your behavior looks like to the outside world."

"What it *looks* like." Charlotte stood up and slapped her hands to her thighs. "Is that *all* you care about?"

"Come now, Charlotte," said Carrie, yanking her back down on the settee.

"Peter Marié is far too old for you—besides, you know his reputation. He'll never marry you."

"Good," she said. "I don't want to get married."

"Nonsense. And you should know, young lady, that people are starting to talk."

"So what?" said Charlotte. "Let them talk. I don't care."

"Well, I *do* care." A flash of anger rose up inside Caroline. She was shaking and handed off her cup to Hade, fearing she might spill her tea.

"Don't you see?" said Charlotte, not backing down in the least. "I don't care what society thinks. All those matrons are wasting their lives. What do they do all day other than make social calls, throw parties and wait on tenterhooks for their precious invitations to arrive from Mrs. Astor?"

"Honestly, where is this indignant behavior coming from?" Caroline stared at her.

"Oh, I'm sorry, Mother." Charlotte gave off a mean-spirited laugh. "Are we expected to bow down to you, too? We're your daughters, not your loyal subjects. And I'm not afraid of you. My goodness, even Father is terrified of you. Everyone's terrified of you."

Caroline was silenced, at a loss. She closed her eyes and waved her hands. "Go, go," she said. "Leave me be." The knot in her stomach coiled tighter.

Once again, she felt trapped between her mother's world and the here and now. Were her daughters really so out of line? Were their actions the catastrophe she was making them out to be? Honestly, she didn't know anymore. So her girls were flirtatious—maybe Caroline would have behaved the same way if she'd had their beauty, their confidence instead of being shy and too insecure to have even tried. She had modern girls, forward thinking, perplexing. Lately Charlotte had been talking about wanting to feed the poor, and Carrie wanted to study the artwork of great masters. *But whatever for?* Caroline wanted to say. The poor would only be hungry again, and it wasn't as if Carrie was going to become an artist herself.

She heard the girls' footsteps, the stomping, the groan of the drawing room door, and when she opened her eyes again it was just her and Hade, who stood at her side, still holding her teacup. He had witnessed the children's occasional temper tantrums, their adolescent outbursts, but this was the first time he'd ever seen one of them talk back to her. She was embarrassed, and knowing she couldn't ignore what he'd seen, she turned to him and said, "I'm sorry you had to witness that. I don't know what's gotten into Charlotte."

"Miss Charlotte can be a very high-spirited young lady." He offered a subtle bow as he handed back Caroline's teacup.

"Hade?" She looked at him and hesitated for a moment before asking, "Are you afraid of me?"

Hade offered a faint half smile and with his deep voice said, "I highly respect you and admire your strength, but no, madam, I am not afraid of you."

Caroline sipped her tea, still pondering. "Hade?"

"Yes, madam?"

She paused as she was about to do something unnatural for her. She was accustomed to everyone asking *her* for advice and now she was the one who needed help. "Was I too hard on them just now?"

She watched his shoulders pull back as he drew a sudden breath, suggesting that he also found this break in her formal veneer unprecedented. Perhaps even uncomfortable. It was the first time the two of them had discussed anything other than menus and household needs. After a thoughtful moment he said, "Your daughters are of a certain age. They're growing up. Bound to make mistakes. That's how we learn, isn't it? I recall my own daughters making a few mistakes when they were growing up."

Daughters? Hade has children? She realized she had never considered his life prior to him coming into hers. And what about

Mrs. Hade? There had been a wife—or maybe there still was an es-
tranged one. She'd never before thought of Hade as someone's husband. She simply couldn't think of him that way. It was no different
than not thinking about what was under a priest's robe, or what her
parents had done to conceive her. She could not think of Hade as a
red-blooded man. It would require a complete reframing of someone
she'd always thought of as only her butler.

"I myself was known to make a mistake or two when I was their
age," Hade said now, bringing Caroline back to the moment. "Sometimes we need to allow our children to falter."

"I see." She felt a bit shocked. Though he hadn't come right out
and said it, she realized that Hade had just told her, *Yes, you were too
hard on them.* Aside from her husband and, of course, her mother,
Caroline was used to everyone agreeing with her, telling her what she
wanted, or what they *thought* she wanted to hear. Everyone tried so
to please and impress her. Perhaps they *were* all afraid of her. But not
Hade. It was strangely refreshing to have someone finally tell her the
truth. Yes, Charlotte had spoken her mind, but that was all anger and
disrespect—meant to wound her. But just now Hade had dared to
calmly point out that she—Mrs. Astor—had been wrong.

Until that moment, she didn't realize how much she'd missed being treated like Caroline, *like Lina.* In a world where everyone wanted
something from her, whether it was an introduction for their daughters or an invitation to her balls, it made her wonder who she could
trust. Which acts of kindness shown her way were sincere? Which
were only to curry favor? Most of all, though, she wondered if anyone
truly liked her.

She needed a friend, a true friend. And Ward McAllister didn't
count. Though he knew her better than most—though she confided
in him and at times swore he was the only one who truly understood
her—Ward could be just as bad as the rest. Especially lately. There
was a time when they were equals, partners in preserving society, but

now he only saw her as Mrs. Astor, not Caroline, not Lina. Ward knew that without her, the self-proclaimed social arbiter would have nothing to arbitrate. And truth be told, she needed him as well to help her uphold society. So they leaned on each other, two sides coming together to form an apex. They knew they had to move as one lest the whole thing collapse.

"Will there be anything else, madam?"

Caroline refused to look at him. She felt so exposed, so flustered, and had already made herself far too vulnerable. All she could do was close her eyes and dismiss him with a wave of her hand. And yet, when she heard the door close behind him, she wished she had asked him to stay.

CHAPTER SEVENTEEN

Alva

NEW YORK, 1878

AFTER COUNTLESS COURT FILINGS and emergency family meetings, Jeremiah finally backed down and settled the lawsuit for $600,000—$200,000 of which was in cash with the remaining $400,000 placed in a trust controlled by Billy.

Willie, with his $2 million safe at hand, surprised Alva one night, coming home with a set of blueprints for their new home. Handing the baby off to the nurse, she eagerly looked over Willie's shoulder at the plans he'd rolled out on his library desk.

"Now see this here?" He pointed to the upper right-hand corner. "This is where the ballroom will be, and this over here is the dining room. You'll be able to comfortably seat fifty guests in there. Maybe more."

She clasped her hands, truly tickled. "Oh, Willie K.!" At last she'd have a home she would be proud to entertain in, a home she could decorate any way she liked. A place to dazzle and impress—a most important asset if she was going to make her play for the reins of society. She walked around the desk to view the blueprints from every possible angle, and with each new glance, her excitement grew.

At least it did until the following week when she was invited to luncheon at Cornelia Stewart's palatial mansion on Thirty-Fourth Street and Fifth Avenue, across the street from the Astors' brownstones. It was the first time Alva had ever been inside Cornelia's home. As the liveried butler showed her into the drawing room, Alva was greeted by Cornelia, another redhead, though her hair was more coppery than Alva's. She wore a strong floral perfume and an enormous emerald brooch. Cornelia's late husband had been the dry goods merchant Alexander T. Stewart. His store was still thriving, one they all frequented. In fact, the muff Alva had with her that day had been purchased at his store.

Alexander had been a wealthy man, but not as wealthy as Willie and yet *just look at how they lived!* Alva was positively spellbound. The whole time Cettie Rockefeller was talking to her, Alva was admiring the Parian marble. While Ophelia Meade told her a bit of gossip about Mr. Brandon's latest mistress, Alva was making note of the gilded whitewood furnishings and the fresco ceilings that had been commissioned from Mario Brigaldi, a prominent Italian artist.

Later, while seated at a long table, Alva struggled to stay engaged in the conversations around her, to get through her vermicelli soup, the lobster rissoles, roasted lamb and Neapolitan cakes. She was still taking in the details of the magnificent dining room while envy churned in the pit of her stomach. The plans for her new house that had once delighted her now seemed bland in comparison to the Stewarts'.

After luncheon, as Alva's carriage made its way down Fifth Avenue, she couldn't shake the dreadful feeling creeping up on her. By the time she returned home, she was clobbered by the horrible realization that all her husband could give her—even with his inheritance—was never going to be enough. True to form, just as she'd once envied anyone with a prettier rag doll, a faster wagon, a fancier dress, Alva wanted to have the best, to be the best. So Alva didn't just want a house *like* the Stewarts'. No, she wanted one that was even bigger, even better.

She feared she'd never be fulfilled. It happened every time. Just when she thought she had all that she wanted, that her cup had indeed runneth over, some trapdoor inside her would open and let everything drain out, leaving her empty once again. And that's when she would up the ante. No sooner had her husband inherited $2 million than she wanted $2 million more. It was obvious now that she was destined to be unhappy, unfulfilled. She was insatiable, her desires too vast. If she ever wanted to be content, she was going to have to learn to settle for less and be grateful for what she had.

Alva wrestled with this for the next several days. After all, who was she to have such lofty dreams? What right did she have to demand so much from the world? How quickly she had become accustomed to the Vanderbilt riches—plentiful food, the finest jewelry, clothing of the best fabrics and designed by the most talented couturiers. The more she had, the more she wanted. She was becoming greedy, taking such luxuries for granted, which she swore she'd never do. She had to right her ways. And quickly.

She tried convincing herself that a grand home wasn't important. And yet she'd seen what owning a magnificent mansion like the Stewarts' had done for Cornelia. Before building that house Cornelia Stewart was considered a swell—a swell of the worst kind. Flashy and ostentatious. The Knickerbockers had refused to open their doors to her. But all that changed with the house—the house that had already eclipsed Alva and Willie K.'s best efforts.

She would have to find another way to get ahead, a way based on her own merits, her own wits. She told herself it would be more gratifying that way. *Wouldn't it be?*

But all those mental calisthenics fell apart one afternoon during a visit with Jeremiah. While Willie and the rest of the Vanderbilts wanted nothing more to do with him, Alva had settled back into her friendship with him. After all, he was an outsider, as was she.

She arrived at his hotel room at the Glenham on Fifth Avenue and Twenty-Second Street, where he'd been living for the past year after selling his townhouse in order to pay his lawyers.

"How were you able to get away?" he asked, letting her inside.

"I told Willie I was visiting *a friend.*"

"Oh, we're so discreet, aren't we," he said. "Just like a husband and his mistress. But without the copulating."

She laughed, shrugging off her coat, taking a seat at a little three-legged table in the corner, near the only window. A full ashtray and a half-empty bottle of whiskey were resting on top, along with two glasses.

"Is it too early for a drink?" he asked.

"What do you think?"

"That's my girl," he laughed, pouring her a whiskey. "To us," he said, tilting his glass to hers.

They started up right away gossiping about Alice and Cornelius, about Billy and Louisa. When he mentioned that Billy was spending $3 million to build two mansions—one for him and one for the daughters, Alva sat up straight.

"For Margaret and Florence?" Alva gave him a puzzled look. "What about us? He didn't even *offer* to help us with our new place." She looked at Jeremiah's flattened expression and caught herself, leaning over to squeeze his hand. "I'm sorry. You're the last person I should be complaining to."

"Darling, I'll commiserate with you about those stingy Vanderbilts all day long." He laughed as if this was much funnier than it actually was. And he kept on laughing, which turned into a violent coughing fit before he finally broke down into a series of heaving sobs.

"What is it? What's wrong?"

Jeremiah apologized as he dried his eyes. "I'm surprised I held out this long. I've been crying like a baby all morning."

"What's going on?"

He propped his cigarette in the corner of his mouth while he re-filled his glass. "Remember that $400,000 that went into my trust?"

She nodded, bracing herself.

"Well, I tried to make a withdrawal and it turns out, thanks to Billy, I can't touch a penny of it. I'm only allowed to specify in my *own* will who that money goes to. So how do you like that?" He laughed even as his face grimaced. "I'm worth more dead than alive." He looked at her, his eyes rimmed with fresh tears. "I'm broke. Well"—he shrugged—"not *entirely* broke, but how long will that pittance I ended up with last me?"

"Listen to me"—Alva had inched closer in her chair, taking Jere-miah's hands in hers—"I have some money set aside. It's not much, but if you ever need it, you come to me, you understand? I mean it."

He patted her hand. "Now why would you do that for me?"

"Maybe it's my way of rebelling against the mighty Vanderbilts."

The next day, Willie K. came home in a foul mood. Brushing past the butler, he plunked down his top hat and gloves and hurled his walk-ing stick at the rack in the corner.

"What's the matter with you?" Alva had been in the drawing room, reading to Consuelo. After handing her off to the nurse, she went to Willie's side. "What is it? What's wrong?"

"I've never been so humiliated in all my life," he said, reaching for a decanter of bourbon. "I can't seem to catch a break."

"What happened?"

"James invited me to sit in on a poker game at the Union Club." He poured a generous drink and took a long pull. "Those bastards wouldn't even let me in the door. Van Alen's fine—they let him join the club, but they won't even let me visit as a guest. I'm sick of being treated like a second-class citizen in this town." He ran his fingers through his hair. "You'd think after all this time, after the inheritance, they would see that I'm as good as any of them. I'm sure as hell wealthier than most of them." He took another drink. "And then I heard they even accepted Alexander Stewart's membership—they were going to let him join if he hadn't gone and died on them. They'd accept him—a dry goods merchant—but not one single Vanderbilt . . ."

Willie was still ranting, but as soon as he'd mentioned Alexander Stewart, Alva's mind flashed back to Cornelia's mansion. That house had opened doors for them, including, apparently, the door to the Union Club.

"Willie," she said, leading him over to the settee, "I have an idea, a way that would get the Vanderbilts respected in this town and would surely get you into the gentlemen's clubs."

He was brooding, hardly hearing her at all. "They're still punishing all of us for the Commodore's behavior. They think we're uncouth, a bunch of savage beasts."

"Let me handle this, will you?"

"There's nothing you can do about it."

Alva wasn't sure if by *you* he meant there wasn't anything *anyone* could do, or if he meant *you—a woman*. Either way, it ignited a challenge in her.

After that, Alva took matters into her own hands and hired an architect, Richard Morris Hunt. At their first meeting Hunt adjusted his spectacles and examined the drawing she'd provided, covered with arrows pointing to sections with callouts like *chimney, buttress, pillars, more archways.*

"Mrs. Vanderbilt," Hunt had chuckled, his full mustache covering his top lip completely. Removing his spectacles, he had sat back in his chair and said, "Is this a home you wish to construct or a castle?"

It wasn't long after that first meeting that Alva discovered she was pregnant again, and by then she had convinced Willie that they were going to need a bigger house than the one they'd started building. Despite her fatigue and bouts of morning sickness, she and Hunt approached the project with a renewed sense of urgency, eating boiled chicken and mutton from a cast-iron pot at his desk while they sketched out the final details.

At the end of October 1878, Alva and Willie's second child was born. A son this time and more traditionally named, William Kissam Vanderbilt II, but from day one they called him Little Willie.

Shortly after he was born, while both children were with their nurse, Alva decided to show Willie K. the plans for the new house. Standing in the dining room, she unrolled the blueprints, laying them out on the table, the curled ends weighted down with a pair of brass candlesticks. Alva proudly presented her French château. She'd been involved with everything, the wainscoting, the arched lancets and round rose stained-glass windows, the ribbed vaulting, the colonnades and spires and every detail down to the last finial. All this time she'd been anticipating building something truly opulent, and on a scale that no one in America had ever seen before.

Willie looked at the floor plan and then up at her. "Have you gone mad?"

"But even you said we're going to need a bigger house. Especially now with the new baby."

"A bigger house is one thing," he said. "What you have here is ridiculous. It's a monstrosity. Where would you even put a place like that?"

"Richard found a perfect spot. Right on Fifth Avenue. A little farther up in the Fifties."

He looked again at the blueprint and scratched his head. "And what does something like this cost? It must be $2 million."

"Actually, it would probably be $3 million."

"What!"

"Or more." She smiled and fluttered her lashes.

Willie looked at her in disbelief. "That's absurd. You know I can't afford that. Even with my inheritance."

"But it's not as if you'd have to come up with the money all at once—and he said a house like this would take at least two years to build, anyway. If we needed a little help, we could always go to your father."

He walked away from the table and dropped down in a chair, resting his elbows on his knees, his head in his hands.

"Oh, Willie, don't you see?" She went to his side. "You're thinking too small—and I'm not just talking about the house. I'm talking about *everything*. You just have to trust me."

He smiled and reached up to touch her cheek. "I do trust you. You know I do."

"Then let me build this house. Let me do it for us. Together, you and me, we could rule all of New York."

CHAPTER EIGHTEEN

Caroline

CAROLINE'S CARRIAGE ARRIVED OUTSIDE her mother's townhouse on West Twenty-Third Street. She had moved from Lafayette Place and Great Jones Street several years ago, and Caroline was only too happy not to have to step foot inside her childhood home ever again.

When she was growing up, her mother was either tending to sick children or mourning the ones she'd lost. Caroline had never even known some of her siblings who'd died. There was Henry, gone before his first birthday. Augustus from influenza; Archibald, run over by a carriage; Elizabeth in childbirth; Cordelia passed from consumption; and Catherine from some mysterious undiagnosed illness. If Caroline's mother wasn't pregnant, she'd been in mourning and sometimes she was carrying one child while grieving the loss of another. Black bunting hung outside, mirrors always covered, clocks stopped at the time of each family member's death. It was a morbid house, heavy, filled with sorrow. Children in the neighborhood said it was haunted.

For the most part, when Caroline was a young girl, her care had been left to a stern governess who sent her to the servants' quarters when she misbehaved, which turned out to be no punishment at all. Smithy, the family butler, brought her lemonade and fresh biscuits. The maids, Sissy and Abigail, called her Miss Lina and doted on her. Caroline sometimes sassed her governess just to be sent back downstairs. But soon the novelty wore off. She grew bored watching them at work and eventually persuaded Sissy and Abigail to let her help fold laundry, dust the furniture, make up the beds. A pile of bed linens whose edges she'd lined up perfectly filled Caroline with an immense sense of accomplishment. Nothing in her privileged upstairs world—certainly not her studies nor music lessons—delivered such immediate and satisfying results.

And now, years later, Smithy, Sissy and Abigail were still working for Caroline's mother, who was getting up in years. Because it was harder for her to get around, to climb in and out of carriages, up and down the stairs, Caroline made regular visits to see her. Each time she arrived, those same kindly servants who had once lavished affection on Miss Lina now only saw her as Mrs. Astor. She'd wanted to throw her arms around Smithy, now stoop shouldered with more wrinkles than crinkled tissue paper. She was saddened by the way he led her into the drawing room with the formality reserved for strangers.

Her mother was in a high-back chair, clutching a lace handkerchief in her liver-spotted hand. Her cane was hooked over the armrest. A footman—someone Caroline didn't remember from childhood—appeared with teacups on a sterling silver tray.

After he'd left, Caroline's mother announced that she was going to host an engagement party for Helen and Mr. Roosevelt. "As her grandmother, it's the least I can do. I didn't *want* to even acknowledge Emily's wedding. Good heavens—why you didn't stop it, I'll never understand," she said now, waving her handkerchief. "You should have stepped in, used a firmer hand."

Caroline never told her mother about General Van Alen and the duel. And regardless of what her mother thought, no one could deny that Emily and James appeared to be a harmonious couple. The two of them, along with baby Mary, were forever going on picnics, or attending birthday parties, puppet shows and the sort. Honestly, she'd never seen Emily so happy.

"Well, at least Helen has chosen well," her mother said. "She's always been such a sensible girl. So is Carrie. That one is wise beyond her years. Now we just have to do something about Charlotte."

"Oh, Charlotte." Caroline shook her head. "She shows no interest in society. She wants to serve the poor and the needy."

"What does she know about being poor and needy? It's time she turned her attention to finding a husband."

"She tells me she has no interest in marriage."

"No interest in marriage?" Her mother drew a deep, incredulous breath. "Charlotte is a beautiful girl but she can't afford to wait any longer. You must step in this time or she'll end up a spinster."

Caroline feared her mother was right. She turned away and looked at the mantel, lined with photographs of her father and dead siblings.

"What about the Drayton boy?" her mother asked.

"From Philadelphia?"

"Isn't Charlotte friendly with him?"

Caroline thought. "She *knows* him, but I'd hardly say they're friendly."

"He comes from a fine family. The Drayton lineage is sterling."

"But Charlotte is headstrong. She's just as stubborn as her father and—"

"Oh, Lina, do you hear yourself? Come now, you're only making excuses. You can't allow Charlotte to just go along her merry way. It's time she settle down, have children. Take her place in society. For goodness' sake, you absolutely *must* step in this time. It's your responsibility as her mother."

The next morning, Charlotte came downstairs for breakfast wearing an old dress, with a fraying hem and sleeves. Every time she wore it,

Caroline asked her to throw it out, but Charlotte continued to wear it proudly, as if it were a banner. As of late, she no longer wanted to dress like an Astor. Didn't want to be mistaken for a spoiled rich girl—which of course was exactly what she was. But she wanted to cut a more noble image, like a missionary, especially while running food drives for the needy, attending suffrage rallies and marches— places where she'd never meet suitable men.

Caroline held her tongue, and merely told Charlotte that she had invited the Draytons for dinner the following week.

Charlotte didn't say anything and focused her attention on her egg cup, clearly not understanding that this dinner had anything to do with her. With her entire future.

"I've asked them to bring their son, Coleman, with them."

"Oh." Charlotte set her spoon down. "Coleman?" She said his name as if she were asking, *Is that the best you can do?*

Carrie turned and looked at her older sister—something passed between them, something understood that needed no words. The two of them had a language of their own just like Emily and Helen.

Charlotte raised one eyebrow in response and pushed her plate away. She didn't finish her breakfast, said she'd lost her appetite.

One week later, the Draytons arrived. Twenty-six-year-old Coleman wasn't a bad catch at all as far as Caroline was concerned. He was handsome with a strong chin and gentle pale blue eyes. A bit jittery, though, constantly smoothing down his mustache or patting down the lapels of his dinner jacket. William said he found Coleman's constant fidgeting maddening and stayed in his study until he was called in for dinner.

Caroline had warned Charlotte ahead of time not to spout off about votes for women and her other causes, but a few comments had slipped out over the bluepoint oysters.

To Caroline's surprise, Coleman had jumped right in. "They

blame it on the Panic of '73," he'd said. He was very animated, hands gesticulating so, she thought he might knock his wineglass over. "But they need to look at what caused the depression in the first place."

"Exactly," said Charlotte. "It goes back to all that speculative investing in the railroads."

"Not to mention the decline in the silver market."

"And don't forget about all the property lost in the Chicago fire," added Charlotte.

Coleman nodded. "It's all so intertwined . . ."

Caroline didn't know if she was impressed by Charlotte's knowledge or embarrassed that she was discussing such subjects at the dinner table. Either way, it was obvious she and Coleman would never be at a loss for conversation, and Caroline decided that the two of them were quite well suited for each other.

The following day, unbeknownst to Charlotte or Coleman, Caroline had arranged a meeting with the Draytons to discuss their children's future. The adults agreed that the two should marry. One week later, the Draytons' lawyer, a young, eager sort who looked like he'd yet to hang his diploma on the wall, rode the train from Philadelphia to New York with a three-page financial agreement in hand. It was settled.

Charlotte was in her bedroom, posing for Carrie at her vanity, her hairbrush suspended inches from her blond curls as she gazed thoughtfully in the mirror. Carrie was sitting on the floor, propped up against the side of the bed, knees bent, sketch pad resting on her thighs. They were chattering about something but went quiet as soon as Caroline appeared in the doorway.

She peered over Carrie's shoulder. "You've captured her eyes quite well," said Caroline. "This one might be good enough to frame."

Carrie smiled as she smudged and blended the charcoal pencil, highlighting Charlotte's cheekbones.

"Carrie, dear, would you give me a moment alone with Charlotte?"

"Can't I stay? I won't say a word."

"No you may not. Besides, you shouldn't sit like that. It's bad for your posture."

Carrie gathered her pencils and sketch pad, letting her sister know she'd be back to finish the drawing. As soon as Carrie closed the door, Caroline said she had good news: the arrangements with the Draytons had been finalized and she should expect a proposal within the week.

"What?" Charlotte set her hairbrush down, staring at Caroline through the mirror. She seemed completely caught off guard. "Was this *his* idea or yours? Does Coleman even *want* to marry me?"

Caroline heard someone out in the hall and presumed it was Carrie with her ear pressed to the door. "Why else would he be proposing? And you do think he's handsome, don't you?" Caroline asked. "And very smart."

"Well, yes, but . . . ." She was about to chew on her cuticle and thought better of it, dropping her hand to her lap. She seemed utterly confused. "Shouldn't we get to know each other better? What if we find out we don't like each other? Shouldn't I at least *like* the man I'm supposed to marry? And what about love? When I marry—*if* I marry—it should be to someone I'm madly in love with. Someone I can't live without."

"And what if that man you're *madly in love with* never comes along? What then?"

"Then I'll be a spinster. I'd rather that than be sold off like a piece of chattel."

Caroline frowned, blaming this all on William. By making Charlotte his favorite, by always treating her with the importance normally reserved for sons, he had given *his Charlie* a sense of entitlement. She actually believed she could put her foot down on this matter. She believed it, and now it was Caroline's responsibility as her mother to stomp on it.

"This is not up for discussion, young lady. You're twenty years old. It's time you get married. Pretty as you are, you can't afford to wait much longer." Caroline once again sounded just like her mother. "Well?"

"Well what?" Charlotte shot her a harsh look. "Don't you see—I want to do more with my life than be someone's wife, someone's mother. Is that so wrong?"

Caroline thought for a moment. "No, my darling, it's not wrong. Not wrong at all. I think it's perfectly understandable for a woman— especially an ambitious woman like you—to want more for herself. That's why society is so important. You need to get more involved. You could do a great deal of good there."

"*Society?*" Charlotte laughed. "How can society possibly be enough?"

"Because we *make* it enough. It's what your grandmother did and what I've done and your older sisters do, too."

"But society is an illusion. Aside from a handful of charitable events, society doesn't help anyone outside your circle, and I'm sorry, but that's not enough for me."

"But it's *all* we have." Caroline's chest grew tight. Yes, she could appreciate that Charlotte wanted more—Caroline had wanted more, too. But they had to face reality. In Caroline's eyes, all Charlotte's marching, all those lectures she'd attended were just another form of illusion, no different from Caroline serving society. They were two sides of the same coin: two women looking to bring meaning to their lives, even if that meant they had to invent it out of thin air.

"Charlotte, the sooner you accept things as they are, and quit bucking up against everything, the better off you'll be. This proposal is for your own good."

"You really think so, don't you?"

"I'm your mother—don't you think I want what's best for you? Don't you think I want to see you happy?"

Charlotte looked at her, and Caroline could see that something had hardened within her. The air between them thickened, and when it was obvious that Charlotte wasn't going to fire back, it threw Caroline. Something was going on behind those big blue eyes, and Caroline found it unnerving.

When she couldn't take it anymore, Caroline broke the silence. "Well? Am I to assume you'll accept Coleman's proposal? You'll agree to marry him?"

Charlotte's expression didn't change. "I don't suppose I have a choice in the matter now, do I?"

An hour later, Caroline walked by Charlotte's room and heard her daughter inside crying to Carrie.

Before the guests began arriving for Helen and Rosy's engagement party, Caroline's mother insisted on having a family photograph taken. The photographer, a tall, slender man in a snug-fitting vest and brown tweed trousers, set up his tripod and began posing everyone in the parlor. He seated Caroline's mother in front with Helen and Rosy to her left, Caroline and William to the right. He scooted Coleman Drayton closer to Van Alen and then scooted Van Alen closer to Emily, who had baby Mary in her arms. He moved Carrie next to her aunt Augusta and put Jack in the back row next to his uncle John and cousin Waldorf.

The photographer stood before them, squinting one eye, sizing them up as if he were the camera's lens. "Lovely," he said. "Just lovely. Stay just like that." He jogged back to his tripod and ducked beneath his dark curtain. "Ready, everyone? On a count of three—"

"Not so fast," said Caroline's mother, tapping her cane to get everyone's attention. "Far be it from me to raise concern, but has anyone seen Charlotte?"

The family photograph was put on hold while everyone went off in different directions, searching the house. Coleman, in his usual frenetic manner, began looking behind curtains, under tables, as if his wife-to-be were a child, playing hide-and-seek. Meanwhile, Caroline and her mother took the main floor, her mother rising out of her chair with herculean force. She kept pace with Caroline as she went room to room, her mother displaying more vigor than she had in months.

"Charlotte? Charlotte, where are you?" Caroline called out as they left the music room and entered the drawing room.

"She has to be nearby. She was with you all when you arrived," Caroline's mother muttered. "How does one misplace a grown child?"

Caroline turned and saw Carrie standing near the front door, pointing. "She's outside."

Caroline threw open the front door and there was Charlotte, waiting out front. Caroline called to her just as she took off running in the opposite direction. Caroline stepped onto the stoop and saw that she was running toward a man coming up the walkway. It wasn't until he cleared the shadow of a tree that Caroline recognized him. It was Duncan Briar.

Caroline saw what was happening, but she couldn't get herself to move. Charlotte looked back at Caroline, her sister and her grandmother, but she kept going, heading toward Duncan Briar.

"Charlotte?" Caroline's mother called out. "Charlotte, where do you think you're going? Lina, what is going on? Charlotte? Charlotte, you get back here."

It was hearing her mother take charge, knowing that she was standing right behind her, witnessing it all, that prompted Caroline into action. Under the pressure of her mother's watch, Caroline rushed down the front steps. If ever she was being tested, forced to call upon all her negotiating and diplomatic skills, this was it. She could hear her mother's voice inside her head: *Be firm, Lina. Take charge of this. It's for her own good.*

"What do you think you're doing, young lady?"

Charlotte stopped, just inches from Duncan. "I'm sorry, Mother, but I'm not going to marry Coleman."

"Oh, come now. Stop with this foolishness."

Duncan pulled Charlotte protectively to his side. "Mrs. Astor, if I may say something—"

Caroline turned to Duncan. "Actually, no you may not. In fact, Mr. Briar, if you don't mind, I'd like to have a word with my daughter. In private."

"He's not going anywhere," said Charlotte, clinging ever closer to him. "Whatever you have to say to me, you can say it in front of Duncan."

"Fine, have it your way." She sighed, fighting to keep her voice even. She heard the *clickety-clack* of horse-drawn carriages approaching; their guests were starting to arrive.

"I thought you'd be more reasonable, more mature about all this, but I can see now that you leave me no choice. You say you don't want to marry Mr. Drayton, then we'll have to make other arrangements."

"What do you mean?" She gripped Duncan's hand.

Caroline dreaded what she was about to say, but the words were right there—her mother was right there, too. "Since you sympathize with the poor so much, maybe you'll enjoy being one of them."

Charlotte's hand slipped from Duncan's as the color drained from her face.

"If you don't marry Coleman Drayton, you'll be on your own. I mean it, Charlotte. You won't get a dime of your inheritance and not a penny from here on out. And—"

"Mother, how can—"

Caroline raised her hand. She wasn't finished yet. "And if Mr. Briar agrees to leave here—leave New York, that is—I will make arrangements to help him secure employment with another family elsewhere."

"And if I don't wish to leave?" he asked, gallantly, foolishly.

"Then I'll see to it that no proper family in this country will hire you."

"But, Mrs. Astor, I have to work."

"Perhaps you can shovel manure for $2 a day."

"Mother! It's not Duncan's fault."

"I suspect you're right about that, but nonetheless, Charlotte, you have a very big decision to make. You can choose to live in poverty with your Mr. Duncan or you can marry Mr. Drayton."

"But, Mother—that's blackmail."

"Yes, I suppose it is."

"How can you do this? That's not fair."

Caroline stared into her daughter's eyes. "I have news for you, Charlotte. Life isn't always fair."

THE
SOCIETY
PAGES

1880–1884

CHAPTER NINETEEN

Society

NEW YORK, 1880

THEY CALL IT *SOCIETY NEWS*, but we call it what it is—gossip! And gossip is nothing new to us. Why, we've been whispering, cackling and spreading the most outlandish rumors about friends and foes alike for as far back as we can remember. Only now, reporters at the daily newspapers and weeklies act as though they've invented this concept, and they do seem to find us endlessly fascinating. Frankly, they can't stop writing about our comings and goings.

They report on everything from the balls and dinner parties we attend to the menus we serve, the flowers we display and of course the gowns we wear down to the brocaded silk trim. They investigate us rather thoroughly, and it seems that a disgruntled footman or maid is only too happy to mention that so-and-so's husband frequents a brothel in Murray Hill, and so-and-so's wife gets into the brandy before noon. But of course, the most engrossing stories come from none other than Ward McAllister, who simply cannot keep his mouth shut.

That man loves talking to the press, and he isn't always kind. After one of Lady Paget's recent extravaganzas, he said to *Town Topics*, "THE BOEUF BOURGUIGNON—IF YOU COULD MANAGE TO CUT THROUGH IT—

WAS DREADFUL, AND SHE DID NOT PROPERLY FRAPPÉ THE WINE." The week before he had lambasted Penelope Easton in the *World*, saying, "THE HOSTESS WHO SERVES SALMON DURING THE WINTER, REGARDLESS WHAT SAUCE ACCOMPANIES IT, DOES GRAVE INJURY TO HERSELF AND HER GUESTS." The *New York Times* also recently quoted him saying, "A DINNER INVITATION, ONCE ACCEPTED, IS A SACRED OBLIGATION. IF YOU DIE BEFORE THE DINNER TAKES PLACE, YOUR EXECUTOR MUST ATTEND."

It seems that if we're not reading about Ward McAllister's pompous pontifications, we're reading about the construction of Alva Vanderbilt's future mansion. Just this morning we open our newspapers and see the headline: THE VANDERBILTS TRANSFORM FIFTH AVENUE. The *New York Times* has called it AN IMPRESSIVE UNDERTAKING. The *New York Herald* said it was expected to be VAST AND EXPANSIVE. The *New York Enquirer* called it a work of SPLENDOR AND GRANDEUR IN THE MAKING.

Not since the construction of the Stewarts' marble mansion has a private home been so generously celebrated in the press. And back then, that had set off a building frenzy among us as we all raced to build mansions of our own. The Knickerbockers thought it was a vulgar display of wealth. We knew they laughed at us, joking about how we were all going bankrupt trying to outbuild and outspend each other. But it certainly hasn't taken long for those very same Knickerbockers to follow suit.

Ever since the Vanderbilts broke ground on their mansion, we've noticed the Brownfields have added gables out front and the Belmonts and Chews have both put up columns at their homes, hoping they'll appear more stately. Rumor has it that even Mrs. Astor is thinking about making some enhancements to her townhome as well.

They'll never admit it, but we know the Knickerbockers are trying to keep up with Alva and with us, the nouveau riche. A bit of the tail wagging the dog.

CHAPTER TWENTY

Caroline

BY THE START OF a new decade Caroline had married off three of her four daughters and was a grandmother many times over with yet more grandchildren on the way. One thing about the Astor women—they were a fruitful lot.

Emily had a four-year-old daughter and a two-year-old son and had just announced that she was pregnant again. Helen had a one-year-old boy and was also expecting again, and Charlotte had a three-month-old daughter. Though all the girls had nurses and maids to help with everything from baths to diaper changes, Caroline had encouraged her daughters to be as involved with their children's care as she had been with her own. Caroline's growing family kept her busier than usual, her mornings spent going from her mother's house to her daughters', visiting them all before she tended to her correspondence and other social engagements.

On some mornings, such as this one, all the married daughters and their children congregated at Emily's townhouse on Fifth Avenue. While on her way, Caroline's carriage passed the construction site of Alva Vanderbilt's future home, occupying an entire block. The press had referred to it as THE VANDERBILTS' FIFTH AVENUE, and it appeared as though Alva was about to take over the city. Each time Caroline's carriage made its way uptown she saw more scaffolding going up and more Indiana limestone being hauled in. The street was constantly congested, blocked off by horses hauling lumber and other materials as well as dozens of stonecutters and carpenters milling about. At first, Caroline had dismissed the construction as a nuisance and inconvenience to those traveling north. Though really, she thought, *Who comes up this far north anyway?* If it weren't for her daughters, she'd have no reason to venture past the Forties.

Several times Caroline had spotted Alva standing in the midst of it all, instructing the men. *Alva*—that name kept turning up in the newspapers, in conversations, and something about her—beyond just being new money—rubbed Caroline the wrong way. Alva Vanderbilt was pushy, and she got under her skin in a way that Mamie Fish and the others never had.

"I would have been here sooner," Caroline said to Emily when she arrived, handing her parasol and hat to the butler. "Traffic was dreadful this morning."

"Charlotte and Helen aren't even here yet."

"I'm not surprised. That Alva Vanderbilt has all of Fifth Avenue backed up with her workers."

"Oh, come now, Mother." Emily frowned playfully, hiking little James up on her hip while Mary stood close at her side. "You never fail to find fault with Alva Vanderbilt, do you?"

"One needn't look too hard to find fault with her." Caroline figured she was entitled to make a sarcastic remark here and there, given all the nasty things she'd heard Alva had been saying about her, criticizing everything from the state of Caroline's marriage to the height of her wigs.

"Then I don't suppose you'll be joining us for the dinner party I'm hosting next month."

"Oh, Emily, you're not inviting the Vanderbilts, are you?"

"I have to. You know how close James and Willie are. Besides, I rather like Alva."

"But what about *your* friends? You know Francine Bryce and Edith McVickar—not to mention the others—will never dine at the same table with Alva Vanderbilt."

"It will be fine, Mother. I've been to plenty of parties where the McVickars *and* the Vanderbilts have been in attendance."

"Mixing everyone together isn't proper. I don't care if other hostesses do it, you shouldn't," she said, following Emily into the morning room.

The floor was peppered with baby blankets, picture books and corn husk dolls. The table was strewn with papers. Emily handed little James off to Caroline while she tidied up the papers. "I was helping James keep his ledger," she explained. "I just found a $27 error. In his favor."

"Well, then I guess you've earned your keep," she laughed, peppering little James with kisses, though she was still miffed about her daughter socializing with that Vanderbilt woman. It simply wasn't right, and Emily's husband shouldn't have put her in that position to begin with. She was about to tell Emily that when Charlotte arrived.

For all Charlotte's reluctance to marry—particularly to marry Coleman—she seemed content enough. The only person she really confided in was Carrie, who never said a word to Caroline about her sister's complaints or if she missed Duncan Briar or if she blamed Caroline.

"Where's my darling granddaughter?" she asked.

"I left her with the nurse—I couldn't listen to her crying anymore. I'm exhausted," said Charlotte, pouring herself a cup of coffee, set up on the sideboard. "That nurse is useless. I've been up all night with the baby," she said, joining them in the sitting area. "She's hungry. She's fussy. She's hungry again. I'm so tired—I don't know which end is up."

"One time," said Emily, laughing, "right after Mary was born, I was so tired, I actually tried to burp my husband."

"I remember those days with you girls." Caroline smiled. "Seems like only yesterday when Helen and Charlotte would be in their bassinets and, Emily, you would watch them sleep, wouldn't take your eyes off them. When you and Helen got a little older, the two of you would hold hands and twirl round and round in a circle. Charlotte, you would try to break in, but they wouldn't let you."

"I guess some things never change," said Charlotte, laughing. "I still can't break in on the two of them."

"Oh, sometimes they'd let you play with them," said Caroline, remembering all three of her girls on their rocking horses having imaginary races. "And then Carrie came along and you all acted like she was a little doll. You all wanted to hold her, cuddle her, take turns reading to her."

They were still reminiscing when Helen waddled into the room even before the butler could announce her. She was pushing Tadd in a baby buggy, parking it over by the fireplace. Caroline's first thought was that she was seven months pregnant and shouldn't have been rushing around like that.

"Oh, Emily, I'm so sorry. It's just awful."

"What's awful?" Emily's face went blank.

"Haven't you seen today's edition of the *World*?" Helen reached into the buggy for a folded newspaper, which Tadd had teethed on, and handed it to Emily.

Emily's eyes rapidly shot from left to right while Caroline read over her shoulder: POKER GAME LEADS TO BAD BLOOD.

Two sentences in and Caroline clasped a hand to her mouth. According to the article, James Van Alen had lost badly in a poker game, had become belligerent and stormed out of the Union Club while still owing Mr. Tennyson Livingston $50,000. They said James was on the verge of bankruptcy because of his gambling debts.

"Is it true?" Caroline asked, her hand having moved down to her throat.

"Of course not." Emily set her son down and drew a deep breath. "James is good for the money. Mr. Livingston will get his $50,000."

"So, then it *is* true."

"No, it's not true," said Emily. "Not exactly."

"Well"—Charlotte shrugged—"he does play a good deal of poker."

"He plays once a week at the club—that's it." Emily dropped the paper and began pacing. "Oh dear—what am I going to do? They're making James out to be a compulsive gambler. He's never welched on a bet and he never will."

"And did you see the part about you, Mother?" Helen picked up the newspaper and read: "'We can only assume that Mrs. Astor will be unable to defend her son-in-law's egregious behavior this time.'"

This time? It was true that in the past Caroline had publicly defended him—claiming she didn't notice that he spoke with an accent and explaining away the monocle by saying he was nearsighted and couldn't find spectacles that fit properly. He was Emily's husband after all, and for her daughter's sake, she'd tell all who would listen what a wonderful son-in-law she had. Still, as Caroline read on, she thought, *Why did they drag my name into this?* Thanks to the press, Caroline felt as if she was always being watched. People knew where she lived now, and one afternoon she'd found complete strangers looking through her downstairs windows. After that, she ordered the drapes be drawn shut at all times. Now whenever she went out in public, she kept her face covered by a veil.

Emily called the maid to take the children, and after they were gone she said, "My husband doesn't deserve this. Why are people so vicious? My own father has never even given him a chance."

"Well," said Charlotte, "you knew Father hated James when you married him and—"

"Oh hush," said Caroline. "Your father does not *hate* James."

"The press is out to destroy him," said Emily. "He's a sensitive man. This will devastate him."

"You have to do something about this," said Helen, looking at Caroline as if she had some magical powers, some invisible shield that could protect them all—and she wished that were true, but the press was too formidable, even for her.

Caroline turned away, feigning interest in a family portrait on the wall, recalling the times she and William had mocked Van Alen. Sometimes Caroline had even poked fun at her son-in-law simply because it gave her some common ground with William. Instead of protecting her daughter, Caroline had been cruel; her jabs at Emily's husband were merciless and at times even exaggerated in hopes of fusing her own fractured marriage. *What kind of mother does such a thing?* The guilt grabbed hold of her, and though she still had plenty of misgivings about James and all the Van Alens, she knew that for Emily's sake she had to do something to spare her son-in-law from the press.

"You pay that story in the paper no mind," she told Emily.

"You do realize, though," said Charlotte, "this isn't going to stop with just that one article, Mother. This is just the beginning. I'm afraid the newspapers are going to have a field day with this and there's nothing even you, *Mrs. Astor*, can do about it."

Was Charlotte right? Caroline couldn't accept that. She was still the most powerful woman in New York and had always had the ability to sway public opinion. But the press presented a new challenge. She wasn't sure how the game was played anymore, but she knew someone who did.

The following day she summoned Ward McAllister to her home. "Thank you for coming on such short notice," she said after Hade had shown him into the library.

"But of course," said Ward. "Don't you know, I'm always at your disposal, my Mystic Rose."

Ward was wearing lavender kid gloves with a complementary

violet boutonniere in his lapel. The tall collar on his white shirt stood at attention, and like most society men, Ward was swept up in the latest fashion trends. Even Jack, on the brink of manhood, tried desperately to keep up with the modern styles, but those popular snug-fitting creaseless trousers, like the ones Ward was wearing that day, did Jack no favors. The boy could not control his appetite even though he knew his weight held him back. Poor Jack required a mounting block to get on his horse, and each time he laughed, his belly shook like aspic.

"Before I forget," Ward said, taking the chair opposite Caroline, "I have something very interesting to tell you. You'll never believe what just happened." She could see that he was wound up even before he sprang back to his feet, passing his walking stick from hand to hand as if it were a theatrical prop. "As I was leaving the Knickerbocker Club earlier today, a reporter from *Town Topics* approached me."

Caroline didn't say a word. *Town Topics* was quickly becoming one of the most widely read weeklies in the city.

"This reporter said I was—and I quote—'a wealth of information' where society is concerned."

"That you are," she said, feeling nostalgic for the days when the two of them had plotted out the first Patriarch Ball, how they'd labored over every detail of her annual clambake. Together they had made a serious study of all the ways in which polite society was to behave. Now her dear friend and business partner was more concerned with high fashion and seeing his name in the society pages. He'd even recently lent his name to a newspaper advertisement for Dr. James P. Campbell's Safe Arsenic Complexion Wafers.

"Believe it or not, the reporter said I should write a book—my memoirs."

"Your memoirs?" She suppressed the urge to laugh.

"Oh yes. And then, don't you know, he started asking me about *you*."

"Oh?" She certainly didn't like the sound of that.

"He was quite interested in speaking with you, but naturally I told him that was out of the question. 'Mrs. Astor does not give interviews. She's extremely private, a lady of absolute elegance and style,' I said." He paused, beaming at her.

She didn't respond and found his servile manner most off-putting. It was as if he expected something in return, just like everyone else who tried to flatter her. This saddened her greatly because she thought their relationship more genuine and not reliant upon the need for pandering.

"I said explicitly that 'Mrs. Astor never speaks to the press.'"

This was true. If it were left up to Caroline, her name would never have appeared in the papers. The first time she saw her name in the *New York Times* had been her wedding announcement. The second time it was a lengthy article about her annual ball, and in thirteen separate mentions, she had been referred to as Mrs. William *Backhouse* Astor Jr. Each time she saw William's middle name, there in black and white, it conjured up visions of outhouses. That same day she'd ordered her social secretary to have new calling cards engraved and had insisted that reporters and others only refer to her from now on as Mrs. William B. Astor Jr.

"Now tell me," Ward said, "what was it you needed to see me about?"

For a moment Caroline had almost forgotten the whole point of their visit. "Well," she said, "I need your help with a sensitive matter." Even as she said those words, she felt the absurdity of thinking she could trust him. Though there was a time when she most certainly did trust him. In the past, she'd talked to him at length about Emily's marriage and the duel. About Charlotte and Coleman Drayton— especially since William had wanted nothing to do with his future son-in-law. Ward had been the one to assure her that in both cases she had done the right thing. He'd always been there to listen and provide guidance when there was no one else to turn to.

But now, with those reporters and gossip columns, Caroline had to be careful. Not that she thought Ward would ever intentionally betray her, but when it came to gossip, Ward McAllister couldn't help himself. Still, he was the most likely person to help her with this, so she gestured for him to have a seat.

"I'm certain you saw the article about James Van Alen in the *World* yesterday."

"Oh, indeed I did. That was a rather unfortunate incident, don't you know. But then again, James Van Alen . . ." He shook his head as if nothing more needed to be said.

"Emily is beside herself."

Propping his chin on his walking stick, looking like a lovesick boy, he said, "Tell me how I may be of assistance."

"I'd like you to contact one of your reporter friends, perhaps the fellow you spoke with earlier today, and let him know that Mr. James Van Alen is in fine financial standing. In fact, he's making a rather substantial endowment—$100,000—to the Frankfort Children's Orphanage."

"My goodness. I had no idea." McAllister sat up, a hand pressed to his chest. "Is he really?"

Of course he wasn't. Caroline was writing the check, but she just looked at Ward and said, "My son-in-law has been greatly misunderstood. He's a fine man, a gentleman, and I'm coming to you, asking for your help. You *need* to get word of Mr. Van Alen's generous contribution to the orphanage into the newspapers."

Ward nodded without hesitation and tweaked his necktie. "Consider it done, my Mystic Rose. Consider it done."

CHAPTER TWENTY-ONE

Alva

CONSUELO AND LITTLE WILLIE had just gone off with their governess, and Willie K. had left for his father's stables to see one of Billy's new phaetons. Alva took advantage of the quiet to write her friend Consuelo, whom she now referred to as Duchy—despite her official title being Viscountess Mandeville. Eventually she'd be the Duchess of Manchester, and in the meantime, it was the only way to keep from confusing everyone about the two Consuelos in her life.

After she'd sealed the envelope, she heard the doorbell, and a few moments later her butler appeared with Jeremiah playfully poking his head inside the room. "Is the coast clear?" he asked.

Alva laughed, sprang out of her chair and hugged him, because that's what they did—hugged like long-lost friends—even if they'd just seen each other the day before. He sat down across from her with a cup of coffee, served in Minton china, and reached for the copy of *Town Topics* on the pile of newspapers.

"My, my," he said, spreading the newsprint out before him, "someone's been getting quite a lot of press lately."

"Isn't that something?" She smiled, knowing it was no accident. She'd taken great pains to get her name in there; befriending reporters—dropping off bottles of champagne and boxes of cigars to those whom she could always count on to cover her every move.

"Good lord"—he sounded flabbergasted—"they even wrote about your latest shopping spree at Stewart's. Is *that* even considered news?"

"It is when you spend as much as I did."

"Well, la-di-da." He set that paper aside and reached for the next one. "What's the latest on the new house?"

She sighed. "More delays."

"Not again."

Alva planted her elbows on the table and rested her head in her hands. "I met with the architect yesterday. He's guessing we're still three years away from completion. *Three more years.* How are we going to manage in this space for another three years? I feel like I can't breathe in here."

"I know just what you need," said Jeremiah, tossing the paper aside and brushing imaginary dust off his hands. "Come with me. I have a surprise for you."

"I'm not up for any surprises." She caught herself grinding her teeth—usually a nighttime activity performed while fast asleep.

"This will cheer you up. I promise."

Reluctantly she followed him outside. At the end of the walkway, leaning against the side of the gate, was a high-wheeler bicycle.

"Where did this come from?" Alva asked, placing her hand on the giant wheel.

"I won it."

"You *won* it?"

Jeremiah shrugged. "I bet a man this morning that a young lady in the park wouldn't give him her name."

Alva laughed, despite her mood. "Is there anything you won't gamble on?"

"Come on," he said, standing the bike upright, "let's go for a spin."

"Do you even know how to ride this thing?"

"I'm a natural." He reached for the handlebars and placed one foot on the mounting peg as he pushed the bicycle forward to give him a running start. Swinging his other leg in place, he leaped up on the seat. "Come on," he shouted, "get on board."

She looked at the apparatus, bewildered. "How?"

"The mounting peg. Just climb up and hold on tight."

She had to admit she was intrigued by the challenge. Hiking up her dress, she stepped onto the peg and placed her hands on Jeremiah's shoulders. The bike wobbled back and forth and Alva yelped, hanging on for dear life. It took a moment before they found their balance and then off they went. Jeremiah pedaled out onto Fifth Avenue. Alva had lost her hat back near Forty-Second Street. Jeremiah offered to stop but she wanted to keep going.

"Faster! Go faster!" she shouted. She imagined they must have been quite a sight—and she loved the wind blowing back her hair, making her eyes tear. People on the street were pointing and gasping, as if they'd never seen a woman's ankles or petticoat before.

Jeremiah laughed, calling back to her from over his shoulder, "I can't wait to see what the press has to say about this."

A few months later, the Academy of Music announced that they were adding an additional row of boxes and putting them up for sale. Once again Alva attempted to buy her way in, but even after she offered the outrageous sum of $30,000, the Academy board passed. And she knew who was driving the vote: Ward McAllister, August Belmont and, of course, Mrs. Astor. But the Vanderbilts weren't alone. The Rockefellers, the Morgans and the Goulds were among the twenty-three families to have earned the dubious honor of being denied.

Alva lay awake, her teeth clenched, her mind grinding over the rejection. The whole thing made no sense to her, especially when everyone knew the Academy was in dire need of money. And the nouveau riche had money—plenty of it. If Mrs. Astor and the board would only let them in, they'd have the funds to rebuild the entire theater and then some. She repeated that thought to herself over and over again and then suddenly—there it was! She bolted up in bed. It was so obvious. Why hadn't she thought of this before?

The next day Alva went to see her father-in-law. His office was decorated with stuffed antelope, mouflon and deer heads on the walls. He had a fondness for marble sculptures, mostly of nearly naked men, their muscles taut, bows and arrows drawn. Billy was seated behind an enormous mahogany desk flanked by two celestial leather globes on gilded stands. The wall behind him sported a map of the country showing all his railroads.

"I have an idea and I want to present it to you." He didn't say anything, didn't try to stop her, so she kept going. "I think we should get everyone who was denied a box at the Academy to pool their money and together we can build a new opera house of our own."

Billy leaned forward, folded his big meaty hands on the desk and simply said, "Alva." *You silly, precious little thing, you.*

"I'm quite serious about this."

"And it's a very ambitious idea, but it's out of the question. We're not in the business of building theaters and opera houses."

But she wouldn't let it go. "Think about it," she said. "It would be an investment for all of us—all of *you*," she corrected herself. "Everyone knows that the Academy is crumbling before the Knickerbockers' very eyes. You could build a theater that would put theirs to shame. And you could put it in a far more fashionable part of town."

Billy sat back, staring at her without saying a word. She sensed he was a bit annoyed. He had his finger marking his place on a ledger and seemed anxious to get back to work. Alva found his gaze unnerving and looked away, her eyes following the routes of the New York Central, the Burlington and Quincy Railroads. When she glanced back at him, Billy was stroking the tendrils of his whiskers. "It seems like an awfully big undertaking."

"Maybe for someone else. But surely not you. You've never been one to shy away from big projects. And just think what you'd be doing for this city. You'd personally be adding to the cultural fabric of New York. How many men in this town can make that claim?" She saw the hint of a sparkle in his eye—he had liked the sound of that.

Billy rubbed his brow. "Let me think about it."

You do that. She had planted a seed and now all she had to do was wait for it to germinate.

As it turned out, she didn't have to wait long.

One week later, on the twenty-eighth of April, Billy called a meeting to discuss the matter with those prominent businessmen whose families had also been rejected by the Academy. They all gathered in a private dining room at Delmonico's. Willie would have preferred that Alva didn't attend the meeting, but she had insisted, vowing to keep her mouth shut.

Billy welcomed everyone and proceeded to lay out the scenario, of which they were all too aware. Alva sat with the other wives, at the opposite end of the table, hands folded in her lap. Her father-in-law continued to set the stage and when he said, "We all know that the old Academy is crumbling before the Knickerbockers' very eyes," it set off a round of chuckles, and Alva was flattered that he'd borrowed her line.

He pushed on. "If the nobs won't allow us to be included, then the time has come for us swells to take control of this situation and establish our own opera house. What's to prevent us? We certainly have the means."

"That we do," Cornelius agreed, reaching for his brandy snifter.

"I question if the timing is right for a new building," said John Pierpont Morgan. He was an enormous man right down to his nose, which Alva couldn't stop staring at. It was badly pitted and discolored. "We might be acting in haste," he said.

The men agreed and, despite her promise to Willie, Alva couldn't keep quiet any longer. "But don't forget," she said to Billy with all the

Southern charm she could muster, "remember what you said about the Academy of Music being next door to Tammany Hall?" Billy looked at her, stumped, not remembering because, in fact, they had never had that conversation. "Remember?" she said, feeding him his lines. "Remember how they have anarchists and union men picketing out front? And how ladies no longer feel safe going down there. Not to mention the performers."

Billy nodded and took over. "Those anarchists alone make the timing perfect for building a new theater in a safer, more fashionable location."

"But where?" asked Jay Gould.

"Perhaps that vacant lot up north that you were telling me about— the one at Broadway and Thirty-Ninth Street," Alva suggested, as if she hadn't already inspected the location herself.

The meeting adjourned without any definitive decisions having been made, but the men did agree to meet again the following week. When they gathered that second time, Alva again took her seat with Cettie Rockefeller, Fanny Morgan and the handful of other wives.

"I've been giving this a good deal of thought," said Jay Gould, his fingertips stroking a patch of white in his otherwise dark brown beard. "I think opening a new opera house on Thirty-Ninth and Broadway makes considerable sense."

"And don't forget," said Otto Kahn, "we'd be protecting the ladies from the picketers and all that nonsense outside Tammany Hall . . ."

Alva sat silently, listening to them regurgitate her very argument from the week before. They had taken ownership of her idea, and that was exactly what she'd needed them to do. She'd known all along that they simply couldn't have heard it from a woman and had to make it their own before they'd buy into the plan. By the time that meeting had adjourned, all twenty-two men seated around the table had agreed to invest $50,000 apiece and appointed Billy as the acting chairman.

———

Alva wasn't done yet. The next day she went to see her father-in-law again and told him she had some concerns about building the new opera house.

"It's just that you're much too busy to oversee the construction, not to mention the decorating. I would suggest Willie, but you see, he's left all those details for the new house up to me . . ."

She followed him out to his livery stables, the hay and twigs snapping beneath her shoes as she stepped around the piles of manure. Billy had twenty-four carriages in an array of colors, some with blue underbodies, others red or yellow; a different carriage for every occasion. The phaetons were for his morning jaunts to watch the sunrise from the pier. The broughams were for his afternoon ventures to play cards or inspect a bit of railroad track. The victorias and landaulets were for outings with Louisa. They were all mounted on the stable walls, and Alva had no idea how his coachmen got them down.

"Judging from the work I've been doing on the Fifth Avenue house," she continued, "I can tell you that it's going to be an extremely time-consuming project. And tedious. I've spent hours selecting lumber, stone, marble for the fireplaces, even things like the doorknobs and the thickness of the windowpane glass . . ." She purposely mentioned the most mundane items she could think of.

Billy gave one of the charmaine wheels a spin with his hand. Alva wasn't even sure he was listening to her. She followed as he moved on to the horse stalls, of which he had sixteen. A red bay's head appeared through one of the windows.

She was focusing now on the aesthetics. "The interior, as you know, has to be done just right. Why, I'm sure you can picture the great hall, the staircases, the upholstery on the seats, even the curtain, right down to the embroidery." She smiled, knowing he hadn't stopped to think about any of that. "All the men are so busy, I don't know that any of them have the experience or the time to see this construction through."

Billy looked at her like he was already getting a headache from it all. She waited for him to say something. When he didn't, she continued. "As you know, I've been working with Richard Hunt on the Fifth Avenue house. I could speak to him and—"

"No need," Billy said, stroking the horse's muzzle. "We've already awarded the new opera house to Josiah Cady."

"Oh." She tried not to let her disappointment show. She skirted around to the other side, hoping to get Billy's full attention. They were already moving ahead, making decisions without her, and that couldn't be. It was time to be direct. "I have a vision for this new opera house. I can see exactly how it should be designed. I know how to communicate with the architect, the workers, the contractors and the masons."

"I'm sure you do, Alva. I'm sure you do." He patted the horse's neck.

"Other women might like to have their hands covered in jewels but, I tell you, I'd rather have mine in mortar."

Billy laughed. "All right. I get it, I get it."

"I just know I could—"

"Alva, relax. I said okay. You can do it. You take charge." He smiled. "Go on, jump in with both feet."

Alva thanked him, but she would not celebrate her victory until after she'd left the stables and was sure Billy was out of earshot. Then she let out a cheer that sent a flock of birds, perched on the fence, soaring into the sky.

CHAPTER TWENTY-TWO

Caroline

NEW YORK, 1881

CAROLINE STOOD STILL WHILE her maid tended to the buttons on yet another black gown. Her mother had passed away six weeks before, in her sleep, on her own terms, when she was good and ready. She was eighty-nine years old.

At first Caroline felt none of the things she thought she should or would. No excruciating sorrow or paralyzing grief. She had managed to push all emotion aside and had thrown herself into planning the wake, the funeral, settling her mother's estate, readying her own house for the two-year mourning period. She'd been icy cold about it, all business. Though she was the youngest, Caroline took charge of everything, believing that her two sisters had been through far too many family burials.

All of her mother's servants had attended the funeral. They had lined up, reverent, heads bent, some crying over the loss of the woman they'd cared for nearly all their lives. Smithy had to have been close to ninety himself. And Abigail and Sissy weren't much younger. The others were newer hires that Caroline didn't know, even by name. But as for Smithy, Abigail and Sissy—what would happen to them? Did they have family that would take them in? Surely they were too old to stay in service. No one would hire them. These were the things Caroline had decided to worry about as they laid her mother to rest.

She hadn't shed a single tear until one week after the funeral when Caroline had found herself with nothing to do, nothing to organize or fix. It was three o'clock in the morning. Though her eyes burned, her mind wouldn't quiet. No matter how much she willed it, sleep would not come. She surrendered, got up and inched her way downstairs. As she approached the sitting room, she saw a wedge of light beneath the door. When she stepped inside, Hade sprang from his seat and dropped a deck of cards, the jack of hearts landing faceup on the carpet.

"Madam, forgive me." He was in his bathrobe and slippers, as was she. And without her wig. All she could think was that he was staring at her thinning hair. But perhaps he was too embarrassed for himself to worry about her appearance.

She was about to turn away, when he said, "I was just playing a little solitaire and having some warm milk. It helps settle the mind." He had already gathered up the fallen cards. "May I prepare a cup for you?"

She thought for a moment. "Actually, yes," she said, wondering what had been keeping him awake at this hour. Naturally he must have had worries of his own—maybe something with his daughters, a friend in need? She had no idea what thoughts drifted through his mind when he wasn't focused on her. Realizing she knew more about her mother's servants than her own got her thinking about Smithy, Abigail and Sissy. Smithy could sew buttons faster and better than any tailor she knew. Once he fixed a button it was there for life. Abigail made the best muffins, fluffy and moist. Sissy was a stickler for cleanliness.

"Hade," she said on a whim, thinking aloud, "I'd like to bring on some of my mother's servants."

He thought for a moment. "But we're completely staffed at the moment, madam."

"I realize that. But surely we can make room for three more."

"If you wish."

She knew it was impractical, but it was what her mother would have wanted. "I do wish to do that. And as soon as possible."

"Very well."

After he left to prepare the milk, Caroline reached for the deck of cards and shuffled them, trying to remember the last time she'd played solitaire, or any card game, for that matter.

When Hade returned with a tray of biscuits and a pot of steamed milk, he was back in his uniform, hair combed. For all she knew he might have even shaved.

"Will there be anything else?" he asked as he poured her a cup and set it down before her.

"Do you play cooncan?" she asked.

"I beg your pardon?"

"Cooncan? Do you know how to play?"

He cleared his throat. "Uh, yes. As a matter of fact . . ."

She held out the deck to him. "Neither one of us can sleep. We might as well play a hand or two."

"Very well, madam." He stiffly sat down and after sorting out the unneeded eight, nine and ten cards, he shuffled the deck and dealt the first hand.

They sat in silence but Caroline didn't mind whatever awkwardness prevailed. She was grateful to be absorbed in organizing her hand, melding her cards into sets and sequences. She drew a seven of hearts, which she'd melded with her seven of spades and seven of clubs, allowing her to place down the first set.

"Your turn," she said, discarding a three of diamonds.

"Thank you, madam." He nodded and practically bowed. "I'm afraid I haven't any use for that," he said in his ever-deep voice, picking the top card off the deck, enabling him to place down a sequence and a set before discarding the six of clubs.

The first hand ended in a tie, and after Hade won the second hand, he started to rise from his chair. "I'm afraid I've kept you later than expected. I shall let you retire—"

"Two out of three," she said with an arched eyebrow.

He sat back down. "I believe it's my deal."

He cracked a minor smile.

At some point during the third hand—she wasn't sure when the switch happened—Hade relaxed, dropped all the formalities and stopped thinking of her as his employer and more as his competitor. He would lay down a card with great zeal. "Ha-ha!" or "Aaah!" She in kind played her hand with equal passion: "Take that!" Or if a turn went the wrong way: "You devil, you!" By then she was so absorbed in the game that she'd all but forgotten she was sitting there in her dressing gown and slippers.

When she discarded the five of diamonds, he snapped up the card with a resounding "Yes! Precisely what I needed." He laid out one melded set after another, finishing it off with a winning sequence that made him full-on smile. "One more hand," he said, sliding the cards to her for shuffling.

"This is for all the money," she said.

"All the money!" Hade roared with laughter. "I'm afraid you have much more to lose than do I." He twitched his mustache and laughed some more. It was the first time she'd ever heard him laugh. It struck her again how very little she knew about this man and how one-sided their relationship was.

They continued playing cards until all the biscuits were gone and the pot of steamed milk was empty. When the grandfather clock struck six, they both looked at each other, somewhat astonished.

"My goodness," she said. The sun was on the verge of rising.

"Forgive me," he said, a slight blush coming up on his cheeks. "I'm afraid I lost complete track of time." He was on his feet, clearing the empty biscuit dishes and napkins, the cups and saucers. Whatever parts of Hade had slipped out during their card game were now buttoned up and put back into place as he bowed and lifted the serving tray, carrying it off to the kitchen.

It wasn't until after he left the room, presumably to get the house ready for the day, that Caroline felt something cold and terrifying zeroing in on her, something she knew she wasn't going to be able to escape. There, in the quiet of the hour with dawn breaking through the parting of the curtains, her mother's death pummeled her. Caroline broke down in gasping sobs that came on like a thundercloud—violent and short-lived.

After she'd finished weeping, Caroline felt she had shed more than just tears. Something had cracked open inside. There was an unexpected lightness that came over her as if a great burden had been lifted. Caroline had always known she could never take the place of her mother's lost daughters and sons, and yet that was what she'd tried to do her entire life. There hadn't been a single decision, or a move made, without considering what her mother would think. How many sacrifices had Caroline made, how many compromises for her mother's sake? She had loved her mother and would miss her, but now that she was gone, Caroline was free.

Immediately that thought flooded her with guilt. Caroline had never felt more conflicted, moving through her days with her emotions seesawing. It took another few weeks of this back-and-forth before she found that the lightness had returned. Returned for good, she thought.

Suddenly she was presented with a world of possibilities. Now, six weeks later, she stood in her dressing room, before her closets filled with gowns and tea dresses in dark blues, grays, browns and black velvet. She had no bright colors—not a single one—and it dawned on her that as a child, she'd only ever seen her mother in black for mourning. Caroline's tastes in dark colors had been her attempt at a show of unity.

In the past Caroline had subscribed to the notion that a true lady didn't call attention to herself with flashy fashions. That had been her mother's belief and thereby Caroline's as well. But nowadays, even the most dignified society ladies favored more beading and ornamentation, and as her daughters often told her, "Styles change, Mother."

She decided they were right. She would change, but within limits. She wasn't about to have opals and pearls sewn into her gowns like Mamie Fish and Alva Vanderbilt, but Caroline decided, after she was out of mourning, on her next trip to Paris, she would consult with Charles Worth for her wardrobe. Her one weakness, however, was diamonds. He could include as many diamonds in her gowns as he saw fit, which would complement her ample collection of diamond stomachers, tiaras, necklaces, bracelets and rings—she did adore her diamond rings.

Even before her mother died, when she couldn't decide which ring to wear, she'd wear several—sometimes three or four at a time. And why not? No one—other than her mother—would have dared to say she couldn't, and soon enough others were following her lead. Mrs. August Belmont wore rings on every finger over her gloves; so did Mrs. Bradley Martin. Now she would wear rings and bright colors and spangled gowns. When she was out of mourning, she would emerge as a new woman.

CHAPTER TWENTY-THREE

Caroline

CAROLINE FELT A BURST of energy and excitement she rarely showed outwardly as she raced up the long staircase. Two months after her mother's passing, Emily had gone into labor. It was rebirth, renewal, a declaration that life goes on. Caroline couldn't get to Emily's room fast enough.

Helen was already in with her sister, sitting at her bedside. Emily's dark hair had been braided in two neat plaits, hanging down past her shoulders, just as she'd worn them when she was a little girl. Emily's maid came in, moving stealthily about the bedroom so as not to disturb them. She had drawn the drapes and turned down the lamps before stoking the fire, sparking a surge of orange embers.

"Shouldn't be too much longer now, Mrs. Astor," the midwife reported, standing off to the side, folding towels and linens. She was a stout redheaded woman who had delivered all of Caroline's grandchildren. She suddenly remembered how much the midwife liked to chatter while waiting for the deliveries. Perhaps she thought it was a welcome distraction.

". . . Now I've already bathed her and helped her empty her bowels. Voided her bladder, too . . . ," the midwife said, mixing up the bichloride solution. Caroline observed the bottle of Lysol on the bureau, next to a tub of lard and the straight razor she'd used. "I've already got the bed ready . . . ," she said, pulling back the covers to show where she'd placed a rubber mat, fastened to the mattress with safety pins. "The bedsheets were heated in the oven. It's the best way to sterilize them," she said. The midwife took two sheets and tied them to the bedposts closest to the headboard. "Gives her something to tug on when the contractions get too strong."

Emily reached for Caroline's hand, gripping tight as more perspiration sprang up on her face, her chest heaving as she groaned.

"Shush now. Calm yourself. You must be—" She was going to say *strong* but stopped herself. That was something her mother would have said.

Since her mother's passing, Caroline had come to reevaluate so many things, including Emily's marriage. Anyone could see that she and James were in love, raising a fine family. If Caroline had been wrong about James Van Alen, maybe she'd been wrong about other things, too. Was it the end of the world if Emily had a Vanderbilt at her dinner table, if Charlotte marched in the streets and if Carrie wanted to paint bowls of fruit and anything else that would sit still long enough? What harm would it do to loosen up her hold on them, make room for—

Emily let out a scream, the veins in her neck pulsing.

"Use these," instructed the midwife, placing the sheets she'd strung through the bedposts into Emily's hands. "That's what they're there for."

It took another three and a half hours before Emily delivered a healthy baby girl. Helen went downstairs to tell the others the good news while the midwife tended to the baby. Caroline wasn't sure if Emily was sleeping or just resting, too tired to speak or open her eyes. Her skin was so pale, almost translucent blue.

"Nothing more you can do for her now," said the midwife, removing the blood-soaked bedsheets, balling them up in her hands. "She needs to get her strength back is all. And you—if you don't mind my saying—you could use some rest yourself, Mrs. Astor."

She hated to leave Emily, but the midwife was right. Caroline was exhausted and excused herself. As she stepped out in the hallway, she took a moment to savor the quiet and realized with an overflow of gratitude that she was now the grandmother of six. And Charlotte was due again in the spring. Caroline closed her eyes for a moment; they were dry and burning. She had a stiff neck and a dull headache, too. It had been daylight when she arrived and now the lamps were turned up, flickering shadows across the floorboards. From the hallway window she could see that it was dark outside. She had no idea what the hour was until the grandfather clock at the foot of the stairs chimed ten times. As she made her way closer to the staircase, she heard the others talking down in the sitting room, their voices jovial, light, filled with celebration.

"Mrs. Astor?" The maid stood just outside Emily's room.

Caroline turned around and froze. Something in the maid's eyes, in her pallor, sent a jolt through Caroline. She suddenly realized something was missing. The crying—it was quiet. The baby wasn't crying. *The baby. There's something wrong with the baby.* Her heart was pounding. She didn't remember how she got from the end of the hallway to the bedroom, but as Caroline reached the door, she heard the infant let out a wailing shriek. *Oh, thank God.* The baby was fine. Everything was fine.

But when Caroline opened Emily's door and stepped inside, a fresh panic arose. The baby was still crying and yet the room seemed quiet. Too quiet. There was a thickness in the air, a heaviness she couldn't explain, but it was like moving through quicksand. The midwife was holding the baby. The maid twisted her fingers and lowered her head but not before Caroline saw that her face was damp with tears. That was when the darkness rolled in and the two women faded to the background. Before the midwife said the words, even before Caroline had rushed to her daughter's side, she knew. Her baby, her Emily, was gone.

No matter how her husband or daughters tried to coax her, Caroline refused to leave Emily's body. For three days she sat in the parlor with the drapes drawn shut. She had no idea whether it was day or night because every clock throughout the house had been stopped at nine fifty-nine, the exact moment of Emily's death—just as her mother had done after each one of her children's deaths. Before Emily was laid to rest, Caroline had taken a snippet of Emily's hair and tucked it inside a locket that she would wear for the next two years of mourning.

Caroline had insisted on a private funeral. A guest list, more exclusive than the one for her annual ball, was drawn up and notices were hand delivered. "I won't have my daughter's funeral turned into a spectacle. This is not going to be a social event where strangers can come and gawk."

During the service William had sat beside Caroline, a somber expression on his face, eyes straight ahead. She was sure that to some he appeared cold and unfeeling. Caroline might have thought that, too, had he not reached over and skimmed the top of her hand, letting his fingers rest atop hers for just a second or two before that same hand, suddenly clenched, was pressed to his mouth. It was as if he'd tried to gather all his grief inside his fist, too afraid to let it out. He was an Astor man. Astor men didn't cry, didn't show emotion, so he dealt with his grief the only way he knew how, and after the burial, he boarded his yacht hoping the sea and enough whiskey would drown his sorrows.

Back at her own home, the dark door badges, indicating to all that the family was in mourning, had already been hanging for Caroline's mother. Now it was impossible to believe they were hanging for her daughter as well. In the days that followed, Caroline saw what Emily's death did to her sisters. Emily had died in childbirth, and Charlotte was six months pregnant and terrified. Helen, having lost her sister and best friend, told Caroline she didn't want to have more children.

"I've already discussed it with Rosy," she said.

"Oh, darling, but just because . . ." Caroline's words trailed off. She knew what Helen was thinking. There had always been an invisible tether between the two sisters; what happened to one seemed to affect the other. When Emily got a cold, Helen always came down with it, too. When one had a bad dream, the other woke down the hall with a start.

"If this happened to Emily, it *will* happen to me, too. Rosy and I have been blessed with Tadd and little Helen. We can't risk having any more children."

Even Carrie had come to Caroline, tiptoeing into her room barefoot one night, unable to sleep, asking *how* it had happened, *why* it had happened—all the questions Caroline had no answers for. So she took Carrie in her arms and held her close, already bargaining with God to spare this one, to spare Helen, Charlotte and Jack, too.

Having covered every mirror in her house, out of respect for the dead, Caroline dressed blindly each day in her heavy black gowns. She spent her time mostly by herself in the library with the curtains closed, the lights dimmed, the logs ablaze in the fireplace. It may have seemed to others that she just sat and stared for hours on end, but what they didn't realize was that Caroline was hard at work. She was looking and waiting for a sign; the flickering of a lamp, an unexplained draft, the sensation of touch that would send a shiver down her spine. She was waiting to hear from Emily, needing some indication that her daughter was still connected to her, that they could still communicate, that her beautiful girl was at peace.

Caroline heard the loud gong of the front door bell. A log gave off a sharp crackle, shooting sparks past the bronze andirons onto the marble floor, where they dulled and died. She heard footsteps in the hallway and realized she'd been crying. Caroline quickly composed herself, clutching her silk handkerchief between her fingers after she'd dabbed her eyes. The footsteps drew closer, so heavy she thought it was William. *Is he back?* Her heart lifted as the footsteps stopped. The doorknob turned.

"Madam?" Hade entered the room, setting a tray on the table before her. "I brought you some chocolate biscuits and tea."

She watched him tending to the fire, realizing that aside from her children, he was the only other person she talked to on a daily basis. Being in mourning she had excused her social secretary, who was in Europe for six months. Her lady's maid and the rest of her staff—even Smithy, Abigail and Sissy—tiptoed about, not wanting to disturb her. She felt so isolated, and though she had wanted to strictly observe the traditional practices, Caroline was beginning to question the wisdom of being in full mourning. Being alone for so long with one's thoughts spelled trouble.

"If ever the grieving should be kept busy, too busy to think, it's during our time of mourning," she said, unaware at first that she was speaking out loud. "Without balls and dinner parties to plan, the opera and ballet to attend, one is left with little to do but think. Thinking"—she shook her head—"thinking can be a dangerous thing."

"Indeed," Hade said, pouring her tea. "Best to always keep one's mind occupied as best one can." He set her teacup on a saucer and handed it to her.

After he left, Caroline reached up and touched the locket about her neck that contained Emily's hair. She squeezed it, as if it had magical powers, and kept waiting for her world to turn right again. For things to go back as they once were. Emily's absence felt as if it were something temporary. Something still not quite real. Any minute now she expected her to come through the door. *How could it be that she is gone forever?*

That Hade also suffered from insomnia was, for Caroline, a blessing, and in those days of mourning, it wasn't unusual for the two of them to sit down in the middle of the night and pass the time with a few hands of cooncan. Other times they'd sit in the library, where he would read aloud to her, both their slippered feet sharing the tapestry-covered ottoman between their wingback chairs.

Somewhere along the line she had begun calling him by his first name, Thomas, rather than Hade, and he in turn now called her Mrs. Astor rather than madam. She thought Thomas had a marvelous reading voice, rich and deeply resonant. They discovered a mutual love of Russian novels, and after completing *War and Peace* they had moved on to *Crime and Punishment*.

One night, even though she was tired and probably could have drifted off, she fought sleep, and at midnight, she went to her dressing table for her wig before heading downstairs. She went into the library and waited. And waited. It had never occurred to her that Thomas wouldn't be there. She felt foolish for so desperately wanting her time with him, but his company had been the only bright spot while she was in mourning.

In mourning. These past few months had opened her eyes. Now she understood how her mother must have felt, over and over again. Losing a child—it wasn't natural, it wasn't right. For the first time she understood why her mother was the way she was. She had needed all the rituals, the traditions and routines to hold her together. Caroline understood that now, because when Emily died, she had taken Caroline's lightness with her. All that newfound joy and freedom were gone, along with looking to the future. She wasn't ready for change. She didn't want it, couldn't handle it. Now what Caroline needed was stability. She needed things to stay exactly as they were. She was struggling every day, clinging to the tried and true, things she could depend on.

That night, while waiting for Thomas, Caroline crawled back inside her mother's world and pulled the lid shut.

CHAPTER TWENTY-FOUR

Alva

NEW YORK, 1882

WHEN EMILY DIED, ALVA took it hard. It wasn't that she and Emily were so terribly close, nothing like Alva and Duchy or Alva and Jeremiah, but still a friend. And so young. And a mother, a wife, a sister and a daughter. With everyone else Alva had lost, from her mother to the Commodore, there'd been time to prepare, to enter the sickrooms, sit by their bedsides, hold their hands and say her goodbyes. Emily had gone so quickly, so unexpectedly. The shock was what she couldn't get past. It made her realize how precious and unpredictable life was, that nothing could be taken for granted, and yet she still did all the time.

She had wanted to attend the funeral, but of course, she and Willie weren't invited. Instead, they'd paid a condolence call to James where the three of them sat around the fireplace, reminiscing about the dinners they'd all shared, about the birthday parties for the children, their christenings, how every year, the day after Christmas, they'd all get together and exchange gifts and drink mulled wine, laughing over one thing or another. Emily's laugh—once you got her going she couldn't stop, and that had always made Alva laugh all the harder. Oh, how she'd miss that about Emily. James had choked up now and again, having to remove his monocle in order to wipe his eyes. When the nurse brought the baby out and placed her in James's arms, Alva had nearly burst into tears herself.

The next day, Alva mustered up the courage to drop off her calling card for Mrs. Astor with the left-hand corner turned down in a show of sympathy. She'd wanted nothing in exchange, only merely to pay her respects, and for once Alva didn't take it personally when Mrs. Astor hadn't responded or acknowledged the gesture.

Time moved on and while Mrs. Astor remained in mourning, Alva, like so many up-and-coming hostesses, made the most of the Grande Dame's absence from the social scene. Alva was busy. She paid social calls, attended teas and luncheons and made exorbitant donations to the other matrons' charities, but mostly, she went back and forth between two construction sites. Of the two projects, she had far less influence over the new opera house.

From the start, Alva thought Mr. Cady was wrong for the job, and she'd been right. The board members, especially her father-in-law, only pacified her when she showed up at their meetings, voicing concerns over the design for the facade. They'd nodded when she said it had no style and the stone was all wrong, but didn't do a thing to remedy it. She realized there was nothing she could do about the exterior now, but she wasn't about to keep quiet on the interior.

Bypassing the men, she met directly with the architect at Broadway and Thirty-Ninth Street. The sound of hammering was coming from all directions as she walked alongside Mr. Cady, passing the sawhorses, ladders standing two stories high, the slabs of marble and massive steel support beams.

She reached into her satchel and retrieved a sketch she'd drawn the night before. "Now this is what I had in mind for the ceiling." She handed him the piece of paper. "As you can see, I've indicated where the fresco begins, and see how it runs right to the edges here?"

He squinted, studying the paper. "I'll be sure and ask Mr. Vanderbilt what he thinks."

"Mr. Vanderbilt trusts my opinion." Alva smiled.

"I'd still feel better dealing with Mr. Vanderbilt on all this."

"I'm certain you would, but I can assure you that won't be necessary."

When she walked to the edges of the shells that would become the boxes, she frowned. She had envisioned something much more elaborate. "Mr. Cady, do you and Mrs. Cady enjoy attending the opera?"

"Ah, yes," he said, somewhat perplexed by the question. "Mrs. Cady especially does."

"And I'll just bet Mrs. Cady enjoys watching the audience as much as the performers."

"I beg your pardon?"

"Well, as you know, and as I'm sure Mrs. Cady will attest, part of the magic of attending the opera is seeing who else is there. We want to see the dresses, the jewels. Everything! The boxes need to extend out far enough so that our most important guests will be on display as much as the performers."

"You said, *extend* the boxes farther out?"

She giggled demurely. "Just listen to me telling *you* how to build a theater box when I'm sure you're already well aware of the problem."

"But, Mrs. Vanderbilt, according to the blueprints—"

"Isn't it wonderful that blueprints can be altered? Now let's talk about the stage. Did you see my note about the distance between the stage and orchestra pit?"

"I did but—"

"It's going to look divine, Mr. Cady. Everyone's going to be singing your praises, saying what a marvelous job you've done." She took a step toward him, and when she brushed a bit of plaster from his lapel, he jumped back as if she'd pinched his bottom.

A flustered Mr. Cady excused himself after that, and Alva continued on alone. She walked through the stairwells and hallways, the taste of plaster and marble dust in her mouth. She didn't care. She felt more at ease in the midst of a construction site than she did at one of those society luncheons. At least she could shape and alter the appearance of the opera house. That was easy. Transforming society and dealing with the opera house's founding members was another matter.

By the time November arrived, the stockholders gathered for a meeting to elect their board of directors. They met that night at Sherry's, a new restaurant that had just opened on Thirty-Eighth Street and Sixth Avenue. They had a private room, and Alva, her sister-in-law Alice, Lucy Clews, Cettie Rockefeller and Helen Gould were all crowded into the rear, sitting on hardback chairs while the men sat at the table with their brandy snifters.

"If there's no other pressing business," Billy said, his fingers laced together, "shall we begin the nominations for our board of directors?"

One by one various gentlemen stood and put forth the names of those they felt best suited for the role. Cornelius nominated John Rockefeller, Jay Gould nominated Willie, someone else suggested Henry Clews, and on and on it went. When Billy said, "All those in favor, raise your hand," Alva's hand shot up, making the room erupt in a burst of gasps and nervous laughter.

"Alva, please," whispered Alice. "Put your hand down. You don't get a vote. This is just for the men."

Alva's hand dropped to her lap as if it were made of lead. They probably thought she was embarrassed, but their snickering and laughter only infuriated her. She knew no one would have nominated her for a position because she was a woman. She hadn't even expected that, but given her involvement with every phase of the building, given that the whole idea of a new opera house had been hers to begin with, she thought she'd at least be given a vote. She looked at the other wives, their hands primly resting in their laps, docile and maddeningly content.

———

Alva brought Jennie and Julia with her one afternoon to show off the
progress on the new house. Armide was back in Mobile. Her sisters
stayed a good three feet behind Alva as she walked them past several
drays lined up, piled high with wood, marble and steel. The smell of
lumber and manure wafted through the air. There must have been
fifty carpenters and twenty-five masons balancing high up on ladders, sculpting the Indiana limestone in order to achieve the French
château effect she wanted. She had never seen so many different
chisels and mallets. Several workers stopped what they were doing
just long enough to say good day and tip their caps.

"Now that rooftop will be trimmed in copper, all the way around,"
she said to her sisters. "And wait till you see the inside."

"What in the world is she going to do with a house this size?"
Julia asked Jennie, loud enough for Alva to hear.

"Easy now." Jennie rested her hand on Julia's shoulder.

"Well, I'm sorry, but I don't see what's wrong with the house she's
got. Still nicer than any place she's ever lived before."

Alva turned and glared at her. "I'm standing right here, Julia. If
you have something to say, you might as well say it to my face."

"All right then." Julia marched up to her and planted her knuckles
to her hips. "I think you're getting a little too big for your britches. All
your husband's money is going straight to your head. Sometimes I
look at you, Alva, and I don't know who you are anymore."

"Come on now, you two." Jennie stepped in between them, her
arms stretched out to keep them apart.

"And I'll tell you something else," Julia said, not backing down,
which was rare because Julia, the youngest, had almost always cow-
ered before Alva. "All that money—it's not going to make you happy."

"This is exactly the kind of house Mama would have wanted me
to have," Alva fired back.

"If Mama were here, she'd be downright disgusted by your greed."

"You're just being ugly now," Alva snapped. "You're plain jealous is all."

"Jealous." Julia laughed. "Jealous of what? You and your snobbish friends? You and this ridiculous house? Just what exactly am I jealous of? You're still not on Mrs. Astor's guest list. You're still on the outside looking in."

"I suppose you think that, too?" Alva said to Jennie.

"Now don't go putting words in my mouth, Alva. I think it's lovely. If this is the kind of house you want, why then I think it's just fine."

"Well, now I don't even feel like showing you the inside."

"That's fine with me," said Julia, folding her arms. "I've seen more than enough already."

"Oh, come on now, you two." Jennie was still standing between them. "Let's just go see the inside and get it over with."

Alva was still stinging from Julia's remarks. If her own sister—who couldn't have cared less about society—knew that Alva was still outside the circle, then everyone knew. She wasn't fooling anyone.

CHAPTER TWENTY-FIVE

Alva

ON A COLD DECEMBER morning, Alva and Willie were finishing up breakfast when Oliver Belmont sauntered in. The two men had an appointment to look at a new Friesian horse that Willie was interested in purchasing. Willie had recently become friends with Oliver, though for the life of her, Alva couldn't understand why. Not only was Oliver a Jew, a rarity in their circles, but his father, August Belmont, was among those who'd blocked them from joining the Academy of Music.

Oliver was only twenty-four, nearly ten years younger than Willie, five years younger than Alva. She supposed he would be handsome once he matured, but for now, he had a round baby face with hardly a hint of whiskers. Yet, despite standing barely five feet tall, he'd managed to woo one socialite after another, including the stunningly beautiful Sara Swan Whiting. Rumor had it they were engaged. Alva had to admit that Oliver had a certain *something*, and she wasn't sure if she found him annoying or intriguing. Either way, Sara must have seen that *something* in him, too. Alva would have assumed that Sara was enough to make any man settle down, but Oliver behaved as if he were still in the Naval Academy, always running around and carrying on until the wee hours of the morning. She worried that Oliver was a bad influence on her husband, who seemed to take on a different persona in Oliver's presence. When Willie was out with Oliver, he tended to return home with a large gambling loss, smelling of liquor and perfume.

"Good morning. Good morning," said Oliver, helping himself to a sip of Willie's coffee. "Overslept," he said by way of explanation as he reached for a slice of toast, spreading a thick layer of butter and jam on top. "Had to leave the house without breakfast today." He raised his toast as if cheering with a glass of wine.

Alva smiled to be polite.

"Well," said Willie, "shall we be going?" He stood up and squared his bowler on his head.

"Have I mentioned lately that I've always looked up to you?" said Oliver, popping a crust of toast in his mouth. "But then again," he laughed, "when you're my height, you look up to everyone." He laughed some more as they bid Alva adieu.

His self-deprecating sense of humor—one more thing she didn't like about Oliver Belmont.

After they left, Alva went back to sipping coffee, and while she sorted through the mail, she came across an envelope addressed to her in Duchy's familiar handwriting. It had been months since she'd heard from her friend, and Alva had lost count of the number of letters she'd sent that had gone unanswered. Slicing the envelope open, she unfolded the stationery and began to read.

After the obligatory apologies for not writing sooner, she congratulated Alva on getting the new opera house off the ground:

> From what you told me, it sounds like you've got those
> men eating out of the palm of your hand. Has your father-in-
> law even realized yet that you moved him around like a chess
> piece? You always have been clever as a fox. First Billy
> Vanderbilt, next, I imagine, is Mrs. Astor . . .

If only, thought Alva. She still hadn't a clue as to how to win that woman over. She continued reading and when she reached the postscript—*Coming for a visit the second week in March*—Alva felt a rush of excitement. And it wasn't only about seeing her friend. No, it was bigger. And just like that, a whole new idea—fully formed and waiting for her—had been sparked. She could feel herself tingling because of it.

The viscountess was coming to town! The viscountess was coming to see *her*! Everyone—Puss, Tessie, Ophelia, Penelope, Lydia—everyone would want to see her. Those who didn't know her would surely want to meet her.

The timing couldn't have been more perfect. Alva's new home would be completed by then, and if ever there was cause for celebration, this was it. Who wouldn't want to attend a ball with the Viscountess Mandeville? Alva had tried so many other avenues to get herself and the Vanderbilts recognized by society, and nothing had worked. But now she had a different approach. Alva had found her angle. The wheels were already turning. Her friend was right—she *was* clever as a fox. If she'd manipulated Billy, she could do the same with Mrs. Astor.

With Duchy's visit and the new house, Alva finally had a way to get society's attention and make them come to her.

CHAPTER TWENTY-SIX

Society

NEW YORK, 1883

AS SOON AS ALVA tells us she's throwing a masquerade ball in the spring that will make Mrs. Astor's look like a barn dance in comparison, we begin to ponder our costumes. We meet with dressmakers and wigmakers, jewelry designers and prop masters. We leaf through history books, looking for figures from the past that we think might inspire the most impressive costumes.

Tessie wants to go as Queen Elizabeth I but so do Mamie and Lady Paget. Why so many wish to be illegitimate *and* a virgin is a mystery to the rest of us. Penelope and her husband are going as George and Martha Washington; Lydia and her husband will go as incroyables and merveilleuses appearing barefoot with rings on their toes and Greek tunics. Penelope has laid claim to Joan of Arc, which means Ophelia will have to rethink her costume.

We hear this is going to be the biggest ball ever held in a private home and that the guest of honor is going to be Viscountess Mandeville, whom we remember as plain old Consuelo Yznaga. Those of us with daughters know this is a golden opportunity for luring husbands.

"Well, I just better be invited," says Mamie.

"Then you might try *not* insulting Alva for once," says Tessie.

"Me? What about you?" Mamie snaps back.

Their exchange makes us all take a moment to reflect on our previous encounters with Alva. For some, petty jealousies have gotten in the way of common courtesies. A few of us have been less than gracious. Others, like Mamie, have outright snubbed her. But it's clear to all that Alva is a formidable woman on the rise in society and that we'd best get on the right side of her.

Thoughts of Alva's masquerade party consume us for days on end until on one cold, wintry morning, the first week in January, we pick up our newspapers and see the headline: CREPE BADGES REMOVED FROM ASTOR HOME. We go on to read:

THE MOURNING PERIOD HAS OFFICIALLY ENDED AND PLANS ARE UNDERWAY FOR MRS. WILLIAM B. ASTOR'S ANNUAL BALL. SOURCES SAY INVITATIONS TO THE COVETED 400 GUESTS WERE HAND DELIVERED THIS MORNING . . .

CHAPTER TWENTY-SEVEN

Alva

ALVA STARED AT THE headline for a second time and read the article, top to bottom. Mrs. Astor was back. Sitting at her table, Alva could feel her entire body tensing up, her jaw clenched, pulse racing.

She set the newspaper aside and dared herself to shuffle through the mail that her butler had delivered earlier that morning. She went envelope by envelope, foolishly hoping that Mrs. Astor's invitation would be among them. But of course it wasn't.

Alva hurried through her morning toilette and called for her carriage. It was snowing but not terribly cold; mostly the flakes turned to slush upon landing. She glanced out the window at the paperboys on the corner, standing next to stacks of wet newspapers.

When they finally reached the Glenham Hotel, she had her driver pull over. Thankfully Jeremiah was home. Letting her into his room, filled with stale air and dust-covered surfaces, he looked rather glamorous in a satin floor-length smoking jacket she'd never seen before.

"Where did this come from?" she asked skeptically, tossing her hat and gloves onto the bed. "I thought you weren't gambling anymore."

"Oh, don't be such a worrier. I'm on a winning streak."

"I've heard that before." She turned toward him. He smelled faintly of whiskey despite it being the middle of the day.

"I'm up. *Significantly*," he said with a great hand flourish.

"Don't forget, you're on limited funds now."

"I was just about to roll a cigarette. Why don't you have one with me?" As he retrieved the tobacco from a dented-up blue tin resting on the chest of drawers, Jeremiah started going on about the poker game he'd sat in on the night before. ". . . So then I had a flush, and right after that, unbelievable, the dealer—you're not going to believe this—I end up with a full house. You should have seen me. I was—" He stopped and looked at her. "Are you even listening to me?"

"I'm sorry." She shook her head. "I'm in a foul mood."

"Another fight with Willie?"

"No, I did not have *another* fight with Willie." Though they had been arguing more than usual lately. Ever since he started running around with Oliver Belmont, who had recently divorced Sara Swan Whiting after barely being married a year. They said he abandoned her in Paris and took up with a dancer or singer—she couldn't remember which. "It's not Willie," she said, watching Jeremiah meticulously sprinkle the tobacco inside the paper. "It's *that* woman."

"Oh dear. I assume we're talking about Mrs. Astor?" He laughed as he released another pinch of tobacco.

"I'm just furious. I can't believe she didn't invite me to her ball. Again."

"How can you be so sure you're not invited?"

"The invitations already went out—this morning. Hand delivered."

"Ouch!" He made a face.

She didn't appreciate his attempt to lighten her mood, and he knew it.

"Well," he said, offering her the cigarette, "I think you've worked your way into the fringes of society as best you can, but let's face it"—he struck the match—"society will always look down on you as new money." He paused while Alva leaned into the flame. "Now remember, don't inhale."

But she did anyway and coughed out a cloud of smoke.

"Here," he said, handing her a glass of whiskey.

"What are you trying to do, kill me?" She pushed the glass away, still choking, her eyes tearing up.

"A good belt of this stuff"—he downed the whiskey—"never killed anyone."

Alva recovered, letting out a few more coughs, and dabbed her eyes. "That woman has kept me out of the Academy of Music and—"

"And the Patriarch Balls, too," he said, as if she needed reminding of that.

She was stewing while he prepared another cigarette for himself, lit it and leaned back in his chair, exhaling a plume of smoke toward the ceiling. "But what can you do about it?" he asked, crossing his long legs, letting his satin slipper dangle off his foot. "She's never going to let you into society, you know that."

"That's what you think. You have no idea how far people will go to get an invitation to this ball."

CHAPTER TWENTY-EIGHT

Caroline

LESS THAN TWELVE HOURS ago, Caroline's townhouse had been filled to capacity with some 400 guests, mingling, dancing, dining at her annual ball. The festivities had gone on late, the last to leave climbing into their carriages at dawn.

Caroline was still in bed, surprised when she glanced at the clock and saw that it was a quarter till two in the afternoon. She couldn't recall the last time she'd slept past noon. Caroline was always faithfully awake at half past eight, regardless of how late the balls went the night before. She was one of those people who prided themselves on needing only four hours of sleep a night, as if that were a sign of strength, endurance.

But on that bone-chilling January day, she was dragging, her body stiff, her head throbbing. *What is the point of getting dressed yet anyway?* Even from her bedroom she could hear her staff shuffling about, moving furniture back in place, sweeping the floors. Downstairs in the kitchen, she pictured the china and glassware being washed, dried and put away. She figured someone must have been taking down the garlands and packing up the floral arrangements that would go directly into the trash. *Pity.* But she hated wilting flowers. Limp petals made her sad, and she couldn't bear it that day.

In the past, she'd always felt a sense of accomplishment after her ball, but on that day, she felt let down. Waldorf and his wife had put in their appearance, as if they were doing her a favor. They were among the first to leave at three o'clock. Thankfully everyone had the good taste not to ask where William was. He rarely attended her balls anymore, and she wasn't sure if she was disappointed or relieved. She didn't need him causing any drunken scenes, and yet, she wondered where he'd been, who he'd been with and if he had managed to find his way home last night. She cleared the thoughts from her mind and wondered instead if Thomas was directing her staff to work as quietly as possible so as not to disturb her. He was always protective of her in that way. She wished William were more like that. How pathetic that her butler should be more concerned about her than her own husband.

She was focusing on William, but she knew that wasn't what was really bothering her. The ball had been a success, just the same as every ball she'd been throwing for the past ten years. But one thing was different this time and she couldn't deny it. Even as she'd sat at the top of the stairs beneath her six-foot portrait, receiving her guests, she was aware that her annual event had been eclipsed by Alva Vanderbilt's upcoming masquerade ball at the end of March.

Caroline had purposely left Alva off last night's guest list, but still that woman had managed to make her presence known. In fact, she was constantly intruding on Caroline's life these days. All night long she'd overheard people talking in rapt anticipation of Alva Vanderbilt's ball at Petit Chateau. *Petit Chateau*—Caroline scowled. No one *named* their city homes. It simply wasn't done.

The event was two months away, and already everyone was all aflutter over the guest of honor, Viscountess Mandeville. Caroline resented the encroachment and found everyone's preoccupation with the Vanderbilt ball most upsetting. The *New York Times* had already declared it THE SEASON'S MOST ANTICIPATED BALL. In the past, they'd said that about Caroline's ball. She decided she didn't care. She was still the head of society and she had no intention of attending Alva's masquerade ball.

Later that afternoon she sat at her dressing room table, her black pompadour wig, which she'd worn the night before, resting on its stand. Looking in the mirror, she observed how gray she'd gone and how much her hair had thinned. Her lady's maid hadn't mentioned it, but over time, Caroline had become aware of the pale, ever-widening spot on the crown of her head, the size of a coin. Though her hats and bonnets had camouflaged the situation at first, in the end, the only remedy was a wig. Or wigs, as it turned out, for now there was a separate closet that housed the various styles in varying shades of browns and blacks. The fragile condition of Caroline's hair and her need for wigs was something that she and her maid addressed without ever discussing outright.

With her fingertips, she worried her center part, growing wider all the time. When she couldn't look anymore, she reached for her wig, squaring it on her scalp just as Carrie appeared in the doorway. Through the looking glass Caroline could see that something was terribly wrong.

"Heavens, child"—she turned around, facing her—"what's wrong? Are you unwell?"

Carrie's shoulders were slack.

Caroline pushed away from her dressing table and went to her daughter's side, placing her hand on Carrie's forehead, feeling for fever. Her daughter had just returned from practicing her quadrille for the Vanderbilts' ball, of all things. Carrie and her friends were performing an homage to the king of Prussia, Frederick the Great. Caroline felt Carrie's forehead a second time. "You haven't got a fever."

"I'm not sick."

"What is it then?"

"All the girls were talking about the Vanderbilt ball at rehearsal."

"This is what you're so upset about? That silly ball?"

"Oh, Mother, why do you hate Mrs. Vanderbilt so?"

"I don't hate her," Caroline said, trying to sound indifferent. "I simply have no use for her."

"I don't think you understand. Alva Vanderbilt is shrewd. She's calculating. They're all saying she's out to take over society. To take it away from you. They're all saying how she has a new vision for society. Charlotte's been hearing talk of it, too. You can't afford to have her as an enemy anymore. You either need to join forces with her, or risk losing your position. And I'm sorry, but if you do lose your position, what happens to the rest of us? We're going to be has-beens."

"Oh pish-posh." Caroline waved off Carrie's concern. "That will never happen."

"But it's already starting. All my friends—they've all received their invitations to the Vanderbilt ball and I haven't."

"Your invitation just hasn't arrived, is all."

"No, you don't understand. The others received their invitations more than a week ago. It's obvious that I'm not going to be invited. How am I going to tell the others? We've been rehearsing our quadrille for weeks. You have to find a way to mend fences with Mrs. Vanderbilt."

Caroline felt a barb run down her spine. "There'll be other balls," she said without much conviction.

Carrie looked up, glassy-eyed. Caroline hated for her daughters to be weak and Carrie knew that. "As you said, there'll be other balls. I'll be fine." A tear slid down her cheek. "But what about you? What about your future?" And with that, she covered her face in her small, pale hands and wept so hard her shoulders shook.

A lump rose up in Caroline's throat. "Well, there's obviously been some mistake," she said.

Carrie hiccuped, breaking into another spasm of tears.

Caroline was seething. She felt manipulated. How dare Alva Vanderbilt punish Carrie like this? She would not tolerate this kind of societal warfare.

CHAPTER TWENTY-NINE

Caroline

THE NEXT DAY, CAROLINE called on Ward McAllister. No one under-stood the intricacies of society better than Ward, and he knew Car-rie, even loved her like a daughter. Caroline was certain that, together, they could figure out a solution. The two were huddled in his library, surrounded by heavy dark paneling and plush velvet drapes that let in a single slant of sunlight. Tea service on a silver tray was perched on a table between them. Caroline was demanding they call for all of society to boycott the Vanderbilt ball.

"On what grounds?" Ward looked at her skeptically. "Just because your daughter wasn't invited? Come now, Lina."

The look on his face made her realize how ridiculous she sounded. "But Carrie is brokenhearted. I have to do something. And now she's worried that Alva is going to take over society." Caroline laughed as if that were absurd.

"Well"—McAllister plucked a sugar cube with a pair of gold tongs—"it's no secret, that *is* part of her grand plan. She is very crafty. You need to watch her."

So it *was* true. Something shattered inside her, like glass break-ing just beneath her skin. She'd thought Carrie was exaggerating, being overly dramatic. Caroline tried to play it off as nothing, dismiss-ing the notion by rolling her eyes—*rolling one's eyes*! Such a pointless gesture, a weak display of disapproval that she had always detested, and yet here she'd gone and done it. "Well, from what I hear," she said, "this is going to be more of a circus than a ball anyway." Normally she was better at keeping her opinions to herself and immediately regretted having said anything. She sounded petty and defensive.

"It may be a circus, don't you know," said McAllister, stirring his tea, "but you can't escape the chatter about costumes and invitations and all." McAllister scooted forward in his chair as if their discussion was about to take a significant turn. "I've just come from the *New York Times*, and they told me that Alva Vanderbilt has invited them to a preview tour of Petit Chateau."

"Oh, that house is an embarrassment," said Caroline with a shudder, failing once again to rein herself in. She couldn't help it—Alva had become a thorn in her side. Caroline had never given much thought to any of the other women who had tried to topple her, but for some reason Alva, with that massive Vanderbilt fortune behind her, was beginning to concern Caroline. "That house is a brazen declaration of that woman's insecurities."

"I couldn't agree with you more," said McAllister. "But it is an astonishing display of wealth. The moment I stepped inside I saw how—"

"Inside? You've been inside? You mean to say you've called on Alva Vanderbilt?" She felt her eyebrows rise.

"Oh." He waved his hand as if it were nothing. "Mrs. Vanderbilt merely wanted my advice on the ball, don't you know."

"I see." Just a few weeks before, Ward had dismissed Alva's masquerade ball as a gauche gimmick. She felt a pang of jealousy and an absurd sense of betrayal. She loathed the idea of having to compete with Alva Vanderbilt for Ward's attention. She had already tried that game with William's various mistresses and failed. Caroline's heart was sinking, and she scolded herself. *Stop it. Just stop it!* She was Mrs. Astor, for goodness' sake. She was beyond having to vie for anyone's attention. "I still can't understand why Alva Vanderbilt would punish Carrie like this."

"Well, if you ask me, it's fairly obvious. Mrs. Vanderbilt has been turned away at your doorstep how many times now?"

"What difference does that make?"

"All the difference in the world. And I must say"—he drew a deep sigh—"this is a very ingenious play on the part of Mrs. Vanderbilt."

"What are you saying?"

"She's going to make you come to her. If you wish for your daughter to attend the ball, you have no choice but to call on Mrs. Vanderbilt."

Caroline heard herself gasp. It was clear that Carrie and Ward both knew that she had caused this problem and that she could also remedy it. But what it would take from Caroline to right the situation was too great a price to pay. Yes, Carrie's immediate happiness hinged on an invitation to the ball, but her daughter would recover, whereas Caroline's very position in society depended on her holding her ground.

Surely Ward understood what was at stake, but it was obvious that he was being seduced by Alva's extravagance. Caroline felt as though she'd lost her anchor, and now it was up to her, and her alone, to preserve society.

She had to find a way to convey to Carrie that making that one seemingly small gesture—paying a social call to Alva—was a signal to all that Mrs. Astor was recognizing that the Vanderbilts were now part of society. And if she'd had concerns about Alva before, she knew that calling on her would be her ultimate downfall. If Carrie and others thought that Alva was going to take over society, Caroline's calling on her would be playing right into Alva's hands.

———

Caroline didn't sleep that night. The wind was howling outside her bedroom window, a tree branch scraping against the panes of glass. She tried reading, but it wasn't the same as when Thomas read to her, and even after her eyes grew heavy and closed, her mind returned to the tug-of-war between her daughter and society.

As society's leader she took her responsibilities seriously. The Knickerbockers were looking to her to guard their customs and values. She knew her mother would never have forgiven her for bending to the pressure. How could she let the Vanderbilts in? Especially after all the terrible things Alva had said about her and now, knowing that Alva wanted to take her place.

It was one o'clock in the morning when she got up and inched her way downstairs. That hour of moonlight and the way its shadows played off the walls had become all too familiar to her. She entered the library, and sure enough, Thomas was up. It was as if he'd been waiting for her. As he swung his feet off the ottoman, she noticed he had a copy of *Wuthering Heights* in his lap.

"Warm milk?" he asked.

She nodded.

After he headed to the kitchen, she rearranged figurines in her curio cabinet, placing her bronze Hercules to the right of Alexander the Great and then switched it out with a fourteen-karat-gold lion figurine. But she didn't like that any better and put it all back the way it was.

When Thomas returned with a pot of steamed milk, she closed the curio door and sat down, gesturing for him to join her. "Children," she said with a sigh. "They can try one's patience, can't they?"

"I should say so. My daughters are grown now, but there was a time when they put me through the paces," he said, placing a delicate teacup on a saucer, pouring the steamed milk that looked thick as cream. "They were both quite young when their mother died."

"And you never remarried?" she asked, which surprised them both, as it wasn't in her nature to pry.

"The three of us got on just fine on our own," he said, handing her the cup of warm milk. "I learned to braid their hair, and we had plenty of tea parties." He smiled sadly.

"I'll bet you were a wonderful father. I can't imagine William ever doing any of that. Can you?"

"Well, why would he have? He had you." Thomas leaned forward in his chair, and still smiling, he said, "I've seen how you are with Miss Carrie—and with all your children. If I may be so bold," he said, covering his heart with his hand, "I have never seen a more devoted mother. Or a mother who loves her children more."

Caroline set her cup aside, touched, maybe even embarrassed by the compliment. "Oh, Thomas," she said, changing the subject, "what will I ever do with myself if you suddenly get over your insomnia and start sleeping eight hours a night?"

"I highly doubt that will ever happen, Mrs. Astor," he said with a warm smile.

"But if it does—"

"I shall never abandon you," he said in a voice so tender, it squeezed her heart.

For a moment his eyes had hold of hers and would not let go. His face changed completely when he said that, and Caroline felt the boundaries of their association stretched to its limits. All the precise edges of the rules that governed their world were going soft. And it wasn't as if it were a romantic moment, and yet it was a most intimate one.

She excused herself after that, went upstairs, and for the first time in weeks, she slept soundly through the rest of the night.

The next day Caroline rang for her driver and set out in her new carriage, a victoria with two stallions bred in Kentucky. The carriage, etched in gold with a purple interior and its sleek black horses, was so distinctive that everyone knew it by sight. So when she pulled up to Fifty-Second Street and Fifth Avenue, there was no mistaking who had arrived at Petit Chateau.

As Caroline looked out her carriage window, she saw that the home was even larger and grander than she'd originally thought. The white facade looked as if it belonged in Paris. Years ago, old New York would have written this off as an absurdity, but times and tastes had evolved, and Caroline realized that her brownstone had become absolutely passé.

She handed the coachman her engraved card that simply read *Mrs. Astor* in a tasteful Old English script. Caroline watched as he passed through the magnificent gate and reached for the doorbell pull. She wondered what she might say to Alva when at last, the butler, dressed in as fine a livery as she'd ever seen, answered the door. Caroline saw the way he produced his silver tray and how her coachman placed her card on top. The butler bowed and closed the door once more.

Caroline waited, a slight breeze carrying the scent of horses with it. The stallions stomped and snorted, wrangling their harnesses. When the Vanderbilts' butler returned and opened the door, she only saw that her driver had offered a small nod before coming back to the carriage.

"I'm afraid Mrs. Vanderbilt is unavailable just now," he said.

Caroline was stunned. It had never occurred to her that Alva might *not* receive her. Her face burned, and thankfully her coachman had the good sense not to linger, immediately taking his seat on the box and steering her carriage away. The implications of what had just happened were too great to fathom. She had just acknowledged the Vanderbilts, thereby letting them into society. And she'd done it for nothing. Carrie was no closer to attending the ball, and Caroline had severely undermined her position.

By the time she returned home, Caroline was quite distressed. Though outwardly everything seemed the same, she felt her world spinning. She detested change and unpredictability. It set her on edge, and to calm herself, she needed something to bring to order. She started with her library, instructing her footmen to organize the books according to height.

She stood in the center of the room amid stacks of books piled on the floor, the sideboard and end tables. When the library was finished, she moved on to her art gallery, which also doubled as her ballroom. She paused at the fireplace to peruse the room, standing by her favorite candelabras, two magnificent gilded pieces of art that William had given her as a wedding present. She decided all the paintings should be rehung according to artist; all the Jean-Baptiste-Camille Corots in one section, the Ferdinand Roybets next to those, the Emile van Marckes on the south wall next to the Jules Lefebvres, and on and on it went, well into the night, until all one hundred paintings were exactly where she deemed they ought to be. Her staff was exhausted, and she should have been, retiring finally at two in the morning with a cup of tea and a newly released serial of Maupassant's *Une vie*, which Thomas read to her in French.

The next day, Thomas knocked gently on her door. "Mrs. Astor, forgive me, but this just arrived." He handed her an ivory linen envelope. "I thought perhaps you might like to present this to Miss Carrie yourself."

There it was, addressed to Mrs. Astor in lovely calligraphy.

Mr. and Mrs. William Kissam Vanderbilt request the honor of Mrs. William B. Astor and Miss Carrie Astor's presence at their masquerade ball to be held on the twenty-sixth of March, at ten o'clock at Petit Chateau.

CHAPTER THIRTY

Alva

IT WAS A GAMBLE. Alva had baited Mrs. Astor with a trail of bread crumbs that led from the Grande Dame's townhouse right to Petit Chateau. It had worked but now Alva was anxious and jumpy, her nerves brittle. She was quick to snap at the children and members of her staff. Her ensuing guilt over having done so only compounded her stress.

She looked at the clock on the fireplace mantel for the fourth time in the past five minutes. Right about now Caroline Astor would be receiving her invitation. And then what? Would she come to the ball? Would she rip the invitation in two? It was anyone's guess. If only a reporter had seen the Astor carriage out front the day before—that could have been some security, but there'd been no mention of Mrs. Astor's visit in the morning papers. She was tempted to feed the story to the reporters herself but wasn't sure it was wise to force their hand. There was a risk that the whole thing could backfire. She felt paralyzed and decided the best thing to do now was just wait and see. If Mrs. Astor did come to the ball, her plan would have succeeded, but if she didn't show, Alva would have only provoked her and completely nixed her chances of ever being welcomed into the smart set, which was her main fear about alerting the press herself.

The irony here was that Alva had been waiting years for Mrs. Astor to pay her a visit and now she'd gone and missed it. But the only reason Alva hadn't received the Grande Dame was because Alva had been with Jeremiah. She'd spotted him lurking about the front gate that day. At first she almost hadn't recognized him, a tall, gaunt, bearded man in an ill-fitting suit. A prowler, she'd thought, until she did a double take.

"What's happened to you?" she'd asked, rushing him inside before anyone else saw him. Up close he had looked even worse. His hair was stringy, and he had dark crescents beneath his eyes, bruises along his cheek and jaw. "Did you get into a fight? Are you all right?"

He had laughed it off, ignoring her question by gazing up at the vaulted ceilings and whistling through his teeth. "I had to come get a look at your palace for myself before the ball."

"What's going on?" she demanded.

He'd looked around, eyes shifting as if making sure no one else was around. "You said one time, 'If you ever need anything.'" He'd chuckled. "Well, I need *something*."

"What? Anything."

"My inheritance? Remember that $200,000? Well"—he made a flippant gesture with his hands—"it's gone."

"All of it?" She'd looked at him like a disappointed parent, and in truth, she was disappointed. He knew that was all the money he had to live on, and she didn't have to ask how he'd spent it.

"I'm broke," he'd laughed. "Turns out my credit's no good in this town anymore." He sat down, practically collapsing into a chair. As he dropped his head to his hands, his glib attitude shifted into a panic. "I owe a whole lot of people a whole lot of money." He'd let out a sob—a single agonized sob—and mumbled, "They beat me up and threatened to kill me if I don't pay them back. Might not be a bad idea. Didn't I always say I was worth more dead than alive?"

"How much do you owe them?"

"I've already borrowed what I could—cleaned poor George out, too. I've ruined that poor man's life. I never meant to hurt him—I love him. I truly do."

She'd grabbed hold of his wrist, forcing him to focus. "How much do you owe?"

He shook his head in response.

"Tell me, Jeremiah. How much are we talking?"

"'Bout $90,000"—shoulder shrug—"give or take."

Knowing Jeremiah, that *give or take* could have been another $90,000. She went to her hatbox and gave him $10,000 that she'd stowed away through the years. "This should buy you some time while I get you the rest."

"And how on earth are you going to do that? You know Willie won't give you a penny if it's on my behalf. Besides, you have your big ball to prepare for."

"Never mind about that. I'll sell a painting, or a piece of jewelry." They had only just moved in two weeks before, and with the exception of an armoire coming from Paris and a tapestry coming from Nice, everything was in place. She was thinking those were the very pieces she might send back in order to get Jeremiah some of the money. "Somehow, I'll get you the rest," she'd said. "And in the meantime, promise me you'll stay out of the bars and no more poker."

So that day when Mrs. Astor came calling, Alva had been with Jeremiah and had told her butler that she wished not to be disturbed *under any circumstances.* After Jeremiah left, she learned of Mrs. Astor's visit and fretted, thinking she'd missed her opportunity. But then when she thought about it, not being available to meet with her had actually been a blessing in disguise. Not receiving the Grande Dame had made Alva more elusive, plus it gave Mrs. Astor a taste of her own medicine.

The following afternoon, Alva was preparing to welcome a host of reporters from the *New York Times, Town Topics* and various other newspapers. She was giving them a sneak peek of Petit Chateau in order to get added publicity for her masquerade ball. Those reporters had always been good to her, as she'd been to them. Alva never missed a birthday or a chance to shower them with a lovely timepiece, a pair of cufflinks, a rare bottle of brandy.

At two o'clock that afternoon her butler ushered in half a dozen newspapermen, and Alva greeted them one at a time, as if she were receiving guests for a formal affair. When asked, she explained that Willie K. would be joining them shortly. He had been called away to his father's office but she was expecting him back soon. While she took them on a tour, calling out details of the gilded trim, the frescoed ceilings, the Corinthian pilasters, they shouted out questions about the guest of honor, what costume the hostess would be wearing, asking for any hints about the party favors and the menu.

The interview continued with no sign of Willie. She was perturbed. He knew how important this was to her. As the questions slowed, the reporters found themselves back where the tour began. One by one they left before Willie put in an appearance.

And when he did return home, she was furious until she came down the grand staircase and saw the look on his face. "What is it? What's wrong?"

"It's Uncle Jeremiah."

Alva froze in place while her mind raced, wondering if Willie found out she was bailing him out of his gambling debt. Or maybe he'd been roughed up again. Maybe he was in the hospital . . .

"I'm sorry," Willie said, coming closer to her.

She looked into his eyes, and her heart went still, a prickly sensation overtaking her.

"I'm sorry," he said again, shaking his head. "They found Uncle Jeremiah this morning. In his hotel room. He's dead."

Alva heard herself gasp, a sharp intake of air that shot her full of pain. She reached out, holding on to the banister as she sank to the bottom step. "How? What happened?" All she could think was that his creditors had caught up to him.

Willie took a moment. He looked around the great hall before his eyes finally landed on Alva. "He shot himself."

Alva held her face in her hands, breathing hard as she rocked in place. She didn't remember Willie sitting down beside her, but now his arms were wrapped around her, trying to hold her still. *Why, Jeremiah? Why did you do this?*

Later that day, she got her answer. His suicide note, found on his nightstand, reiterated what he'd said to her time and again: he was worth more dead than alive. And in Jeremiah's mind, now at least his one true love, George Terry—to whom he'd left the $400,000 trust in his will—would have the money to pay off Jeremiah's debts and live comfortably on what was left. Alva was heartbroken. As far as she was concerned, the Vanderbilts—especially Billy—had blood on their hands.

She wandered about the rest of the day, an aching pressure building in her chest that she kept pressing back down until, at last, she couldn't fight it anymore. She had barely made it to her room before the tears let loose. Flinging herself across the bed, she buried her face in a pillow to muffle her sobs and then her screams, her grief tangled in anger. How could Jeremiah have left her? How selfish of him. How cowardly. If only she'd known he was suffering so. Could she have possibly saved him?

Not since her mother died had she felt this kind of anguish and loss. Who was she going to smoke cigarettes and drink whiskeys with in the middle of the afternoon? Who was going to commiserate with her about her in-laws? How could it be that they'd never again walk arm in arm through the park or down the broken sidewalks of some newly discovered neighborhood? And what about his sardonic wit—how would she manage without that?

She finally peeled herself off the bed, went into the bathroom and splashed cool water on her face before sobbing again into a hand towel. When she was able to compose herself, she remembered her masquerade ball was less than a week away. She was supposed to have checked in with the florist, the chef and the wine merchant that afternoon, but none of that mattered now. She didn't care about her ball and couldn't imagine going through with it.

Now she was crying again, overwhelmed by the thought of bringing everything to a screeching halt. She turned on the tap and ran more cool water over her face. When she glanced in the mirror, she swore she saw Jeremiah looking back at her, frowning. "Don't you dare think about canceling your ball," she heard him say. "I'll never forgive you if you do."

CHAPTER THIRTY-ONE

Caroline

THE VANDERBILT BALL WAS called for ten o'clock, but the quadrilles wouldn't begin until midnight, and just as Caroline never arrived at the opera a minute before the second act, she and Carrie would not step foot inside the Vanderbilt mansion a moment sooner than was absolutely necessary.

As their carriage made its way up Fifth Avenue, Caroline saw people congregating along the side of the road. At first she thought they were all in costume—sack coats and woolen shawls—but then she realized they were just commoners from the poorer neighborhoods, there to watch the guests arrive. One block farther north, the crowd grew larger. Police officers were there to contain the onlookers. Carrie pressed her face to the window, her excitement as palpable as Caroline's curiosity.

When they drew closer still, Caroline saw the city's finest carriages lining the street. If she didn't know better, Caroline would have thought she was in Paris with all the liveried coachmen and footmen assisting guests. An enormous awning stretched from the doorway to the curb along with a thick red carpet there to protect everyone's delicate footwear.

As she and her daughter made their approach, Caroline heard the orchestra music spilling forth from the mansion and *good lord* people were dancing in the great hall by the staircase. A woman dressed as a hornet with a diamond in her cone-shaped headdress was fluttering about, stinging guests and laughing as if she'd already gotten into the punch. A man dressed as Daniel Boone was chasing Mother Goose with a tomahawk made of flowers. A woman, whom Caroline would later realize was the other Mrs. Vanderbilt—Cornelius's wife, Alice— was dressed in a white gown studded with diamonds that shimmered like tiny lightbulbs, and in her hand, a genuine electrical torch gave off a glow each time she pressed a switch hidden inside her pocket. There was a carnival-like atmosphere in the air, and everyone was laughing and carrying on recklessly. It was as if the costumes shielded their identities, giving them permission to do away with decorum altogether. Caroline shuddered. People never would have conducted themselves in such an undignified manner at one of her balls. *Never!*

Unlike the majority of the guests, hiding behind their disguises, Caroline was in plain view for all to see. She hadn't given much thought to her costume and, frankly, hadn't had much time to prepare it, opting at the last minute to wear a Venetian gown. It was a Rococo style in purple velvet, with a dramatic neckline cut low enough to display her four diamond necklaces. She drew a deep breath, feeling everyone turn her way. The wide-eyed glances told her that no one had expected her to be there.

As Carrie excused herself to prepare for her quadrille, Caroline saw that Puss Strong had come dressed as a puss herself, complete with a taxidermy cat on her head and several tails sewn into the back of her gown. She was making her way toward Caroline when, thankfully, Ward McAllister intercepted, cutting in front of Puss and practically galloping to Caroline's side, all dignity abandoned.

"Welcome, welcome," he said, as if he were the host, which irked Caroline to no end. She didn't like his embracing this charade of an affair. "My Mystic Rose has arrived, and now the real ball can begin, don't you know."

"And who, pray tell, are you supposed to be?" she asked, scrutinizing his outfit, uncertain what was more absurd: his powdered wig, the enormous plume protruding from his cap, the bright orange stockings or the pleated gorget framing his head. Were it not for that *Mystic Rose* and the *don't you know*, she might not have recognized him.

"Why, I am a member of the French nobility." He offered a grand bow that was entirely out of character for Ward McAllister. She gave him a disapproving glance as he straightened up. "Step right this way," he said, still acting his part.

Passing through the great hall to the salon, Caroline willed herself not to glance up and admire the calcium lights illuminating the room along with the largest arrangements of flowers she had ever seen, orchids and bougainvillea everywhere she turned. It was also quite obvious that Alva Vanderbilt didn't want a single guest to overlook her very expensive Louis XV furnishings. Caroline did her best to look unmoved. She had to retain a sense of superiority and would let it be known that she was not impressed, when in truth, she was immensely so. It seemed the only way to cope was to feign disgust—even if only to herself.

Suddenly there was a round of applause as a trumpeter began to play and a flock of white doves appeared from behind a curtain. Just as they flapped their wings and started taking flight, they revealed the hostess herself, Alva Vanderbilt, in grand preposterous style. Caroline assumed that Princess de Croy standing next to her was Viscountess Mandeville.

After the doves cleared her view, the first thing Caroline noticed was that Alva was also wearing a Venetian gown. Hers was a lemon-and-white brocade, and she had Catherine the Great's pearls about her neck. Alva looked like a princess, but Caroline reminded herself that she was still the queen.

Through the crowd of adoring guests, Caroline and Alva locked eyes. It was like a matador facing off with a bull. Alva stood, waiting to receive her guests alongside the viscountess, and Caroline felt propelled toward her. The side conversations had stopped. All eyes were on Caroline and Alva, everyone waiting to see what would happen when the two came face-to-face.

Alva spoke first, her Southern accent syrupy sweet. "I'm so pleased that you could join us tonight, Mrs. Astor. Especially on such short notice. I do hope you'll forgive my not receiving you that day when you came by."

Touché. Caroline took a moment before responding. "Mrs. Vanderbilt, you seem to have outdone yourself tonight," she said with a regal nod, and then turned away, only to be greeted by a masked man in yellow tights and a floor-length cloak.

"Isn't this marvelous?" he said. "I'm mad as hops to see you here." The accent gave him away. James Van Alen was all smiles. "How splendid that you've put your collieshangies aside. Emily would have loved that."

Emily! For a split second, Caroline expected to see her daughter standing next to him.

"Emily was forever in Alva's debt," he said. "That day in Newport, we might have lost her had it not been for Alva . . ."

Oh, Emily. The ache in Caroline's heart made it hard to focus on what Van Alen was saying and yet, she longed to talk about her daughter just to keep her memory close and alive. She was about to ask Van Alen to slow down and explain it all, when Carrie appeared and Van Alen vanished, swept away by another masked man.

"Mother," said Carrie, "may I present Mr. Wendell Perkins."

"Mrs. Astor, it's a true honor." He offered a ceremonial bow. He was wearing a diamond aigrette as if he'd stepped out of the days of Henri III.

Caroline sensed that Carrie wasn't truly interested in this young man. Judging by the way she'd haphazardly introduced him to Ward as well, Caroline could tell that Wendell Perkins was just another admirer, wanting to meet Carrie's mother. Still, Caroline and Ward exchanged pleasantries with the young man until the first quadrille began, and Carrie and Wendell excused themselves to prepare for their own presentation.

As soon as they left, Ward McAllister's gossipy nature took over. "What was that business Van Alen was saying about Alva and Emily?"

"I haven't a clue."

"Well, I assure you, I will get to the bottom of it at once." And off he went.

Caroline's head began to throb; the pulsing of her temples seemed to be keeping time with the orchestra as they moved into the ballroom for the quadrilles. The majority of the presentations left much to be desired as far as Caroline was concerned. She found the Mother Goose and hobbyhorse routines unintentionally laughable and the Dresden quadrille far too dark. The last dance, the one Caroline thought was the most impressive, and certainly the most dignified, was Carrie's star quadrille.

It was nearly two in the morning when the footmen made their way through the crowd, distributing party favors. Caroline and the other ladies were presented with diamond-encrusted brooches and matching bracelets. Caroline remembered the days when silk fans and boutonnieres were considered fine favors. She found Alva's flaunting most distasteful, as was Ward McAllister's obvious delight with his new ruby cufflinks.

As the hour grew later, many of the gentlemen—and a good number of ladies, too—had consumed an excessive amount of claret and champagne and were acting a fool; one of the Marie Antoinettes was clonking people on the head with her scepter, as was Little Bo-Peep with her crook. Napoleon Bonaparte was arm-wrestling with Amadeus Mozart while onlookers cheered and clapped. Never in her life did Caroline imagine she'd see the day when society's most respected citizens would behave in such a way. Such a spectacle. She caught herself staring and at one point even laughing, both tickled and appalled. The whole thing was just that absurd.

When they were called downstairs for supper, Caroline had regained her composure and was now bracing herself, imagining to what lengths Alva had gone to impress society. The dining room was enormous with a vaulted ceiling and a hundred or more round tables, each graced with cobalt-blue-and-gold Royal Worcester china, a plethora of crystal glasses and fourteen-karat-gold cutlery. Each table had an enormous centerpiece of American Beauties, which had always been Caroline's flower of choice. She considered it to be *her* flower and felt a bit encroached upon.

A commotion across the room interrupted her thoughts as she saw one of the footmen gracelessly traipsing about, nearly knocking over one of the Catherine the Greats. Apparently a pair of doves from Alva's grand entrance had escaped and were now flapping about the dining room. As the footmen tried to wrangle the birds, one of the doves landed atop Puss's mummified cat hat. Puss didn't seem to notice. *With enough champagne, what was one more creature perched upon one's head?*

Ward McAllister ran—*he ran*—to Caroline's side, nearly breathless and eager to tell her what he'd learned. "So I spoke with Van Alen, don't you know . . ." He was saying something about Newport, something about Cliff Walk, jabbering on when Caroline stopped, unable to listen because she saw that her seat was on the dais, next to Alva's. She should not have been surprised. She was always seated next to the hostess. But this was different. Caroline knew that she was being used as a prop, there to make a statement, put on display, and there was nothing she could do about it. All who saw her coming stepped back, making way for her.

Ward took his seat on Caroline's other side and proceeded to tell her about Alva rescuing Emily that day on Cliff Walk.

"What?" Caroline looked at him.

"That's right. Emily slipped and fell. Alva just happened to have been passing by and ended up saving her life . . ."

Caroline listened as the commotion around her faded to background noise, muffled and dimmed. She tried to absorb what Ward was saying but couldn't make sense of it all. *Emily was on Cliff Walk? With Alva Vanderbilt?* One thought led to another as she vaguely remembered that day in Newport when Emily came home limping with scratches and bruises on her face. Alva had been with her. For some reason she remembered the black-and-gray-striped bathing costume. *It was true. Alva really did save Emily's life.* Caroline brought one hand to her mouth, the other splayed across her chest. She could feel the rapid heartbeats beneath her fingertips.

Ward went on, whispering to her, but Caroline was lost in her own thoughts. She was struggling to reconcile her resentment and anger toward Alva with her sudden gratitude for rescuing Emily.

There was another round of applause as Alva and her husband—dressed as the Duke of Guise—entered the dining room. Caroline felt the energy shift as the couple made their way to the dais. She was still letting Ward's news sink in. Caroline had to admit she was somewhat surprised, maybe even impressed, that Alva hadn't exploited the incident with Emily. Maybe Alva had better judgment than Caroline had given her credit for. It didn't make Caroline like her any more, but it did stir within her a genuine feeling of appreciation.

After Alva curtsied and her husband bowed, the couple took their seats, and the footmen began bringing out the first course. Caroline was sitting so close to Alva she could smell her perfume and see the exceptional cut and clarity of her diamonds. It was only a matter of time before they would have to acknowledge each other, and when their eyes met, Caroline knew it was up to her to speak first.

Had it been anyone else, Caroline would have apologized for her past actions against Alva, for Caroline was never afraid to admit when she'd been wrong. But Caroline had already swallowed her pride by attending the ball and now, looking into Alva's blue eyes, she couldn't bring herself to say she was sorry. The best she could do was say, "Thank you." And to indicate that she was not thanking Alva for the invitation to her ball, she added, "Thank you for what you did for Emily. I didn't know." And with that she started on her turtle soup.

CHAPTER THIRTY-TWO

Alva

AT FIRST ALVA DIDN'T know to what Mrs. Astor was referring. But then she understood. Someone—probably James Van Alen, since no one other than Willie knew—had told her about Cliff Walk.

"I was happy to help," Alva said, not quite sure that the Grande Dame had heard her, for she kept her eyes fixed on her soup.

And that was it. Not another word was spoken between them.

Throughout the meal, Alva glanced around the room, amazed at how her children's gymnasium had been transformed into such an elegant dining hall. She was serving a nine-course meal prepared by the Delmonico's chef himself, something that no hostess had ever done before. She couldn't help but recall the times when she didn't know where her supper would come from or if her family would be turned out on the street. *Imagine, recovering from such a humbling setback.* Alva had dreamed of this night, had craved it as much as she'd once craved a morsel of food. This was a moment she wanted to mark in her bank of memories, to never be forgotten. Here she was, with Mrs. Astor seated next to her, in her palace of a home. She wished that Julia were there, but she hadn't even bothered to acknowledge the invitation. Last Alva heard, her sister had moved to Brooklyn and was devoting herself to the suffrage movement. Alva looked about the room for Jennie and Armide, hoping they would at least understand the significance of this evening. Despite what Julia thought about the house, Alva knew her mother would have been proud. This was exactly the sort of life she'd always intended for her daughters—all of them, not just Alva.

There was no denying that Alva had achieved exactly what she'd set out to do, what even Alice Vanderbilt couldn't have done. She had gotten the Vanderbilt family admitted into society's highest echelon. She'd won and now she was waiting for that validating effervescence to bubble up inside her like a swallow of champagne. She waited. And waited. *So where was it?* Alva felt underwhelmed to say the least. She watched the festivities whirling around her—the feasting and dancing, her husband and Duchy laughing jovially—and yet Alva found such little satisfaction in her triumph.

Losing Jeremiah must have had something to do with it. Earlier in the evening she thought she saw him. Could have sworn he was one of the King Lears. It was just too hard to fathom that she'd never see him again, that she'd never had the chance to say goodbye. She felt tears building up behind her eyes and willed them away.

Mamie Fish interrupted her thoughts. She'd come dressed as Elizabeth I, her gown made of gold with a silver farthingale and a matching neck ruff that made it impossible for her to turn her head. In typical Mamie style she said, "I hope you and Willie don't end up in bankruptcy after this ball." She laughed, making everyone nearby turn around.

"Oh, go on, Mamie," said Alva without cracking a smile. "I'm serious"—she gestured in the direction of the ballroom—"go on."

But Mamie stayed where she was, undeterred.

Soon Puss joined them, holding one of her many tails in her gloved hands.

"I'm so glad you were able to get that bird off your cat," said Mamie with another sharp laugh.

Puss patted her hat as if making sure the taxidermy was still in

place. "Now, Alva, tell us about the new opera house. Is it still scheduled to open in October? Do you know who will be performing yet?
Are you pleased with the seating . . . ?"

Alva was still fielding questions when Oliver Belmont appeared at
her side, dressed in yellow-and-red-silk tights and a black velvet
cloak. "Mrs. Vanderbilt, may I have the honor of the next dance?" He
leaned in and whispered, "You look like you need rescuing."

And she did.

"I'm warning you," he said, leading her onto the dance floor, "I'm
very light on my feet."

In fact, Oliver Belmont was indeed light on his feet, a far better
dancer than she would have expected. If he was at all self-conscious
about dancing with a woman taller than himself, it wasn't evident.

"You've pulled off quite a victory tonight," he said. "So what's
wrong? Was the foie gras not to your liking?"

"What do you mean?"

"You haven't smiled much tonight."

"That's because I'm exhausted."

He nodded, unconvinced. "So what's next?"

"Next?" she laughed. "You mean *this* isn't enough?"

"Nah"—he smiled and twirled her around—"not for someone
like you."

"Someone like me? What does that mean?"

"Nothing. Nothing at all."

"No, tell me."

He sighed. "All right. Very well. You, Mrs. Vanderbilt, are never
quite satisfied with what you've got. I know that because you remind
me a little of myself."

She was facing him now, his gaze fixed on hers. She'd never really
noticed how lovely his eyes were. Or how comfortable she was with
him, which suddenly made her most *uncomfortable*.

She looked across the way and saw Willie K. waltzing with Duchy, who, in Alva's mind, was the grandest of all the Princesses de Croy. She was smiling, laughing at something Willie just said, and it pleased Alva to see her friend enjoying herself. She was grateful that Willie was keeping an eye on her, especially since the viscount had been unable to attend.

When the dance ended, Alva thanked Oliver, though she wouldn't have minded a second dance with him.

No sooner had she returned to her hostess duties than Ward McAllister came up to her explaining that Mrs. Astor had left early, at half past three. "And don't you know, the press left right behind her . . ."

While he was talking, Alva thought about all the reporters scrambling back to their desks, writing up their articles that would appear in the next day's society pages. She looked around, distracted by her various guests: Oliver Belmont was now waltzing with Puss; Alice Vanderbilt's light switch had stopped functioning, and Cornelius was attempting to fix it; Mamie and Tessie Oelrichs were bickering over who had first decided to come as Elizabeth I. Ward was still talking about Mrs. Astor when Alva excused herself to steal Duchy away from Willie. In the midst of some 1,500 people, she felt lonely and wanted a quiet moment with her friend.

As the evening wore on, Alva was exhausted and, frankly, a bit bored. Her wig was heavy and hot, and her gown was digging into her waist. Willie was offering guided tours of the house as if he'd been the genius behind it all. Everywhere she looked she saw bits and pieces of discarded costumes: a trampled mask in the hallway, plumes that had come loose from someone's hat, a gentleman's gloves, a white powdered wig that turned out to be Willie K.'s. The hour was growing late; it was nearly dawn. Soon her staff would be setting up for the morning buffet, and then, after all the planning and all the anticipation, it would be over. Done.

———

Hours later, the last of her guests were gone. Willie K. had passed out just before daybreak, having to be escorted upstairs by a footman. The sun was coming up now, and other than the servants who were putting her house back in order, Petit Chateau was eerily quiet. As tired as she was, Alva knew she'd never be able to sleep. She started back at the beginning, reliving the evening moment by moment, already rewriting her personal assessment of the ball. Her mind canceled out those instances where she'd felt disappointed or flattened. She negated any details that were less than spectacular, less than perfect, until her memory had crystallized the unprecedented success that she hoped her ball had truly been. But of course, the press would have the final say on that.

It was going on eight o'clock in the morning. Willie and the children were still asleep, and Alva was wide awake, a nervous energy festering inside her. When she couldn't take the quiet another minute, she reached for her overcoat and satchel and stepped outside into the morning air.

The red carpet that had been pristine the night before was now trampled on by thousands of footsteps. It was a cold, crisp day already set in motion: children being marched off to school by their governesses; businessmen in their bowlers, carrying attaché cases and walking sticks; carriages and hacks maneuvering up and down Fifth Avenue.

Alva saw a newsboy standing on the corner beside stacks of papers held together with fraying twine. Her heart began beating a bit faster. She felt like an actress or an opera star anticipating her opening night review. Those newspapers held her fate, and after buying one of each, Alva, still dressed in her Venetian gown, her wig and her pearls, sat down on a nearby bench and began scouring the papers one by one until she came to the one article, the only one that really mattered.

There it was, a quote from her harshest critic, someone who rarely spoke to reporters:

> "WE HAVE NO RIGHT TO EXCLUDE THOSE WHOM THE GROWTH
> OF THIS GREAT COUNTRY HAS BROUGHT FORWARD, PROVIDED
> THEY ARE NOT VULGAR IN SPEECH AND APPEARANCE," SAID
> MRS. WILLIAM B. ASTOR AS SHE WAS LEAVING PETIT CHATEAU,
> ADDING, "THE TIME HAS COME FOR THE VANDERBILTS."

CHAPTER THIRTY-THREE

Alva

SEVERAL MONTHS AFTER HER masquerade ball, Alva discovered she was pregnant again. And though plagued with morning sickness, she refused to let her delicate condition interfere with the traction she was gaining in society. Petit Chateau had accomplished exactly what she'd hoped it would. She had recently been invited to dinner parties, balls and other events that had previously been denied her. With her one fancy dress ball and Mrs. Astor's presence, Alva had moved to the top of nearly everyone's guest list.

But Mrs. Astor remained lukewarm at best. Despite her declaration to the press, Mrs. Astor had yet to extend a personal invitation to Alva for so much as tea, let alone to one of her exclusive dinner parties or balls. It had infuriated Alva, but she also knew it was just a matter of time before Mrs. Astor would have to come around. Each day more calling cards arrived for Alva, and her engagement book was filling up weeks and months in advance.

And it wasn't just Alva who'd found herself embraced by society; all the Vanderbilts benefited from what she'd done. Especially Willie. She didn't have to say, *Told you so*, when suddenly the men's social clubs invited him in, including the Knickerbocker, the Union Club and the New York Yacht Club.

Now that the construction of Petit Chateau was completed and they were finishing up the opera house, she was eager to work on another project. She wanted to build a new cottage in Newport, but Willie wasn't in favor of the idea, especially when she was expecting. He complained that construction absorbed all her attention and took her away from him and the children. Even she couldn't deny that he was right about that. She could pore over blueprints, losing track of time, oblivious to her children waiting at the table for her to join them for luncheon, or standing by her desk with a book in hand waiting patiently for her to read aloud with them. Willie would ask if she was coming up to bed soon. "Five minutes," she'd say, stunned when he'd reappear an hour or two later, already in his bathrobe, his cowlick sticking up, indicating that he must have already fallen asleep for a bit.

Now without blueprints to consume her, she was obsessed with the opening of the new theater—the Metropolitan Opera House.

"For the inaugural season," Alva said, addressing Billy and the other board members, "we absolutely must hold the grand opening on the same night as the Academy of Music's opening season performance."

The men looked at her wide-eyed and openmouthed. Someone— she wasn't sure who—gasped. Alva refused to look at Willie and figured he'd reprimand her later.

She was thinking of how to soften the request when Billy said, "Why the hell didn't I think of that?"

"But on the same night?" asked Willie. "How can we possibly do it on the same night?"

"Don't be ridiculous," said J. P. Morgan. "It's brilliant."

"The Academy can't possibly compete with our new theater," said Cornelius. "Everyone's dying to see it. That old hall will be empty on opening night."

"And the old money will be seething when they hear," said Mr. Gould.

"But," insisted Willie, "what are we going to do for talent?"

Alva glared at him. Why was he challenging this when everyone else was in favor of it? Was it resentment? Did he feel threatened? What happened to the adoring boy she'd married? She wished he could just be proud of her.

"Don't you see," Willie persisted, "in terms of talent, we'll be left with second fiddle. I've heard they've already hired Christine Nilsson to perform for their opening night."

"Don't worry about the talent," Alva said. "I'll take care of that."

On a clear Monday night, the twenty-second of October, when those loyal to old New York money went downtown to the Academy of Music, Alva's carriage arrived outside the new Metropolitan Opera House. She was dressed in a royal-blue gown with a gold-and-silver-embroidered basque. The gown had been designed in Paris by Madame Buzenet, and Alva's local dressmaker had let out the seams to make allowances for her child on the way. She was on the arm of Willie K., smiling for the press, which lined both sides of Broadway, between Thirty-Ninth and Fortieth Streets. She wondered if anyone was covering the arrivals at the Academy.

Once inside, Alva stood back and watched everyone marveling at the great hall. It was so spacious, they could have tucked the entire Academy into the first floor. Now that the massive crystal chandelier had been installed, the intricate carvings along the gilded molding were much more prominent, impossible to miss. She was also pleased with the feel of the sumptuous crimson carpeting beneath her feet. Though she'd fought the architect every inch of the way, the Metropolitan Opera House had her name written all over it, and everyone knew it.

She watched as people entered the auditorium. They were delighted to see not one, not two, but *three* tiers of luxury private boxes awaiting the very best of society. And for once, because of Alva, her circle would be among those fortunate enough to sit there. Just as she'd instructed Mr. Cady to arrange it, every guest in those boxes found that they were on display as much as the performers.

The tide was starting to shift, and Alva took the moment to luxuriate in it. She glanced about and saw Puss stroking Mr. Fritzy, who sat primly on her lap, showing off his diamond collar. Ophelia happily fluttered her silk fan back and forth with one hand while nudging her husband awake with the other. Lydia kept toying with her pink and brown topaz brooch, which she told Alva had been designed by her friend Louis Comfort Tiffany. Penelope was so delighted to be there she didn't seem to care that her husband was peering at another woman across the way through his opera glasses. Alva watched those women sitting just a bit higher in their plush seats, shoulders back, heads held high. They were no longer second best; now they were right where they'd always wanted to be.

Alva settled back, watching Christine Nilsson perform the role of Marguerite in *Faust*. When Alva had offered double what the Academy was paying, the opera star had agreed on the spot.

During the intermission, Alva and Willie were joined by Oliver Belmont, who had escorted Miss Louise Baldwin that night. With her honey-colored hair, she was a stunningly beautiful debutante whose popularity was rivaled only by Carrie Astor's. Alva thought Oliver and Louise made for a smart-looking couple, and Oliver was particularly handsome that night in his silk top hat and white cravat. Over the past year or so, the roundness of his face had given way to more definition and the hint of a strong jaw to come. He truly did have lovely eyes. Lovely and yet sad. Alva recalled that dance they'd shared at her ball when he told her she reminded him of himself, *never quite satisfied with what you've got*. She, too, now recognized that same restlessness in him and wondered how long it would be before Oliver would move on from Miss Baldwin to the next socialite.

"You're looking ravishing tonight, Mrs. Vanderbilt." He bowed to kiss Alva's hand, just as he'd done countless times before, but this time it gave her a tiny unexpected prickle, a spark.

"Why, Mr. Belmont, I didn't expect to see you here this evening," she said. "I thought for sure you'd be with your daddy at the Academy." She smiled, cocked her head and added a bat of her lashes before realizing that she was flirting with him.

"My heartfelt congratulations on tonight's opening," he said with the briefest nod to Willie before shifting his attention back to Alva. "And don't you worry, Mrs. Vanderbilt, I will be sure and let Father know that you've given him a run for his money."

As she watched Oliver and Louise Baldwin make their way through the lobby, she wondered what his father's reaction would be when he learned that his son had come to her opening. *Her opening.* She thought of it that way. And part of her did wonder if it was because of her that Oliver had come.

When she and Willie were about to return to their seats, she spotted Mr. and Mrs. Stuyvesant Fish attempting to sneak out before the fourth act. "And where do you think you're going?" Alva asked Mamie, only half-teasing.

Stuyvesant's face flushed as Mamie gave off a shrill chuckle, waving her kerchief. "You know I hate the opera. Three acts of *Faust* is about all I have the stomach for."

Alva smiled even wider. *Three acts of* Faust. That was laughable. Everyone knew that while Mamie said she hated opera, she attended the performances on Monday evenings as religiously as she attended Sunday Mass. Alva knew exactly where Mr. and Mrs. Fish were heading. She was well aware that others, too, including Puss, Tessie and Lady Paget, were planning to shuffle back and forth between the two theaters. They were all hedging their bets on the off chance that the Academy would outshine the new opera house. Everyone wanted to be at the right place at the right time.

"If you hurry," Alva said to Mamie, "you'll be able to catch the fourth act. Oh, and do be sure and say hello to Mrs. Astor for me."

CHAPTER THIRTY-FOUR

Society

ACROSS TOWN, THOSE OF US who have defected enter the Academy's theater and work our way to our seats on the main floor. Tucking in the many layers of our expansive gowns, we sidestep down the narrow rows to our fold-down chairs with the squeaking hinges and the worn-out springs that are getting a bit too familiar with our behinds.

We see Mrs. Astor in her private box, naturally accompanied by Ward McAllister. Mrs. Astor is wearing a forest-green velvet gown covered with diamonds along the bodice. Someone who saw her entering the theater said her train is embellished in fourteen-karat-gold beads. Even from the main floor we see her three diamond necklaces and her diamond harp brooch. And if by chance anyone missed that, the diamonds adhered to her wig are sure to catch their eye. Each time she shifts in her seat, her bejeweled gown catches the light and shimmers, making it impossible to look at anything or anyone other than her.

By the start of intermission, Mrs. Astor and Ward McAllister remain in their seats while people line up to visit her box. It's very obvious that the line is much shorter than usual. We imagine that neither Mrs. Astor nor Ward McAllister will acknowledge this truth any more than they'll speak about the number of empty seats there are in the theater. It must be too horrific to admit that many of their regular subscribers have opted for the new opera house over their beloved Academy. It must fill them with sentimental sadness, for there was a time when there was never a question of where one should be on a Monday night. But all that is changing now, because of Alva Vanderbilt.

For years now we've listened to Alva going on and on about the new opera house. She made sure we knew it was all her idea. And she wasn't shy about her triumphs, either—how she'd gone up against her father-in-law and the other board members. We pooh-poohed her at the time, but now, to think she'd been the driving force behind it all, to think she'd been given such responsibility, leaves us speechless. Even jealous. But also hopeful. It makes us take a breath and—for better or worse—reexamine our lives.

Each, in our own way, begins to question what we are doing with our time here on earth. While our husbands and fathers spend their days on their yachts or at their gentlemen's clubs, or locked away in their offices, we convince ourselves that we have important work of our own. After all, our balls and nine-course dinner parties don't plan themselves, now do they? And if we weren't so damn busy doing that, how else might we fill our days? Would we study philosophy and ancient Greece? Write great works of literature? Compose operas? Find cures for smallpox and malaria?

If Alva can build an opera house, just think what we could do if given the chance.

CHAPTER THIRTY-FIVE

Alva

NEW YORK, 1884

IN 1884, ON THE sixth of July, Alva and Willie welcomed Harold Stirling into the world. And on the fifteenth of July, just as soon as Alva felt strong enough, she welcomed the press to Petit Chateau to meet the newest Vanderbilt heir. At least that was how she'd explained it to Willie and how she set it up with the reporters.

It had been a difficult pregnancy, and Alva had been prescribed bed rest for the last three months, which had felt more like three years. With each passing day, with no luncheons, no dinner parties, balls or theater to attend, she felt herself drifting further and further away from the life she'd known. She feared that all the progress she'd made in society would be lost. Even more than that, she feared that Mamie and Tessie would take over that spot she had so painstakingly carved out for herself. Her remedy was to bring the press to her, get her name back out there before everyone forgot about her.

Reporters from the *New York Times*, the *World*, the *Sun*, the *Evening Telegram*, *Town Topics* and various other newspapers gathered in the great hall of Petit Chateau. Though many of them had been there before, they were still captivated by its sublime grandeur. Alva had become so accustomed to the mansion, she no longer saw its magnificence. Instead, she was critical, thinking the molding wasn't quite right in one of the parlors or the draperies weren't hanging properly in the study. Those minor imperfections festered and magnified in her mind. It was good to see her creation through the fresh eyes of the press. And that day, the summer light was coming in through the double-arched windows as if she'd trained it to enter her home that way, the sun's rays landing just so.

With the handsome little red-faced Harold swathed in a fine cashmere blanket and nestled in Alva's arms, she stood before the grand staircase. Seven-year-old Consuelo was to her left, six-year-old Little Willie to her right, while she answered a flurry of questions: *How was she feeling? Who was Harold named after? How did Consuelo and Little Willie feel about having a new baby brother?*

The baby was growing restless and started to fuss and then cry. His shrieks grew louder, making Little Willie fidgety while Consuelo covered her ears. Eventually Alva had to hand the baby off to the nurse and dismiss the other two children. Now it was just her and the reporters, which was really what she had wanted all along. But as the questioning shifted from the baby to society, something also shifted inside Alva.

She couldn't put her finger on what it was exactly. When a reporter asked if she planned to return to Newport for the balance of the season, and others asked if she would be attending the Livingstons' coaching party and Mrs. Astor's annual clambake, Alva grew weary. The light that she'd marveled at earlier was now glaring in her eyes. She heard herself answering each of the questions, but the words seemed to be coming from somewhere outside herself.

She realized she no longer wanted to be on display. Suddenly, everything she'd been sheltered from while pregnant, everything she'd thought she'd been longing for, came rushing back. She knew she'd never be invited to Mrs. Astor's clambake, and in that moment, she didn't care. In fact, she felt a little relieved. Alva was just beginning to realize how fatigued she was. After taking a step back from society, she wasn't quite ready to reenter its drama.

She thanked the reporters, and after they left, she was all alone. The house was quiet and she was grateful for that nothingness. That very nothingness that had nearly driven her mad now made her feel safe and protected. For the life of her, she couldn't say what it was all these months that she'd been missing.

The Third Avenue line had recently made its way as far as the Bronx, but Alva loathed the elevated trains and instead rode in her carriage. Such a swelteringly hot day. There was a slight breeze, but it wasn't enough to bring relief. Alva had canceled her plans to return to Newport, in part because of the baby but mostly because she wasn't ready to face society just yet. She needed to ease back into its harsh rays. So she had stayed in the city, but on days like this, she ached for the salty sea breeze.

It was the eighteenth of August. Her mother had died on this date just one week shy of her fiftieth birthday, but the sickness that had ravaged her body made her appear much older. Alva wished she could remember her mother in healthier days without the sunken eyes, the hollowed-out cheeks, her rawboned torso, her chest rattling with each labored breath. Alva shook her head to clear the image, trying to think of other things. She and Willie had been talking again about building a new cottage in Newport. Or rather she had been talking about it. He was still resisting the idea, saying the cottage they had was good enough.

Alva sighed and closed her eyes trying to recall the last time she'd visited her mother's grave. She couldn't remember. She wished her mother had lived long enough to know Willie K. and her grand-children! Though she would have gotten on Alva about Consuelo's posture. She could hear her mother's voice: *Don't let her slouch like that.* She would tell her that the boys took after the Smith side of the family despite Alva's mother-in-law insisting that Harold looked like Willie when he was a baby. Alva couldn't see the resemblance. Harold was a good baby, though, a sound sleeper with an easy temperament. In that respect he was definitely more like his father.

When Alva opened her eyes, they had arrived outside the cemetery. The coachman jumped down, unlatched the catch on the massive wrought iron gates and pushed them open. The dirt pathway forked off in various directions, surrounded by rolling green hills, home to fields of headstones.

With a bouquet of flowers in hand, Alva climbed down from the carriage and headed over to her mother's gravesite. As she made her way toward the large granite monument, she saw her sister Julia kneeling in prayer. She wasn't surprised. There was a time, before Alva began spending her summers in Newport, when all of them visited their mother's grave together on the anniversary of her death.

Julia stood and turned around just as Alva stepped forward and placed the flowers on the headstone.

"I was hoping you would be here," Alva said, standing shoulder to shoulder with her sister.

"You just missed Armide and Jennie."

Alva nodded, wondering if Julia had lingered, waiting in hopes that Alva would show up. It had been two years since they'd seen each other. They were both too stubborn to have reached out to each other directly, but arranging a *chance meeting* allowed each to preserve her pride.

For a moment, they just stood silently until Alva said, "Remember how Mama used to dress us up, make us wear white gloves and sip tea on the front porch?"

Julia laughed. "I mostly remember Mama yelling at you to get down from the trees. *Alva! You git down here and quit showing the whole world your petticoat.*"

"Ah, yes," said Alva. "And then she'd whip me."

"And the next day you'd get back up and do it all over again."

"Well, I *did* like climbing trees."

"You liked seeing what you could get away with," she laughed.

"Perhaps." They both smiled as Alva placed her arm about Julia's waist. "It's good to see you," she said. "I just wish it didn't have to be here."

Julia nodded, leaned in closer to Alva. "You're looking good."

"No." Alva shook her head. "I'm fat. I just had another baby."

"I heard. Jennie and Armide told me. Congratulations."

"Maybe you'll come see him someday? After all, you are his aunt."

She paused, considering it. "I would like that. Yes, I would like that very much."

They went silent again, and Alva suspected that Julia didn't know what else to say any more than she did. She'd forgotten how much Julia resembled their mother, with her red hair a shade deeper than Alva's, her eyes a darker blue.

Looking straight ahead, Julia said, "I'm sorry about the things I said to you that day when you were showing us the house. I hear it turned out beautifully. I read all about your big ball . . ." Her voice trailed off for a moment before she said, "I really am sorry about everything."

"Are you getting on okay?" Alva asked, sidestepping Julia's peace offering so that she herself wouldn't have to apologize.

"I'm doing some writing," Julia said.

"Writing, huh?"

She shrugged. "Just short little pieces. For a women's journal."

"Well, good for you."

Another awkward silence fell over them. Alva observed the fraying sleeves on Julia's dress. The fabric on her shoes was worn; one of the embroidered flowers was gone save for one petal.

"I don't have much on me right now," said Alva. "But—"

"What?" Julia kept her eyes straight ahead.

"If you come by the house tomorrow, you can see the children. Meet little Harold, and I can have Willie give you some money."

"Money?"

"However much you need. I know Willie would be happy to help you out." Jeremiah flashed through her mind. Willie wouldn't have given him a dime, but this was different. Willie had always liked Julia, and she was responsible, wouldn't squander it . . .

Julia didn't say anything, but Alva felt her sister's body go stiff. "What is it? What's wrong?"

Julia turned and looked at her. "For a moment there, you were starting to sound like yourself again. You were doing fine until you mentioned the money. You just had to bring that up, didn't you?"

"Now, Julia—"

"You were always so ashamed of being poor. I never understood that. We were still the same people, we just had less money. And it wasn't like we were poor because we were bad people or because we did something to deserve it. We just had a streak of bad luck is all. Could have happened to anyone. I thought you would have learned something from that."

"I did. I learned that I never want to be poor again."

"You still don't get it."

"Oh, come on now, Julia. I'm just trying to help—"

"I don't need your help. I didn't ask for it. I don't want your money. And I'm not impressed by your big fancy house or your clothes or all your wealth, so you don't need to flaunt it." She turned and started to walk away.

"Julia . . . at least let me give you a ride back."

"No thank you. I'd rather take the train."

She watched her sister walk away, and it was only her pride that kept Alva from chasing after her. Did Julia think Alva had forgotten what it was like to go hungry, to go without? If she hadn't married Willie, who knows what might have become of her?

There was a time when all she wanted was to take Mrs. Astor's place. Now, for the life of her, she couldn't understand why. It was all such a silly game. Julia had just made her realize that she no longer knew how to reach out to people just as herself. She always relied on her money, thinking she had to impress them. It was exhausting. Something as simple as paying a friendly social call required wearing just the right dress and jewels. She thought about how much she'd spent on Emily's wedding present, on all the birthday presents for her children. She'd done the same for Tessie's children and had thrown elaborate dinner parties for Ophelia and even Mamie—whom she didn't really like—and so many others that she'd lost count. When Consuelo became Viscountess Mandeville, Alva worried Duchy would no longer think she was worthy of her friendship. In part, she'd even thrown her masquerade ball hoping to prove herself to her oldest, dearest friend. She'd even tried to buy the press. Though she never doubted her bond with Jeremiah, she wished she'd spent more time trying to understand his troubles, rather than trying to pay them off. There was no denying it; Alva led with her money because, without it, she didn't believe she had anything of value to offer.

Alva turned back to the headstones, watching her mother's and father's names blur through her tears. She felt lost as she dropped to her knees, praying for guidance, help in finding her way back to herself again. And she prayed that, despite it all, her mother would still have been proud of her, and that her father would have realized that a daughter was just as good as a son after all.

CHAPTER THIRTY-SIX

Caroline

"WHY?" CARRIE ASKED, STANDING in her father's library, hands on her hips. "Give me one good reason."

Caroline looked up from her needlepoint. A deep vertical crease had formed between Carrie's brows. William cleared his throat, not saying a thing. Orme Marshall Wilson had just asked for Carrie's hand in marriage, and William said no and had the young man escorted out of the house.

Orme may have been handsome, intelligent and well-mannered, but his family had amassed their fortune in the railroads, which was a strike against him. Plus, his father was known as a swindler who'd made a good sum of money during the Civil War by selling soldiers woolen blankets that had turned out to be cotton. Besides, the Wilsons were friendly with the Vanderbilts.

"But you let Emily marry James," Carrie said, her voice still calm, reasonable, but those eyes steely, unwavering. "Well?"

Caroline looked at William, his fingertips pressed into the arms on his club chair. They had never told their children about the duel. William didn't want them knowing that the only reason they'd let Emily marry James was to save their father from imminent death. He didn't want them thinking he'd been a coward.

"This is different," said Caroline.

"How so?" Carrie folded her arms. She didn't raise her voice. She seemed so composed, so determined.

Caroline glanced back at William. His fingertips were turning white. "It just is," Caroline said, pushing her embroidery needle through the hooped fabric. "For one thing, Orme Wilson is a fortune hunter." It was true. All the Wilson boys were known for acquiring even greater wealth by marrying into families with money—mostly new money. They were known as *the Marrying Wilsons*.

"Your mother's right," said William, getting up from his chair, going to the sideboard and pouring himself a drink. "All he wants is your money."

"Please don't insult my intelligence," said Carrie. "I know he loves me for *me*. And I love him."

Caroline paused her embroidery needle. "Your father and I are only thinking of what's best for you."

"If that's true, you'll let me marry Orme."

"Get the idea out of your head," warned William. "You are not marrying him."

"This conversation is pointless." Carrie turned and started for the door.

"You get back here, young lady," said William.

But Carrie kept walking, stopping just before she reached the doorway. "I think it's best that I leave now," she said, looking back over her shoulder. "If I stay another minute, I'm likely to say something we'll all regret." Throwing the French doors open, she walked out to the hall, dignified and measured as she climbed the stairs. She was completely in control until they heard her bedroom door bang shut all the way down in the library.

Caroline looked at William, who was refilling his glass. "I'll go talk to her," she said.

Standing outside Carrie's room, Caroline straightened the portraits that had been knocked off-kilter when Carrie slammed her door. She was trying to reason with Carrie, trying to convince her to let her inside.

"Go away, Mother. Please, just leave me alone."

"Carrie." She knocked again. "You unlock this door right this minute. I want to have a word with you." Caroline was about to give up, when she heard the light padding of footsteps, followed by the turning of the latch. *Thank goodness.*

Caroline stepped over Carrie's shoes that were lying in the center of the room, kicked off along with her ribbed lavender stockings that were balled up on the floor. Her dress was slumped in the seat of a chair by the open window, the drapes stirring in the breeze. Carrie was down to her union suit, her plaited light brown hair hanging down to her waist. Had it not been for her puffy eyes, the red nose and flushed cheeks from a previous crying bout, Caroline would not have known she'd shed a tear. When she came face-to-face with Carrie, her eyes were dry, her position unflappable.

"I know it's hard to understand, but this is for the best," Caroline said.

"I know what's best for me. I'm not like Helen and Charlotte. Helen married Rosy just to please you. Charlotte married Coleman because you left her no choice, and she's been miserable with him ever since. You broke her heart when you sent Duncan away, and you have no idea how she's suffered with Coleman. I'm sorry, Mother, but I'm not backing down on this. I can't. This is my life and I *am* going to marry Orme."

Carrie was so matter-of-fact it was unnerving, and Caroline knew she had to be equally composed, even more so. "If you feel so strongly," said Caroline, tranquil, outwardly calm, "then I suggest you and Mr. Wilson elope."

Carrie looked as if she'd been expecting this. She was prepared. "That won't serve either one of us, Mother, and you know it. Society doesn't look favorably upon elopements, and I'm sure you'd rather not have the family dragged into a scandal. I was raised an Astor and I'm not willing to give that up. I won't have society turn its back on me. I plan to marry the man I love *and* have my place in society. And we both know I can't have that without your blessings."

Caroline was taken aback. Carrie's rational reasoning had thrown her off. She'd dealt with her daughters' anger, their hysterics, their childish antics, but this was a cool, even exchange and she realized that Carrie had learned all this from Caroline herself. The way she held Caroline's gaze, the irritating logic she used, the steady cadence to her voice. It was much the same way Caroline argued with William. She didn't know how to respond. So she left Carrie, sitting on her bed, staring at the wall. She'd try talking to her again later.

When it was time for supper, Carrie refused to come downstairs and didn't eat a morsel from the tray that Thomas had taken to her room. The next morning, she hadn't touched her breakfast, either.

"You have to eat something," Caroline said.

"I'm not hungry."

Now it had been three days since Carrie had eaten anything. Not a bite of food, not a drop of water. Trays were taken to her room and removed hours later, untouched. When glasses of water and cups of tea were brought to her, Carrie simply turned her face away.

"What is this?" Caroline asked. "What are you trying to prove?"

"I'm going to marry Orme. And I *expect* you and Father to give us your blessing. It's just that simple."

So it was a test of wills, Caroline's versus Carrie's. One thing Caroline knew was that her daughter had the upper hand. She was in control of the situation, and all Caroline could do was wait it out.

After two more days, she became concerned. Carrie hadn't even had so much as a sip of water. She was complaining of a terrible headache but still refused to eat or drink anything. On the sixth day, when Caroline saw that Carrie was running a fever, she sent for the doctor.

"Your daughter is suffering from severe dehydration," he said, stepping out into the hallway after examining Carrie. "She's very weak. Her blood pressure is extremely low, and unless you can get her to eat, I'm afraid we'll have to induce feeding."

After the doctor left, Caroline went back inside Carrie's room. "You have to start eating. This has gone on long enough."

"Do I have your blessings to marry Orme?"

Caroline refused to budge and sent for Charlotte, who came by later that day.

"Maybe you can get through to her," said Caroline, following Charlotte upstairs.

"Mother." Charlotte stopped and turned around, her expression telling Caroline she wanted to talk to her sister in private.

Caroline raised her hands in surrender, despite feeling left out, even a bit hurt. After Charlotte slipped inside Carrie's room and closed the door behind her, Caroline found herself standing alone in the hallway. She went to her dressing room and began organizing a drawer of hatpins. For nearly half an hour she arranged them according to length but, of course, that fell apart when she took it further, attempting to divide them again by style, the emeralds and sapphires on the gold stems intermixed with the silver stems. Abandoning the task as hopeless, she went back out to the hallway—Carrie's door was still shut and she could hear the girls whispering back and forth. Caroline returned to her room, sorted through the day's mail and waited some more.

An hour later Charlotte appeared in the doorway.

"Well?" said Caroline, setting her pen down. "What did she say? Is she going to eat?"

Charlotte shook her head. She looked exhausted. "It's no good, Mother. I tried but she won't listen."

The next day the doctor came back. This time with his nurse.

Together the three of them went into Carrie's room. "Young lady," the doctor said, "unless you agree to start eating, I'm going to have to force-feed you. It won't be pleasant. Do you understand?"

Carrie shook her head, her mouth shut.

"Very well then, let's get started."

"Wait"—Caroline spoke up—"let me talk to her. Carrie, listen to what the doctor's saying. You must start eating. You don't want him to force you."

But Carrie just looked at her mother and shook her head.

"Have it your way, then." The doctor reached into his bag. "You've left me no choice."

Once again Caroline asked the doctor to wait. "She'll come around—I know she will. Couldn't we wait just a little longer?" She looked at all the heavy apparatus he was pulling from his bag. "Is this absolutely necessary?"

The doctor looked at Caroline. "It's absolutely necessary unless you want your daughter to die."

Die! Caroline knew it was serious, but until that moment she'd been denying that this was a matter of life and death. She couldn't go through this again. She couldn't lose another daughter.

"Carrie, did you hear what the doctor said? You'll die—if you don't eat, you'll die."

"You might want to wait out in the hall until we're finished," said the doctor, moving ahead.

But Caroline refused to leave and stood in the corner watching the nurse hold Carrie still while the doctor strapped her arms down. Carrie fought with what little strength she had left, kicking out her legs. The doctor raised a horrible-looking metal clamp.

"Now open up."

But Carrie kept her mouth sealed shut.

"Come on now, Carrie," he said.

She had no fight left in her as the doctor pried her jaw open and shoved the metal clamp inside her mouth. With the twisting of the screws on either side, the clamp forced her mouth open wider and wider. The alarm in Carrie's eyes was unbearable for Caroline, and when she saw the doctor pull the tube from his bag, she wanted to stop him but froze in place, helpless. When he forced the tube down Carrie's throat, she started choking, her eyes flooding with tears as blood trickled from her mouth where the clamp had cut her. As soon as the feeding began, Carrie's eyes bulged even wider and her restrained body writhed as she gagged.

"Now calm down," said the doctor. "Relax or it'll just come back up on you and we'll have to do it all over again."

Carrie was so weak, so pale. So very pale.

For a moment, Caroline was back at Emily's bedside, her daughter's face so pale, her body so still. Something clenched deep inside Caroline's heart. There was nothing she could have done to save Emily, but Carrie—Carrie had brought this on herself. Or was it Caroline who'd caused it?

As much as she didn't want Carrie to throw her future away, Caroline would be damned if she let another daughter die in front of her eyes.

"Stop it! Stop! Oh, my dear God, stop it!" She pulled the funnel from the doctor's hand. "Marry Orme," she said, pushing the doctor out of the way as she pulled Carrie close. Holding her frail body, Caroline rocked her daughter in her arms. "Go on, marry him. Just don't you dare die on me."

THE
FOUR
HUNDRED

1890–1894

CHAPTER THIRTY-SEVEN

Society

NEW YORK, 1890

AS WE USHER IN a new decade, we no longer know where the smart set leaves off and we begin. The line between *them* and *us* is starting to blur and oftentimes that line is crossed. Puss was actually invited to Carrie Astor Wilson's latest dinner party. Mrs. Astor was there and Puss reported back that "she has very tiny teeth." Ward McAllister promised Lydia the first autographed copy of his memoir. And many of us have been to luncheons, dinners and balls where Mrs. Astor is seated on one side of the hostess and Alva on the other. It's as if we have two queens now.

Not that Alva or Mrs. Astor seems too pleased with the new arrangement. They continue to spar in their own ways; Alva hurls insults behind Mrs. Astor's back, and Mrs. Astor humiliates Alva with her haughty rebuffs.

We hear, though, that Mrs. Astor is not quite as restrained when it comes to dealing with her nephew, Waldorf. Rumor has it the two are engaged in a feud of their own. And over a calling card!

The trouble started several months ago when Mrs. Astor had her new calling cards engraved to simply read *The Mrs. Astor*. Well, Waldorf thought it was disrespectful to his mother and his wife, who are also Mrs. Astors. Honestly, how absurd! We all know who *The Mrs. Astor* is. She isn't Augusta. She isn't Mary. She's Caroline Webster Schermerhorn Astor. She's earned that title. Still, the two of them, Mrs. Astor and her nephew, had a big row over it and we thought that was the end of it. But no!

Waldorf inherited a fortune after the recent passing of his father, making him one of the three wealthiest men in the country. A mantle he now shares with Cornelius and Willie Vanderbilt who, by the way, inherited the majority of Billy Vanderbilt's $232 million estate when he passed five years ago.

But back to the present—Waldorf has decided to use his newfound wealth to retaliate against *The* Mrs. Astor. He has torn down his father's home and has plans to build a hotel—*of all things*—on that very site, right next door to Mrs. Astor's townhouse. If there's one thing we know about *The* Mrs. Astor, it's that she's exceedingly private. The thought of living next to a hotel must have her unhinged.

CHAPTER THIRTY-EIGHT

Caroline

CAROLINE OPENED THE DOOR to her library and saw dust motes dancing in the sliver of sunlight coming through the parting of the drapes. Despite her staff cleaning the house top to bottom every morning, by noon each day she could see that a fresh film of dust had settled onto the furniture, dulling the rich luster of her mahogany tables, the hardwood floors and millwork. Even with the windows closed, the dirt found its way inside, not to mention the noise: the deafening sound of chisels and mallets against the striking blocks, the grinding of the mortising machines running, the steady hum of the saws and hammers. It went on five, sometimes six days a week and started early in the morning, lasting well into the afternoon. She could feel the constant pounding reverberating inside her chest, throbbing in her temples. At times the foundation of her house shook, leaving the crystal chandeliers tinkling and her precious artwork hanging crooked on the walls.

The racket outside her window was relentless, and just when the pounding seemed to fall into a steady pattern that she could almost push to the background, there would be a jolt, mixing it all up. If chaos had a sound, this was it. She ran her fingers over an end table, leaving a clean track in the dust. She was disgusted. They were still only in the early stages of construction. She figured it would be another year or two before Waldorf's hotel was completed.

The hammering and thunderous pounding came to a sudden stop, replaced by an eerie calm. It was so quiet she heard a bird chirping. The construction workers must have been on their lunch break, and so Caroline took that time to settle into her reclining chair and started reading Ward McAllister's memoir, *Society as I Have Found It*.

When he'd first told Caroline that he was going to follow that reporter's advice and write his memoirs, she cautioned him to tread carefully. Though he assured her he wasn't going to name names, she was uneasy about the book. And yet, she had to admit she was curious. The day it was published, Caroline had sent her social secretary to the bookstore for a copy, which had sat on her shelf for the past week. Caroline's calendar was surprisingly light that day and it was the first opportunity she'd had to begin reading.

The memoir was over 400 pages, beginning with his childhood and upbringing, all told in tedious detail. Just five pages in and already she was bored. As she read on, his prose became more self-indulgent, and she grew embarrassed for him. Caroline found herself wincing as she read about his travels abroad and his command of etiquette. Frankly, the book was so poorly written that she was surprised anyone would have agreed to publish it. Thankfully she hadn't suggested that she and Thomas read it aloud together. *Why make us both suffer?* But Caroline was not one to abandon a book, feeling an obligation to finish what was started, so she pressed on despite the construction noise, which had resumed.

She was slogging through the pages, feeling a bit detached, until she came to CHAPTER XVII, A GOLDEN AGE OF FEASTING. She recognized herself immediately, even before he got to the part where he'd referred to her as a "Grande Dame." Bits and pieces jumped out at her:

AT THIS PERIOD, A GREAT PERSONAGE . . . HAD DAUGHTERS TO
INTRODUCE INTO SOCIETY . . . SHE POSSESSED GREAT ADMINIS-
TRATIVE POWER . . . CIRCUMSTANCES FORCED HER TO ASSUME
THE LEADERSHIP . . . HAVING A GREAT FORTUNE, SHE HAD THE
ABILITY TO CONCEIVE AND CARRY OUT SOCIAL PROJECTS . . .
QUICK TO CRITICISE ANY DEFECT OF LIGHTING OR ORNAMENTA-
TION, OR ARRANGEMENT, SHE . . . MADE THESE BALLS WHAT
THEY WERE IN THE PAST . . .

In the past? Caroline was speechless. Mortified. She felt betrayed.
He said he wasn't naming names but he had still exposed her and
violated her privacy. The more she read, the more furious she became.

By the time she'd reached CHAPTER XXVI, AN ERA OF EXTRAVAGANCE,
where he described Alva Vanderbilt's masquerade ball, Caroline was
beside herself:

WE HERE REACH A PERIOD WHEN NEW YORK SOCIETY TURNED
OVER A NEW LEAF. UP TO THIS TIME, FOR ONE TO BE WORTH A
MILLION DOLLARS WAS TO BE RATED AS A MAN OF FORTUNE, BUT
NOW, BYGONES MUST BE BYGONES. NEW YORK'S IDEAS AS TO
VALUES, WHEN FORTUNE WAS NAMED, LEAPED BOLDLY UP TO
TEN MILLIONS, FIFTY MILLIONS, ONE HUNDRED MILLIONS, AND
THE NECESSITIES AND LUXURIES FOLLOWED SUIT.

Caroline was so agitated she had to pause and collect herself before she could continue reading about a certain masquerade ball and
the hostess who had unseated the queen.

CHAPTER THIRTY-NINE

Alva

THE NIGHT BEFORE CONSUELO's thirteenth birthday party, Alva went to her daughter's bedroom carrying a big box, lavishly wrapped with a pink satin bow. Consuelo was fast asleep when Alva placed the box on her bed, gently shaking her awake. With sleep in her eyes, her dark hair strewn across her pillow, Consuelo began to stir.

"Happy birthday eve," Alva said, perched on the edge of the bed. Now that Consuelo was becoming a young woman, Alva had something special to give her, something she wanted her daughter to open in private, and it couldn't wait for the morning. Celebrating the eve of her children's birthdays was something her mother had always done for Alva and her sisters. She'd crawl into bed beside them or pull them onto her lap, or as they got older, she'd sit with them at the table, teacups between them, while she'd recount their births, which she no doubt edited for their sake. Alva had arrived early and fast. *You were in such a hurry to start torturing me*, her mother used to say playfully.

Consuelo sat up, the pillows propping her up from behind.

"Well, go on, open it."

Consuelo smiled as she carefully removed the bow and peeled back the wrapping paper.

"You're not a child anymore," Alva said, reaching over to help

Consuelo lift the lid off the box. "You're a young lady now and this is exactly what you need."

Consuelo reached inside the box and pulled out a steel pole contraption with leather straps. She turned to Alva. "Mamma? What is it?"

"It's going to straighten that posture of yours. Now stand up and let's put it on." She sounded excited, as if it were a new dress to try on. "C'mon now." Alva threw off the blankets. "Let's make sure it fits good and snug."

Consuelo gingerly stepped out of the bed, her bare feet landing on the hardwood floor. Alva stood next to her, instructing Consuelo to turn around as she tugged on the leather straps and aligned the pole with her spine.

"Oh, Mamma, it's so cold."

"Now just stand still. It's almost on." She held the pole in place, while fitting the brace about her hips to stabilize it. Lastly, she placed the leather straps over her shoulders and about her forehead. "There. Now how's that?"

"It hurts, Mamma. It's pinching me."

"Oh, you'll get used to that. It's the surest way to correct your posture." She saw some correlation between her daughter's curved spine and the way Consuelo always conformed and bent to the stronger will of others. Alva hoped the brace would not only straighten Consuelo's spine, but also give her a backbone, a dose of confidence to stand up for herself. Though Alva didn't necessarily want Consuelo to be like she was as a child—oh heavens no—she did want her girl to fight for herself, to say no to Alva. Just once.

"Straight posture is a must for a young lady searching for a husband," Alva said, still inspecting the fit.

"But I'm not searching for a husband."

"Maybe not yet. But it's never too early to start thinking about your future. You're going to marry well. We just have to straighten that spine of yours." She helped Consuelo out of the back brace, crawled back into bed with her firstborn, and then, like her mother had done, Alva recounted the day Consuelo was born.

When she was done, Consuelo's eyes were heavy with sleep. Alva reached over, kissed her forehead and turned down the lamp. "Happy birthday. Sleep tight."

After she'd checked in on the boys, she went downstairs to her sitting room and was just starting to read Ward McAllister's memoir when Willie K. came through the front door, held up by Oliver Belmont, the two of them reeking of whiskey. Willie's hair and clothes were rumpled, his words slurring together, making no sense whenever he attempted to speak. Alva was disgusted and could hardly bring herself to look at him.

After the footman helped Willie to his room, Oliver turned to Alva and said, "Don't be too hard on him. It was *all* my doing."

"Sure it was," she said with a harsh laugh, folding her arms across her chest.

"I realize you're perturbed. And"—he raised his hands—"rightfully so, but I swear the girl was with me."

The girl? There was a girl involved? That hadn't even crossed her mind. Something caught in Alva's chest, squeezing hard.

"I swear she was with me. Willie hardly said two words to her the entire night."

"Thou dost protest too much."

"No, no," he laughed drunkenly. "I swear Willie was a perfect gentleman, whereas I, on the other hand, was an absolute scoundrel."

She looked at him, so cocksure, so convinced he could charm his way out of this. "You? A scoundrel, Mr. Belmont? I'd like to see that."

"Oh, would you now?" He raised a suggestive eyebrow.

That little gesture of his threw her off-kilter. She excused herself, hopefully before he noticed the blush surfacing on her cheeks.

Alva didn't sleep well that night. She was disturbed by *the girl* who was supposedly with Oliver. There had been another girl in Willie's past, a woman, really. It was about five years ago, right after Billy died and Willie inherited all that money. Alva heard that Willie had been seen at Sherry's with this other woman. A brunette, about Alva's age. Willie of course denied it, but then he turned around and bought that $650,000 yacht and named it the *Alva* just to make himself feel better for being an unfaithful husband.

She thought they'd moved beyond that, but now she was worried again. She tossed about, thinking how Willie seemed more distant lately, and tried to remember the last time they'd had relations. Then, out of nowhere, she caught herself thinking about Oliver Belmont. That suggestive eyebrow of his taunted her, rising over and over again.

The next day, during the party, Alva observed the festivities with a sense of detachment. Conversations barely registered with her as she stood back and watched Consuelo, the guest of honor, talking with Mamie Fish and Lady Paget, with Ophelia Meade and Penelope Easton. Her daughter was blossoming into a woman before her eyes. She was as beautiful as her father was handsome, but more than that, she had her own style, demure but endearing. Alva saw how gracious Consuelo was, how at ease she appeared. Her daughter had the makings of a natural hostess. All the things that Alva had worked so hard to master seemed innate to Consuelo. Alva should have been pleased. After all, she'd fought to get into society for the sake of her children—especially her daughter. But she could see now that one day, Consuelo would outshine her, and that left Alva with an undeniable and shameful pang of jealousy.

Alva kept a smile on her face, but she was sinking. Oliver, whom she'd tried to avoid, sought her out, crossing the room with such swagger she would have thought he was six feet tall.

"I hope you've found it in your heart to forgive me for delivering your husband to you in such a compromised state last night."

"You're forgiven," she said, though she didn't mean it. "I have just one question for you: Who was the girl?"

"A gentleman doesn't kiss and tell."

"A gentleman?" she laughed, forgetting herself for a moment. "I thought you were a scoundrel." *Now why did you go and say that? And why is he smiling like that?*

She excused herself and went back to worrying about Willie K., keeping an eye on him throughout the night: Who was he talking to? Was he standing too close to Lydia? Was he laughing a little too gaily at something Tessie just said? Where was he now? Who was with him? It was agony.

After the cake had been served and the last guests left Petit Chateau, Willie K. came up to Alva and stood behind her. All night long she'd been waiting for him to come to her, pay her some attention, and now that he had, she didn't want it. She knew he was going to place his hands on her shoulders even before he did it, and it took all her will not to shrug them off.

"You've been awfully quiet tonight," he said.

"Have I?" She was grateful that her back was to him. She could feel heat coming up on her cheeks. He was acting as if nothing were wrong, as if he hadn't been out half the night with Oliver and some *girl*. And even if he'd been a perfect gentleman and Oliver was the scoundrel, shouldn't Willie have apologized? Explained himself? She'd wanted to confront him, but women—wives—didn't do that.

Though Willie didn't say anything, didn't apologize, he must have known she was upset because, with his fingers gently kneading her shoulders, he said, "I've been thinking about Newport. About what you were saying about building a new cottage up there."

"Oh?" For years now, she'd been begging Willie for a new cottage in Newport. She had tried reasoning with him, explaining that she was bored, that she needed something more stimulating. Something for herself. She'd pleaded, being sweet as punch, and it had gotten her nowhere. She'd tried bullying him into it, too, and still he'd re-fused.

"I think it's time," he said.

If that wasn't the sound of a guilty man, she didn't know what was. She turned and looked at him.

"How would you feel about designing a brand-new place?" he said. "From the ground up."

Before she could stop herself, she was hugging him, thanking him. He was no fool, but neither was she. Alva had just gotten what she'd wanted, her reward for being the good, obedient wife.

CHAPTER FORTY

Caroline

IT HAD BEEN A week since Caroline finished *Society as I Have Found It*. By then others had read it, too, and the mocking of Ward McAllister had begun, as uproarious as the construction next door. The press was merciless, running headlines such as THIS NOB IS A SNOB and THE FRAPPÉ FLOP. One article in *Town Topics* suggested that MR. MCALLISTER IS CANOODLING WITH MRS. ASTOR. Caroline was horrified. For many reasons, but especially that one, she had been avoiding Ward, forgoing a week of balls, dinner parties and opera performances. She didn't want to be seen anywhere near him, and what's more, she didn't know what to say to him.

She thought he would have been devastated by such criticism and public shaming, but if so, it wasn't at all apparent to Caroline the day he finally appeared at her home.

He looked prim and crisp, a yellow boutonniere in his lapel, a new walking stick in hand. He was full of apologies, not for what he'd written about her, but for his not having called on her sooner.

"But don't you know, I've been in such demand with my book." The steady pounding next door hadn't let up since he'd arrived. "That racket is maddening," he said, turning toward the window. "Now tell me"—he faced back around—"how have you been? I've been splendid, don't you know. All the fanfare has been exhilarating." He smiled, as if he hadn't picked up a newspaper or visited a gentlemen's club during the past two weeks.

He was chattering away and pacing before finally settling into the chair opposite Caroline's. She braced herself for the inevitable question, and sure enough, he leaned in on his walking stick and said, "Now tell me, what did you think of my book?"

Caroline was silent.

"You *have* read my book, haven't you?" He was incredulous at even having to ask.

Caroline had never lied to Ward and she wasn't about to start now. "I have."

"And?"

She could see how very eager he was for praise. Caroline looked into his eyes and said, "I think you've gone too far."

"Oh, I know," he chuckled, seemingly unaware that she was warning him. Or maybe he just didn't want to acknowledge it. "Bookstores can hardly keep it on the shelves."

Caroline looked at him, amazed. He seemed lost in a cloud of his own making. Well, she was about to shatter his illusions, tell him exactly what she thought of his pompous memoir and how offended she'd been by the things he'd written, when William and Coleman Drayton burst into the drawing room.

She was startled. *Why on earth are the two of them together?* William detested Coleman's company. A jolt of adrenaline shot through her. Caroline was on her feet, her heart racing. "What's happened? What's wrong? Is it Charlotte? The children?"

William turned to McAllister. "If you'll excuse us, Ward."

"Oh dear, no." Caroline felt her legs go weak as she dropped back down in her chair.

"I have to be running along anyway," Ward said, cocking his bowler just so. "I have a meeting with my publisher."

After he left and Thomas had closed the double doors, Coleman took a seat beside Caroline, his leg anxiously jouncing up and down. Together they watched William walk over to the fireplace and rest his elbow on the mantel.

Their silence was unnerving. "Will someone please say something? Tell me what's going on."

William cleared his throat and finally said, "I'm afraid that Coleman has some distressing news about Charlie and the state of their marriage."

"Oh?" *That was it?* She felt relieved. Every marriage had its problems. She and William were proof of that. This idea of marrying for love was such a modern concept. Caroline couldn't comprehend it. Marriage was a practical union, a means by which to continue the family bloodlines, perpetuate the family wealth. Helen understood that. She and Rosy had made a fine marriage and family together. But Carrie had followed her heart and Jack had, too. Her son had recently become engaged to Miss Ava Lowle Willing. Caroline didn't approve of the match, but she did see that Miss Willing had a positive effect on Jack. For once he seemed interested in something other than food and had reduced his husky frame down to a slender, fit physique like the rest of the Astor men. Caroline realized with a stab of guilt that it had been love and affection her son was starved for, not food.

So Charlotte and Coleman had their differences. *Pish-posh.* So theirs wasn't a marriage of love and passion. So few were. She knew Charlotte had been unhappy from time to time. Many a wife was dissatisfied with her husband. That's why the children were so important. Frankly, Caroline was surprised that William and Coleman were making such a fuss over the matter.

"What kind of marriage trouble?" she asked finally, somewhat distracted.

Coleman spoke up for the first time. "Your daughter has been carrying on with our neighbor, Hallett Borrowe."

Carrying on! That got Caroline's attention. The shock of it crackled in her ears. She was accustomed to husbands breaking their vows, but a wife and mother? *Never!*

"It's been going on for some time," said Coleman.

Caroline couldn't believe her daughter was capable of such a thing. She looked at William but he wouldn't meet her eye. "How do you know it's true?"

Coleman's cheeks began to color. "I'd rather not say in mixed company. But trust me when I tell you that I have proof. After I discovered the two of them—and in my own home, I might add—I threatened divorce."

"Oh heavens no," said Caroline. This time when she looked at William, he was rubbing his temples, his eyes closed. Divorce would be too great a scandal for the Astor family. "You mustn't even think of such a thing," said Caroline. "These matters can be worked through."

"I thought so, too," said Coleman. "After I found out about the affair, Charlotte wrote me a letter." He produced a piece of Charlotte's stationery from his breast pocket, a trifold, well creased as if read over and over again. "She confessed to her affair with Borrowe—it's all right here, in her own hand." He held out the letter. "She promised to never see him again."

"Very well then," said Caroline. "See? The matter is resolved."

"I'm afraid not. Charlotte is still carrying on with that miscreant. And you should know—he's a married man, too."

"Oh dear God." Just when Caroline thought it couldn't get any worse.

"I can't tolerate that kind of behavior or expose my children to such things. I've tried talking sense into Charlotte, but she claims she can't help herself." He shook his head, tugging on his shirt cuffs. "I have no choice but to move ahead with divorce proceedings."

"No, no, no," said Caroline. "We can't allow that to happen. Especially because of the children. I will talk to Charlotte."

But when she did speak with Charlotte later that day, Caroline's daughter only repeated what Coleman had already said: "I can't help myself."

"Well, you'd best learn to *help yourself*, young lady. Your husband is threatening to divorce you over this."

Charlotte didn't say anything. She seemed more interested in the flowers in her parlor, lazily rearranging the lilies in a cut-glass vase.

"Do you have any idea what a divorce would do to your reputation?"

"Is that all you care about? My reputation?" She stabbed a stem into the vase. "What about my happiness? I'm miserable with Coleman. I don't love him. I never did. You knew I loved Duncan and you forced me to marry Coleman. I was devastated over Duncan. For years. And then I met Hallett. He's the only happiness I've known since I got married."

"Just because you want something doesn't mean you can have it," said Caroline. "What about your children?"

"I know you don't want to hear this, Mother," she said, still busying herself with those flowers, "but I'm glad Coleman found out about Hallett. I *wanted* him to find out about us. I *want* Coleman to divorce me."

"And what then? Hallett is a married man."

"He'll leave his wife—I know he will. He doesn't love her. He'll divorce her and we'll get married."

"Charlotte, you don't know what you're saying. Divorce is not an option."

She finally abandoned the flowers and looked Caroline in the eyes for the first time. "I can't stay in a marriage when I'm this unhappy. I just can't."

You don't have a choice, Caroline wanted to say. Charlotte's biggest problem, the source of her pain, was that she actually *believed* she had a right to have what her heart desired. "If you divorce, you would never be welcome in the world in which you were raised. You would tarnish your children's reputations right along with your own. You would be an outcast, and that, my dear, is a very lonely existence. Much lonelier than staying married to Coleman. And your father will not tolerate it. He'll disown you. I'm certain of it."

Charlotte looked up, her eyes wide, her mouth open. "You can't be doing this to me again. You just can't." As much as she claimed not to care about her family's wealth, as much as she said she didn't want to be another rich girl, it was always the money that pulled her back in line.

"I mean it, Charlotte. You won't receive a penny."

Charlotte looked up. Finally understanding the gravity of what she'd done. "So I'm trapped. Is that what you're saying? I'm trapped in this marriage? Forever?" Charlotte covered her face with her hands, her shoulders quaking as the tears slipped through her fingertips, mumbling incoherently.

"You have to stay in the marriage—that's all there is to it. That is, if your husband will let you."

Caroline knew that the decision was entirely up to Coleman, who had every right to seek a divorce.

Twenty minutes later, Caroline showed up at her son-in-law's office, handsomely appointed and paneled in Circassian walnut. He had a marble bust of himself stationed on his desk, which he leaned up against, arms folded, listening to her offer.

"$5,000," she said. "Annually."

Coleman sighed and looked up toward the coffered ceiling. "In exchange for *what*, exactly?"

"For staying married to my daughter. And for your discretion."

Coleman lowered his chin and uncrossed his arms, stuffing his hands inside his pockets. He seemed to be weighing her offer. He knew what divorce would do to his own reputation, and of course Caroline knew he was considering the children. "What about your daughter's discretion?" he asked.

"Charlotte has given me her word that she won't see him again. She's filled with remorse."

He turned down his bottom lip and with a nod, said, "$7,000. $7,000 annually and I'll stop divorce proceedings."

"Very well."

He raised both eyebrows. "I thought you might have wanted to think about it. I should have asked for $10,000."

Caroline smiled grimly. "I would have paid you $20,000."

CHAPTER FORTY-ONE

Society

NEWPORT AND NEW YORK, 1891–1892

WE ALL TOLD ALVA not to do it. We told her time and again that it was a bad idea. That, in fact, it was a terrible idea. But would she listen? Hardly. She wanted to build a new cottage in Newport, and of all the lots she could have purchased, she bought the one on Bellevue Avenue right next door to Beechwood, Mrs. Astor's cottage.

Clearly she is taunting the Grande Dame, which puts Alva in a bit of a quandary. As much as she wants to be accepted by Mrs. Astor, she wants to usurp her more.

Alva bought that cottage—a modest nothing sort of place—about a year ago and hired Richard Morris Hunt, the same architect who built her home on Fifth Avenue. She's being very secretive about it all, which isn't Alva's style. Usually she's so boastful about everything, but not this. As soon as they tore the old cottage down, she had Hunt put up a fence all the way around the property. This fence has to be at least ten feet high. We can't see a thing going on behind it, and it's not as if we haven't tried. Every now and again while on our daily strolls, some of us have tried stealing looks through the slats, but we can't see a thing.

We're all back in New York now. It's the third Monday of January, the eve of Mrs. Astor's annual ball. We rise to a cold, blustery day, drafts sweeping across our floorboards. The boilers in our cellars are clunking, the coal furnaces working overtime. It's snowing, too. Big, heavy wet flakes that drench all the morning newspapers. They arrive on our breakfast trays crinkly and wavy, despite our staff having ironed them dry.

We lazily go through *Town Topics* and the *World*, and as we set those papers aside, we move on to the *New York Times*. With just a glance, we are all wide awake. An entire pot of coffee could not have given us a morning jolt like this. We look again at the headline: WARD MCALLISTER DECLARES NEW YORK SOCIETY COMPRISED OF ONLY 400 PEOPLE.

The article leads off by quoting McAllister: "THERE ARE ONLY ABOUT 400 PEOPLE IN FASHIONABLE NEW YORK SOCIETY. IF YOU GO OUTSIDE THAT NUMBER, YOU STRIKE PEOPLE WHO ARE EITHER NOT AT EASE IN A BALLROOM OR ELSE MAKE OTHERS NOT AT EASE." So there it is—a declaration. A finite number. A line drawn in Newport's privileged white sand. We wonder, has this clique of 400 always existed, and are we just now learning of it? A secret—like so many other things in their world, that's kept from us? Has this list of names been held in a safe somewhere, perhaps in the bowels of Mrs. Astor's townhouse? And why, on the eve of Mrs. Astor's ball, did Ward McAllister decide to publish the names of those members in high society?

Pulses up and down Fifth Avenue quicken. Heat crawls up our necks as we look farther down the page at the list. It's alphabetized, and we start in the *A*'s, our eyes racing over the columns. Certain names jump out at us: MR. AND MRS. JAMES L. BARCLAY, MR. AND MRS. CHAUNCEY M. DEPEW, MR. SHIPLEY JONES . . . Some of us, like Puss, Mamie and Lady Paget, are relieved and exhilarated to see their names on there. They're in, despite not having a drop of Knickerbocker blood. But Jay Gould is not on the list. Fanny and John Pierpont Morgan are not, and neither are the Rockefellers. Our hearts continue to pound. We see that MR. AND MRS. CORNELIUS VANDERBILT are in. So is GEORGE

W. VANDERBILT. We all expect to see Mr. and Mrs. William Kissam Vanderbilt next, but instead it's MRS. A. VAN RENSSELAER. *Van Rensselaer?* We pause. We back up as if we've misread. *Alice and Cornelius are on the list but Alva Vanderbilt isn't?*

The following evening, the event of the season has arrived. Mrs. Astor's ball! Those of us who, after all these years, have finally received a coveted invitation enter her townhouse not quite sure what to expect. What we find is an enchanted entranceway with more tulips, tropical palms and American Beauties than we've ever seen before. Ivy is wrapped about the marble staircase, and a sea of yellow tulips is stationed in the front parlor along with a chiffonier overflowing with yet more American Beauties.

This business of the list of 400 names looms in the air. We hear people whispering about it. Everyone seems to be on the lookout for Ward McAllister, who has yet to arrive. The big question on everyone's mind is: *Did Mrs. Astor know Ward was going to publish that list?* We can't tell because there she is, ever the consummate hostess, casting all gossip and speculation aside as she receives her guests. She sits on the raised dais, in her favorite throne-like banquette, beneath her life-size portrait. Dressed in her customary velvet, wearing a big wig, she is bejeweled in her diamond tiara, her diamond necklaces, a diamond stomacher and rings on five fingers. She sparkles, giving off a prism of light each time she moves.

By eleven o'clock a line has formed stretching all the way down to the first-floor landing. For those of us meeting Mrs. Astor for the first time, the anticipation is immense. We've waited years for this moment. And now we shall wait the better part of an hour until it's our turn. One by one, she greets her guests with a handshake and a cordial hello. Some get a mere welcoming nod. She manages to say a few words to the Livingstons and Belmonts, but when it comes time to receive Mamie Fish, Mrs. Astor only extends her hand.

It's Mamie who says, "Ward has certainly outdone himself this time, *don't you know*. That man is going to need a stepladder to get over himself. We should change his name to Ward Make-A-Lister." Mamie, who always enjoys her own wit, starts up with that laugh of hers.

Mrs. Astor doesn't so much as crack a smile.

Soon enough Ward McAllister arrives, and we observe him looking terribly proud of himself. He goes to greet Mrs. Astor but she raises her hand to stop him. She is angry. There's no mistaking that, and no mistaking that she had been caught off guard by his list, too. Ward reluctantly retreats, suddenly seeming smaller, his shoulders sagging; all his pomp has up and left him.

Frankly, it's hard for us to feel too sorry for him. He's brought this all on himself, and besides, he's hardly given any of us the time of day. And when he does, it's usually to criticize us for one thing or another. He's been especially hard on Lady Paget, denouncing her latest dinner party in the press because there was no meat course served. The paper neglected to mention that Lady Paget has joined a new non-flesh-eating movement. The next day, she sent Ward McAllister a fish—with the head and tail still attached.

As we continue to mingle, we're all aware of an unspoken emptiness around us, a void because Alva isn't here. Mrs. Astor may have been forced to recognize the Vanderbilts after the masquerade ball, but that doesn't mean she has to welcome them into her home.

Earlier that day, Alva made a point of telling Lady Paget and Ophelia and Penelope and Puss and anyone else she could find that she and Willie had been called out of town at the last minute. How convenient.

CHAPTER FORTY-TWO

Alva

ALVA INCHED DOWN THE hall, hands out in front, feeling her way through the darkness. She might as well have been blindfolded. She'd already turned too quickly coming out of her dressing room and stubbed her toe on the doorstop. She expected to make contact with the carved rounded banister any second, but it kept eluding her. She shuffled forward step-by-step, inch by inch, until finally, her finger-tips found the baluster. She took the stairs slowly, with caution. Throughout the house she could hear her servants also bumbling about in the dark.

When she made it to the first floor, she called out, "Willie?"

"We're back here. In the game room."

Alva followed the direction of his voice, which led her to where he and the children were riding out the night. There was just a hint of moonlight coming through the windows, barely etching the four of them, sitting close together. Willie was in the middle of a ghost story, and when he let out a big, loud *boo*, little eight-year-old Harold screamed and burst into tears.

"Now look what you've done, Willie." Alva couldn't make out Harold's face but she knew that scream, could picture his bottom lip quivering, his eyes squeezed shut.

"Me?" Willie snapped. "You're the one making us all sit in the dark."

"You're going to give them all nightmares," said Alva, pulling Harold onto her lap.

"Then turn up a lamp. Or light a candle for God's sake."

"No."

"This is ridiculous. Just one lamp. One candle."

"So help me, Willie K.," she said, gritting her teeth, "if you reach for that lamp, I'll break your fingers."

It was eleven o'clock. A few blocks south, Mrs. Astor's ball was already underway, and Alva had ordered all lights out at four o'clock, just before dusk. Not a single lamp or light remained on inside the whole mansion.

"But this is silly," said Willie.

But it wasn't silly to Alva. As soon as she saw that her name wasn't on that list, she told everyone she could think of that she and Willie had been called out of town unexpectedly, some sort of emergency down in Mobile. They were catching the five o'clock train, otherwise of course they would have been attending Mrs. Astor's ball.

"But they all know we weren't on that list," said Willie.

"That list is full of holes and errors." Several of the names that Ward gave the *New York Times* were flat-out wrong. Mr. Stanley Dunn had died of a heart attack the year before, and Mr. Herbert Franklin had also passed away; Marjorie Blundt had been entered once under her maiden name and a second time with her married name. "Everyone knows it's not accurate. They could still think we were *supposed* to be on it."

"That's absurd. And surely no one thinks all the servants have left town, too," he reasoned. "They wouldn't be in the house without any lights on."

"We gave them the night off," she growled.

"And how exactly are you going to explain your being back in town tomorrow?"

Oh, you do know how to provoke me, don't you! "We'll tell everyone we came back early," she said, knowing she wouldn't be able to show her face until evening.

"I will never understand you, Alva."

"And *I'll* never understand why *you can't understand* that I would rather sit here in the dark all night than let Mrs. Astor humiliate me. Again."

CHAPTER FORTY-THREE

Alva

ALVA TURNED UP THE fur collar on her overcoat and stuffed her hands deep inside her muff. It had snowed earlier and now the skies were clear, the sun glinting off the new blanket of accumulation, tree branches etched in white. She had just come from Hunt's office in the Village after reviewing the latest plans for the Newport cottage. As she was strolling by Washington Square Park, she came upon a crowd gathered near the arch; mostly women, young, old, some light-skinned, others dark. Some wearing babushkas, their faces lined, hands calloused. Others were dressed more like herself with fashion-able furs and wide-brimmed hats. Alva noticed only a handful of men, mostly police officers. A marching band in formation beyond a snowbank broke into a rousing rendition of "Hallelujah." Some of the women were wearing sashes over their coats and carrying signs and banners high: **VOTES FOR WOMEN**.

Standing before the crowd was a woman whose booming voice defied her petite stature. Alva was cold and hadn't planned to stop until she heard her say, "We as women need to unite in order to change the laws that keep us under our husbands' control." Alva ended up spending the next twenty minutes listening. ". . . We chal-lenge the laws that forbid a married woman to own her own land. We challenge the laws that say a woman cannot sign a legally binding contract. We challenge the laws that say a wife who *does* hold a job—who does earn her own money—be required to turn her wages over to her husband. We do not belong to the men of this world!" Alva marveled at the eruption of cheers and applause. The clapping was contagious, and she couldn't help but remove her muff and join in.

". . . Some say a woman's highest calling is to be a wife and mother, to keep a home. We say 'nonsense.' Some say that if women get the vote, we'll become masculine, we'll sprout whiskers and beards. We say 'utter nonsense.' We *will* get the vote and we *will* show them what we're capable of, what our highest calling truly is."

Alva clapped so hard her palms stung. Wasn't this what she'd been trying to prove ever since that day she'd found her father crying, asking God why he'd taken his only son and not one of his daughters? The band began playing again, and as Alva looked around at the women who'd come there from every corner of the city, she realized they were all the same. It didn't matter if they were rich or poor, young or old, they were all women first and foremost. And all of them were being held back, held down. No amount of money or status could free them.

The crowd began to disperse, and Alva headed up Fifth Avenue, deciding to walk despite the cold. Even though her toes were numb, her fingers stiff, she was exhilarated, filled with a daring energy that she knew couldn't be satisfied by the same old visits to Tiffany's or taking her children ice-skating or sledding in the park. Even with the work she was doing with Hunt on the cottage, she was still restless. She'd been searching for something more, certain there was *something* out there—waiting for her to uncover. Perhaps the suffrage movement was it.

Continuing along Fifth Avenue she found herself enamored of the architecture and the changes to the city. Hacks and carriages were lined up, moving slowly, steam rising from the piles of manure. Pushcart peddlers, bundled up in ill-fitting coats and fingerless gloves, were on nearly every corner. When she came to Twenty-Third Street, she saw the familiar blue awning of the Glenham Hotel and something caught in her chest. *Jeremiah.* She missed him and his reckless counsel, the hours they spent inside his decrepit room, commiserating and conspiring. He'd been gone eight years and she still thought of him every day.

On a whim she decided to go into the lobby, uncertain if she was purposely trying to ruin her good mood, replacing all that optimism with melancholy and nostalgia. *Sabotage or punishment?* She wasn't sure. She walked up the carpeted steps and nodded as the doorman showed her inside. Just as she remembered, the lobby was dark and gloomy, quiet and nearly empty save for a man sitting in a wingback chair, reading a newspaper. Alva wondered if George Terry still lived there. She thought about calling on him, seeing if he was in, when she looked at the big gilded mirror over the fireplace and saw Charlotte Astor—well, now Charlotte Astor Drayton—coming through the doorway.

What would she be doing at a hotel like the Glenham?

A moment later, she understood completely. The man in the wingback chair set down his paper and crossed the room to greet her. Tall, handsome, with a slightly receding hairline. Alva had no idea who he was other than the fact that he was most certainly *not* Coleman Drayton. Alva could feel the spark between them when their eyes met, their lips curved into smiles. And then of course there was no denying that subtle way he'd placed his hand on the small of Charlotte's back just before whisking her into the elevator.

CHAPTER FORTY-FOUR

Caroline

CAROLINE HAD FOOLISHLY HOPED that all the nonsense about Ward McAllister's list would die down, replaced by some other salacious gossip, but the public's fascination showed no signs of abating. If anything, it was just the opposite. She couldn't pick up a newspaper without seeing that list. *That list*—it had taken on a life of its own. It had even become a proper noun, *The Four Hundred*.

It had been reported that Ward McAllister had in fact only provided 319 names and that because of duplicates and other errors, the actual total had been a mere 169 families. That left 81 missing names, and now everyone was stirred up again, curious about those *missing* individuals. She found it all so tedious and petty. Caroline couldn't bring herself to look anymore, and set her morning papers aside on her breakfast tray. Instead, she glanced out her bedroom window, only to see the back of Waldorf's hotel, still under construction.

He was hell-bent on opening his hotel the following year, and last she heard, it was supposed to be a staggering thirteen stories high. It would entirely block her views and would surely bring a bad element to the neighborhood. Technically, it might have been a hotel, but as far as she was concerned, it was a tavern. A tavern with bedrooms.

Thankfully she had only a couple more weeks and the season would be over and she could leave New York, as she did every year.

The last week in February she would retreat to her apartment in Paris, where she was also the pinnacle of the social scene. She'd stay there until July, when it was time to summer in Newport. And it wasn't just the construction she wanted to escape, but Ward McAllister, who had come to her house nearly every day, begging her forgiveness.

"Everyone's turned against me," he'd said, pacing about her drawing room, all his pride now deflated, replaced with desperation. "They've mocked and shunned me, don't you know. You're the only one who can bring me back into the good graces of society. Please, my Mystic Rose, I beg of you."

"There's nothing I can or will do." She'd hated to be cruel, but he had brought this on himself. She'd stood by him after he'd published his absurd memoir, but now, this was asking too much. She was still angry with him, or perhaps she was more disappointed, which was far worse. Despite all his gossiping and pretension, he had been the one person, outside of Thomas, whom she'd confided in. But no more. He was not to be trusted, which was all the more reason why she wasn't going to save him now.

There was a knock on her bedroom door, and much to her surprise, it was William. He was wearing a Harris Tweed hunting jacket and looked as though he'd been outside, his cheeks tinged red. "May I come in?"

"You may." She was stunned and couldn't remember the last time William had stepped foot inside her room. She felt suddenly modest and pinched her dressing gown at her throat. She worried about his seeing her without her wig, her gray hair so thin and limp. She thought she was past caring what he thought of her, but clearly that wasn't the case.

She could tell by the way he held his arm close to his side that his shoulder must have been bothering him. A sure sign that damp, colder weather was coming. In another time, she would have gone over and massaged away the ache, but to do so now would have only been awkward for her and possibly unwanted by him.

He took a chair opposite hers in the little seating area by the fireplace. "I've just spoken with Coleman. Apparently this affair of Charlie's is still going on."

"But she ended it. She told me she did. She gave me her word."

"Well, according to Coleman, she's still carrying on and the man can take no more. He's confronted Borrowe and challenged him to a duel."

"Oh, dear God, no."

"What choice has he got?" William said with a shrug. "Coleman said someone from the *New York World* is reporting that Charlie and Borrowe were seen together at Delmonico's and again at Sherry's and also at the Glenham Hotel."

"No."

"The *World* is prepared to run with it, and you know it's only a matter of time before all the other papers pick up on it, too."

William was right. The headlines were everywhere. One more incriminating than the next: THE ASTOR GIRL SCANDAL, said the *New York Times*. MRS. J. COLEMAN DRAYTON SEEN EMBRACING MR. HALLETT BORROWE IN PUBLIC appeared in *Town Topics*. INJURED HUSBAND CHALLENGES WIFE'S PARAMOUR TO A DUEL was what the *New York Sun* published.

It had been ages since Caroline and William were in agreement, but they both knew something had to be done. Caroline canceled her trip to Paris in order to deal with her daughter, and the day the *New York Times* ran a story, MORE SCANDAL BEFALLS THE ASTOR FAMILY, Charlotte was called into her father's library.

The construction work next door, the intermittent pounding and chiseling, intruded upon them. Charlotte had arrived in a formfitting gown with a satin sash accentuating her bosom, which Caroline found inappropriate. If her daughter wasn't dressing in rags, she was parading around like *that*. But now was not the time to bring it up. Caroline sat up straight, gripping the armrests of her chair, watching William pace, his cheeks flushed red with fury.

"You know your husband has challenged Borrowe to a duel," said William. "You're about to have blood on your hands, young lady."

Charlotte was impenetrable. Even when the newspapers were shoved under her nose—which William had done after reading each headline aloud—Charlotte stared straight ahead, unapologetic. Barely blinking.

"You should know that I've paid your husband—quite handsomely— to stay in this sham of a marriage." William raised his voice, and Caroline wasn't sure if that was out of sheer frustration or in order to compete with the hammering next door. "You have your children to think about."

"And what am I to do?" Charlotte said, finally, matter-of-factly, as if the situation were out of her control. "I'm in love. Don't I deserve to be happy?"

It seemed like such a simple request. She asked as if it were her birthright, and maybe it was, but Caroline had never felt entitled to happiness. Happiness was something you worked toward achieving, it wasn't a given.

"Happy at what cost?" Caroline asked, thinking of her grandchildren. Charlotte had three children, ages four to twelve. "Think of those who will suffer over your pursuit of this selfish love."

"Charlie, I'm not going to say this again. This affair with Borrowe will come to an end, and it will come to an end right this minute."

Charlotte looked at her father, and in an act of sheer defiance, she said, "I'll end my affair, Father, if you'll end yours."

"That's it." William threw his arms up, wincing at the pain in his shoulder. "You shan't receive another penny from me. Do you hear me? Not one penny."

"I don't care. Go ahead, disinherit me."

"Oh, you don't mean that," Caroline said. She couldn't possibly mean that. The threat of losing her inheritance had always been their ultimate point of leverage. Caroline couldn't think of anything to counter with as Charlotte stormed out of the library. Watching her leave, Caroline felt another part of her soul break away. The money—Charlotte's inheritance—was the last tether they had to her. Caroline simply couldn't bear the thought of losing another daughter, and all because of a man.

One week later, Caroline opened her newspaper and there it was: MRS. ASTOR PAID MR. J. COLEMAN DRAYTON $7000 TO HALT DIVORCE PROCEEDINGS. Caroline was horrified. She reached for the *New York Sun* only to see ASTOR GIRL DISOWNED OVER ILLICIT AFFAIR.

The following day, after William escaped it all and had left for the Everglades, Coleman came to see Caroline. As soon as Thomas showed him into her sitting room, she could tell that something new had developed.

"That good-for-nothing coward, Borrowe, left town," he said, handing her a newspaper he'd been angrily rolling and twisting into a cylinder.

She let the paper flop open and saw another headline: COWARDLY BORROWE BACKS OUT OF DUEL AND FLEES FOR EUROPE.

"He's gone abroad," said Coleman. "They say he's gone to Europe just to dodge my challenge to a duel."

Caroline couldn't say she was surprised by this and wondered why Coleman was. His vigorous pacing was making her anxious. "Would you like some tea?"

"And that's not the half of it," said Coleman, ignoring her.

"Why don't you have a seat? Let me ask Thomas to bring you some tea. Or perhaps coffee?"

But Coleman continued to babble, explaining that he'd attended a Giants game at the Polo Grounds earlier that day, and when he'd returned home Charlotte was gone.

"What do you mean *gone*?"

"Gone—*gone*! She's run away."

"Run away?" Caroline nearly dropped her teacup.

"She's gone. She's left me." He shook his head as if he himself could not believe it. "And she's left her children, too."

This time Caroline used both hands to set her cup aside. It was impossible to fathom. Her daughter wouldn't do that—a wife and mother simply did not do such a thing. It wasn't true. It couldn't be. "I know my daughter isn't perfect, but Charlotte would never leave you and her children. This is beyond—"

"I tell you she's gone to chase after her lover, that coward."

"No, no, you must be mistaken. Perhaps she's gone to Newport early." *Yes, that was it.* "Charlotte's always enjoyed the peace and quiet up—"

"I have proof." He grimly reached inside his pocket and handed Caroline a letter.

Caroline looked at it, which was really more of a note. Just a few words in her daughter's hand:

> *Dear Coleman,*
>   *I've gone to find Hallett. Do not follow me.*
>
>   *Charlotte*

"As if that weren't enough—"

"Oh, dear lord, there's more?" Caroline felt her heart seize up.

"You might want to take a look at today's edition of the *New York Sun*."

Caroline's stomach dropped as she clutched Charlotte's note. *No more press. Please, let there be nothing more in the press.*

"I've been alerted that the *Sun* obtained Charlotte's love letters—"

"Love letters?"

"Apparently, Hallett Borrowe's valet found *love letters* that Charlotte wrote to Borrowe, and he sold them to the *New York Sun*. They've already published one of them in today's paper." He winced. "It's a good thing Charlotte's run off. What she's written to that philanderer is disgusting. Disgraceful. No lady of her upbringing should ever embrace such salacious thoughts."

Caroline wasn't a fainter, but the last thing she remembered before the world went blank was Charlotte's note to Coleman slipping from her fingers.

CHAPTER FORTY-FIVE

Society

EVERY NEWSPAPER IN TOWN has published Charlotte Astor Drayton's love letters—word for titillating word. The intimacies described make us blush as we read them again and again. How Charlotte ACHES FOR THE FEEL OF HIM, how she CRAVES THE TASTE OF HIM, how he makes her body DO AND FEEL THINGS SHE DIDN'T KNOW WERE POSSIBLE. She claims her ENTIRE BODY PURRS FOR HOURS AFTER HE'S LEFT HER BED.

Purrs? Our bodies most definitely do not purr. In fact, we didn't know our bodies *could* purr. We are on tenterhooks to see what happens next in *The Astor Girl Scandal*. Lydia gobbles it up just like she would one of her romance novels. To be honest, we all do, though admittedly, we have no idea what Charlotte Astor Drayton is referring to—this aching for *the feel of a man? Craving his taste?*

We don't dare speak of the specifics, oh heavens no, but our curiosities are working overtime. It is beginning to dawn on us that we are missing out on something. That there is more to the marital act than we've been led to believe.

CHAPTER FORTY-SIX

Alva

WHILE ALL OF NEW YORK was still gossiping about the Astor girl's love letters, Alva's dearest friend, Duchy, who by now was a genuine duchess—the Duchess of Manchester—came for a visit with her son and twin girls. Her husband, George Victor Drogo Montagu, the eighth Duke of Manchester, had recently passed away unexpectedly. He was only thirty-nine and was now succeeded by his fifteen-year-old heir.

Duchy was understandably down and irritable, snapping at her girls to sit up straight, stop fidgeting. She'd swatted her son's hand away from his mouth each time he habitually chewed his cuticles. She'd been especially curt with Willie, and Alva noticed how she pulled away when he'd first greeted her with a familiar kiss on her cheek. Normally the two of them would stay up half the night, drinking whiskey, smoking cigars and singing while she played the banjo. But not this visit. Her banjo had stayed in its case even after Alva had begged her to play a song or two for everyone. Duchy had only shaken her head and said, "Maybe later."

On the last morning of her stay, Duchy turned to Alva and said, "I didn't love him, you know." The two were having their coffees when she declared this, out of the blue. "His Grace was graceless," she said with a sad laugh. "It probably sounds horrible to say this—

and you mustn't repeat it—but I'm not grieving his death. Really, I'm not. Sometimes I think I'm a little relieved."

Alva's eyes opened wider. "That is horrible and luckily for you, I won't repeat it."

"I've taken lovers—you should know that, too," she said, puckering her lips in a way that showed every line around her mouth.

"I suspected as much," said Alva.

"Everyone's making such a big fuss over the Astor girl. Honestly, don't they realize that this sort of thing happens every day?"

"Not with the Grande Dame's daughter it doesn't," Alva said, reaching for her coffee cup. She was about to take a sip when she saw a storm gathering in her friend's face, the eyelids hooded, her jaw clenched. "What is it? What's wrong?"

Duchy took a lingering moment before setting her coffee aside. "I'm going to tell you something. And I want you to stay calm."

Alva's heart pumped a beat faster. Her thoughts were racing—*Is Duchy sick? Is it one of the children?*

Duchy reached for Alva's hand, which made whatever she was about to say seem even worse. "I didn't want you to hear about it from anyone else."

"Good God, what is it?"

"It's about Willie." She paused. "Alva, he's been seeing another woman."

A tiny tremor rippled through Alva. She tried to pull her hand away, but Duchy held it even tighter in place.

"She lives in Paris."

The tremor intensified. Willie had just returned from Paris the month before. He'd said he'd been sailing.

"Her name is Nellie Neustratter."

Alva freed her hand from Duchy's. She was shaking now and gripped the arm of her chair.

"He's got her set up in a home in Paris. A magnificent château. I hear it's huge. And she's got servants. The whole bit."

Alva stood up and went to the window, pressing her forehead against the glass. She had suspected other women, sometimes swore she smelled perfume on him. He'd always denied it and she'd managed to brush it aside. But this was different. A mistress. With a home in Paris. Servants and God knows what else. This explained why Duchy had been so cold to Willie.

"And everyone knows?" asked Alva, the humiliation beginning to dawn on her.

"Enough people know."

Alva thumped her forehead on the windowpane. She turned and faced Duchy. "How long have *you* known?"

Duchy shrugged, cocked her head to the side. "He's a rat. He doesn't deserve you."

"And you waited until now, until your last day, to tell me?"

"I wanted to be long gone by the time you confronted him."

"And what makes you so sure I'll confront him? Most women just look the other way. They don't say a word about this sort of thing."

"But you're not like most women, Alva."

Duchy was barely out the door when Alva did confront Willie. She found him in his library, on a rolling ladder, getting a novel off a top shelf. She waited until he climbed down, and grabbed the book, ripping it from his hands.

"Hey," he said with a start, giving her an indignant look. "I was—"

"Nellie Neustratter," she said, casting the book aside. It clattered, sounding like it might have broken something. She kept her eyes on him, watching his face turn ashen.

"Alva, I—I—"

"Don't try denying it."

He hung his head, leaning up against a bookcase for support. "Well?"

There was a long silence.

"I'm sorry," he mumbled.

"How long has it been going on?"

He shook his head, ran his foot over the carpet and mumbled again, "I don't know—a year, maybe longer."

Alva thought she might be sick on the spot. "And you love her?"

He looked up, as if shocked, as if her question were absurd. "No. No, I don't love her. I love you."

Alva laughed bitterly. "You buy her a house and servants—and that's not love?"

"That's just money, Alva. It doesn't mean anything."

"How can you possibly expect me to believe that?"

"Alva, c'mon now." He stepped forward and reached for her shoulders. "I do love you. I do."

"Then why?"

His eyes glassed up. "You kept pushing me away. You've made everything so hard. I felt like I was always letting you down. I couldn't build you a big enough house or buy a big enough yacht. I couldn't please you no matter how I tried. And she—well, Nellie was just someone to turn to. But that's all. I swear—I never once stopped loving you."

They stayed in the library and talked until the light outside the window had changed, the setting sun casting longer and longer shadows across the room. Alva knew she was difficult, demanding, but she hated playing the fool.

They continued to talk, their voices sometimes spiking into shouting matches, sometimes reduced to whispers. It was late. They were exhausted. They found themselves sitting in the dark. The thought of her husband kissing another woman, touching another woman, brought on waves of nausea. She'd once loved this man with everything she had. And because of this Nellie Neustratter, she didn't know if she could ever feel that way about him again.

She'd made a promise before God to love, honor and obey, and that wasn't a promise she could easily forsake. But how could she tolerate this? "I want you out—I want you out of this house and out of my life. I'm getting a lawyer. I'm getting a divorce—"

"Now, Alva. Be reasonable. I don't want to lose you," he said, grabbing hold of her hands. "I'll end it with her—get rid of that house—of everything. I promise I'll never go to Paris again without you."

Alva didn't know of a single wife who had ever divorced her husband. *A divorce.* A public scandal. Could she do it? She was a proud woman but realized her pride would only make matters worse. It was bad enough that half of Paris was talking about her husband's affair; soon news of it would find its way to the States and probably into the press. The society pages loved writing about wealthy men and their mistresses. That would be bad enough. But divorce—well, divorce, especially one that she instigated—was a far greater scandal.

In the end, Alva's decision to stay with Willie was more about saving face than saving her marriage.

CHAPTER FORTY-SEVEN

Caroline

NEWPORT AND LONDON

THE HAMMERING OUTSIDE HER window woke Caroline with a start. She had dozed off in the solarium and, for a moment, thought she was back in Manhattan. But it was July now and she was at Beechwood, her cottage in Newport, only to find herself surrounded by more construction. Thanks to Alva Vanderbilt's new cottage going up, the dust and noise had followed Caroline from the city to Rhode Island.

Caroline did her best to ignore the noise, sipping the tea that Thomas had just brought her while she leafed through her engagement book. She turned to a page and drew a diagonal line through the four previous lines and tallied them up: 145. It had been 145 days since Charlotte disappeared. In some ways she found it hard to believe it had been that long—the trauma still stinging fresh as a paper cut. In other ways it seemed as though Charlotte had been gone forever, time stretching out in slow motion, dragged down with fits of worry.

She was just thankful that the gossip surrounding her daughter's affair had all but vanished along with her. Society was fickle, and after Charlotte's love letters had been published, a new scandal emerged. Now everyone was chattering about Mr. Gordon Bennett, who had arrived at a party so inebriated that he mistook the fireplace for a latrine, thereby extinguishing the roaring flames while guests looked on, horrified. And of course, there had also been all that talk about Willie Vanderbilt and his mistress, Nellie Neustratter.

Shortly after Charlotte had left town, Caroline and William met with Coleman, offering him $20,000 this time not to file for divorce, lest another scandal turn up in the newspapers. He had reluctantly agreed. "But only for the sake of my children."

Caroline pressed her fingertips to her temples. Now if only someone knew where Borrowe had gone, they could find Charlotte and bring her home. He was somewhere in Europe—that was all they knew. Could have been France or England. Possibly Italy. It was impossible for Caroline to sit back and do nothing. She had already canceled her trip to Paris but was reconsidering it. Maybe she could go and look for her? Although, if the Pinkerton detective couldn't locate Charlotte, what chance did she have of finding her?

Caroline closed her engagement book and chucked it aside. She missed Charlotte but she was angry with her, too. How could she have done this to her family and especially to her children? But still, Charlotte was her daughter, and there was no amount of wrongdoing that would ever change that. Caroline had always thought there was no greater force on earth than a mother's love. She'd experienced it, going days without sleep when her children were sick, never leaving their bedside, finding energy for one more bedtime story, patience for one more tantrum. How was it that Charlotte didn't feel that bond with her own children? How could she bear being away from them? And how could it possibly be that Caroline now had six motherless grandchildren? Each time she thought about those poor children, she nearly broke in two.

A loud banging started up next door, assaulting Caroline's sensibilities. While Bellevue Avenue was the most fashionable street in Newport, Caroline deeply resented that Alva had felt the need to build right next door to her. The disruption was atrocious, the clangor and dust relentless. Thomas had already informed her that a slab of the Vanderbilts' marble had landed in her rosebushes.

Caroline had no doubt that her rival's cottage would be extraordinary, and there was no escaping the anticipation mounting around Newport. Even at Bailey's Beach people were talking about Alva's new cottage and the ball she was going to throw upon its completion that August. Normally Caroline would have hosted her clambake in August, but given everything with Charlotte, not to mention Ward McAllister, she couldn't bring herself to do it this year.

Thomas entered the room just then with the day's delivery of calling cards and mail. The first envelope she reached for was from Ward McAllister, which she set aside, unopened, along with his previous letters. Honestly, it didn't matter if she answered him or not, because the man continued to appear on Caroline's doorstep even after she'd instructed Thomas to turn him away. Maybe if Ward backed off, she would have found it in her heart to forgive him, but his constant pestering and begging had made him a pathetic, groveling annoyance. They both knew she was the only one with enough clout to do it, but restoring Ward McAllister in society's good graces was not her responsibility.

Among the various invitations to balls, lawn parties, dinners and charity functions was a letter from Consuelo Yznaga, now Lady Montagu, the Duchess of Manchester. At first Caroline thought the post had been delivered in error and that it was intended for Alva next door, as she knew the two were friends. But it was addressed to Mrs. Astor, so Caroline unsealed the envelope and began to read:

> *Dear Mrs. Astor,*
>   *I wanted to inform you that I recently encountered your daughter Charlotte here in London. At the risk of being too familiar, I must tell you that circumstances have not gone in*

her favor. Apparently, her reasons for coming to Europe have
not gone well. Her gentleman friend, as it turns out, is no
gentleman. I shall not even write his name but suffice it to
say, he has left Charlotte in a rather bad way. I regret to
report that I found her in quite a state with no money and
only the clothes on her back. Frankly, to look at her, one
would never guess her to be a member of the Astor family. I
gave her whatever I had in my change purse at the time—
and convinced her to take it. She refused to tell me where she
was staying, and when I offered to provide her with a ticket
to return home, she broke down, weeping, saying that she
could not possibly return to America after what she'd done.
As of the writing of this letter, she is here, in London. Please
forgive me for this intrusion but as a mother myself, I could
not help but write to you. I pray for Charlotte's well-being.

> *Most sincerely yours,*
> *Consuelo Montagu*

Caroline sat with the letter, unable to shake the thought of Charlotte all alone and penniless in London, too afraid to return home
where she belonged. Caroline had to go get her, but she couldn't do
it alone. When William returned later that day from the matches at
the Polo Club, she showed him the letter.

"I'm going to London and I need you to come with me," she said
before he'd spoken a word. "That's the only way Charlotte will come
back and you know it. She was always your favorite, and she needs
to know you'll forgive her. She needs to hear that from you."

The next day Caroline and William set sail for England. It was the
first time in more than a decade that Caroline had stepped foot on
William's yacht, the *Ambassadress*. William had built the 235-foot

schooner in 1877, and the press had aptly called it a "floating palace." Her husband had spared no expense, importing teakwood for the upper and lower decks, French walnut for the grand staircase, gold and marble fireplace mantels for the smoking room and library.

The weather was bad that day but Caroline, who had always publicly claimed that seasickness kept her from joining William on the *Ambassadress*, wasn't fazed by the choppy waters. Instead, she stood on the promenade deck, her chamois gloves gripping the brass railing, looking out at the whitecaps. The sky was overcast, heavy with a thick band of clouds as far as she could see. She was thinking of Charlotte as the wind gusts toyed with her hat, salt water misting her face.

She heard footsteps coming up behind her on the deck. She looked over her shoulder and saw that it was Thomas. He gazed at the horizon, squinting as if he were looking directly at the sun even as the sky darkened.

"Mrs. Astor, perhaps you should come in from the deck."

"I'll be in shortly," she said.

Something about the sea, even a rough one, gave her a new perspective, a humbling one. Her world wasn't all that significant when compared to the ocean's vastness, its constant motion and sheer power. A few minutes later, a rumble of thunder sounded in the distance as a bolt of lightning branched out across the sky, unleashing a torrent of rain, quarter-size drops bouncing on the deck. Thomas raced over with an umbrella and hurried her inside.

The storm intensified over the next few hours, raging on, and later that night, Caroline listened to the violent waves lashing out, pounding against the hull. The sea rocked the yacht, causing the lamps in her cabin to flicker, making it nearly impossible to read. She'd thought about asking Thomas to read with her, but doubted he'd have any better luck, so she marked her place and set the book aside. She hadn't been able to concentrate anyway and not because of the weather. She rested her hands on the upholstered arms of her chair and glanced about the bedroom, admiring the ivory-and-gold Louis XV furnishings, trying not to think of William's various lady friends who had stayed there before her.

Someone knocked on her door and she assumed it was Thomas or maybe one of the stewards, checking in on her.

Instead it was William, looking a bit sallow. "May I come in?"

"Is everything all right?"

He didn't answer and instead stood there, leaning against the doorjamb for balance as the yacht bobbed back and forth. He'd been in his library most of the day and well into the evening. She'd expected him to be full of whiskey by now but couldn't detect even the slightest smell of liquor coming off him. He seemed perfectly sober.

"I thought I should check in on you. In case you're frightened or—"

"Oh, I'm not frightened."

"You never are, are you?"

She looked at him and paused. *Was that a smile she detected?*

"You are fearless," he said. "Not afraid of anything. You really are as strong as they say, aren't you?"

Caroline was taken aback. She didn't know what to do with his compliment. For years she'd been starved for his attention, and here he was giving it to her, and she couldn't take it in. She was about to change the subject, when he did it for her.

"Lina, I'm afraid I've failed our girls."

"Failed them?" Her voice ticked up a notch. "What has gotten into you tonight?" She realized he had inched his way inside her cabin without her having noticed it and was standing now just a few feet from her. She thought about asking him to have a seat but that seemed presumptuous, as if she thought he was planning on staying when perhaps he'd only wanted to say his piece and leave. She couldn't decide what to do, so she did nothing and he continued standing before her, talking.

"As a man gets older," he was saying now, "he's bound to have regrets. Let's face it, I haven't been much of a father. Or a husband for that matter."

She couldn't have agreed with him more. "You've been a good provider," she offered, trying to be kind.

"A provider, huh?" He laughed, but his eyes were sad. "You have every right to be angry with me."

This time she was the one with the sad laugh. The lamps flickered so, they nearly went out but then recovered to full strength.

He brought a hand to his mouth and smoothed down his horseshoe mustache. "Lord knows you deserved better than I've given you."

"Oh pish-posh," she said. "No point in going over that now."

They lapsed into silence just as a massive wave hit them starboard. The tea in her cup sloshed overboard into the saucer.

"You did the right thing," he said.

"About what?"

"You were right about letting Emily and Carrie marry the men they loved. We've seen what happens when the families arrange the marriages, haven't we? We shouldn't have forced Charlie to marry Coleman."

"*We* didn't force her," said Caroline. "*I* forced her."

He bobbed his head, not necessarily agreeing or disagreeing. After a long pause he said, "Maybe the heart doesn't make a perfect match for society, but in the long run, the heart knows best." She wasn't certain, but thought his eyes were misting up. "If I had it to do over again with Charlie . . . with Emily . . ." He shook his head, unable to get the words out.

She stood up, reached over and touched his hand, suddenly feeling the need to comfort him. She'd never seen him so vulnerable, and it stirred something inside her. Another wave rocked the yacht, and Caroline stumbled forward, falling against his chest. The awkwardness was nearly unbearable. It was as if she were pressed up against a stranger. They both mumbled apologies, and as she stepped back, he came forward. She saw her own surprise mirrored in his eyes, and the next thing she knew, he had his arms around her and was kissing her. She was startled at first. Long ago she'd dreamed of kissing him again, and now she was. It took a moment to find the pleasure in it and accept the reassurance she'd so desperately needed. He wanted her again. When he removed her dressing gown, she turned shy as a schoolgirl. She didn't dare speak or question *why—why now*—for fear he'd stop.

Afterward he was tired and asked if he might just lie down beside her and rest his eyes for a bit. And that was what he did. With his head on her sturdy shoulder, the heat rippling off his body, he fell asleep while she lay awake, confused and stirred up, listening to the storm whipping against the starboard.

In the morning, the waters had calmed and William complained of a chest cold, saying he wasn't quite feeling himself. He left Caroline's cabin, acting as if the previous night hadn't happened, so she, too, acted as if it hadn't happened. She wasn't going to leave herself exposed and let him see her disappointment. She looked at the situation from every possible angle. She even considered that maybe he *did* still care but that she'd given him the impression she *didn't*, and so now he was pretending indifference.

At luncheon she took a chance, asking how he was feeling and if he wanted a mustard plaster for his chest. "I'd be happy to apply it if you'd like."

"That won't be necessary."

He was cordial.

She was deflated.

Even if the mustard plaster hadn't been necessary, wouldn't he have used it as an excuse for them to be together again? But he had dismissed it, finished his lunch and gone back to his cabin, or library, he didn't say where. He was just gone.

She scolded herself. Even though he was her husband, she should have denied him, should have saved her dignity. Now he'd made her feel things she thought were beyond her. Her heart was the heart of a young girl's once again, and she couldn't let that be. She was angry with him, but even more so, she was angry with herself for having allowed it to happen.

By the time the *Ambassadress* docked in London, Caroline and William had resumed their usual roles. Not another word was said about what had happened on the ship. Now the business at hand was finding Charlotte.

While waiting to hear from the detective, Caroline and William spent two days wandering about town, calling upon friends and discreetly making inquiries. As they made their way to wharves on Lower Thames, Caroline kept a kerchief pressed to her nose and mouth, trying to ward off the briny stench of Billingsgate Fish Market. They later stopped at the Fenchurch Street train station, where Caroline searched the platform for passengers exiting the steam locomotives, but there was no sign of Charlotte. That night Caroline would be haunted by the flower woman they'd seen at Ludgate Circus, fearful that Charlotte would end up like that, perched on the brick road, surrounded by baskets of daisies, daffodils and petunias for sale.

The next day Caroline felt herself dragging, her hope growing weaker as she hunted the crowded streets for her lost daughter. When they arrived at Piccadilly Circus, she spotted a woman that made her heart lurch forward. *Oh thank goodness! There she is! Charlotte!* She was standing by the statue of Eros, her face slightly obscured by her blond curls, but Caroline knew it was her. She was certain of it. She was about to call out when a breeze cleared the hair from the woman's face. Caroline's heart sank. A stranger. A stranger who really didn't look anything like Charlotte at all. When they returned to their hotel that day, Caroline retreated to her room, brokenhearted. Just when she was resigned to never finding Charlotte, William heard from his Pinkerton man.

The following day, the detective, a short man with a thin mustache and neatly trimmed goatee, escorted Caroline and William to the St. Pancras Hotel. William was especially quiet that day, hardly saying a word. He claimed he hadn't slept well and that his stomach was bothering him. He blamed it on something he'd eaten, saying he'd never liked the food in England.

The hotel's gothic clock tower was visible from blocks away. This was the last place Caroline would have thought to look for Charlotte. It was a very expensive hotel, and the duchess said in her letter that Charlotte was penniless.

When they arrived, the detective went first, and Caroline and William followed, pushing through a revolving door that spilled into a plush lobby accented in gold leaf wallpaper and an enormous staircase. Rather than going to the luxury rooms on the first floor, with their Axminster carpets and oversize beds, the Pinkerton man took them through a maze of back stairwells and narrow hallways leading to the top floor. William was breathing hard, perspiring. He held on to the jamb for support when the detective turned the knob and slowly opened the door.

Caroline's heart lurched. There she was. Her Charlotte, in a tiny room, sitting on a cot-like bed with her back to them. When Caroline stepped inside, she stubbed her toe against the wooden chamber pot in the corner. Charlotte heard the noise and turned around. Caroline stifled a gasp as Charlotte's eyes instantly glassed up. Her daughter looked terrible; her face was drawn and pale. She had purple half-moons beneath her eyes. When Charlotte stood up, Caroline took her in her arms, startled by the feel of her bones. She had lost so much weight that her dress hung off her like a rag. Caroline took hold of Charlotte's hands and noticed her wedding ring was gone. She would later learn that Charlotte had pawned it along with her other jewelry in order to keep the hotel room.

William, still propped against the doorjamb, excused his Pinkerton man. "We'd like some privacy if you don't mind." The detective left the room, but William still hadn't spoken to Charlotte. Finally, he stepped inside and closed the door with great effort.

Charlotte returned to the side of the bed, buried her face in her hands and wept.

"Now, now," said Caroline, expecting William to reassure Charlotte, too, but he wasn't ready yet. In his stubbornness, he crossed his arms, keeping his chin tucked close to his chest.

"The important thing is that you're all right," said Caroline.

"But I'm not all right, Mother. Don't you see?" She looked up, her lashes webbed with tears. "I've ruined everything. *Everything.* I have nothing left. I should have never come here. I knew it was a mistake as soon as I arrived. Hallett told me our relationship had become too complicated, too messy. He said I had tarnished his reputation and that the duel was my fault. He said that because of me, he wouldn't be able to step foot back in New York City without having to draw a pistol. Oh, he hates me now and—"

"Enough!" said William, his voice booming. "Good God, Charlie, stop feeling sorry for yourself. I can't listen to this whining. Now buck up, girl. It's time to get you out of this hellhole. Get your things. We're taking you back home to your husband and children."

"No. I can't—I—"

"It's not up to you, young lady," said William. He was furious. Beads of perspiration appeared on his forehead, his pallor off. "You're going home."

Charlotte shook her head. "I can't go back to Coleman. I don't love him. I've never loved him. How can I go back to him?"

"Because your children need you," said Caroline.

"But I've been disgraced. I can never show my face again in New York."

"Charlie, I tell you, I have heard—" But William stopped short, cutting himself off midsentence. Caroline thought he was going to back down, change his mind, for he almost never lashed out at Charlotte like that. But then his eyes flashed wide, wide enough for Caroline to see that he was in an absolute panic. Something was wrong, and before she could reach him, before she could even ask, he clutched his chest and gasped for air. There was a resounding thud and the room shook when William's body dropped to the floor.

Caroline stood on the promenade deck of the *Ambassadress*, looking out at the ocean. The calm and gentle waters were a complete contrast to the weather they'd experienced the day she and William set sail. New York seemed so very far away, and though Charlotte was at her side, Caroline had never felt more alone. She couldn't shake the fact that her husband was belowdecks, lying in a casket.

So much time lost, squandered away on things that in the long run hadn't mattered. Why hadn't they made more of an effort to include each other in their lives? Why hadn't they bent just a little more to each other's ways? She would have gone to the Everglades if only he had gone to the opera. They could have found a balance. She was sure of that now. Call it a sixth sense or hunch, but Caroline realized that on some level William must have known he was about to die. What else could have explained his being so sentimental and reflective in the days before? Why else had he come to her bed one last time? But damn him. Damn him for leaving her after there had been a glimmer of hope at righting all that had been wrong between them. So much had been given and taken away in a flash.

"Mother?"

Caroline cleared her throat and looked away, listening to the breeze catching in the sails, the sound of water lapping against the hull.

"Are you *crying?*" Charlotte asked, her voice suggesting it wasn't possible.

"Oh, it's just the sea air." Even when her mother died and when Emily passed away, Caroline had refused to let her daughters, or anyone else, see her cry.

Six days later, when the *Ambassadress* arrived back in New York, Jack met Caroline and Charlotte at Pier Twelve down by the North River docks. It was a sunny day; the waterfront was crowded with sailors, dockworkers, fishermen and passengers. Seagulls squawked and swooped down on the piers, and everywhere Caroline looked, she saw more yachts and steamers. *Life goes on* and that made her want to scream—*Don't you realize my husband is dead!*

When Jack took Caroline and Charlotte back to the house on Thirty-Fourth Street, the mourning badges were already hanging. The sight of that dark bunting made William's passing all the more real. As she walked up the front steps, she felt herself going back in time, back to when she'd lost her mother. And Emily. She had never expected to find herself in this dark place again so soon. She was already feeling pulled under by the weight of two more years of mourning.

CHAPTER FORTY-EIGHT

Society

NEWPORT

AS THE NEWPORT SEASON nears its end, we have our invitations in hand. Not to Mrs. Astor's clambake—she's still in mourning, so that's been canceled. No, this year, the event of the season is being hosted by Alva. It's cloaked in mystery, though. We have no idea what to expect. All we know is that Alva is throwing an enormous ball to celebrate the completion of her new cottage. She's named it Marble House, and none of us have set eyes on it yet. Hence the mystery. She still has it hidden behind that maddening fence.

Alva has also been just as secretive and close-lipped about Willie's affair. We hear he has a lover. In Paris. Nellie something or other. We expected better of Willie, but then again, we expect better of our own husbands as well.

These men—they underestimate us. They think we don't know about their mistresses, or if we do, that we don't care. Oh, please, we care. And we punish them for it in our own way. We tuck those crisp greenbacks in our pockets and later doctor the weekly ledger of household expenses that they approve without suspecting a thing. Small victories but through the years, those dollar bills add up. Tessie saved enough for a lovely pair of satin square-toed Julien Mayers, and she walks a little taller in those shoes knowing she earned them. In a sense.

So why would Alva, in the midst of a marital scandal, throw a big bash? We say, *why not!* How many of us have done the same—hosted a dinner party or reception, praising our husband's devotion to offset gossip about our own marriages? We deflect, divert attention and do whatever it takes to distract.

It goes without saying that if Mrs. Astor weren't in mourning, she would have done the same. Hosted a magnificent ball or dinner party in Charlotte's honor to repair her daughter's good name. But, because of her husband's passing, the Grande Dame's hands are tied, and besides, the damage has already been done. No amount of celebration can counterbalance this business about Charlotte Astor Drayton's divorce.

The gossip columns can hardly keep up with the scandal. We follow it all day by day. Some absolutely relish the Astor name being smeared across sixteen different newspapers. Already there is talk about the whole sordid affair even tarnishing Mrs. Astor's reputation. This of course has Mamie, Tessie and Alva all jockeying for position.

It storms on the day of Alva's ball, and after the rain moves out, the fog rolls in. Across the street, Ophelia tries to get a glimpse of the cottage, but Alva has guards stationed all around to keep nosy passersby from getting an early look. As the sun begins to set, mosquitoes—big as horseflies—hover everywhere, looking to feast. Cornelia Martin peers out her bedroom window to see a team of two dozen or more workers starting to take down the exterior fence surrounding Marble House. One by one those wood panels are pulled down, chucked into a mountain of cedar waiting to be hauled away. But for now, because of the fog and darkness, Alva's cottage remains hidden and mysterious as ever.

At eleven o'clock that night, we arrive at Alva's only to be kept out front, on the lawn. Hundreds of us are lined up all the way back to Bellevue Avenue. It's muggy, swelteringly hot. The night sky is charcoal black and starless. Alva doesn't have a single light or lamp on inside the cottage. Only the orchestra music and Alva's elegantly liveried staff serving us champagne and sherry indicate that anything festive is underway. When the last of her guests have arrived, we see Alva signal her butler, who signals the head footman, who throws a master switch, and with a flash of brilliance, all of Marble House is illuminated. We are awestruck, applauding, giving off a chorus of *oohs* and *aahs* while the orchestra plays.

The doors are thrown open and we eagerly enter the great hall, anticipating what awaits us. If we thought Petit Chateau was something, Marble House is beyond compare. Five years in the making and it shows. The Tuckahoe marble sparkles so, it takes our breath away. We walk through an austere archway leading to an intentionally dark, medieval-like study that Alva calls the Gothic Room. It is something to behold, with stained-glass windows surrounding Alva's most priceless antiques, statues and chalices.

As we move on, Puss can't get over the gilded garlands along the ceiling and the fountain with its bronze accents. Peggy is enamored of the tapestries, and Tessie is clearly impressed by the sienna marble throughout. Just when we think it can't get any more grand, we see the luster of the twenty-two-karat-gold walls and ceiling in the ballroom. It's Mamie Fish who goes up to Alva and laughs as she says, "Leave it to you not to go overboard and make this place too gaudy." We're quite certain that coming from Mamie, Alva takes this as a tremendous compliment.

CHAPTER FORTY-NINE

Caroline

NEW YORK, 1893

IT WAS A FRIGID January afternoon, eight months after William's death, and a chilly draft seemed to permeate the entire house. Caroline was at her desk, tending to her daily correspondence, when Charlotte walked into the room. While warming her hands before the marble fireplace, Charlotte announced that she was moving back to Europe.

Caroline set her pen aside and looked at her daughter nonplussed. "Whatever for?"

"There's nothing here for me in New York." She wrapped her shawl closer around her shoulders. "I *mustn't* attend any suffrage or political rallies. I mustn't *go* anywhere, *do* anything. I'm bored to tears here. I haven't been invited to a single ball or a dinner party in months."

"That's because you're in mourning."

"That's not the only reason, and you know it."

Caroline did know it. After William's death, Caroline had sent a very reluctant Charlotte back to Coleman, instructing her daughter to beg his forgiveness. But Charlotte's jilted husband would have none of it, and no matter how much money Caroline offered, it wasn't enough to appease him. Coleman had filed for divorce, claiming adultery and desertion, leaving Charlotte without custody of her children and her reputation tarnished.

Charlotte dropped into a chair opposite Caroline's desk and laughed bitterly. "How terribly ironic. I never even *liked* going to those things. I never cared and now, I'd give anything for an invitation to one of their silly affairs."

"I know this has been a difficult time for you," Caroline said to Charlotte, "but you can't run away. And especially not while in mourning. That will only stir up more talk."

Charlotte folded her arms, her shawl slipping off her shoulders. "Very well then. I'll stay until we're out of mourning. But then I'm leaving. I'm going back to England."

What about your children? You'll never have any hope of seeing them again if you leave. But Caroline held her tongue, taking some comfort in knowing that at least this time, Charlotte wouldn't return penniless and end up living in a hovel. Despite William's threats to disown Charlotte, in the end, he couldn't do it. At the reading of his will, it was announced that William had left the house on Fifth Avenue to Charlotte, along with $850,000, the same amount he'd left to Helen and Carrie. Jack, his only male heir, had received the balance of William's $50 million.

A log in the fireplace crackled, spitting red-hot embers that soon turned to ash when they hit the marble floor. Caroline looked at Charlotte, exasperated, and finally said, "You're a grown woman. I can't stop you. But I urge you to consider what you'll be leaving behind—your own flesh and blood."

"But I need to get away from New York. I need to go someplace where I can put all this behind me and start over."

Caroline was still discussing the matter with Charlotte when Thomas knocked, announcing that she had some visitors. He stepped aside and in walked Jack and Carrie.

"What brings you here?" Caroline asked, pleased at first to see them until the expressions on their faces made her sit up, her heart beating faster.

Carrie closed her eyes, and her shoulders began to shake. Caroline couldn't tell if she was laughing or crying. Then Jack stepped forward, placing his hand on his sister's arm, as if to say, *Let me.*

"Mother," he said, "I'm afraid we have some terrible news." Jack wiped his eyes with his fingers and pressed a fist to his mouth—just the way William used to do whenever he was choked up. Jack was pale, and watching his eyes glaze over sent a chill up Caroline's back. "It's Helen. She's—"

"Not Helen." No. It couldn't be Helen. She'd just seen her.

"I'm afraid she's gone."

She had a cold. *A simple cold. A bad cough was all . . .*

"We just came from Rosy's. She died this morning."

Hearing it out loud made Caroline gasp. She felt she was falling and gripped the arms of her chair, holding on. Everyone was talking all at once. Someone was crying—she wiped her cheek, her fingers dry. Everything was happening outside her, and she didn't know if time was standing still or moving too fast to grab hold of. A pool of blackness was spreading across her desk. *When did my inkwell spill?* She wanted to sop up the mess and began opening drawers, frantically searching for a rag that she knew would never have been stored there. Cleaning up that mess was all she could focus on. But she could no more put that ink back inside its bottle than she could bring Helen back.

Caroline had been shattered by the news of Helen's death. She'd nearly collapsed that day, and after they told her, Thomas and Jack helped her to bed, where she'd stayed for days, barely able to eat, unable to think of anything but losing another child. It wasn't natural. Children weren't supposed to die first. Carrie and Charlotte

checked on her the next day and the day after. Caroline was incon-
solable.

After Helen's death, Caroline experienced a kind of anger she'd
never before known. Emily. William. And now Helen. She was convinced that God was punishing her. Her family was cursed. She feared
she was destined to repeat her mother's hell and knew she couldn't
bear another loss. For two years she dressed each day in black, her
body cloaked in grief.

The first winter seemed to last forever. The long cold nights blurred,
one right into another. Sleep was unheard of, and though she recalled
Thomas reading to her, later on she would not be able to remember
a single book, the characters or plots. Spring came, then summer, but
the warmer weather only spelled longer days to endure before the
cycle repeated.

It was the finality of death that she wrestled with the most. It was
so permanent. Her loved ones were gone, gone forever. Looking back
on those dark days, she had no idea how she'd managed to get through
them. She hadn't been living, she'd only been marking time.

Losing another daughter had certainly caused Caroline to reexamine her priorities. Life was so fleeting, so fragile, and in the grand
scheme of things, what difference did it make if someone used the
wrong fork, or served the wrong wine? So what if her daughter was
divorced? Was it better for Charlotte to have lived a life of misery? In
the end—did *any* of this matter? Maybe William had been right all
along—society was frivolous. And yet, she was so conditioned by it,
she didn't know how to be any other way. Still, in her darkest hours,
she wondered if Helen knew she would die young. When Emily
passed away Helen had said, *If this happened to Emily, it will happen to
me, too.*

Over and over again, Caroline questioned if her dear sweet Helen—
who had always tried to do the right thing, to please everyone around

her, to keep the peace—had truly lived the life she'd wanted. Or had she been living only for Caroline just as Caroline had lived for her mother?

She couldn't undo the past, but now she knew that it was time to set them free—all of them. Rest in peace to those gone, live in peace to those still here.

CHAPTER FIFTY

Alva

NEWPORT

IT WAS DUCHY'S FORTIETH birthday, and Alva decided to throw a little dinner party for her. Nothing too elaborate or too large. Just a handful of friends. True friends. The past few years, with His Grace's passing, had been hard for Duchy, and she'd been spending more and more time in the States. Sometimes she brought the children along; mostly she didn't. Alva tried not to pass judgment, though she couldn't have imagined being separated from her children for that long.

Duchy had been dreading this birthday. In addition to the dinner party, which Alva hoped would cheer her up, she'd bought Duchy a new banjo, especially made for her with a mother-of-pearl fingerboard, gilded frets and a burl walnut veneer for the resonator.

"Oh, Alva, you shouldn't have. It's beautiful. Just beautiful." Duchy played a few chords. "What a wonderful tone it has." She thanked Alva again and set the banjo back inside its velvet-lined case.

That was it? Alva was puzzled and then irked. If only Duchy knew how much trouble she'd gone to, not to mention the considerable sum she'd spent. Alva thought a little more enthusiasm was in order, a bit more appreciation. She thought Duchy would have played song after song, just like she did at lawn parties and on picnics. She loved to play and used to lead everyone in sing-alongs until her fingers needed a break.

Alva tried chalking it up to birthday malaise and did her best to let go of her disappointment. It continued to niggle at her, though, as they spent the rest of the day lazing around the cottage before heading to the beach and back in time to get ready for the party.

Duchy wore a lovely blue gown trimmed in matching feathers and sapphires. She looked radiant, happy and at ease. The prospect of a party in her honor seemed to have lifted her spirits considerably.

By eight that night they were all in the Gothic Room. It was a hot, muggy evening and they had the doors thrown open, while they enjoyed their aperitifs before dinner. Alva couldn't help but notice that Duchy and Oliver were sitting rather close together. He'd just said something that made her laugh, and there was an intimacy to it, like an inside joke. Alva turned and began making polite conversation with Puss and Ophelia, Penelope and Lydia, but all the while her stomach was roiling. She could hardly believe that she was jealous of Duchy.

She realized that if her friend had been more gracious about the banjo, she probably wouldn't have been upset. But no doubt about it, Alva was still angry and told herself this burst of emotion was more about the banjo than anything else. But it wasn't just the banjo. It was Duchy. She wasn't herself and hadn't been for some time. Duchy had repeatedly hurt Alva's feelings, leaving letters unanswered, passing judgment on Marble House's furnishing, mocking Alva for commissioning the French painter Carolus-Duran to do her portrait. It was as if Duchy was testing the strength of their friendship. That bond they'd always shared seemed to be bowing, on the verge of snapping in two.

Alva excused herself on the pretense of checking something in the kitchen. She needed air, needed a moment to collect herself. She ended up looking in on the children, and when she went back downstairs, she saw Duchy slipping out of a shadowed alcove; one of her blue feathers had escaped from the trim and floated along the floor. Something about that feather landed heavy on Alva's heart. She had a feeling that Oliver was about to step out behind her. *And so what if he does?* Oliver's being with other women shouldn't have bothered her. And she shouldn't begrudge Duchy her happiness—especially after losing her husband. Besides, the only person more restless than Oliver was Duchy—it would never last . . .

She was trying to convince herself of that when she saw that it was not Oliver Belmont emerging from the alcove, but rather Willie; his hair rumpled, a blue feather stuck to his lapel. Alva felt the wind knocked out of her. The room tilted as stars danced across her vision, her pulse doubling its speed. *Willie K. and Duchy.* She stood there, frozen, trying to comprehend it all. She was clobbered. *Silly little trusting fool.* Sure, he'd ended it with Nellie, but now he'd taken up with her best friend.

Think, Alva. Think. She had to be smart about how she handled this.

"Excuse me, Mrs. Vanderbilt." Her butler interrupted her thoughts. "Everyone is waiting for you in the dining room. Your guests have all been seated."

Alva took another moment, still struggling to recover. "I'll be right there."

As she made her way back toward the dining room, she saw the banjo resting in the corner. She picked it up, plastered a smile on her face and entered the dining room, cast in the warmth of rose-colored marble. Everyone was seated around the table in her bronze Louis XV chairs that weighed seventy-five pounds each. They were anchored on the thick carpet and certain to render her dinner guests moored wherever they landed, unable to scoot any closer to the table, or get away without the assistance of a strong footman.

With an exuberance that alerted everyone to the sense that something was amiss, Alva said, "Why don't we have the birthday girl play us a little song before the first course is served?" An awkward murmur rippled around the table; such an unusual way for a hostess to start dinner. Alva couldn't bring herself to look at Willie. She handed the banjo to Duchy, who hesitantly accepted it as if it were a stick of dynamite.

Tentatively, with her eyes on Alva, as if trying to read her, Duchy played the opening chords of "Ole Dan Tucker."

"Oh, no, no"—Alva cut her off—"that sounds terrible. It's out of tune. Here"—she reached for the banjo—"let me fix that for you." She yanked it out of Duchy's hands and, holding it like an ax, proceeded to smash it against the marble sideboard. Everyone gasped but Alva kept going. The bridge and heel went flying; the resonator split in two. Duchy flinched, trying to get out of her chair, but she was trapped by the weight of it. She had to sit there and take it.

When the neck broke in two and all Alva had left was the head-stock, she turned to her best friend and said, "Next time you decide to make love to my husband, please have the decency to do it somewhere other than in my home."

CHAPTER FIFTY-ONE

Alva

ALVA HURRIED OUT OF the dining room and down the hallway to the back staircase that led to the belly of Marble House. Even with the giant copper pots simmering on the stove and the kitchen filled with scullery maids and cooks, it was cooler down there than upstairs, the stone walls blocking out the heat. The wine cellar was cooler still. It was a deep, dark room, save for the lamps casting shadows along the wooden racks filled with bottles of claret and burgundy, champagne, and sweet dessert wines from Portugal.

She went inside to escape and sat on a bench, leaning forward, elbows planted on her knees, fingertips pressed into her forehead. Did she really just smash that banjo to pieces? Yes, she did. Did she regret doing it? No, she did not. As she sat in the wine cellar, she realized that Willie's affair with Duchy had to have been going on for some time. That visit with Duchy, when she'd been so cold to Willie, when she'd told Alva about Nellie—Duchy had done it to punish Willie. He hadn't only been cheating on his wife, he'd been cheating on his mistress, too. Alva was reliving that conversation with Duchy when she heard footsteps outside the wine cellar.

The door creaked open. She looked up and saw Oliver.

"Are you okay?" He stepped inside the cellar and bent down so that she was forced to look him in the eye.

She attempted a weak smile. "I think I've just reached a new low."

"Don't talk to *me* about new lows. You've got me by three inches." He straightened up and laughed.

She didn't. "You shouldn't do that."

"Do what?"

"Poke fun at yourself."

"Oh." He shrugged, rubbed his chin. "I figure I'll crack a short joke before someone else has a chance to do it."

His candor touched her, made her feel more inclined to be honest herself. "I made a fool of myself tonight, didn't I?"

"Nah, but I have to tell you, you play one helluva banjo."

She laughed sadly. "My husband is a louse. And Duchy is even worse. She stabbed me in the back."

Oliver reached for a bottle, clearing the dust off the label with his fingertips. "I think this calls for a drink."

"In here?"

"What better place for wine than in a wine cellar?" He grabbed the corkscrew hanging by a chain at the side of the door.

"I don't think there's any glasses in here," she said as he turned the screw and pulled the cork clean.

"I don't mind your germs if you don't mind mine." He took a drink and passed the bottle to her.

"You are bad, Mr. Belmont, aren't you?" she said, gingerly taking a sip of the wine.

The two sat, passing the bottle back and forth, discussing Willie and Duchy, his short-lived marriage to Sara; things they never would have shared had they not already finished off that first bottle. Occasionally they heard servants moving about. They didn't care; they kept on talking.

Oliver opened a second bottle, and halfway into it, he reached over and caught a droplet of wine on her bottom lip with his thumb and held it there, gently running it back and forth. Such a small gesture but it set off something inside her. At first she was afraid to let her eyes meet his and instead focused on his mouth, the slight parting of his lips, their fullness. When she couldn't fight it anymore, she leaned into his touch and did the thing she realized she'd been wanting to do for a very long time: she kissed him. She kissed Willie's best friend.

The next day, Alva did what no wife had done before. She told her husband she was going to divorce him.

"Divorce me?" Willie hadn't even gotten his coat and hat off when she confronted him. He'd left Marble House the night before, presumably with Duchy. She had no idea where he'd been and she didn't care. "Can you at least do me the courtesy of letting me sit down and have a drink before you start attacking me?"

"I don't owe you any courtesies." She stormed after him, out of the great hall and into the sitting room. "I mean it," she said. "I want a divorce."

"Don't say that." He fixed himself a drink and took a long pull. "Look, I know you're upset and I understand—"

"No, you don't understand, I *am* going to divorce you."

"Alva, calm down. I know what we did was wrong. She's sick about it. So am I. It just happened."

"You're a liar. It didn't *just* happen. It's been going on for God knows how long."

He raised his hands, wincing. "It won't ever happen again. I promise. It was a mistake. We can get past this. I know we can."

"Well, I *can't*. I *can't* get past this. I don't *want* to get past this. I don't love you anymore, and I don't want you in my bed—I don't want you in my life."

Willie faltered, as if she'd hit him, and after he recovered, he turned mean. "You've lost your mind. You're a woman. A wife doesn't divorce her husband. And don't forget, Alva, you can't divorce me without bringing yourself down, too. You're too proud, you'll never do it. You'll be kicked out of society so fast it'll make your head spin."

"You might find this difficult to comprehend, Willie, but I'd rather risk losing my place in society than be forced to stay in this marriage with you."

SOCIETY
AS WE'VE
KNOWN IT

1894–1908

CHAPTER FIFTY-TWO

Alva

NEW YORK, 1894

FOR THE PAST YEAR, Alva and Willie had been living separate lives. He'd moved out, and other than to see the children, he hadn't been back to Petit Chateau or Marble House.

Duchy's best and numerous attempts to apologize hadn't changed a thing. There weren't enough tears or begging, nor enough telegrams or letters for redemption. As far as Alva was concerned, the friendship was irreparable. She knew the anger and bitterness would eventually burn itself out of her, leaving behind a heap of sadness that she wanted to put off for as long as possible. Sadness would turn her soft and more likely to forgive, and neither one of them was deserving of that. Especially not Duchy. In fact, she thought Duchy's betrayal was worse than Willie's. Friends didn't do that to friends.

She thought about Willie's friendship with Oliver. At first she blamed the kiss on the wine and thought she was getting even with Willie for his affair with *her* best friend. But deep down Alva knew that kissing Oliver wasn't an act of drunken revenge. It had been real. And magical. Even now, his kisses stirred her to the core. What she felt for Oliver was part emotional salve and part raw desire for a man who had sneaked up on her and stolen her heart. She wanted a future with him, and that alone gave her the courage to go through with her plans.

But divorce was harder than she'd expected. Her own lawyer had tried talking her out of it, claiming it would harm her reputation more than her husband's. *If you divorce him, there won't be a hostess in all of New York or Newport who will welcome you into her home . . .*

Alva knew certain women would not have approved of her divorcing her husband. She'd been expecting that and had prepared herself for it as best she could. What she was not at all prepared for, however, was a visit she received one day from Tessie and Mamie. At first she'd been so pleased to see them, but when they refused to even step inside her house, she felt suddenly clammy and cold.

"I'll make this brief," Tessie had said. "Given the news of your divorce, we, all of us"—she gestured as if to an imaginary chorus of women—"have agreed that your company is no longer welcome at our upcoming teas or parties."

"Oh, and you needn't bother replying to any recent invitations," said Mamie. "Your name has already been removed from our guest lists."

Alva had felt her face turning red, but she didn't crack. She couldn't afford to. "In that case," she had said, clearing her throat, "I suggest you take your leave before I have you thrown off my property."

That had only been the start of it. Alva couldn't make it through a day without being rebuffed. Even a simple visit to A. T. Stewart & Company had resulted in a public shaming. One day, under the dome of the grand emporium on the sixth floor, Alva was all too aware of the women with their hand fans up, covering their mouths while they whispered back and forth about her. And then it was Peggy Cavendish, of all people, who came forward and said in a loud, stuttering voice, "H-h-how dare y-y-you march in h-h-here as if y-y-you've d-d-done nothing w-w-wrong."

Alva turned, shoulders back, her chin held high as she took painfully slow measured steps out of the emporium. When she reached the mezzanine, she doubled over, her face slick with tears.

She didn't understand why they were so offended by her. Especially when for every one woman who criticized her, there were two more suffering in their own loveless marriages. How many wives had been humiliated and heartbroken by their husbands' adultery? Hadn't they all heard the stories about the first John Jacob Astor having orgies in his house with his wife sleeping upstairs? What about Charlotte Astor Drayton—was she the only woman who longed for a man other than her husband? Or just the only one brave enough to pursue him? Couldn't they appreciate that Alva had taken it upon herself to be the first—that if she could divorce her husband, they could divorce theirs, too?

CHAPTER FIFTY-THREE

Society

EACH DAY WE READ more about Alva and Willie's divorce, skipping over news of the current financial crisis for which there seems to be no end in sight. Not that you'd know it to look at us. The depression certainly isn't causing us to curb our appetite for the finer things. If anything, we seem to be indulging more than ever before.

Many of us were at Carrie Astor Wilson's Hat Ball, where we arrived in the most original hats imaginable. One gentleman's top hat was three feet high; another woman's plumes were so enormous, they got tangled in a chandelier and had to be cut free. And not to be outdone, Mr. and Mrs. Henry Clews threw a Servants Ball, where we dressed in carefully designed rags made of satin and silk. Many of us ladies carried buckets as evening bags while the men converted brooms into walking sticks. Then Tessie Oelrichs threw her Bal Blanc, where she served only white food and displayed only white flowers. We ladies dressed in all white, including white wigs, and the gentlemen were restricted to wearing solid black. If one of the men appeared in a white shirt, or carried white gloves, he was turned away at the door.

Following suit, there was the Rouge Ball, the Royal Blue Ball and a ball dedicated to just about every other shade imaginable. It kept us quite busy with our dressmakers. With all the primary colors taken, Puss decided to do something truly original and hired an elephant for her ball and had given each of us a fourteen-karat-gold bucket filled with peanuts so we could feed the animal as it trudged past us.

Perhaps one of the most unique entertainments of all was the Dog Ball, thrown by the flamboyant Harry Lehr. The Field Spaniels, English Setters, Fox Terriers, Saint Bernards and Great Danes arrived with diamond collars, satin bow ties, and hats perched between their ears. With the dogs gathered around a table off to the side, we owners looked on while the pets slurped from individual water and food bowls. One of the little Pointers overindulged on the mutton and passed out under the table. Aside from some attempted mating caused by a Spaniel in heat, and an accident by an overly excited Collie, the Dog Ball had been a huge success and the talk of the town.

We can hardly imagine who or what will top that, but we know something even bigger, even more outrageous must surely be in the works.

CHAPTER FIFTY-FOUR

Alva

ONCE UPON A TIME the press had adored and celebrated Alva. But no more. The very people who had built her up and helped to establish her in society were now first in line to tear her down. She could hardly believe the things they'd written about her—saying she was greedy and ruthless, a conniving liar. They urged other women not to follow her example, claiming *it would destroy the institution of marriage and do irreversible damage to the American family.*

Alva took Mamie and Tessie's advice and stopped attending all social functions, losing the nerve to show her face in public. And by then, the usual onslaught of invitations had come to a screeching halt anyway.

Oliver said he didn't mind and she was inclined to believe him. As far as he was concerned, they could run away to Europe until the whole thing blew over, or else stay in night after night. He just wanted to be with her. He didn't care if she was a socialite or not. He might not have cared, but she did. Alva spiraled downward, staying in bed most of the day, not bothering to join the children for luncheon like she normally did. There were times she wondered if it was all worth it, if she would have been better off staying in the marriage. And yet, she'd gone this far; she couldn't undo the damage to her reputation.

One day Alva's sisters, even Julia, arrived at Petit Chateau. They'd come to rally around her, hoping to cheer her up and take her mind off things.

"When was the last time you left the house?" asked Jennie.

"Get your hat and gloves," said Armide. "You're coming with us."

"Where are we going?"

"You'll see," said Julia, taking her hand.

They went on foot, walking through lower Manhattan, traversing streets she'd never been down before, Pearl Street and then Doyers. It was filthy: piles of manure everywhere, rubbish flying about, dirty-faced children playing in the street. A crude, crooked sidewalk of broken stone was overgrown with furry moss, and the scent of burning leaves hung all around them.

They ended up at a rickety building, covered in sooty-looking limestone with a rust stain running down the side caused by a leaking pipe. They entered and were led downstairs to a room packed with men and women sitting on long hard benches. The air smelled of cedar and cigars, though Alva didn't see anyone smoking at the time. A man was standing up at the front of the room, talking about an eight-hour workday and giving instructions for a protest the following day.

Alva looked around at the people, especially the women, their faces hardened, eyes bloodshot with dark circles underneath. She imagined they were chambermaids, or maybe seamstresses working in crowded, dirty factories. They wanted an eight-hour day, and she wondered how many hours a day they were working now. She pictured them standing on their feet or, worse yet, down on their knees scrubbing floors, cleaning up rich people's messes. She felt guilty—like she was the enemy—but she also felt inspired because these people weren't sitting back feeling sorry for themselves. They weren't victims. They were at least trying to do something about it.

"And you mean to tell me," Alva said on their walk home, "that there's meetings like that going on all over the city? Everyone was so energized in there!"

"See," Julia laughed, "there's more to life than your stuffy dinner parties and fancy balls."

Over the course of the next week, Alva's sisters took her to poetry readings, and lectures on everything from ending monopolies to the suffrage movement. She found it all so interesting, fascinating really. It was like scaling a wall and peeking over the hedge where a new world awaited—such possibilities on that other side.

Eventually, though, her sisters, one by one, were called back to their lives in Mobile, in New Jersey and in Brooklyn. Without them, when left on her own, Alva regressed to that dark place where they'd found her.

As the days and weeks passed, she realized that life—especially society—was getting on just fine without her. She read about all the balls and wondered if people even remembered that she'd started the trend of themed balls more than a decade ago with her masquerade ball. Did they recognize that it had been her ingenuity and creativity that had inspired it all?

The gossip columnists couldn't get enough of these parties. While the front page of every newspaper reported on the devastating economic depression, the society news sections were devoted to grandiose entertaining. Alva tried to imagine all the people—some of the people she'd met with her sisters—crowded into boarding rooms and tenement houses, reading about these lavish balls and nine-course meals when they could barely afford to feed themselves. There was more coverage given to their fashions and antics than to the anarchists and populists criticizing the rich, underscoring the growing disparity between the haves and have-nots.

What Alva found most ironic was that as the divide between rich and poor widened, the chasm between the Knickerbockers and the nouveau riche seemed to be narrowing. The more Mrs. Astor tried to keep the two separate, the more women like Alva had forced both halves together. They were becoming one, a high society united against the critical and hostile masses.

Though she found herself back on the outside looking in, Alva recognized that society had entered a whole new tier of extravagance, one that even the wealthiest among them would never be able to sustain. She wondered if the conspicuous consumption they feasted upon would be the very thing that would eventually choke the life out of them.

Weeks later, Alva had just left the stables out back and was still smelling of manure and the horses she'd been grooming when her butler announced she had a visitor.

"You'll have to forgive my appearance," Alva said, dusting off her hands. "I wasn't expecting company."

"Oh, come now, it's just me."

"Just me" was Lady Paget. "Haven't seen much of you around lately," she said, wrapping her arm about Alva's waist, the two walking into the drawing room.

"I'm afraid to step outside my house these days," said Alva, taking the chair next to hers. "But please, please tell me everything I'm missing out on."

Lady Paget laughed and dropped into a golden velvet bergère armchair, her bracelets jangling like wind chimes. "I'm sure you heard all about the Horse Ball at Sherry's."

Alva had indeed. Who would have thought one of New York's finest restaurants would ever be inhabited by horses? "And how was it?"

"They had a trough filled with caviar, and the horses had a bottle of champagne and crystal glasses in their saddlebags," said Lady Paget. "It started out wonderfully but"—she raised her hands—"what a disaster. They couldn't keep up with the manure, and then a horsetail cleared a table with one swish. The ball ended early. I was home by three."

Alva sighed, and pulled off a straw of hay clinging to her jodhpurs.

"Now tell me how you're getting on," asked Lady Paget.

"Honestly, I've been better. Everyone told me this would happen," she said, twisting the piece of hay. "Willie is still the toast of the town and I'm a pariah. Why is it always the woman who's to blame? I'm ruined. Frankly, I think you're very brave to have come here—I hope no one saw you arriving."

"Oh, nonsense," said Lady Paget. "You're not done for yet. You're forgetting you still have a secret weapon."

"Oh really," she said. "And what might that be?"

Lady Paget cocked her head and smiled. "Your daughter."

"Consuelo? No, no. I'm trying to keep my children out of this whole mess. I don't want to involve them, especially not Consuelo."

"But she's lovely and it is time to find her a husband." Lady Paget prided herself in being something of a matchmaker and claimed to have a sixth sense about these things.

"I don't know what Consuelo finding a husband has to do with anything. Besides, I know she's rather fond of Winthrop Rutherfurd. Unfortunately."

"Winthrop Rutherfurd?" Lady Paget laughed. "Winthrop Rutherfurd won't get you back in society. But a duke will."

"A duke?" Alva scrutinized Lady Paget's impish grin. "What are you up to?"

"Supposing I were to tell you that my friend Charles Richard John Spencer-Churchill, the ninth Duke of Marlborough, is looking for a wife."

Alva inched forward. "Go on."

"Sunny—the duke—is looking to settle down. It's time."

"And you think Consuelo would be a suitable match?"

"Let me just put it this way: He inherited the family's palace—it's a behemoth—and it's in dire need of money to keep it from utter ruin. He needs a bride—a bride with money." She tilted her head. "And you, my dear, can offer him both."

Alva collapsed back in her chair. "You're asking me to *sell* my daughter?"

"Oh, of course not. Don't be ridiculous. Sunny is a wonderful man. Very charming. Handsome, too. He's a far better catch than that Winthrop Rutherfurd."

"That's not saying much." Alva didn't care for Winthrop. He was much too old for Consuelo, thirty-three to her eighteen. He had a reputation of being a fortune hunter and courting lonely socialites whose husbands ignored them. On top of that, he was a gambler, and Alva had already seen what happened to Jeremiah. She didn't want her daughter subjected to a life like that.

"And you know Winthrop is sterile," said Lady Paget.

"No." Alva was shocked.

"Yes." She nodded as if that were worse than all the rest. Alva didn't bother to ask how she knew this intimate detail. "Think of it this way," said Lady Paget, "you'd be rescuing your daughter from a far worse fate. And honestly, it's the only way to get you back in society's good graces. Look at what marrying a title did for me. And, of course, marrying a duke did more for you know who—we won't even mention her name—but it did more for her than all her banjo playing ever could. And need I remind you how enraptured we Americans are when it comes to British nobility? If Consuelo becomes engaged to the duke, there won't be a hostess in this city who wouldn't welcome you. My God, they'll be tripping over themselves just to get invited to the wedding . . ."

Lady Paget kept talking about what the duke could do for her, but Alva was more interested in what the duke would do for Consuelo. Her daughter was so young, putting all her hopes on Winthrop. Alva wanted to open Consuelo's eyes, show her that there were other men in the world, men that were far better suited for her. Maybe the duke could turn her head; maybe she'd actually like him. At the very least, Alva could get her daughter away from Winthrop, and there always was the possibility that she could marry a title—could have the ultimate status for a woman in society. Consuelo's future would be secured. The idea filled Alva with a sense of duty and a great deal of trepidation. Alva knew that if Consuelo married the duke, she herself would forever be in the shadow of her daughter, the Duchess of Marlborough. She knew that her daughter would forevermore be the main attraction, and not Alva. The fact that Alva was willing to give that up, something that had once been her raison d'être, was a measure of how much she loved Consuelo. What had sounded absurd just moments before now made sense.

"How would we even go about this union?" Alva asked.

Lady Paget raised her bejeweled hand. "You leave that to me. It just so happens that Sunny will be here in New York on holiday. I'll arrange a dinner and, in good time, a meeting with him so you can work out all the details. But whatever you do, don't offer a penny over $2 million. That's more than enough to save Blenheim Palace—and your reputation."

The dinner with the ninth Duke of Marlborough went better than expected. He was gracious and notably impressed by Petit Chateau, especially Alva's Baccarat crystal chandelier and platinum-paneled walls in the dining room. The duke was quite handsome. A bit too serious in the beginning, though he relaxed as the evening progressed, even attempting a joke or two.

"I heard a good one," he said at dinner, between the *bouillon d'huîtres* and the terrapin. "Tell me," he said, "why is a dog just like a tree?"

They all looked at one another before Alva said, "I don't know. Why is a dog like a tree?"

"Because they both lose their bark after they're dead."

Consuelo laughed so hard that Alva was momentarily appalled by her unladylike guffaw. But then His Grace told another joke, and Alva realized this was what he did at the supper table. Consuelo would have to get used to that and cache some jokes of her own so she could contribute.

After dinner, when they retired to the music room, Consuelo had impressed him by playing Beethoven's *Moonlight* Sonata followed by pieces by Chopin and Strauss. Alva was pleased. Consuelo and Sunny seemed to be getting on very well.

The next day, the duke joined them for tea, and two days after that, he accompanied Alva and Consuelo to the Metropolitan Opera House for the production of *Fidelio*. The following week, Alva invited him to a reception and another dinner. After each new encounter, Alva would huddle with Consuelo, the two of them crowded into her bed with the coverlet pulled up past their shoulders while they compared notes: *He did bring me flowers. He clearly doesn't like America. He has such a lovely smile. He was obviously bored at the opera. The ladies at the reception all found him charming.* Night after night they did this, and Consuelo hadn't so much as mentioned Winthrop's name.

Six weeks later, just two days before the duke was set to return to England, Alva met with him in the office that had once belonged to Willie. After the duke expressed his interest in marrying Consuelo, Alva took over.

Resting her hands on the desk, fingers laced together, she said, "Shall we discuss the dowry?"

"As you know," said the duke, "Blenheim Palace is facing some financial challenges." He went on to list his needs including the staff and, of course, the palace itself, which was overdue for a complete renovation.

Alva fluttered her eyelashes, and keeping Lady Paget's advice in mind, she started low, offering $1.5 million.

The duke sighed. "Actually, I was hoping to do a bit better."

Alva contemplated her options. She didn't want this opportunity to get away—especially since Consuelo was growing more and more attached to the idea of marriage. "I suppose I could go a *little* higher."

The duke was a tough negotiator and, in the end, the day before he set sail for England, they agreed that Alva would pay him $2.5 million, plus 50,000 shares of Vanderbilt stock and an additional $200,000 a year for the rest of his life. Now that the finances had been settled, they were just waiting for the duke to propose.

One morning, Alva was shuffling through the mail, which had increased significantly since her association with the duke. There were invitations and notes from Mamie, Tessie and several others.

Alva set those aside and came upon an envelope addressed to Consuelo. Clearly the handwriting was a man's, and Alva was hoping it was from Sunny. Without a thought for her daughter's privacy, Alva sliced the envelope open only to find a lengthy letter from Winthrop Rutherfurd, who was abroad, visiting relatives in England. As Alva continued reading, she turned queasy when she reached the part about his *undying love and affection* for Consuelo. Alva was confused. Consuelo said she'd ended it with him right after meeting Sunny. She seemed in favor of marrying Sunny. Had she just been pacifying Alva? Playing her this whole time? Her daughter couldn't be that cunning, could she? And then her eyes moved to the next paragraph, and the knot in her stomach pulled even tighter. Winthrop had detailed their plans to marry. *Marry! Good lord!* They were eloping, one month from the day.

The letter slipped from Alva's hands. The panic was rising inside her, and she thought she might get sick. There was no way her daughter was going to marry Winthrop Rutherfurd. He was a laughing-stock. A philanderer, a fortune hunter, a compulsive gambler. She could see the headlines now: VANDERBILT HEIRESS SWINDLED . . . The room grew hot. Alva turned clammy and nauseated. A marriage to Winthrop would be a source of ridicule and scandal, and Alva had to spare her daughter from that. Consuelo wasn't strong enough to withstand that kind of pressure. Winthrop would break her heart. Besides, Alva had already promised the duke that Consuelo would accept his proposal.

Alva picked up Winthrop's letter and stuffed it in her pocket, and later that day when Consuelo asked if she had received any mail, Alva looked into her daughter's hopeful, doe-like eyes and she lied. She lied to her the next day, too, and the day after that. By the end of the week, Alva had five of Winthrop's letters—each filled with romantic angst and longings—locked away in her desk drawer.

The next day Alva got hold of an outgoing letter that Consuelo had written to Winthrop. Again, casting aside all privacy—a line she'd long since crossed—she tore the letter open and felt her legs turning weak as she read more about their plans to elope. *I have my dress picked out . . . I cannot wait to get away from here . . . So excited to start my life with you . . .* Alva was shaking by the time she finished. She had to do something—she couldn't sit back and watch Consuelo throw her future away. She had to save her daughter from herself.

After an hour of fretting, her panic had escalated and could no longer be contained. She rang for the butler, asking for the key to Consuelo's bedroom.

It wasn't even noon yet and Consuelo was still asleep when Alva locked her daughter's bedroom door. Wringing her hands, Alva paced up and down the hallway. She had no idea what she was doing—it sounded absurd even to her. She was about to reach for the skeleton key in her pocket and unlock the door, put everything back the way it was. Consuelo would be none the wiser. But just then she heard the doorknob turn once, twice, and all the fear came flooding back.

Consuelo jiggled the knob harder on the third try before calling out. "Boya? Boya"—she called for her maid—"can you help me? My door seems to be stuck."

Alva's heart was racing, her hand sweating as she worried the brass key in her pocket. She was light-headed and dizzy. It hurt to breathe. If she didn't know better, she'd swear she was having a heart attack.

"Boya?" The knob turned more violently. *"Boya!"*

Alva dropped the key back into her pocket. "It's not stuck," she said. "It's locked and you're not going anywhere until you stop this foolishness with Winthrop Rutherfurd. I know all about your plans, and I'm putting an end to them right here and now, do you understand?"

There was a beat of silence before Consuelo began desperately pounding on the door. "I love him. I love him, and I'm going to marry him."

"You'll do no such thing. Do you hear me? You're going to marry the duke."

"I won't marry Sunny. I won't do it!"

"Then you'll just stay in your room until you come to your senses."

Alva walked away just as Consuelo began pounding on the door again, demanding to be let out.

Later that afternoon all was quiet when Alva went to check on her. "Well," she said from outside the door, "are you ready to do as you're told?"

"I'm going to marry Winthrop."

"I'm not playing games here, Consuelo. You are not going to marry that man."

"Oh, yes I am. He'll come for me."

"If he does, I'll have him arrested for trespassing."

"You're bluffing."

Alva sighed, resting her head against the door. "Consuelo, I'm warning you—you do not want to push me on this."

She heard Consuelo's footsteps coming closer, stomping across the floor, and watched the doorknob twisting. "Let me out!"

"You know what you have to do if you want out." She paused for a moment. "Well? Are you going to do as you're told?"

Through the sound of gritted teeth—a grimaced expression she could picture in her mind—Alva heard Consuelo say, "I am going to marry Winthrop."

"Fine. Then you have a good night, Consuelo." She walked away while Consuelo screamed and pounded on the door.

Alva hardly slept that night. Twice she got up to unlock the door and then changed her mind. The next day she wrestled with herself, trying to figure out what to do. Realizing she couldn't keep her daughter locked up forever, Alva finally went to Consuelo's room. She found her lying in bed, eyes barely blinking as she defiantly stared at the ceiling, refusing to acknowledge Alva.

"You have no idea what you'd be getting yourself into with that man. He's no good. He's no good for you—I won't let you do it. You cannot marry Winthrop."

"You don't even know him."

"I know that he's too old for you, he has a gambling problem, he'll never be able to give you children, and he'll—"

"What?" said Consuelo, her eyes open wide.

What did she mean, "what?" Had she never heard this before? Alva sensed the tiniest of cracks in her daughter's resolve. Was it possible that Alva had finally raised an argument that was getting through?

"It's true," said Alva. "He's sterile. Didn't you wonder why he'd never taken a wife? It's because no other woman would have him."

Consuelo blinked, her eyes welling up with tears.

This was all it would have taken? Telling her he was sterile? Why didn't I tell her this sooner? "I know what having a family means to you. If you marry this man, you'll never have children of your own. Never."

"But—that can't be true. It just can't be."

Alva reached for Consuelo's hand, bringing it to her cheek damp-
ened by her own tears. "I wish it weren't true. I don't dislike Winthrop, truly I don't," she lied. "But he can never give you the life you
deserve. Why do you think I want you to marry Sunny instead?"

Consuelo sniffled and let loose a cascade of tears before she folded
down into her mother's arms. "It's not fair. Why does it have to be
true? It's not fair . . ."

Two months later, Consuelo's engagement to the duke was announced in newspapers across the country. The date had been set for
the sixth of November, and planning the nuptials had begun for what
the New York Times predicted would be THE WEDDING OF THE CENTURY.

So Alva had gotten her way, but her victory was bittersweet. This
was her daughter—her only daughter—who was getting married,
and all the fantasies Alva had about one day designing her wedding
gown and selecting the items for her trousseau and the flowers for her
bouquet fell flat. Alva had never seen a more indifferent bride in all
her life. And everyone seemed to notice.

Willie begged Alva to call off the wedding. "Can't you see the girl
is miserable? Don't force her, Alva. It isn't fair. A title isn't worth it."

"So easy for you to say. You've never been publicly shunned. No,
you took a mistress and no one slammed their door in your face. Do
you realize what it's taken for me to pry that door back open? Even
just a crack?"

In truth, it was more than just a crack. As Lady Paget had predicted, invitations to balls and luncheons, to dinner parties and teas
came flooding back to Alva. Even the published details of her pend-
ing divorce—her suing for custody of the children, her anticipated
settlement of at least $200,000 per year along with Marble House—
no longer fazed her former critics.

Off the record, Willie had offered her Petit Chateau, but she no
longer wanted it. She didn't want anything of his other than his best

friend. Oliver Belmont she did want. Badly. She would have him, too. And she didn't care that he was a Jew. He loved her and wanted to marry her just as soon as her divorce was finalized.

When he'd first raised the subject of marriage, Alva had laughed and nearly shoved him out of bed. "Don't be ridiculous. We each have one failed marriage behind us."

"All the more reason why we should do it again. We already know what *not* to do."

Alva propped herself up on her elbow. "You're the last person in the world I'd marry. You'll never be ready to settle down with anyone."

"I am with you."

She had been ready to make another joke, when she saw the look in his eyes. "You're serious, aren't you?"

"Don't you see? I finally understand why I *couldn't* settle down before. Nothing—no one—ever felt right. I was always looking for what's next—who's next—because what I had wasn't right. This is the first time in my life that I don't want to run. When I'm with you, I'm exactly where I want to be, where I'm meant to be. When we're together, I'm not thinking about the past, I'm not worrying about the future. I'm not thinking about anything but you and what we have right here, right now in this very moment. And I want a lifetime of moments with you."

That was when she realized that he had articulated how she felt, too. Exactly.

The two planned to marry the following year, and then she would be able to rest easy. She would be Oliver's wife, her daughter would be a duchess, and Alva would have survived the ultimate taboo.

CHAPTER FIFTY-FIVE

Caroline

NEW YORK, 1895

AFTER MORE THAN TWO years, Caroline was out of mourning for William and Helen, and her upcoming annual ball would be her first social engagement and her first opportunity to reinstate Charlotte's good name. In fact, her ball was going to be in Charlotte's honor. Caroline would show everyone that, despite the rumors, despite what may have been true in the past, it was a new day now, a new era for women. She needed everyone to understand that she stood by her daughter.

This, of course, was an easier stance for her to take given Alva Vanderbilt's upcoming divorce. Although Alva was expected to retain custody of her children, whereas poor Charlotte had lost that battle. Caroline had certainly taken that loss harder than Charlotte, which left her baffled. Charlotte's detachment from those children was nearly impossible for her to defend, but still Caroline had to try.

She moved forward with her party planning, disgusted by how ridiculous and extravagant balls had become in recent years. It was as if jeweled favors and zoo animals could compensate for a weak hostess. Caroline's ball would be dignified, and she would show society what it truly meant to be a New York hostess.

Two days before the big event, while she was reviewing the orchestra's song list, Charlotte and Carrie came to her with that doleful look in their eyes.

"Mother," said Charlotte, stepping into the sitting room, Carrie close behind. "Oh, Mother, have you heard about Mr. McAllister?"

What now? "What has he gone and done this time?" she asked, returning to her list.

"He died," said Charlotte bluntly.

"What?" Caroline dropped the orchestra list.

"He was at the Union Club last night," said Carrie. "It happened right in the dining room. He was having dinner by himself and suddenly collapsed at his table. They said he died instantly."

Caroline brought a hand to her chest. For a moment she couldn't catch her breath.

"Oh, Mother," said Carrie. "I'm so sorry. How much more can you take?"

Caroline was stunned but composed—perhaps because she'd already been through far greater losses. But both her girls had gone glassy-eyed, refusing to outright cry, knowing that such a display would have only disappointed Caroline.

"Shall we cancel the ball?" asked Carrie, looking at her sister, who was readily nodding.

"I'll understand if you wish to, Mother," said Charlotte. "We'll wait and have the ball after his funeral. Or maybe wait until spring."

Caroline shook her head. She didn't even have to consider it. "That won't be necessary." It was more important, now more than ever, that she host her ball. There was too much riding on this event—mainly, Charlotte's reputation.

After her daughters left, Caroline sat by herself for a good long while, until the sun began to set. She hadn't seen Ward McAllister in months, and their friendship, if she could have called it that, had been fractured by his memoir and then destroyed by the Four Hundred.

She thought any affection she'd once had for him would have drained out of her long ago, but in the quiet of that room, she felt a tear in her heart.

There was a time when he'd been her only confidant and she, his Mystic Rose. He'd been the first one—even if it was because of her inheritance—to recognize that she could lead society. In a sense he'd been as much a part of her family as her husband and children. He'd been the one who crowned her queen of New York society, and together they had designed a world that served them, delighted them, empowered them.

A lump gathered in her throat as she thought about her losses, first Emily and then William and Helen, and now Ward. It made her think about what lay ahead after this world. Caroline did believe in heaven and hell, and she wondered about God's judgment. Was he as strict as Caroline and Ward had been when it came to society and determining who was acceptable and who wasn't? It occurred to her that by establishing the Patriarch Ball, her own annual ball and especially the Four Hundred, they had excluded many, based on their own criteria, on the randomness of birthright and bloodlines. It all seemed so insignificant now, and she realized, to her horror, that she and Ward had been playing God. And a vengeful God at that.

Two days after Ward McAllister died, Caroline held her annual ball as planned where she honored her *disgraced* daughter in a public and purposeful way. With Charlotte at her side, Caroline received her guests, the two of them seated next to each other beneath Caroline's regal portrait.

When it was time to receive Mamie Fish, Mamie shook Charlotte's hand and said, "I'm sure you'll go places, my dear. And may those places be far, far away from here." She walked away, laughter trailing behind her, thinking she was merely being clever, but Caroline found it rude, even by Mamie's standards.

There was a time when Mamie never would have dared to say such a thing for fear of being banished from society, but it was clear now that Charlotte's sullied reputation had diminished Caroline's authority as well. Charlotte's face flushed, and for the first time Caroline questioned whether her social clout was still strong enough to save her daughter's reputation. Charlotte was on the dais, on display, and might as well have had a scarlet *A* on her chest.

Charlotte wanted to leave, and Caroline was about to let her go, when Alva Vanderbilt arrived. Caroline had invited Alva for a myriad of reasons, but mostly for Charlotte's sake. At least now there were two divorced—or soon to be divorced—women at the ball. In a sense she was using Alva just as Alva had used Caroline to make a statement at her masquerade party all those years ago. It was clear by the way people stopped to greet Alva that society had not only accepted her imminent divorce, but now wholeheartedly embraced the future mother-in-law of the ninth Duke of Marlborough. Caroline's guests even parted the walkway for Alva, just as they'd once done for her. She was mystified and a bit envious of Alva's charisma.

When it was time to receive Alva, Caroline extended her hand, welcoming her.

"Mrs. Astor." Alva smiled graciously, shaking her hand. "It's so very good to see you again."

"You remember my daughter, Charlotte?"

Alva took Charlotte's hands in hers. "Why of course. Charlotte, how lovely you look, my dear." She leaned in and said in a soft voice, "You stay strong, you hear me? Divorce is not the end, it's a new beginning." Then she turned to Caroline. "May I borrow your daughter for a moment?" Before Caroline answered, Alva had turned back to Charlotte. "Let's you and I take a little stroll, shall we?"

Caroline watched Alva help Charlotte down from the dais, the sea of guests parting as the two walked along. Alva was all smiles, stopping every few feet to say hello to this one and that, gesturing toward

Charlotte as if making an introduction. Alva never left Charlotte's side, and those matrons who had just openly rejected Charlotte were now waiting their turn to speak with her. Soon it was almost as if a second receiving line had formed, people lining up to say hello to Alva. And Charlotte.

Caroline remained on the dais, still greeting her guests, but she was very much aware of how Alva's gesture had changed the course of the evening in Charlotte's favor. Standing next to Alva, Charlotte held her shoulders back and her head high, and the hint of that sparkle she'd lost years ago was back in her smile. It was as if the spell had been broken, a dark cloud lifted. There was a time when Caroline was the only one powerful enough to have done such a thing. But that night, her own efforts had paled in comparison to Alva Vanderbilt's.

CHAPTER FIFTY-SIX

Society

IT'S NEARLY DAWN BY the time we return home from Mrs. Astor's ball. After our lady's maids help us out of our gowns, return our jewels to our safes, take down our hair and braid our locks, we lie in our feather beds able to breathe deeply for the first time all day, our angry rib cages puckered and dimpled by the boning of our corsets. We take in the air, letting it fill our lungs and expand our abdomens, thinking about Alva's triumph tonight.

It's hard to believe this is the same Alva Vanderbilt who was cast out because of her own divorce scandal. She has clearly redeemed herself, and in the process, she's paved the way for us, too. The only question now is, *What will we do with our newfound freedom?*

Choice is something we're unaccustomed to; it's almost too much, and at first it makes us freeze up. But another deep breath and we begin to relax, to let our minds dare to wander . . .

Penelope thinks boldly about divorcing her husband, about starting over. Ophelia wonders what it would be like to make a simple purchase without her husband's permission. What a relief it would be to no longer produce a weekly ledger of expenses for his approval. Lydia imagines what it would be like to live the life of one of those heroines she reads about. Peggy feels that winning the vote is too lofty and instead thinks how lovely it would be to smoke a cigarette in public, or even a pipe if she so pleased, letting the aromatic tobacco swirl about her head as the brandy swirls in her snifter. We'd all love to have our own ladies' clubs where we can go to luncheon, play poker, talk politics and gossip. We want all this and more, and we drift off to sleep now, counting possibilities like others count sheep.

CHAPTER FIFTY-SEVEN

Caroline

THE MORNING AFTER HER ball, Caroline awoke at her usual time, half past eight. After her maid brought in her breakfast tray along with the morning newspapers and Caroline had completed her morning toilette, Thomas, looking a bit flustered, came to speak with her.

"Is something wrong?"

"Ah, well . . ." He was stammering, and Thomas, an elegant man, never stammered. "I'm afraid there's been some more trouble next door."

Caroline waited, somewhat annoyed. She had been in such a fog, so lost in mourning, that she'd hardly noticed when her nephew finally opened the Waldorf Hotel. But now she was all too aware of the strange carriages pulling up in front of her house, people of all walks of life traipsing across her lawn.

Thomas cleared his throat. She sensed he was stalling.

"Well? What is it *this time*?"

"I regret to inform you that apparently some of the Waldorf Hotel's patrons relieved themselves on the front lawn last night."

She was aghast. Civilized people didn't do such a thing.

"Forgive me, Mrs. Astor, but I thought you would want to know." He paused to clear his throat. "And I'm afraid there's more."

"More?" She crossed her arms, bracing herself.

"One of the footmen discovered that another Waldorf patron—a perfect stranger—wandered in last night during the ball along with some of your guests. I'm sorry to report that he passed out in one of your guest rooms. And apparently, he misplaced his clothing along the way."

Caroline winced. This was unacceptable. She told Thomas to have her driver bring the carriage around and dashed off to see her nephew, demanding that Waldorf shut down his hotel.

"Well, I'm not about to do that, Aunt Lina." The two of them were in his game room. Waldorf was shooting pool, concentrating on each shot, scarcely bothering to look up when he spoke. "The hotel is extremely profitable. Besides," he said as he made a complicated bank shot, "your old townhouse is a bit of an eyesore. You could do us all a favor and move. I do wish you would tear the old place down and make room for something worthy of this block."

"Beware of what you wish for, Waldorf." Though she remained calm and moved with her regular slow grace, she was fuming. She left the game room, got back into her carriage and rode off, thinking of ways to retaliate.

When she returned home, she told Thomas she was thinking of moving and turning her townhouse into a horse stable. "That would show him," she said. "Can't you just imagine the stench of manure infiltrating every room of Waldorf's hotel?"

"With all due respect, Mrs. Astor, what I cannot imagine is a horse stable with your name on it."

She smiled.

"Have you been to the Waldorf?" he asked tentatively.

"Most certainly not." She looked at him as if to say, *How dare you ask such a thing.* Then she thought for a moment. "Why? Have you?"

He shrugged apologetically. "Only once. It's quite nice but I think you could do better."

"Better how?"

"Well, if Mr. Waldorf Astor wishes to see something more laudable next to his hotel, I say give it to him."

"What are you suggesting?"

"Build another hotel. A bigger hotel. A better one." He smiled and tweaked his mustache.

"Thomas!" Caroline's eyes flashed wide. "You never cease to amaze me."

The next day Caroline enlisted the help of Jack, and together they engaged the services of Richard Morris Hunt to build a new home at Sixty-Fifth Street and Fifth Avenue that Caroline would share with her son and his family.

And starting in the spring, they would demolish her townhouse and begin building a new hotel at Thirty-Fourth Street, right next door to the Waldorf. Caroline's hotel would be larger, seventeen stories compared to Waldorf's thirteen. It would have a bigger, grander ballroom large enough for 1,600 guests, and a rooftop garden, too. Richard Hunt told her it would take two years to complete but Caroline didn't care, as long as its every detail was designed to upstage and dwarf the Waldorf. She was going to name it the Astoria Hotel.

CHAPTER FIFTY-EIGHT

Alva

"TAKE THEM," ALVA SAID to Consuelo the day before her wedding, closing her daughter's hands about the strand of pearls.

"But Mamma, not these, too. These were the first jewels Father ever gave you."

Alva had already given Consuelo all the other jewelry from Willie. Those pearls, once belonging to Catherine the Great, were the last of it.

"I can't accept these," Consuelo said, handing them back to Alva.

"Of course you can. You'll need those pearls after you're married. Don't forget, you're going to be a duchess."

"A duchess." She said it as if the word weighed fifty pounds.

"Ah, what's wrong?"

"I'm sorry, Mamma. I'm just—well, I'm just having second thoughts about everything."

"Perfectly normal," she said rather dismissively, busying herself with the pearls.

"But I can't stop thinking about Winthrop—I hurt him so."

Alva froze in place.

"And, well . . . I still love him, Mamma. I do."

Alva dropped the pearls.

"I know we couldn't have children of our own," said Consuelo, "but there's all those orphanages. So many children without homes . . ."

"Adoption?"

"I know it's not the same but—"

"Your children will have Vanderbilt blood, and that's all there is to it."

Consuelo went silent for a moment, summoning the courage to say, "But you divorced Father because you didn't love him anymore."

Alva toyed with a pair of emerald earrings. There was gnawing in the pit of her stomach. All this had run in the back of her mind, that nagging truth that she was a hypocrite. Up until now she'd found ways to justify it: *Consuelo didn't understand. She was young, only eighteen. She didn't know what real love was* . . .

"I don't love Sunny," said Consuelo. "And I *know* he doesn't love me."

Alva turned very still and set the earrings back down. It finally hit her. The evidence had been mounting even as she tried ignoring the signs, pretending not to see the sadness in her daughter's eyes. The criticisms had been coming from Willie, from his family, her sisters—even from Oliver. For weeks and months, everyone had been begging her to call it off. And now Alva could no longer escape the fact that no one—other than herself—wanted this wedding. She had orchestrated this whole union against everyone's wills. Yes, the groom wanted the money, but any bride with the right financing could have become the duchess. This was a business transaction, not a marriage.

After everything she'd suffered through—telling herself and others that she'd endured the disgrace of divorce on behalf of women everywhere. Women everywhere—but not her own daughter. How could she have let things get this far? She'd stood up for women—nameless, faceless women—and turned around and sold her daughter off.

"Listen to me," she said, taking Consuelo's hands, "I love you more than anything in this world. I want you to be happy."

Consuelo blinked, releasing a trickle of tears.

"If you feel that strongly," said Alva, "if you really think you can't go through with it, we'll call off the wedding. But—"

Consuelo's mouth had dropped open.

"But if we break this off, you cannot marry Winthrop. That would be the greatest mistake you could ever make, and I can't sit back and let that happen. And," she said, "you need to know that it won't be easy on you. There *will* be gossip. There *will* be ridicule. You can be sure the press *will* run stories about it. It could make things much harder for you to marry well in the future. Are you prepared for that?"

Consuelo's shoulders were shaking as she wept into her hands. "I'm so confused. I'm so scared, Mamma. I don't know what to do."

Alva pulled her into her arms and let her cry, tears soaking her shoulder. All she could think was, *Dear God, forgive me for what I've done to this poor child!*

"It's not as though I'm *not* fond of Sunny," said Consuelo, trying to compose herself. "I *am* fond of him, but I don't actually *love* him."

"Sometimes love is not enough. I was madly in love with your father," she said, recalling when she and Willie met, when she'd first set eyes on him. "Love just wasn't enough for us. At least with Sunny you'll have a chance for happiness," said Alva. "And children—you'll be such a wonderful mother. You'd have a title, and your future and your children's futures will be set for life. That's why I've been pushing so hard for this."

Consuelo dried her eyes and sniffled. "Sunny and I do get on well," she said as if trying to talk herself into it.

"That's a strong foundation," said Alva. "Love can always come later."

Consuelo let fresh tears roll down her cheeks. "Mamma, if you were me, what would you do?"

Alva paused. This wasn't a simple question to answer. Alva was as different from her daughter as anyone could be. She thought about what she'd gone through to divorce Willie. The press had torn her apart. There were days she'd found them camped out on her front lawn, waiting to attack. There were days Alva couldn't get out of bed, couldn't eat, couldn't keep from crying. If her daughter left the groom—who happened to be a duke, no less—at the altar, Consuelo's name and character would be dragged through the mud. Consuelo wasn't as tough as Alva. She feared her daughter would never be able to survive that sort of criticism and scrutiny.

Alva drew a deep breath, cupped Consuelo's face in her hands and said, "Honestly, *if I were you*, even though I'd have doubts, even though I'd be scared, *if I were you*, I would marry the duke."

And she did. The next day, Consuelo Vanderbilt married His Grace, Charles Richard John Spencer-Churchill, the ninth Duke of Marlborough.

CHAPTER FIFTY-NINE

Caroline

NEWPORT AND NEW YORK, 1896

WITH HER TOWNHOUSE DEMOLISHED to make way for the new Astoria Hotel and her future home still weeks away from completion, Caroline was cottaging in Newport. It was good to be away from the city, to take in the sea air, and after years of mourning, the more leisurely pace helped her ease back into the social scene.

One afternoon she accepted an invitation to the McVickars' lawn party. Delighted to have her there, the hostess, Maud McVickar, sat with Caroline in the wicker chairs beneath a large umbrella overlooking a robust game of croquet. While the two made idle conversation, a croquet ball rolled their way. Maud stopped the ball with her foot, and as soon as she got up to return it, a handsome young man stepped in to take her place.

Removing his straw boater, he bowed gallantly and said, "Where oh where have you been all my life, Lina?"

Caroline's eyes opened wide in shock. No one had called her Lina in ages.

Then he winked.

She was secretly tickled when he leaned forward, kissed her hand and helped himself to Mrs. McVickar's chair without having been invited to do so. His name was Harry Lehr. He was twenty-seven, gorgeous to look at, charming and witty; a man who didn't take himself or society too seriously. Even before Ward McAllister passed away, everyone sensed that he had fallen out of favor with Caroline, and a number of gentlemen had come forward, eager to take his place. Caroline had been unimpressed. But there was something about this Harry Lehr. Unlike the others, he was not a tad bit intimidated by the Grande Dame. He stayed at her side the rest of the party, showering her with attention. After mourning William and Helen, Caroline found Harry's company as refreshing as Newport's sea breeze.

The following week he paid a social call to her at her Beechwood cottage, and the two of them had tea and chocolate biscuits in the solarium. Thomas was lurking around, fussing with plants and straightening picture frames, keeping a fatherly watch on things. As she and Harry sat talking, and drinking their tea, Caroline wasn't sure if she was more appalled or charmed when Harry shamelessly licked his fingers.

He caught her eyeing him and smiled. "It's a crime to waste even a morsel of chocolate. Isn't it? Go on, give it a try."

Much to her astonishment, she did.

In the weeks and months to come, Harry continued to call on Caroline, both in Newport and back in New York. With each passing day, her stiff joints, her sore back and aching feet reminded Caroline of her own mortality. Time was precious, and with two daughters whose lives had been cut short, she felt she owed it to them, as well as to herself, to ease up and enjoy herself while she still could. She believed that Harry had come into her life for that very reason. And so, at the age of sixty-six, Caroline Astor discovered something new and novel: it was called fun.

Harry was the only one who could get away with saying things to her that no one had ever dared. He told her she was stiff and accused her of behaving like a snob, to which she laughed. When he said, "You have elevated rudeness to a fine art," she giggled like a schoolgirl and playfully slapped his hand.

It was Harry Lehr who finally persuaded Caroline to attend the Metropolitan Opera House. Still bitter over the collapse of her beloved Academy of Music, she had never stepped foot inside the new opera house, despite having purchased a box years before. As was her usual style, she'd arrived late, during the second act of *Tannhäuser*. With Harry at her side, she was more carefree than she'd felt in ages. She'd had an immensely fine evening.

Harry Lehr had also escorted Caroline to the opening of the Astoria Hotel on the site of her former townhouse, next to the Waldorf. That night, while on Harry's arm, she remembered looking across the room and seeing Thomas with not one, but two lovely ladies at his side: his daughters. Seeing those girls with Thomas made her think of William with Emily and Helen.

When they were preparing the hotel's opening party, she had told Thomas she wanted him to attend. "And bring your daughters, too," she'd said. "After all, this hotel was your idea to begin with."

He had respectfully declined.

"I insist."

"But I'm afraid neither my girls nor I would have the appropriate attire for such an affair," he said.

Well, Caroline had remedied that. After much protesting on Thomas's part, she paid for not only a fine tailored suit for him but two extraordinary gowns for his daughters embellished with gemstones and beading, along with a string of pearls for each. Thomas did look dashing, and she noticed several women wondering who this mysterious gentleman was. Caroline had been most amused by that and couldn't wait to tell Thomas that he'd made such a fine impression on society. She also realized that his daughters had never been introduced to society, had never been exposed to such an opulent atmosphere before. If they were at all nervous, no one would have known. They seemed graceful and just as poised as any other guests. It was all just further proof that there was more room inside polite society than she'd once thought.

One evening, while visiting Caroline in her new home, Harry sat in her parlor with a mischievous grin on his face. "Come," he said, summoning her with his index finger. "We're going out for dinner."

Caroline looked at him, bewildered.

Thomas, who had been standing off to the side, spoke up. "I'm afraid Mrs. Astor does not engage in social activities on Sunday evenings."

"Oh, come now, Lina," said Harry, crossing his legs, bobbing his foot up and down. "It's 1896. Stop acting like an old biddy."

"Well"—she could feel Thomas's eyes on her while she looked at Harry—"I suppose I could make an exception. But just this once."

"Marvelous." Harry clapped, springing to his feet. "Let's go. My new carriage is right out front. Just wait till you see it. And please, don't wear that silly veil. Let people see you in all your glory."

The next thing she knew, she was standing out front before his carriage, or at least something that looked like the body of one. "What happened to your horses?" she asked, thinking they'd been stolen.

"This is a Schloemer Wagon. It doesn't need horses. It's motorized, Lina. Imagine that!"

"Motorized?" She was aghast.

"Word is that this machine right here is going to replace the horse."

"Impossible. I don't believe it. Not for a second."

She was skeptical as he helped her inside, and after a series of cranks, the carriage let out an atrocious noise and started to move, on its own, as if some invisible force were pulling it forward. She was terrified. "Where are we going?" she asked, holding tightly to Harry's arm.

"To Sherry's. We're going to dine. In the restaurant. Just like regular ordinary folks."

Caroline was stunned. The only time she'd eaten at Sherry's was at a ball or private affair. She'd seen people dine in public but had never done so herself. She wasn't even sure *how* to go about doing it.

The maître d' showed them to a fine table, elegantly appointed. Caroline felt everyone in the restaurant taking notice of her. Or perhaps they were looking at how very handsome Harry Lehr was. Either way, she supposed she was easily recognized, especially without her veil and with all her diamonds and oversize wig. Caroline was quite taken with the notion of a quaint table for two and a waiter who tended to their needs just as a footman would have done.

After their waiter presented her with a leather-bound menu, Caroline glanced inside and said, "Oh my. Did you see this? They have prices next to every item. How very odd."

Except for the motorized wagon ride, the whole experience was unfamiliar but wholly enjoyable. Caroline loved everything and decided she would take to dining out more often. The next day, news of Caroline's restaurant debut made nearly every paper: MRS. ASTOR VISITS A PUBLIC DINING ROOM. For once she was tickled by the press's attention.

As her friendship with Harry continued, Thomas seemed to be more protective of Caroline, and if she hadn't known better, she would have thought he was jealous. And while Thomas had become a loyal confidant, Harry was a most refreshing companion and always full of surprises.

The one drawback to Caroline's friendship with Harry was that it did put her in frequent contact with Mamie Fish. He enjoyed Mamie's sense of humor, and amazingly enough, the woman's laugh didn't give him a headache. When Caroline received an invitation to attend Mamie's ball honoring Prince Del Drago of Corsica, she told Harry she wasn't interested.

"I've never even heard of Prince Del Drago," she said, but Harry had insisted Caroline attend, and when he set his lovely eyes on her and flashed that devilish smile, she could not say no.

So she went to Mamie's ball, and since Harry was sociable with everyone, Caroline found herself engaged in conversation with Alva and her new husband, Oliver Belmont. Caroline had to admit that this second marriage seemed to agree with Alva. The hot-tempered redhead appeared to have mellowed, or perhaps it was Caroline who had become more genial.

Alva asked about Charlotte. "How is she getting on in London?"

"She's delighted to be back in Europe," said Caroline. Her voice had a queer ring to it, as she was unaccustomed to making small talk in general, let alone discussing her children—especially Charlotte, who had recently met that one man she truly *could not live without*. She and George Ogilvy Haig were to be married later that year.

Alva smiled. "I'm sure you must miss her dearly, as I miss my Consuelo."

Of course, Caroline missed Charlotte, but she took comfort in knowing that her daughter had left New York with her head held high. And that was in great part due to Alva.

Meanwhile, Mamie was holding court, receiving her guests. The line moved along quickly and soon Caroline and Harry were behind a gentleman whom Mamie looked at and said, "Oh, how do you do? I had quite forgotten I'd invited you." She laughed and added, "Well, do make yourself at home, and believe me, there's no one here who wishes you were at home more than I."

"Hasn't she got a marvelous wit?" said Harry.

They were next, and when she shook Caroline's hand, Mamie said, "We were taking bets on whether or not you'd show."

"There's still no telling how long I'll stay," said Caroline.

Mamie laughed and turned her attention to Harry, who took both her hands in his. "You look positively beautiful tonight," he said.

Beautiful? Mamie was many things but beautiful was not one of them. Caroline felt a jealous stab to her heart. Heaven help her. *Jealous of Mamie Fish!* It was absurd. Besides, Harry Lehr was impossibly too young for her—and for Mamie, too. Caroline had heard the rumors about his having that portrait of a nude man in his bedroom, but it didn't matter. This wasn't romantic. It was simply that Caroline had never had such fun ever before in her life. He made her feel young and free-spirited, lively again. She also suspected that it did something for Harry to be the only person who could bring such playfulness out of *The* Mrs. Astor.

Playfulness was one thing, but when it was time to meet the guest of honor, the mysterious Prince Del Drago, Caroline was not expecting to be introduced to a chimpanzee. *A chimpanzee!* Dressed in a red bow tie, a tiny suit with tails and a top hat. Caroline was speechless. Everyone was laughing and looking, waiting to see what the Grande Dame would do. Well, she would do nothing. Caroline stood there, horrified, and frankly terrified of the little beast who stared at her, cocking his head from side to side. When Caroline started to back away, the chimpanzee let out a high-pitched squeaking protest and threw his top hat across the drawing room.

Caroline yelped and nearly tripped over her gown trying to take cover. Her heart was racing. "I think perhaps I should leave," she said to Harry.

"Oh, nonsense, Lina. I won't hear of it. Come now, you're safe with me. I shall protect you."

But as the ball continued, Caroline watched the guests taking turns petting the furry prince and offering him sips of champagne. Mamie laughed the entire evening, especially when the monkey leaped up into the chandelier. He was swinging from the fixture, and

Stuyvesant climbed up on the table, tiptoeing about the stemware and china settings, trying to get the little fellow down. The prince shrieked and retaliated by throwing crystals and lightbulbs all over the room. Guests were jumping and vaulting about, trying to catch them, as if they were prizes.

When a bulb landed in Caroline's wig, she yelped for the second time that evening, perhaps the second time in her life. She nearly fell off her chair and was quite shaken, though no one seemed to notice. Everyone, including Harry, was too fixated on their game of catch with the chimp.

It was only Alva who came over to Caroline's side. "Here," she said, gently helping Caroline to her feet, "why don't we go freshen up a bit."

Caroline was only too grateful to escape the ruckus and allowed Alva to escort her to one of Mamie's dressing rooms. Caroline could still hear the commotion, screams and laughter coming from the ballroom, when she sat down and looked in the mirror. She was mortified to see that a sprig of white hair had escaped from beneath her wig, and hadn't even noticed the bulb still stuck in her hair until Alva began untangling it with her fingertips.

"I do declare that little chimp has got a strong pitching arm," she laughed softly, gingerly tucking Caroline's white locks back underneath her wig. "There," she said, squeezing Caroline's shoulder, both their faces framed in the mirror, "good as new."

Caroline realized that it was simply impossible to go on hating this woman who had been so good to Emily and Charlotte. And now to her. She wanted to apologize for how she'd treated her in the past, but the words refused to come. The best she could do was reach up for Alva's hand and offer a squeeze, thinking if only Alva had known all those years ago that it would have been her kindness, and not her money, her fancy houses or balls, that would have impressed *The Mrs. Astor*.

When Caroline and Alva returned to the main room, she saw that the atmosphere had further deteriorated. Ladies who knew better were taking turns dancing with the hairy little prince while the men stood around clapping, cheering, clanking their glasses of wine and champagne. When the chimp escaped the clutches of Wilhelmina Browning, half the party took chase after him, sending china and chairs crashing to the floor.

Caroline knew then that she'd stayed at the ball too long. While she adored Harry Lehr, she was too old and couldn't keep up with him. She wanted no part of this tomfoolery and realized just how much she missed society as she knew it. And Thomas. She missed him and wished more than anything that she were back home, in her sitting room listening to him read to her.

CHAPTER SIXTY

Alva

NEW YORK, 1897

IT HAD SNOWED FOR three days, and on Wednesday, the tenth of February, 1897, the storm let up but the temperatures had plummeted. As Alva and Oliver approached the Waldorf Hotel, where the Bradley Martin Ball was being held, Alva glanced out the back window of her carriage at a city blanketed in glistening white, sparkling in the moonlight. It was so cold that even her gloved hands inside her mink muff were stiff and chilled. Fifth Avenue was backed up with carriages, and Alva was surprised to see the street lined with men and women, standing knee-deep in snow, braving the bitter temperatures in threadbare coats and woolen hats. All of them protestors—members of the Populist Party—carrying signs: **THE MOST GOOD FOR THE MOST PEOPLE. JUSTICE IS MODERATION. ROBBER BARONS GO HOME.** Policemen were trying to contain them. The crowd was angry, shouting, chanting, "Shame on you," as they threw snowballs and bottles at the elegant broughams pulling up to the hotel.

At one point, Alva made eye contact with a woman standing on the curb. Eyes sunken, lips chapped and quivering from the cold, she held a sign, **ROBBER BARONS ARE GLUTTONS**, and raised an angry fist at Alva that sliced through her like a blade. She was suddenly very aware that her Duchess of Devonshire gown had cost $25,000 and that Oliver's suit of arms, with its gold inlays, had cost $10,000. He'd been complaining how uncomfortable it was since they'd left their home and even had to temporarily remove his pauldrons, faulds and gauntlets just so he could sit in the carriage.

After recently getting such harsh criticism in the news about the ball's extravagance, Alva and others had opted to employ local dressmakers rather than going to Europe as a means of helping the workers in town. But clearly the protestors hadn't seen it that way, and what would they think if they knew that neither Alva nor Oliver would ever wear these costumes again?

The woman outside shook her fist again, and Alva had to look away, her pulse jumping, her heartbeat echoing inside her ears. Something hit the side of their brougham, and Alva jumped, reaching for Oliver. She was terrified as a pair of footmen—dressed in full sixteenth-century livery, powdered wigs and all—cut through the chaos and ushered them inside the Waldorf, shielding them from the flying debris with bumbershoots.

Alva was not able to shake the protestors as she entered the hotel, taking in all the lavish decorations and costumes. It seemed like such a shameful display. She was flooded with guilt as another footman escorted them to the second floor. There Alva found a series of private dressing rooms along with a lady's maid waiting to assist the guests with their costumes and hair, should either have been disturbed during the journey to the hotel. There was a time when she would have given anything to be invited to a ball like this, but just then, seated before the vanity, she found it hard to look at herself in the mirror.

Part of her felt as though she belonged outside with the demonstrators. When she thought back now on Petit Chateau and Marble House, on all her balls and parties, all the clothing and jewelry, she had to admit that Julia had been right. None of it had made her happy. She'd once been as hungry as those people on the street.

Despite Alva's privileged upbringing, she'd been no better off than any of them, and yet, she'd married money, she'd used Willie's wealth to elevate herself, and for what? Once upon a time she'd done it for her mother and then for her children, but any worthwhile sense of purpose had fallen by the wayside long ago. Advancing in society had become a game, a competition with Mrs. Astor, and the challenger in Alva had refused to lose.

CHAPTER SIXTY-ONE

Caroline

CAROLINE HADN'T WANTED TO go to the Bradley Martin Ball. She'd been appalled by recent balls, especially Mamie's chimpanzee ball, and wasn't interested in any more shenanigans. Plus, she was still annoyed that the Martins had chosen the Waldorf over the Astoria Hotel for the location of their ball.

The two hotels, butted up next door to each other, were in constant competition, vying for the same pool of patrons and social events. When Caroline learned that the Martins had selected the Waldorf over the Astoria, she'd been dreadfully disappointed and disgusted by Waldorf's gloating.

She said she wasn't going to the ball, but then Harry offered to escort her, and much as she hated to admit it, Caroline still found Harry Lehr captivating. Besides, the Bradley Martin Ball had promised to be a good old-fashioned masquerade ball. Prior to the Vanderbilt ball nearly fifteen years before, Caroline would have found such a thing gimmicky and outrageous. But now, in lieu of the animal balls, a costume ball seemed quite tame and dignified to her.

On the night of the ball, Caroline wore a full-length mink overtop of her Marie Antoinette costume. Wanting to look especially lovely for Harry, she had gone a bit overboard with her gown, even by her own standards. Her dress was heavily weighted down with diamonds, and after reading in the newspaper that Cornelia Martin's Mary, Queen of Scots gown had cost $30,000, Caroline realized she had outspent the hostess by two. But the look on Harry Lehr's face when he arrived at her home and saw her—that wide-eyed look of admiration and enchantment—told her it had been worth every penny.

Of course she thought Harry was dazzling as ever that night, dressed as George Washington with a white powdered wig beneath his three-pointed hat. His waistcoat was fully embroidered; his sword peeked out from the bottom of his beaver coat. She had refused another ride in that mechanical contraption of his, and so their horse-drawn carriage proceeded toward the Waldorf Hotel.

On the way, Harry told her everything he'd gleaned about the ball. "They sent out 1,000 invitations, and you won't believe this—every couple will have their own private footman. And"—he leaned in conspiratorially, so close that she could smell his wonderfully aromatic shaving soap—"I have it on good authority that Bradley Martin has imported 4,000 bottles of Moët et Chandon. Each guest will have two bottles just to themselves. Can you imagine what that must have cost . . ."

Coming from Harry, this didn't seem like gossip, and he held her spellbound and oblivious to the biting cold, immune to the many changes in her old neighborhood. Her attention was so fixated on Harry that she was only vaguely aware of the crowds that had congregated along the snow-covered sidewalks.

Once inside the Waldorf's lobby, Caroline felt as though she had entered the Palace of Versailles. Everywhere she looked she saw women dressed as queens and princesses, the men as kings and dukes and former presidents. It was as if everyone had stepped out of the pages of history.

Normally, Caroline stood with the hostess as she received her guests—a symbol of society's approval—but given the outrageous balls and dinner parties recently held, Caroline had declined the honor, for fear she would have been endorsing another fiasco. But that didn't appear to be the case at the Bradley Martin Ball. It was such a regal display, she was delighted and felt as if she were back in the arms of the society she'd known and trusted. After she and Harry Lehr were received by Cornelia Martin, they mingled among the other guests.

Harry stayed close by her side, and at first all was fine, the two of them making polite conversation with the various other guests. But by one in the morning, Caroline began to tire. Her bunions were acting up and her lower back ached from the weight of her gown, so she took refuge in a Louis XV chair that had been brought into the hotel as part of the decorations. Glancing about, admiring all the roses and floral arrangements, she spotted Jack, looking slender and fit in his Henry IV costume. Carrie was there as well, dressed as Elizabeth of York, and her husband, Orme, was Henry VII. Despite all the drama that had preceded their wedding, her daughter was happily married. They were talking with John Morgan, whom Caroline supposed was dressed as the Duke of Guise, but she couldn't be sure. She recognized the architect Stanford White as one of the many court jesters, prancing about.

Though she never thought she'd live to see the day, Caroline was beginning to accept that the distinctions between the Knickerbockers and the nouveau riche had all but vanished; the two sides had practically become one. Together, they represented the upper crust, high society—whatever they were called these days. It made her nostalgic, which always made her think about Ward McAllister.

Other than her assigned footman, who had brought her a fresh glass of champagne, no one seemed to notice Caroline sitting off to the side, which was disturbingly odd. She was unaccustomed to being left unattended at a ball, even for a moment. She had assumed that people would come over, say their hellos, relishing an opportunity to speak with Caroline outside of a receiving line. She sipped her champagne, waiting, but everyone seemed caught up in conversations of their own. She opened her fan, moving it back and forth in slow, easy sweeps, perking up when she saw Penelope Easton coming her way. Caroline was about to say hello but Penelope walked right past her, joining a group of other women standing a few feet away. Caroline was embarrassed by her presumption. Puss Strong and Lady Paget—one dressed as Katherine of Aragon, the other as Anne Boleyn— were just across the way, and Caroline surprised herself by doing something she rarely did—she initiated the first gesture, a smile. A smile from Mrs. Astor was akin to being anointed, something that other women would have cherished and later boasted about to their friends. But Caroline was dumbfounded when they offered only a quick hello and drifted by. Was it possible that people hadn't recognized Caroline in her costume? Nonsense, they had to have known it was her.

What is happening here? She was invisible, and the longer she sat there by herself, the more distance she was able to put between herself and the scene playing out before her. The fact that no one was watching her, scrutinizing her every move, gave her an opportunity to relax and see society from a clear vantage point.

For once she got to be the spectator rather than the spectacle. She found it all quite liberating and amusing—oh so amusing! She was positively tickled by all the pageantry, the frivolity. And in her new-found anonymity, she would have loved to get up to join in on the fun if only she could. The weight of her many diamonds and the gold sewn into her gown had anchored her into the chair, and she knew she would need help getting up when they called for supper.

CHAPTER SIXTY-TWO

Alva

AFTER ALVA AND OLIVER were announced at the Bradley Martin Ball and received by their hostess, they entered the grand ballroom as the orchestra played Hungarian court music. The floor was practically covered in rose petals, the crimson juice seeping into the carpets and marble as people trampled over them.

Alva was still thinking about the protestors outside when she overheard a group of women discussing the divine supper that awaited them: *chaud-froid de pluviers, filet de boeuf jardinière, canard, terrine de foie gras, galantine à la Victoria, mayonnaise de volaille.* Twenty-eight courses in all. *Who could possibly eat that much?* What about the people standing out in the cold who could barely afford to put food on their tables? She felt horrid being inside that glamorous hotel, watching people frolicking about with more money on their backs than those protestors made in a year or more. It wasn't right. Nor was it right that Oliver was handed a Figurado cigar wrapped in a $100 bill and that Alva was presented with a diamond bracelet as a party favor. She tucked it inside her pocket, thinking she would give it to one of the women outside later when she left. Maybe they could sell it or exchange it for food or warm clothing.

Even before she saw her, Alva heard Mamie Fish's cackle. "Oh, forgive me," said Mamie, holding up her gilded lorgnette, scrutinizing one of the many Madame Pompadours there that night. "I thought you were someone else. I don't wish to speak with you at all." There was more cackling as Mamie walked on, heading in Alva's direction. Alva turned to avoid her, her eyes landing instead on Mrs. Astor, sitting off to the side, all alone.

Alva hadn't seen her since Mamie's ball for the furry little Prince Del Drago. It was shocking and a bit heartbreaking to see the Grande Dame sitting by herself, so Alva excused herself and went over to say hello.

Mrs. Astor lit up at the sight of Alva, gesturing for her to sit in the Louis XV armchair beside her as she held out a frail hand. "Would you like a champagne?" Caroline asked, signaling her assigned footman as if he truly were her personal servant.

"Are you enjoying the ball?" Alva asked moments later, sipping her Moët et Chandon.

"I'd enjoy it much more if it were held next door at the Astoria."

Alva smiled. "Well, at least there's not an elephant or chimp in sight."

Caroline looked at her for a moment before offering a slight smile and an arched eyebrow. "You're rather funny. I had no idea."

Alva laughed. "And I had no idea *you* knew how to smile."

"Shhh"—she scowled playfully—"don't tell anyone."

At that they both laughed.

"Oh, Alva, if only I were twenty years younger."

Alva? Mrs. Astor had never called her by her first name before.

"Take care of your feet—wear more sensible shoes," she said, pointing to Alva's heels. "That's something no one ever told me when I was your age."

Alva nodded and smiled. "I'll remember that."

Caroline took another sip of champagne. "I never understood what Emily saw in you, you know."

"Oh yes, I was well aware of that," Alva said, much more charmed than offended by Mrs. Astor's candor. "And now?" asked Alva. "Have I changed your opinion of me?"

"What do you think?"

Mrs. Astor wouldn't say it. She didn't have to. Alva had already detected an infinitesimal wink.

The tinny sound of the dinner bell rang, signifying that it was time to move into the grand dining room. Alva rose from her chair and extended her hand to Mrs. Astor. Normally a lady waited for a gentleman to accompany her into the dining room, but, in an unprecedented move, after Alva helped Mrs. Astor to her feet, Mrs. Astor placed her gloved hand on Alva's arm, and the two women escorted each other into the dining hall and took their places at the head table.

CHAPTER SIXTY-THREE

Caroline

NEW YORK, 1905

CAROLINE AWOKE WITH HER usual aches and pains, but on this morning, something else was off. She wasn't feeling right. For a moment she thought she was at Beechwood in Newport and then remembered she was at her new home on Fifth Avenue. A beautiful mansion that she now shared with her son, Jack, and his family. She looked around her bedroom, wondering why everything seemed hazy, gauzy, more dreamlike than real.

Unfortunately, this confusion was nothing new. Ever since she'd taken that fall, stumbling down her marble staircase, she'd felt a fog crowding in around her. It was Thomas who had found her that day, out cold at the foot of the stairs. He'd called for the doctor, and when she finally came to, she didn't remember tripping, but her hands and gown were covered in blood. Her head was pounding, searing pain shooting from her skull down her spine each time she moved. They'd all said she could have broken her neck, but she hadn't suffered even a single sprain or fractured bone, only a concussion that had left her nauseated and exhausted, her body craving sleep. It had taken her weeks to recover, and at times she questioned if she'd ever made a full recovery.

While still in bed, she reached for the pull and rang for Thomas, anticipating her busy day ahead. There was so much left to do before her ball that evening. She would have to meet with her social secretary and Thomas so they could finalize the menu and confirm the flower arrangements, the orchestra and party favors. She was ticking off items in her head when the door opened and William stepped into her bedroom, carrying her breakfast tray.

"What are you doing? Where's Hade?"

"I'm right here, Mrs. Astor. I've brought you tea and toast." He set the tray down before her.

She looked at him again, frustrated and embarrassed by her blunder. *Of course this was Thomas.* William was dead. "Did you remember to notify the orchestra?" she asked quickly, hoping to deflect her error.

Thomas dragged a hand over his mouth, letting his fingers rest on his chin. He wasn't looking at her.

"Well? You *did* schedule them, didn't you? They'll need to arrive here no later than nine o'clock."

Thomas nodded, and when he did finally look up, she saw the hesitation in his eyes. Lately, he had been less than agreeable. She would have to have a word with him about his impertinence.

After he excused himself, Caroline felt the haziness beginning to clear. The confusion tended to come and go, but she couldn't distinguish which was which anymore. Before dismissing him, she had asked Thomas for her mail and the morning papers. Lately she had noticed a steady decline in the number of calling cards she received each day. She told herself it was because of the press and the brouhaha over the Bradley Martin Ball last season. *No, wait—the Bradley Martin Ball was ages ago, wasn't it?*

A breeze stirred the curtains in her bedroom, and Caroline felt herself beginning to drift again. The claws of confusion were grabbing for her once again. She shook her head as if that would keep it at bay and called for her maid to help with her morning toilette.

Gazing in the mirror, she didn't feel nearly as old as she looked. What little hair she had left had long since turned white as snow, and the lines in her face had never been deeper, the circles beneath her eyes never darker. It wasn't until her wig was in place that she recognized herself at all. When it came time for her jewelry, she glanced at the backs of her hands, fingers gnarled, joints so swollen that she couldn't get her favorite diamond rings past her knuckles. She sighed, reaching for her leather Boucicaut gloves to hide them from herself.

After she was dressed, Thomas appeared in the doorway, asking if she'd like to go for her carriage ride.

"Oh, I haven't time for that, Hade. Not today. The ball is tonight."

"Of course." He bowed ceremoniously and led her to the drawing room, where she checked her engagement book, her twisted fingers struggling to cooperate. When she did get the book open and was able to turn to the correct date, she saw a blank page. "Hade?" she called out. "Hade—come here!"

He rushed into the room. "Mrs. Astor?"

"What's happened to my engagement book? I had a luncheon today."

"I'm afraid not today, Mrs. Astor."

"And the ball is this evening. Why isn't that in here? There was definitely a luncheon today. I'm certain of it." She closed the engagement book and shoved it across her desk.

Setting a teacup down before her, Thomas said, "I brought you some extra chocolate biscuits."

She reached for one, when he stopped her. "Allow me, Mrs. Astor." Without another word, he helped her off with her gloves. "There. Now that's much better, isn't it?"

She nodded, and as she sipped her tea, she overheard Hade speaking to someone out in the hallway, mumbling . . . *She's not having a good day.*

She wondered who he was talking to—Jack? Carrie? Had Charlotte come back from Europe to see her? Charlotte was remarried now, happily so, and she'd been trying to reestablish ties with her children, especially her daughter. *Time*, Caroline had said to Charlotte, *give it time*, but Caroline feared she didn't have much time left, and she didn't want to miss a thing. For now, at least, she was still the matriarch, the guiding force over this family. Just as she'd created society, she had, even more importantly, created this family, her legacy: three surviving children, twelve grandchildren and seven great-grandchildren. They would carry on the Astor name, the Astor traditions. It was her family that gave her strength and made her want to hold on.

Thomas was still in the hallway when she called for him. "Thomas?"

"Yes, Mrs. Astor?"

She couldn't remember why she'd wanted him.

"Perhaps you might enjoy a hand of cooncan?" Thomas suggested, sitting down across from her, reaching for a deck of playing cards.

"That would be lovely." She nibbled a biscuit. "Very nice indeed."

While he shuffled the cards, Caroline sat silently, thinking. On some level she was all too aware of things getting away from her. She knew her mind was unreliable, failing her. She knew she sounded like a demented old woman, and it terrified her. She was reminded of some of the nonsense her mother would say in later years, calling Caroline by the wrong name, insisting that someone had taken her cane, stolen her jewelry . . .

Caroline was so terribly confused. She didn't trust herself to speak—afraid of what might come tumbling out. She was on an emotional ledge, one thought away from pure senility. Her heart began racing, her breathing labored as sweat broke out on her brow and along the back of her neck.

"Thomas," she said, barely above a whisper. "Thomas, I'm not done yet. I'm not ready to die."

"I should hope not." He smiled kindly, trying to make light of her comment as he began dealing the cards.

She dropped her biscuit and brought her hands to her face. "Oh dear lord, what's happening to me?"

"You're tired, Mrs. Astor. You didn't sleep well last night, but I assure you, you are positively fine."

"Oh, Thomas, what would I ever do without you?"

"You needn't worry about that." He set his cards facedown and reached for her hand, gently squeezing her fingers. "I'm here, Mrs. Astor. I'll always be right here." He released her fingers, picked up his cards and fanned them out.

After a moment, she felt her breathing return to normal and felt the walls in her lovely drawing room expanding once again. She reached for her cards, and after a hand of cooncan, she was feeling better, more in control.

When they'd finished their game, she said she wanted some fresh air. "Bring the carriage around, Thomas. I'd like to go for a ride."

Once outside she felt better still. The mild breeze and sunshine did her good as they traveled down Fifth Avenue, Thomas sitting right beside her. She was stunned by the number of automobiles puttering about on the road.

"I remember Harry predicted ages ago that those machines would replace the horse. I still don't believe it . . ."

Soon they turned in to the park where children were roller-skating in the distance, women and men cycling just about everywhere she looked. She must have dozed off because the next thing she knew, church bells were pealing in the distance and they were no longer in Central Park. Her head was resting on Thomas's shoulder. She looked around, bewildered, and asked for the time.

"It's just past four o'clock, Mrs. Astor."

"Oh dear. We have to hurry. Guests will be arriving in a matter of hours and there's so much yet to do."

"I assure you, Mrs. Astor, everything is under control."

She ordered the coachman to take them back home, and after she was inside and had her afternoon tea, it was time to perform her evening toilette. The purple Worth gown she'd selected was one of her favorites and just perfect for that evening's ball. She insisted on wearing her diamond tiara, and since her favorite rings wouldn't fit, she opted for one of her diamond stomachers instead.

Before leaving her dressing room, she called on Thomas. "Is the orchestra ready?"

"You look lovely tonight, Mrs. Astor," he said with a slight ceremonial bow.

Caroline turned back to the mirror to see what he was seeing—and there she was, young Lina with the future about to unfold before her. And it was going to be grand.

With that, Caroline left her dressing room, went to the top of her staircase, the very staircase she'd fallen from, and taking a seat beneath her portrait, she waited patiently to receive her guests.

CHAPTER SIXTY-FOUR

Alva

NEWPORT, 1908

THE SUN WAS HIGH above, the sky a vivid blue. The orchestra outside had begun playing "We as Women." Alva grabbed the black chiffon parasol that matched her gown, thinking, *How awful having to wear black on such a hot day.*

Making her way down the long hallway, she exited through the French doors, thrown open to let in the ocean breeze and cool the cottage. Police officers were stationed outside of every room, keeping an eye on her priceless art and antiques while thousands of strangers came to view Marble House.

Long before Oliver passed away, when Alva wasn't tending to society, she had devoted her spare time to visiting tenement houses, hospitals and orphanages. After his sudden death that June, Alva had pushed back against her grief, not allowing it to swallow her whole. Instead, she'd thrown herself and her financial muscle at the women's suffrage movement. She'd already secured a lease for the National Suffrage Association at Forty-Second Street and Fifth Avenue and had given the landlord $5,000 to cover the rent for the entire year.

She was still living at Belcourt, Oliver's cottage, just across the street on Bellevue Avenue. Having never been able to part with Marble

House, Alva had kept her prized cottage, using it mostly to house her too many clothes and all her furnishings, artwork and antiques. Today would be the first time she'd done anything at Marble House in years. And for those who criticized her for *entertaining* while in mourning, well, they didn't understand that this was not a social event. This was an important occasion, and Oliver would have wholeheartedly approved.

Knowing that plenty of people were curious to see her cottage, especially the interior, Alva had decided to host that day's fundraising rally at Marble House. They sold $1 tickets that gave people access to the gardens and all the speeches as well as $5 tickets that included a limited tour inside. More policemen stood guard before the red velvet cords roping off the rooms she deemed private—including her bedroom.

With the blue and white-star suffrage flags flapping in the breeze outside the massive tent and the orchestra playing rally songs, 1,000 or so women—rich, poor, young and old, white, Negro, American and European—walked the grounds, buying pamphlets and buttons, sashes and banners, anything to support the cause.

Alva's friends Puss and Lady Paget were there, along with her sisters. Even Tessie Oelrichs and Mamie Fish put in an appearance.

"Here we are again," said Mamie, with a blasé wave of her hands, "*older* faces and *younger* clothes."

"What a surprise this is," Alva said in return. "And to think I thought you weren't in favor of women's rights."

"Oh, I'm not," said Mamie. "As far as I'm concerned, a good husband is all a woman truly needs."

"Well"—Alva gestured about the grounds—"I'm afraid everyone here today would disagree with you."

Alva looked at all the women who had come together that day. It nearly broke her heart when she thought about all their talents, their passions and ambitions that hadn't been realized simply because

they were women. And there were so many more out there, struggling to rise up and out of their circumstances. Let them vote, own
property, leave their abusive husbands, and pursue their education
and their dreams.

As an ambitious woman herself, Alva had made society her career
because there were no other options. She'd once been a daughter of
privilege whose family had lost their fortune, forcing her to claw and
crawl her way back into society's good graces. She'd made it, all the
way to the top, in fact, but she wasn't done yet.

Excusing herself from Mamie and Tessie, Alva twirled her parasol
and walked toward the tent, eager to hear the first speaker. Society
would carry on without Mrs. Astor and without Alva, too. Society
didn't need Alva Vanderbilt Belmont, but women—ordinary women
everywhere—did.

CHAPTER SIXTY-FIVE

Society

NEW YORK

WE WALK DOWN PEACOCK ALLEY, that long lovely corridor that links the Hyphen, which is what everyone calls the newly combined Waldorf-Astoria Hotel. Its opulence is immense. The onyx mosaic floors echo our every step as we pass a few couples seated on the plush benches butted up against the Corinthian columns.

When we enter the hotel café with its beautiful frescoes and elegant crystal and china table settings, we see that Penelope and Ophelia are already there. It's been ages since we've gathered for luncheon. The last time was at Delmonico's. It had been early summer then, just before we left for Newport. We'd dined outside amid red geraniums and scarlet peonies blooming in the window boxes. It had been a delightful day, and we had all agreed we should lunch together more often, it's just that we've all been so busy as of late.

Puss now sits on the board for the Central Park Menagerie and has currently been fighting to keep the zoo here in the city. Peggy Cavendish volunteers twice a week to help children with speech impediments. Ophelia also does volunteer work, at an orphanage, and Penelope now sits on the board of the Astor Library, which is in great decline.

Cornelia Martin sadly won't be joining us. She and her husband fled New York shortly after their Bradley Martin Ball. When various members of the clergy as well as populists and anarchists criticized them for their extravagance, they started receiving death threats. The last straw was finding their home and carriages vandalized. They're now in Scotland or England—we've lost track.

Certainly no one has thrown a party on such a grand scale since. Some say the Bradley Martin Ball marked the end of the Gilded Age. And that is true, though judging by the jewelry and fashions on display at our table, not to mention the prices on the menu before us, we're all still very well-off.

We feast on such delicacies as mutton stew, fresh tongue of beef, seared lamb with mint, and deviled lamb kidney. Lady Paget, who prides herself on having not touched a piece of flesh food for sixteen years, ordered broiled shad and roe, along with cold lobster tartare.

She looks at Mamie's tenderloin steak béarnaise with great disdain. "How can you eat flesh?"

"Very simply," says Mamie. "With a fork"—she raises her cutlery—"and a knife."

The conversation moves on and we find ourselves discussing Penelope's divorce and her daughter who is attending college. Lydia tells us about the plot for her next romance novel. Each of us has been sworn to secrecy about her writing under the nom de plume Louis W. Sterling. We laugh, we gossip, we share.

The last time we were all together was at Mrs. Astor's funeral in November. She was seventy-eight and had died at home, surrounded by her son, Jack, daughter Carrie and her butler, Thomas Hade. They say that in recent years her butler never left her side, accompanying her on her daily carriage rides through the park. The two had been regularly seen dining at Sherry's and Delmonico's. Even here at the Hyphen. Some say she'd never been happier.

It's the end of an era now that Mrs. Astor is gone, and while society still exists, it isn't what it once was.

There was a time when we blindly followed the protocol as effortlessly as one season follows another. From winter to Newport and back again. The restrictions and limitations of yesterday were largely self-imposed. The very same society we so desperately wanted in on was the same society that told us no diamonds before nightfall, no social visits before two in the afternoon, no denying relations with your husband, no divorcing him, either. It's sometimes hard to accept that in many ways, we had stepped inside the very cage that held us prisoner.

Looking back, it's easy to say that one woman's monotony is another's sense of purpose. Now we regard all the etiquette as quaint. Passé. The next generation is much more lenient and *society as we've known it* will never be the same. Isn't it interesting, though, to note that it now takes three women to do what Mrs. Astor had done by herself for three decades?

Tessie, Mamie and Alva have now taken over society. It's no secret, though, that before she died, Mrs. Astor had handed the scepter to Alva. She told Alva that she was the best person to replace her, but by then, Alva didn't really want the throne. Instead, she shared the honor with two hostesses who would have killed for it. Tessie and Mamie rule their ever-fading empire, and while Alva is still very much the head of society, her attention has shifted to rights for women—all women.

Looking back, we weren't always kind to Alva, though she wasn't always at her best with us, either. We sometimes mocked her, shunned her, gossiped about her ad nauseam. We thought she was too brash, too controversial, too overpowering, and oftentimes, she was. But there were other times—moments—when she was daring and spectacularly brave. We hadn't always had the foresight back then to see where she was heading, where she was leading us. And as it's turned out, her courage eventually made us more courageous, too. She cracked the door open, and we've been crossing that threshold ever since.

We are the wives and daughters of wealthy men, but now we are no longer defined by that. And neither are our daughters. Look how far we've come, and just you wait and see where we'll go from here.

AUTHOR'S NOTE

One of the greatest challenges I faced in writing this book was bringing Caroline Astor and Alva Vanderbilt to life and making them relatable to readers. On paper, they were both obsessed with society and matters that frankly seemed so frivolous and comical. I really needed to dig deeper and deeper to find out what made these people tick and to humanize them.

In some cases, the material was available, despite a lot of contradictory "facts" in the various source materials. Oftentimes there was no information, so I had to fill in a good many blanks myself, and it is in that spirit that I'll attempt to separate the fact from the fiction in this novel.

Caroline's relationship with her mother was a driving force of Caroline's development. While it's true that her mother lost six of her nine children, the dynamics between mother and daughter were those of my own imaginings and not based on any documented events or findings.

It's also true that Caroline's daughters did give her a run for her money. Emily married James Van Alen only after General Van Alen had challenged William Astor to a duel. James Van Alen was a bit of a laughingstock who did indeed speak with a phony British accent and wear a fake monocle. Sadly, Emily did die in childbirth in 1881. Helen was the only daughter with a "respectable" marriage by Caroline's standards and she, too, died young, in 1893 of unknown causes.

Charlotte was a spirited rebel. While her relationship with Duncan Briar is fictional, her scandalous love affair with Hallett Borrowe was real and went viral Gilded Age–style with the publication of her love letters. She did abandon her children and flee to Europe, and William did go to bring her back. What is less clear is whether Caroline accompanied him. For the sake of the narrative, I have opted to place Caroline with him. One thing we know for sure is that William did die while in London trying to rescue his daughter. That brings us to the youngest daughter, Carrie. Caroline's namesake was used as a pawn for Alva's famous masquerade ball, and Carrie was instrumental in Caroline's recognizing the Vanderbilts in society. Also, Carrie did go on a hunger strike when her parents opposed her marriage to Orme Wilson. I do not know that they ever had to induce feeding, but I do know that Caroline gave in and Carrie married him and lived happily ever after.

Ward McAllister's life and memoir have been widely documented, and many of his most outrageous quotes in this novel came directly from him verbatim. He did call Caroline "my Mystic Rose" and was her co-conspirator in all things society up until the publication of the Four Hundred and *Society as I Have Found It*.

Caroline Astor actually was out of town on the night of the opening of the Metropolitan Opera House, perhaps because she knew the Academy of Music couldn't compete with the new house. However, in order to show the juxtaposition of the two, I have taken creative license and placed Mrs. Astor at the Academy on that same night.

With regards to the Met, I have attributed much of its creation to Alva, and while it's true that Billy Vanderbilt, her father-in-law, was one of the founding members, Alva most likely played a much smaller role in its development. She was, however, hands-on in every aspect of the creation of Petit Chateau, Marble House and other Vanderbilt properties. She fancied herself an unlicensed architect.

The string of outrageous themed balls really did occur. The chimpanzee ball has been attributed to various hostesses, mainly Mamie Fish and Alva Vanderbilt. Here again the source materials contradict themselves and so, in keeping with Mamie's character, it seemed more likely to me that Mamie would have hosted the party.

Cornelius Jeremiah Vanderbilt was the ne'er-do-well son of the family. Afflicted with epilepsy, he was institutionalized by his father, the Commodore. He was a compulsive gambler and did contest the Commodore's will after learning he'd inherited only $200,000. He was a homosexual and did commit suicide. While all that is true, I did take some license in terms of Jeremiah's relationship with Alva. I cast the two as outsiders that formed a tight bond between them. There is no documentation of their having a close relationship. Also, in the novel, for the sake of pacing, I moved the timeline of Jeremiah's death from April of 1882 to March of 1883.

Much speculation has been cast upon Alva's marriage to Willie K. Vanderbilt. We know that he had several affairs while they were married, and here again, the facts become a bit sketchy. Some say Nellie Neustratter was a plant to distract from his real relationship with Alva's best friend, the Duchess of Manchester. Others say Nellie was just another one of his mistresses. For the purpose of this book, I chose to follow the historical account that had him involved with both women. Also please note that the nickname Duchy was my own invention in order to distinguish between the two Consuelos in the book. There are varying accounts of when Alva's affair with Willie's best friend, Oliver Belmont, began. I placed it where I thought it worked best in the narrative, but the truth remains that after her scandalous divorce, she did turn around and marry Oliver.

Speaking of marriages, Consuelo Vanderbilt's marriage to the ninth Duke of Marlborough has been well documented and recounted. For that reason, I chose not only to focus on the outlandish things Alva

did to orchestrate the marriage, but to dig a little deeper and specu-
late as to how a mother who loved her daughter dearly could have
justified such actions.

The ladies featured in the Society chapters are a combination of
real and fictional characters. It should be noted that history recog-
nizes two Lady Pagets: Minnie Stevens, an American heiress and
socialite, is the Lady Paget in this novel. There is no record of her
having been a vegetarian. That was *borrowed* from the other Lady Paget
(born Countess Walburga Ehrengarde Helena von Hohenthal), who
often wrote on the subject of vegetarianism.

Much research went into the writing and rewriting of this book.
In addition to reading and watching various documentaries and
movies from this time period (see complete list below), I went to
Newport to see the cottages—which are breathtaking. While there,
we ventured onto Cliff Walk, ignoring the signs that read **STAY ON THE
PAVED PATH. STEEP CLIFFS. HIGH RISK OF INJURY. PASS AT YOUR OWN RISK.**
I was not wearing the right shoes and had many close calls. I'd probably still be stranded out there now had John, my partner in crime,
not practically carried me over the rugged terrain. It was that experience that led to the scene where Alva rescues Emily.

Also, you'll notice the Astor and Vanderbilt family trees in the
front of the book. Because the families were so large and there are so
many duplicate names, I limited the individuals on the trees to those
people in this book.

If you'd like to learn more about the Gilded Age, Caroline Astor
and Alva Vanderbilt, I highly recommend the following:

American Experience: New York: A Documentary Film by Ric Burns
The Gilded Age in New York, 1870–1910 by Esther Crain
*The Vanderbilts and the Gilded Age: Architectural Aspirations,
     1879–1901* by John Foreman and Robbe Pierce Stimson
Alva, That Vanderbilt-Belmont Woman by Margaret Hayden Rector

Alva Vanderbilt Belmont: Unlikely Champion of Women's Rights by
  Sylvia D. Hoffert

Mrs. Astor's New York: Money and Social Power in a Gilded Age by
  Eric Homberger

The Astors: An American Legend by Lucy Kavaler

*A Season of Splendor: The Court of Mrs. Astor in Gilded Age New
  York* by Greg King

Society as I Have Found It by Ward McAllister

The First Four Hundred: Mrs. Astor's New York in the Gilded Age by
  Jerry E. Patterson

The Vanderbilts by Jerry E. Patterson

*What Would Mrs. Astor Do? The Essential Guide to the Manners
  and Mores of the Gilded Age* by Cecelia Tichi

The Glitter and the Gold by Consuelo Vanderbilt Balsan

ACKNOWLEDGMENTS

When it comes to writing a novel, I rely on a host of people for expertise, support and encouragement along the way. So, it is with tremendous gratitude that I thank the following people: Andrea Peskind Katz, Lauren Blank Margolin and Mary O'Malley, for your honest feedback on a very early draft of this novel. You helped steer me in the right direction.

Brenda Klem and Mindy Mailman, for always being there for me. You are my sisters!

Thanks also to my trusted friends and colleagues: Tasha Alexander, Stacey Ballis, Julia and Len Elkun, Andrew Grant, Sara Gruen, Julia Claiborne Johnson, Abbott Kahler, Lisa Kotin, Pamela Klinger-Horn, Jill Miner and Amy Sue Nathan. Also, a big thanks to the members of the Berkley Chicks and the Lyonesses—I'm honored to know such a talented group of women.

I fear I'm running out of ways to say thank you to the amazing Kevan Lyon, my agent who is truly Superwoman! All you need is the cape! There is nothing you can't do and do well. So here again, Kevan, I say thank you. To my editor, Amanda Bergeron, my very own Maxwell Perkins! You went above and beyond to help me shape this book, and I thank you for your patience and faith in me while I wrote and rewrote. To my Berkley family at Penguin Random House—especially Ivan Held, Claire Zion, Craig Burke, Jeanne-Marie Hudson, Tara O'Connor, Fareeda Bullert, Elisha Katz, Sareer Khader and, of course, Brian Wilson. You have given me a wonderful home in the world of publishing, and I am forever grateful for all your support and hard work.

And lastly, my love and gratitude to my family: Debbie Rosen, Pam Rosen, Jerry Rosen, Andrea Rosen, Joey Perilman, Devon Rosen and John Dul, who read every word—sometimes more than once— and rescued me on Cliff Walk.

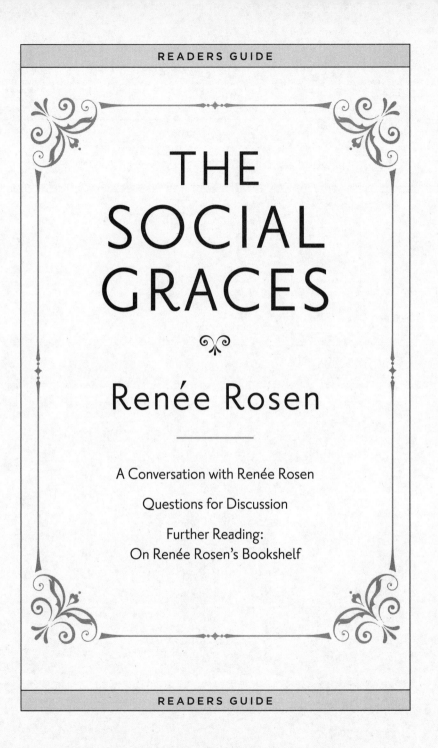

THE SOCIAL GRACES

Renée Rosen

A Conversation with Renée Rosen

Questions for Discussion

Further Reading:
On Renée Rosen's Bookshelf

A CONVERSATION WITH RENÉE ROSEN

How did you get the idea for *The Social Graces*?
Coming up with new book ideas is always more difficult for me than you might imagine. After finishing *Park Avenue Summer*, I was brainstorming on new concepts and my agent mentioned Consuelo Vanderbilt right before my editor suggested doing something in the Gilded Age. After some preliminary research on New York in that time period, it was obvious that the rivalry between Mrs. Astor and Alva Vanderbilt had the makings of a really interesting novel.

What were the greatest challenges you found in writing this book?
There were several, but in terms of the greatest challenge, it came down to the characters themselves. Honestly, when I looked at my cast of characters, I realized I had a group of rather unlikable people. On the surface they came across as spoiled, entitled, greedy and superficial. If I wanted to engage the reader, I was going to have to really drill down to find the humanity in these people and find a reason for us to root for them. That in and of itself took many drafts.

How did you go about conducting your research for this book?
I always start with a baseline of reading, and I had a stack of books on the Gilded Age, the Astors and the Vanderbilts (you'll find a full

list at the end of my author's note), and in addition to that, I watched some videos on the Bradley Martin Ball and the Ric Burns *New York* series, which was excellent.

From there, I knew I needed some hands-on research, so we went to Newport, where I could visit Marble House and Mrs. Astor's cottage (though Beechwood was under renovation when we were there). After touring the mansions and taking in Newport, I went to New York and visited Trinity Church and Trinity Cemetery. Unfortunately, the original homes of Caroline and Alva are no longer there. The Empire State Building sits on the site of Caroline Astor's townhouse, Cornelius Vanderbilt II's mansion is now Bergdorf Goodman, and the Waldorf-Astoria has since been relocated.

What did you find most surprising about Caroline Astor and Alva Vanderbilt?
Oh, there were so many things! I didn't know, for example, that Caroline was such a devoted mother. According to the research, she dearly loved her children and doted on them. I was also surprised by how understated she was early on, before the nouveau riche began exerting their influence. As for Alva, I had no idea that she divorced her husband and remarried, especially during a time when that was considered the ultimate taboo for a woman. I was also surprised that she became so active in the women's suffrage movement.

You've written in various time periods from the 1800s through the 1960s. Do you have a favorite time period? And what's the biggest difference when it comes to writing in the distant past versus the more recent past?
I'd be really hard-pressed to choose a favorite period—I find it fascinating to go back in time, regardless of the era. Typically, I fall in love

with the period I'm currently writing about, because for several hours a day, I lose myself in the work, living back in that era.

Regardless of what years or century a book is set in, I've found that each time period presents its own challenges. When you're writing about the 1800s or the early 1900s, you really have to educate yourself on the most basic things and imagine living without the modern conveniences of electricity, plumbing, etc. And the fashions— people really want to know about those fabulous gowns and hats, and you need to get those right. As you move forward on the timeline, you need to make sure you've got your facts straight because some of your readers will have been alive during the 1930s, '40s, '50s and '60s. If you misstep on even a little detail, you'll pull them right out of the story. They'll lose confidence in you as an author and your so-called authority on the subject.

Since we were under quarantine when you were still writing this book, how did COVID-19 affect your process and your book?
Thankfully, I had just sent the book to my editor the week before the shelter-in-place orders went into effect both in New York and here in Chicago. There was still much work to be done, but I was grateful that the majority of the heavy lifting was already completed. But that said, like everyone else, I was terribly distracted and so very heartbroken over the suffering in this world. It was hard to concentrate. Hard to pull myself away from the news. It took me a couple of weeks to get my head back into the book and even then, I was still easily distracted for those last few rounds of edits.

What's your writing process like? Do you outline? What is the most difficult part for you?

Oh, if only I could outline, my life—and my editor's life—would be so much easier. Unfortunately, my brain doesn't work that way. For me, it's the physical act of writing itself that helps me access my characters so they can tell me their stories. Knowing where to begin the story is always the most difficult part of any book for me. My agent has pointed out that I generally write the first one hundred or so pages over and over again until I find the vein of the story. I've come to accept that this is just part of my process. I'm sure it would be more efficient to outline, but I know I'd never be able to follow it.

QUESTIONS FOR DISCUSSION

1. Mother-daughter relationships play a large role in *The Social Graces*. What did you think of the various mother-daughter dynamics in the novel? Do you think mothers still exercise as much influence over their daughters today as they did in the Gilded Age? Do you think that in today's world daughters are more outspoken with their mothers?

2. Alva's best friend and her daughter's godmother, Consuelo Yznaga, the Duchess of Manchester, has an affair with Alva's husband. In the book, Alva says she feels her friend's betrayal is worse than her husband's. How do you feel about that? Is there a so-called Girl Code between friends? Do you think Alva should have forgiven Duchy?

3. Because women in the 1800s had few opportunities outside the home, they sought positions in society and took these roles very seriously. Do you find this frivolous or an act of survival? Is it fair that the opinion of one society matron could make or break someone's reputation?

4. When Caroline found out that her daughter Carrie had not been invited to Alva's masquerade ball—the event of the season— Caroline was forced to pay the social call that thereby let the

Vanderbilts into society. Do you think Caroline did the right thing for her daughter, or should she have stood her ground? What were your thoughts on the weight of this one gesture made by Mrs. Astor?

5. If you suddenly inherited millions of dollars, how do you think it would change your life, and what would you do with a windfall like the one Willie K. and Alva received?

6. The society pages and gossip columns were a new phenomenon in the 1880s. How do you think the press affected the behavior of the society matrons?

7. A secondary theme of this book is the relationships between sisters. We see it with Alva and her siblings as well as the Astor girls. Whether it was a matter of comradery or rivalry, how do you think these relationships influenced the characters?

8. The Gilded Age was definitely a time of the "haves and have-nots." The divide between rich and poor was vast back in the 1800s. Do you think we're still living in a world of "haves and have-nots"? To what extent are things different now? How are they the same?

FURTHER READING:
ON RENÉE ROSEN'S BOOKSHELF

GREAT HISTORICAL FICTION

The Woman Before Wallis: A Novel of Windsors, Vanderbilts, and Royal Scandal by Bryn Turnbull

City of Girls by Elizabeth Gilbert

And They Called It Camelot by Stephanie Marie Thornton

The Dutch House by Ann Patchett

Valentine by Elizabeth Wetmore

The Sisters of Summit Avenue by Lynn Cullen

OTHER BOOKS I'VE LOVED

The Great Believers by Rebecca Makkai

Writers & Lovers by Lily King

Darling Rose Gold by Stephanie Wrobel

Daisy Jones & the Six by Taylor Jenkins Reid

The Kids Are Gonna Ask by Gretchen Anthony

Dear Edward by Ann Napolitano

Photo by Charles Osgood Photography

Renée Rosen is the bestselling author of *Park Avenue Summer, Windy City Blues, White Collar Girl, What the Lady Wants* and *Dollface*. She is also the author of *Every Crooked Pot*, a YA novel published in 2007. Renée lives in Chicago and is at work on a new novel about Estée Lauder.

CONNECT ONLINE

ReneeRosen.com
🐦 ReneeRosen1
📘 ReneeRosenAuthor
📷 ReneeRosen_